"Hagberg, a maven of mach speed mayhem, intricately moves [the] pieces around his global chessboard, until many bodies, plane crashes, and a running sea battle later, action hero McGarvey wipes out the bad guys. Hagberg's long yarns always muscle their way to the top of the techno-intrigue-warfare genre."

—*Booklist* on *High Flight*

"Hagberg may have out-Clancied Clancy. *High Flight* ends the twentieth century with a bang, Russia versus Japan, with the U.S. caught in the middle. Perhaps it's time. There's a lot of techno and a lot of thrills in *High Flight*. Better strap in and hang on when you go for this ride."

—Stephen Coonts

"A tale of international hi-tech intrigue that draws and grips you like a superconducting magnet....Compelling suspense and visceral drama."

—Bill Pogue, SkyLab astronaut, on *High Flight*

WITHOUT HONOR
by
David Hagberg

TOR

A TOM DOHERTY ASSOCIATES BOOK
NEW YORK

This is a work of fiction. All the characters and events portrayed in this book are either products of the author's imagination or are used fictitiously.

WITHOUT HONOR

Copyright © 1989 by David Hagberg

Cover art by Danilo Ducak

A Tor Book
Published by Tom Doherty Associates, Inc.
175 Fifth Avenue
New York, NY 10010

Tor Books on the World Wide Web:
http://www.tor.com

Tor® is a registered trademark of Tom Doherty Associates, Inc.

ISBN: 0-812-50413-5
Library of Congress Card Catalog Number: 88-50998

First edition: January 1989

Printed in the United States of America

0 9 8 7 6 5 4 3 2

Honor is like an island, rugged and without a beach; once we have left it, we can never return.
—Nicols Boileau-Despéraux

They were men without honor . . .
—Anonymous

PART ONE

1

Flight 451 left Miami International Airport at two-fifty in the afternoon. On time. It was Tuesday, October 13. The weather was warm, in the high eighties, under clear blue skies with a gentle wind from the southeast. Signs were posted here and there throughout the busy airport warning that it was a federal offense even to joke about air disasters or hijackings. But it had been months since any incident had happened anywhere in the world, and even longer for Miami, so there was only a simple, relaxed watchfulness among the security people.

By three the DC-10 had climbed out over the Florida peninsula, the sun glinting on its silvery tail and wings, the cocktail cart beginning to move up the long aisle.

There were only ten persons in first class, among them two Mexican government employees returning from vacation; a professor of languages from the University of Mexico who had come to Miami to attend a conference on ancient cultures; three businessmen from AT&T (one of them of Mexican descent) on their way to talk some sense into the Mexican minister of communications about joint funding of a new satellite that would improve telephone service between the two countries; and two American couples on their way to Mexico City on assignment with the U.S. Agency for International Development, which had gotten a new start six months earlier.

They were served by two stews. One of them, Maria Gonzales, a pretty young girl from La Paz, clearly remembered the American couples because they seemed to be in such high spirits. They joked and laughed across the aisle with each other. And Señor Arthur Jules, the older of the two men, tall, husky, balding, was telling the most outrageous jokes about American-Mexican relations, which even the somewhat taciturn language professor seemed to find amusing.

No, she had not actually been close enough at any time to hear exactly what was being said by Señor Jules (he and his wife, Bernice, were seated in 3A and 3B), or by the other AID employee, Ted Asher (he and his wife, Janice, were seated across the aisle in 3C and 3D), but overall her impression of the two American couples was that they seemed pleasant, very aware, and apparently genuinely interested not only in each other, but in the other passengers in first class, especially the Mexican gentlemen.

Had she any idea why the two Americans in first class had been singled out by the hijackers? She would not even venture an opinion. The very same question was, of course, also asked of the other passengers, most of whom had not even the slightest awareness of the goings-on in first class.

There were three couples from Des Moines, Iowa, who had been vacationing together for the past four days in Miami and Key West, and were on their way to Mexico City on a lark. They had never done anything like this in their entire lives. Howard S.

Morgan, the farm implement dealer in Saylorville (a suburb to the north of Des Moines) had come up with the idea in a bar in Key West the night before. They knew nothing about the happenings in first-class. None of them had ever gone first class in their lives and had no interest in ever doing so, but they all saw the killing.

Marjory Dillard, a woman from Duluth on her way to see her son in Mexico City, sat one row behind and across the aisle from one of the hijackers. Throughout the first part of the incident, she had been busy taking photographs with her Instamatic. The flash unit on the camera did not work, but technicians were able to produce images from the film nevertheless, which proved to be of inestimable value. She never gave first class a thought, and later she was so frightened that one of the two men who had taken over the aircraft would find out what she had done and kill her that everything seemed to pass her by in a blur.

Donna Anderson, just forward of the smoking section, who also saw the killing, was traveling with her two young children on the second leg of her trip to Acapulco, where her estranged husband was said to be living on company funds he had stolen. She was going to him, with the children, in an effort to make him see the light of day and return home to Tallahassee with her. The company was willing to forgive, if not forget, should he return of his own accord and promise to make restitution. Throughout most of the hijacking she was so concerned about the safety of her children that she, too, had little or no awareness of anything or anyone outside her own personal sphere.

Of the others, all of them were naturally aware that they had been hijacked, but only half of them actually saw the shooting take place twenty-five yards from the plane on the runway outside Havana.

By four that afternoon, while flight 451 was still fifteen minutes away from landing at Havana, the FBI Miami office had secured the passenger and crew list from the airline (via computer) and had immediately transmitted the list to its headquarters and archives in Washington, D.C. Who aboard the hijacked aircraft could be the hijacker . . . or hijackers (it still was not known how many were involved)?

A scant fourteen minutes later, as the DC-10 was on its final approach, the passenger list had made its way from FBI Headquarters in the J. Edgar Hoover Building to the State Department on 21st and C streets. This transfer of information was done for two reasons. First, many of the passengers aboard the Aeromexico flight were foreign nationals: did State have anything on any of them? Second, two of the American passengers, Arthur David Jules and Theodore Alvin Asher, were employees of the U.S. Agency for International Development, a State Department operation.

Both men's names were flagged in State's computer. It was true, in a technical sense, that they worked for AID. But that simply was their cover. In actuality both Jules and Asher were field operatives for the Central Intelligence Agency.

During those first few critical moments it very nearly leaked that the two Americans were undercover. However a bright supervisor of some years experience at State, whose name was never mentioned on any report, picked up the telephone and called his friend Robert LeGrande, chief of the Western Hemisphere Division of Operations at Langley, to advise him that a couple of "friends" were involved as passengers in a hijacking. Even as they spoke, the State Department supervisor was deleting the flags from the operatives' names, assuring their anonymity at least for the moment. State would continue to make all the appropriate noises as if the two were in fact AID employees, but the CIA would take their debriefing in hand if and when they were returned, which of course never happened because they were murdered.

Stewart Burger, a junior AID official working out of the Miami office, was immediately dispatched to the airport to take charge of Bernice Jules and Janice Asher. He knew nothing other than that they were the wives of the two murdered AID employees, although Albert Thompson, a CIA operations man who happened to be in Atlanta that afternoon, was flown by military jet to Miami where he tagged along, unobtrusively, to ensure nothing was said by either woman.

By early evening of that same day, a special investigative unit of the FBI was set up under the direction of John Lyman Trotter, Jr., who was acting assistant director of the bureau's Special Investigative Division. Trotter was a fairly rare breed in that he not only had the slick political savvy necessary for survival in Washington, but he had genuine talent as well, though over the past few years he had found himself bending his own principles with increasing frequency in order to satisfy an insatiable bureaucracy. He was tall and thin (almost cadaverous), and anything but good-looking, behind thick, wire-rimmed glasses perched atop a huge, misshapen nose. By way of compensation for his looks he had very early on become good at what he did . . . which was finding out things that had to be found out. His wife, who had killed herself three years ago (or so the rumor went) had done so because she could not bear the strain of living with such a highly charged

man. He literally drove her crazy, which in some
odd, perverse way, had increased his reputation as a
power in Washington; as a man with such a devout,
all-consuming singleness of purpose that not even his
private life came before his work.

Trotter drove immediately from his home in Arlington to his office, where he began gathering his
staff, who in turn began feeding him the first bits and
pieces, just as they came in.

"Don't worry about analysis, or any sort of so-
phistication. I want, I need, details. Now!"

The media had gotten on to the business, of
course, and already the networks were not only reporting the hijacking and the mysterious killing of
two Americans, they were all trying to analyze what
this meant in terms of the very complex U.S. relationship with Cuba.

Trotter was of no mind for such nonsense. He
had begun his investigative career some years ago in
the CIA, transferring to the bureau during the
shake-up in the Carter years, when pragmatism was
a dirty word. He had a very good idea, early on, that
Jules and Asher could very well be Company men
using AID as their cover. Two telephone calls to the
State Department, including one to a very angry under secretary, produced the grudging admission that
Jules and Asher may have been more than anyone
was being told. A third call, this one to Lawrence
Danielle, deputy director of operations at Langley,
verified the fact that Jules and Asher were indeed
Company operatives who had been on their way to
Mexico City where they were to have taken up AID
posts at the embassy.

"Is there a connection between their identities
and their murders?" Trotter asked. "I just want to
know that much, Larry, because it looks goddamned
suspicious to me."

"We're working on it, John, believe me. Donald has got this place secured like a fortress. We're at war here. Can you understand that?" Danielle said it as if he were out of breath.

"Apparently the Cubans themselves shot them down right on the runway. Them, as well as the hijackers. What the hell was going on down there?"

"We had no indications, I assure you. Otherwise we would have made different arrangements to get them to Mexico City."

Trotter sighed deeply. "I'm taking charge of this investigation from here. Personal charge. You and I will have to liaise on this."

"Don't go charging off in all directions. Donald is going to want to talk to you," Danielle said hastily. Until Donald Suthland Powers had been appointed director of Central Intelligence by the president, Danielle had been acting director. There was universal agreement in Washington (in itself a rare thing) that Powers was the right man for the job at the right time. Things were getting done.

"We'll have to set up a common ground," Trotter said.

"It'll be on your turf. We have to keep the investigation out of our corner. At least for the time being," Danielle said. "I'll talk to Donald now."

The anonymous little man from across the river showed up that night. He was given clearance and a security badge, over Trotter's signature, and the nonpublicized collaboration between the FBI and the CIA began its intense, eight-day run. Trotter was in charge, with the help of his "expert," as Danielle came to be known, and if anyone could produce results it would be such a team. Within the first twenty-four hours they had brought together most of the facts, leaving the refinements and their ramifications to be worked out on the run.

* * *

In one sense, the hijacking could not have happened at a more propitious time for the United States. We had bungled the Bay of Pigs business in the sixties; we had muffed the rescue of our POWs from the hellish prison camp outside Hanoi in the seventies; and of course the Iranian hostage situation was still painfully fresh in everyone's minds. But America was on the road back. The Reagan administration had taken a hard-line stand with a hostile world. Had the Iranians grabbed our embassy in 1985, the hostages would have been freed within twenty-four hours; probably over a lot of dead bodies, but freed nevertheless. We were beginning to stand tall, and this incident seemed tailor-made to show our new strength of purpose. In another, larger sense, however (certainly no one could have predicted this), the hijacking ultimately resulted in arguably the most sinister and certainly most tragic of consequences.

The actual hijacking itself was an incident whose moment-by-moment details few of the passengers seemed able to agree upon. The consensus collated from the testimony of everyone on board did, however, allow investigators to come to a number of generalized conclusions and quite a few reasonable assumptions.

It went smoothly. All seemed to agree on at least that singular fact.

"We didn't really know anything was happening, at first," and variations on that theme were quite common statements.

The woman with the Instamatic shot one frame of the hijacker who had been seated near her. It showed him with a large, ugly-looking automatic in his left hand. Analysts later were able to identify the gun as a Graz Buyra, the KGB's weapon of assassination. But it was eight days before they realized how the two hijackers got their weapons on board, information which was, of course, never made public. An Aeromexico employee, Manuel Garcia Lopez, had brought the guns onto the aircraft the day before, while it was down for maintenance in Mexico City, stashing them in the waste paper-disposal compartment in the aft, port-side head. Lopez was never apprehended. It was believed he made his way to Cuba the very evening of the hijacking.

The most serious conclusion, at least in the early days, was that the two hijackers had had help. Organization. Backing. Planning. One of them had been tentatively identified (from the woman's photographs) as Eduardo Cristobal Valejo, a small-time hood who had overseen a wide variety of illicit transactions out of Mexico City ... anything from smuggling a few grams of cocaine to an occasional truckload of marijuana across the border at Piedras Negras into Texas. This hijacking was too big for him to have planned it. And how did a small-time hoodlum come to possess a Soviet assassination device in the first place? The other man was never identified. The woman's photographs of him were unclear and showed only the back of his head. Nor were the Ident-a-kit drawings made from descriptions by the crew of any help. So, for a time before the investigation began to be overshadowed by other, larger concerns, the second hijacker came to be known simply as the *mystery man*, a title that perhaps did him too much justice, for almost certainly he, too, was a small-time hood and not some international terrorist.

The actual time of the hijacking was one of the few facts that was nailed down solidly. At exactly 3:23 P.M., when flight 451 had flown nearly a hundred miles out over the Gulf of Mexico off Florida's west coast, the two hijackers (who had already retrieved their weapons) got to their feet.

Valejo, seated near the rear of the plane, walked to the aft galley where he showed his automatic to the two stews there, telling them the flight would be diverted to Havana. There was no noise, no fuss or bother, and none of the passengers, at that point, suspected anything untoward was happening.

At the very same moment, the second hijacker, the *mystery man*, got up from his seat, moved carefully through the first-class section, and opened the door onto the flight deck. The door had been left unlocked in flight, contrary to regulation. He closed and properly locked the door, pulled out his weapon, and announced in clear English but with a Mexican accent that this plane was being taken over and would head immediately for Havana's José Marti International Airport.

In the retelling the crew on the flight deck were quite clear and concise. They were professionals, trained for such an eventuality, so that at no time did they attempt to do anything that would create any further danger. They treated the hijacker with the utmost respect and regard, they told investigators.

Captain Vincent May (the only non-Mexican member of the crew) immediately radioed Miami Flight Control, advising them that they had been hijacked and were being diverted to Havana. No mention was made of a bomb, or of weapons, or of the number of hijackers on board. The Miami controller who took the call turned all his flights over to other controllers so that he was free to handle only this flight . . . standard operating procedure. His supervisor immediately telephoned Havana Air Traffic Control to advise them of the incoming hijacked flight, and then in quick order he telephoned the Federal Bureau of Investigation in Miami, the Mexican Air Control Authority, the Aeromexico representatives at both airports, and finally Miami International Airport security.

The subsequent events seemed to gather their own terrible momentum. At the very same moment that Lawrence Danielle marched up to the seventh floor to inform the DCI of the event, flight 451 rolled to a stop on the far side of the terminal at José Marti International Airport. Within seconds the plane was surrounded by a dozen military vehicles from which emerged more than a hundred soldiers and civil police officers, all armed, all at the ready.

It was like a dream after that, Maria Gonzales, the first-class stew, told investigators. The forward hatch of the aircraft was opened, boarding stairs brought up, and she clearly remembered the thick, damp odors of the warm, tropical day, intermingled with the harsher odor of burnt jet fuel. The hijacker who had stationed himself in the aft galley hurried forward, the big automatic in his left hand raised so that everyone would be sure to see it and therefore try nothing silly. He was met in the first-class compartment by the hijacker who had issued the orders from the flight deck.

There was a bit of confusion at this point. Maria Gonzales told investigators that the hijacker who had been aft pointed his gun at the two Americans— Señors Jules and Asher—and motioned for them to get to their feet, which they did without a fuss. Janice Asher, who had been hysterical all through the incident, nevertheless gave her version in which her husband had leaped up in an attempt to disarm the hijacker, who struck her husband in the head with the weapon. Asher had to be helped off the aircraft. Bernice Jules, on the other hand, told authorities that the hijacker who had emerged from the flight deck had pointed his gun directly at her, right between her eyes from a distance of less than fifteen feet, and motioned for her husband to get to his feet, which he naturally did. She could not remember if Ted Asher had gotten up or not. Of course, he had to have, because he was shot down on the tarmac.

From that point on, the consensus from the passengers and crew was that the two hijackers and the two Americans got off the plane, started away, and at some point one or all of them were seen making a dash for one of the civilian cars that had pulled up, followed by several seconds of intense gunfire in which all four were killed.

It sounded like corn popping in another room, Marjory Dillard said. She did not actually see the shooting, but those passengers on the port side of the aircraft who were able to witness the terrifying event recoiled in horror. About that she was quite clear.

Within the hour the bodies had been taken away in four ambulances, and the Cuban authorities came aboard to begin their preliminary questioning. The wives of the two slain Americans went crazy. They wanted to be with their husbands. The crew only got them calmed down after a long time, Maria Gonzales said. She and first officer Hernando Prañdo managed to administer Valium from the aircraft's first aid locker, and when they got back to the States the next day they were placed in Miami's Mt. Sinai Hospital. The following day they were flown to George Washington University Hospital, and by that evening they were home with their families: Bernice in Wilkes-Barre, Pennsylvania, and Janice in Georgetown, away from the press so that an agency psychologist, Charles Ruff, could have the time and the privacy for a proper debriefing.

Each of the other passengers was questioned by
the authorities through the following two days. They
all stayed at the Miami Airport Hilton at Aeromexico's expense but under FBI supervision.

Everyone agreed that the Cuban authorities had
treated them with the utmost kindness and understanding during their twenty-four-hour stay at a
nearby hotel. The questions were routine, the food
passable, and their hosts polite.

Now back in Miami, the DC-10 was literally
stripped in an effort to find out how the weapons
were brought on board. The crew was thoroughly
questioned, and in Washington files on every single
person aboard (so far as such files were available)
were gone through with a fine-toothed comb. It
wasn't until the beginning of the second week, however, that it was discovered how Manuel Lopez, the
Aeromexico maintenance employee, had brought
the weapons onto the plane. But by then he was long
gone. It was theorized that the very evening of the
hijacking he had made his way to Cuba. Someone
thought they recognized him in Havana, but it was
another dead end. One of many for Trotter's team,
such as the origin of the Soviet assassination devices
both men carried.

By this time the hijacking was old news. Mines
had been placed in the Strait of Hormuz, the Israelis
were talking seriously about going back into Lebanon to stop, once and for all, terrorist strikes on their
settlements. And there were new rounds of talks
with the Russians about the Star Wars defensive
measures which Reagan was asking Congress to support with billions in research funds.

Through all of this Trotter became a very dissatisfied man. He did not like loose ends, and although he was forced by the press of other important
business to order most of his investigative team to

stand down from the hijacking and to spend more
and more of his own time on an ever-increasing
work load, hardly an hour went by when he did not
give serious thought to Lawrence Danielle and what
his old friend had *not* told him. Jules and Asher were
agency operatives on their way to assignment in
Mexico City. That much Danielle would verify. But
beyond that there was nothing as to the nature of
their assignment, or if they were killed because of it.
Trotter was enough of an old hand to know when to
stand down, when not to poke his nose into areas
closed to the bureau, but it galled him nevertheless
that he had been used to take all the heat away from
Langley. His career hadn't really suffered for not
having brought the hijackers' real motives to light,
but there was a blemish on his record. And if there
was anything Trotter despised, it was lack of preci-
sion.

The last of the hijacking business, at least as far
as concerned the bureau, came late on Friday, November 15, a full thirty-three days after the hijacking, in the form of a meeting of the minds, in a
manner of speaking. It was a meeting that nevertheless was on an informal basis and was therefore
never recorded. Lawrence Danielle, who had become quite aloof from the FBI's investigation after
the first few days' flush of information and speculation, showed up at the Alexandria home of an angry
Trotter who was willing, able, and just about ready
to bring pressure to bear on the agency through Justice Department channels.

"I resent being toyed with like this, Lawrence,"
he cried at the beginning. "You of all people surely
understand that to be a policeman . . . an effective
policeman . . . one needs adequate information. No
source must be sacred."

It had been a rather constant theme of his, almost from the first, when he began to realize that there was more to this business than met the eye. (Actually from the moment the woman's photographs had revealed the type of weapons the hijackers carried.)

A Mahler symphony was playing softly on the stereo in the large, pleasant living room. Trotter had fixed them each a drink, and they sat by the fireplace. It was nearing Thanksgiving and was quite chilly. Danielle had thrown his overcoat carelessly over the back of a chair and had taken up a position on a corner of the couch. His actions and manner were irritating just then.

"There's nothing we can do, publicly, that would help us," Danielle began. His voice was soft. Hoarse. He sounded worn out. "In fact there are certain . . . shall we say, delicate matters on the burner now."

"Christ, their shooters were signatures chiseled in stone on the cave walls for the entire world to see," Trotter shouted. His blood pressure was rising. He could feel it. His face was flushed. "Someone is bound to make the connection."

"That is certainly possible," Danielle said.

"Then what do you expect of me?" Trotter said. Much later he recalled that at that moment he felt as if he were rushing headlong down a narrow, darkly blind alley. At the far end was danger. He knew it. Could feel it. Yet he could not stop himself.

"We don't expect anything more of you than what you've already done, John. Just your very best effort. It is appreciated."

Trotter rolled his eyes. He could not believe his old friend had said that. "Save that for the virgins. Just save it for the kids."

Danielle, who at fifty-five was ten years Trotter's senior, sat forward, his drink cradled in his small, delicate hands. "The agency is out of this investigation as of now."

"I'm left holding the bag. Is that what you've come all the way out here to tell me?"

"Let this business run its natural course—"

"Unnatural, if you ask me," Trotter interrupted.

"The hijackers are dead, the maintenance man who supplied the weapons is gone, and the two fine Americans killed in the heat of the moment have been buried. Passions were high. Havana has apologized. Leave it at that."

"State is pressing."

"Let them press, John. It will pass."

"Herbert Danson was by today, actually came by my office, sat me down like a schoolchild, and gave me my ABCs." It still rankled. "The *New York Times* is pressing them for more information. It somehow leaked that there were photographs."

Apparently unperturbed by this news, Danielle nodded. "I know," he said. "Donald asked me to stop by tonight to have a little chat with you."

This was the payoff then, Trotter thought. They were bloody well trying to buy him off. Christ. "Then have your chat and get the hell out of here."

Danielle looked genuinely pained.

"I have an investigation petering out here with holes in it large enough for a Mack truck. Meanwhile, you sit over there in your palace with all the answers. At least point me in the right direction."

Danielle nodded sadly, finished his drink, and set the glass down.

"Another?" Trotter asked, but Danielle shook his head. He seemed to be weighing his words with care.

"Norma will have dinner waiting." He stood up and got his overcoat.

Trotter got to his feet. He felt very frustrated, yet here was an old friend whom he had wounded. "Listen, Larry, I'm sorry."

Danielle waved off the apology. "No need for that, John, I understand. Believe me, I do."

Trotter nodded.

Danielle was staring at him. "If there was one question . . ." he said.

"What?"

"If there was one question for which you had an answer, our very best answer mind you . . . would that help?"

Trotter would forever retain the impression that he was being manipulated at that moment by a man who knew exactly what he was doing and had known all along that their meeting would come exactly to this point. But he could not help himself. The offer was too tempting.

"They carried Soviet weapons. Where did they come from? Who supplied them with the hardware?"

"CESTA."

The word meant nothing to Trotter, though he had a visceral feeling he knew what was coming next. "KGB?"

"More than that. The Soviets have their networks in the Caribbean. Banco de Sur, El Rodeo. But CESTA is more than that." Danielle spoke very slowly, precisely, each word measured carefully, a rare and precious substance to be handled with the utmost respect. "CESTA is composed of the intelligence-gathering systems of all the Warsaw Pact nations, sharing responsibilities as well as product."

"Based in Mexico City."

Danielle nodded.

"And who runs this super organization? Who is the man in charge? The brains?"

At this Danielle shook his head. "That's all, John. As it is, I've overstepped my charter."

The symphony on the stereo was over. The silence held an ominous note. "Then let's go after them, Larry. You and I."

"Stay out of it, John. As one friend to another, I'm telling you to stay clear. There'll be a lot of fallout in the months to come. The man with the clean hands and clear conscience will come out on top."

Before Danielle turned and walked out of the room, Trotter suddenly realized that there was something about his old friend just then that he had never seen before. The way the older man held himself, the set of his shoulders, the hooded expression in his eyes, the tightening of his jaw. It took a moment, though, before Trotter recognized just what it was he had seen, and the effect on him was profound, deeper than any mere words could adequately describe. But forever afterward Trotter would swear that at that moment in time he had seen fear written all over the deputy director of Central Intelligence Agency operations.

That very night, Donald Suthland Powers stood alone at the window in his office on the seventh floor of the Central Intelligence Agency's Langley complex, trying to see into the future. He was short, somewhat stoop shouldered and slight of build, with a squarish, scholarly face, thick eyebrows, and absolutely the most penetrating, intelligent blue eyes that had ever peered across the DCI's desk. At fifty-six he wasn't so terribly old that he had slowed down, yet he was of the age when he could begin looking back at his youth, to a time when the future was a bright penny still untarnished. Since the president had appointed him DCI a year ago, his goals had seemed very clear. At least they had until this night. Terrible goals in the sense that he was a general waging a war in which casualties were being incurred, but exciting in that the endeavor was right: his president and his nation were behind him.

He had spent most of his life in service to his government in one capacity or another, but never from such an awesome position of responsibility and never with such a strong, clearly defined mandate. For the first time, though, the future wasn't clear to him.

"Perhaps you should speak with Trotter," Danielle had suggested. "He'll stand down. He'll give us the room."

Powers was frightened. He needed time. Use the considerable Powers charm, he counseled himself. The power of this office, of your experience and charisma. There would be a lot of fallout. Jules and Asher were only the first. They had been lost in the opening salvo. There would be more, many more. Could he stand it?

God knew he had tried to get out of the agency after his father died. For a year in Hartford, operating the Political Action Think Tank, he had very nearly succeeded. But when the president called him back to arms, he had not been surprised or very saddened. Here was where he would wage his battles. From this very fortress was where he would expiate the sins of deadly competition, nuclear confrontation, and, on a smaller but much more intensely personal scale, the murders of Jules and Asher. They would be the cry to arms. The point around which all of them would rally.

Powers had allowed himself in the years past, rising in the ranks of the agency to deputy director of intelligence before his short-lived retirement, to play the game according to the rules: to honor the status quo. Push a little in Turkey, or Iran or Lebanon, but give a little in Afghanistan, in Poland, and in the Caribbean Basin. But it was over. The honeymoon had ended. The opening shots had been fired in a war that could no longer be denied.

Kennedy had held his Cuban missile crisis. Here now was another crisis. Much subtler, perhaps, but none the less deadly for its obscurity.

Powers turned away from the window. In appearance as well as in intellect, he was reminiscent of William F. Buckley, Jr., with perhaps a bit of William Colby thrown in. He listened now to the ghosts of ten thousand decisions made from this office and wondered if, indeed, he was the right man for the job.

"Baranov," Powers said softly, no longer able to hold the memory in check. They had done battle before, and it was said he was back in Mexico City. Back at the helm of CESTA. They said he was just an agent runner. A network man, not another Andropov, but Powers knew differently.

He looked again at the window, but this time he focused on his own reflection in the glass. He looked haggard. Worn-out. His daughter Sissy told him he wasn't eating his Wheaties. But Katy Moss, his secretary, and Lawrence Danielle both knew the trouble . . . or thought they did. When you're frightened, push ahead; it's the only cure. Whoever had said that never sat behind this desk, Powers decided. And through the entire season he would stop at odd moments to think back to this very evening. To the beginning.

2

A frigid winter had given way to a nasty spring in Lausanne, Switzerland. Kirk Collough McGarvey, an expatriate American in his early forties, lay awake in bed on an early April morning, morosely listening to the hiss of the rain against the windows and the breakfast sounds of Marta Fredricks in the kitchen. Tall, husky, he was the archetypical form of the disgruntled American living overseas: his hair was too long; he wore an unkempt beard; and his clothes always seemed a bit too shabby, ill-fitting, and hastily chosen. In the several years he had lived here he had taken on the manner of a somewhat bemused scholar whose concentration on his studies left little time for the more mundane day-to-day routines of modern life. In his role, he would have fit in well in the intellectual community of any university or exclusive English boarding school for gifted scholars. But it was nothing more than a role, a protective barrier against a world he figured had gone quite mad; a role that was beginning to wear quite thin, however.

Last night he had been cruel again. He and Marta had argued bitterly, and he had said some things he wished he hadn't, no matter their truth.

She had stood her ground and taken every bit of it, which had increased his blind rage.

"Fight back, for Christ's sake," he bellowed. "Don't stand there taking the bullshit." God, how he despised meek compliance. Namby-pamby subservience. Downtrodden acceptance of whatever any asshole wished to dish out.

Yesterday had been a bitch of a day. It had begun at the bookstore when a haughty Swiss customer pretended that she could not understand his French. He had turned her over to his partner, Dortmund Füelm, whose French was nearly nonexistent. The woman, confronted with a gentleman of her own nationality, suddenly blossomed like a wilted rose having been given a fresh spray of cool water. The post had come around noon and included a longish, nasty letter from his ex-wife's lawyer in Washington, D.C., saying that it was once again time for him to increase the amount of his alimony and child-support payments. If need be, the attorney hinted, the matter could be brought into the Swiss courts, which probably would not be effective in jarring loose money, but it would certainly be an embarrassment to him. The between-the-lines message was that the attorney was sleeping with Kathleen and was taking McGarvey's intransigence personally. He was probably a Washington up-and-comer who deserved Kathleen, though McGarvey wondered if the poor sod understood that he was being used by a woman who was probably the most self-centered bitch in a town devoted to self-service. That very afternoon he had whipped off a particularly scathing letter, but better sense stayed him from posting it until he could calm himself down. He walked over to the Lausanne Palace Hotel for a late lunch on the terrace with its magnificent view. But his peace did not last. Dortmund's beautiful though bratty twenty-eight-year-old daughter, Liese, had followed him and now barged right up to his table.

"Aren't you going to ask me to join you? Buy me some lunch?" she said. She worked for an engineering firm nearby. "Or wouldn't Marta approve?"

Instead of the leisurely filet of sole and half bottle of pouilly-fuissé he had contemplated, the two hours seemed to drag interminably with the egocentric kid prattling on about how he should dump Marta and move in with her.

"Daddy adores you, of course, but if you didn't want him to know, it could be our little secret."

"No secrets."

"Fine," she said, brightening even more. "Then we'll tell him that . . ."

"We'll tell him nothing, Liese, because nothing will happen."

Finally managing to disentangle himself by three o'clock, he walked up to the library to continue the research he had begun six weeks ago on Voltaire, who had lived and worked for a time in Lausanne. But he found that his concentration had been shot to hell; reading a rare edition (with notes in the margin) of *Candide*, his mind bounced back and forth between Kathleen, Liese Füelm, and Marta, so he gave it up and was back home by four-thirty.

"Bad day?" Marta asked innocently when he came in. She was ten years younger than he but looked even younger than that, and had a glow about her. She was tall, not unattractive, with long dark hair, wide eyes, and sensitive lips. She carried herself with an athletic grace. In the winter she skied, in the summer she swam, and year-round she jogged five miles each morning, rain or shine, after which they would have breakfast and then often make love.

"Kathleen has sent a lawyer after me, and Liese is up to her old tricks again," he said, throwing off his coat, and opening a beer.

Marta smiled. She was fixing their dinner. "There's nothing your ex can do to you in Switzerland. As far as concerns Liese, why don't you jump her bones. She'll back off fast enough. She's only flirting, you know."

"Fucking. That's your goddamned answer for everything, isn't it?" McGarvey snapped. "Christ on a cross!"

She looked up, her eyes bright. "I'm sorry, Kirk . . ."

"Yes, you are."

She had started to cry then, which really set him off, so he had proceeded to take her apart, piece by piece, bit by bit, attacking her eating habits, her physical fitness insanity (as he called it), her sense of clothing style or lack of it, her constant prattling about totally inconsequential shit, and her sex-solves-everything juvenile attitude. And she stood and took every bit of it. Had it been him on the receiving end of such a tirade, he would have lashed out. She had not, which made him even angrier.

It was his turn to be sorry this morning, though he knew it didn't really matter. He suspected he could say or do almost anything to her, and she would remain. Out of love, or loyalty, or for some other, darker reason?

"You awake in there?" she called from the kitchen.

He reached over to the night table, got himself a cigarette, and lit it before he answered. "Just coffee, Mati. It's all I can stand."

He could hear her laughing. It was a musical sound.

She appeared in the doorway with a cup of

coffee in hand, a big grin on her face. Her hair was pinned up, and she had changed out of her jogging suit into a thick robe.

"You were a real shit last night, you know," she said.

"I know," he said, turning away. It was hard to face her. He had drunk too much, and this morning he had a splitting headache. So why couldn't he tell her he was sorry?

Her grin faded and she came the rest of the way into the bedroom, setting the coffee down and perching on the edge of the bed. She reached out and touched his knee beneath the covers. "What is it, Kirk?"

"Nothing," he mumbled.

"It worries me when you get like this," she said. "Do you want me to talk to Liese?"

McGarvey laughed, though there was no pleasure in it. "It's not that."

She studied his face. "What then, boredom?"

"Yes, that."

"You're forty-four and your life is passing you by. You're no longer in the fray, is that it?"

McGarvey said nothing. It seemed like years since his life had even had a semblance of real purpose. Yet in the seventies when he worked for the Company he had been just as frustrated: only it was in a different way. The Carter administration had ended it for him. A dozen places, a hundred faces all passed through his mind's eye with the speed of light. Santiago, Chile, had been the end. Afterward he had been recalled, and within six months he had been dumped. Overexuberance. Taking matters into his own hands. Operating outside his sanctions. Failure to keep a grasp on the world political climate.

"I talk in my sleep. That's it, isn't it?"

"All the time," she said.

"Do you write it all down, Mati? Have you got a little black book?"

She started to rise, but he sat forward and grabbed her arm.

"I want to know."

"Why are you doing this, Kirk? Haven't you had enough? Do you forget what you were like when you got here? You were a wreck."

"And you were Joan of Arc riding in on your white charger, your armor all polished, your sword sharp, raised to do battle. Are you telling me that, Mati?"

Her nostrils flared and there was a momentary spark in her eyes, but her control was marvelous, and she ended her little battle by merely shaking her head. "We can't go on. Not like this."

McGarvey released her arm and lay back on the bed. Christ, he felt rotten. Marta was almost certainly a watchdog of the Swiss federal police, sent to his side so that they could keep track of him. Former Central Intelligence Agency operatives made a lot of people nervous, especially the Swiss, who valued their clandestine CIA banking operations above all personal considerations.

Was she his watchdog? Or was it love he saw in her eyes?

"No, we can't," he said.

She got up from the edge of the bed and went back into the kitchen.

He sometimes thought of that part of his past as the glory days. And they were that, weren't they? he asked himself. Ruefully he had to admit a certain nostalgia, even though he understood that the reality wasn't anywhere near as exciting or interesting as his memory of it.

Why did he get out in the first place? The end was coming long before they kicked him out. He could have changed things to prevent it. Only he was too blind, too stupid, to see it. Stewart had made a great show of fighting for him. Yet, later, after Alvin had bought it in Geneva, McGarvey had heard that Stewart had bad-mouthed him all over the agency. It was Washington. It was the power that had corrupted them all. The ends justified the means, didn't they? By then Phillipi was out, Mason had been killed short of the runway at Andrews, and like the meek inheriting the earth, the quiet but sly Danielle had been bounced upstairs.

McGarvey threw back the covers, got out of bed, and padded into the bathroom, where he looked at himself in the mirror. Already there was a lot of gray creeping into his hair, flecks of it throughout his beard. There were bags under his bloodshot eyes, and the beginnings of a paunch were showing, though his legs and arms still had something left to them.

It occurred to him that his life had happened in three quantum jumps, each more debilitating to him than the last. The first stage was his childhood and youth, which ended with the death of his parents in a car crash. His sister was given their cash, their stocks, and their bonds, but he was given the ranch in western Kansas which he sold for something under three quarters of a million dollars. Living on the interest, he had enjoyed a certain financial independence from that moment on, but the loss of his parents and the harsh disapproval of his sister, who had wanted the ranch kept in the family, had left him out in a spiritual wasteland. The second devastation had come with his dismissal from the Central Intelligence Agency because he had killed a tinpot general in Santiago on orders that had changed, unbeknownst to him, in midstream. Now this, his retirement to ostensibly the most neutral

place in the world, was the third stage. He had the
feeling it was also coming to an end, and when the
finish came the results would be catastrophic for
him, as had the ends of the first two stages of his life.

Marta came to the doorway. "I can't help if you
close up on me," she said softly.

He looked at her reflection beyond his in the
mirror. He was afraid of her. Afraid that after all she
was nothing more than a Swiss police watchdog sent
to keep track of him. And even more afraid that she
was not pretending that she loved him.

His sister said he could not understand what a
commitment was . . . what it meant. "Do us all a
favor, Kirk, and grow up."

"Like you and Al?"

"Why do you think the ranch was left to you?"

"I don't know."

"Mom and Dad hoped it would change you.
Settle you down."

McGarvey focused on Marta. "Sorry," he said.
"I'm sorry."

3

"Boredom." He spoke the word aloud as he turned the corner in the rain and trudged down the stairs below his apartment block. Perhaps Marta was right. Or perhaps he missed the States. It had been five years since he'd been back. Not the McDonald's, or the *Three's Company*, or the jostling machinations of an upwardly mobile population—those weren't things to be missed—rather it was the feel of the country, of her cities. Telephone operators who honestly understood English, little things like that. A decent martini. Supermarkets. Sears. Penney's.

Two young girls sharing an umbrella came up the stairs. McGarvey had to step aside to let them pass. He turned up his coat collar and at the bottom hesitated a moment to look down at the lake before he continued. Before too long it would be summer.

He and Marta had a small sailboat. Perhaps they'd take a trip across the lake to Evian on the French side. Last summer had gotten away from them, as had the summer before and the winters in between.

He stopped short. That was it. Time was passing like a wide, slow-moving river, deceiving in its flow. You never realized the volume of time that was going by until moments such as these when you suddenly awoke, face to face with your own mortality.

A trip back to the States was certainly possible. Füelm was capable of running the shop. It would get him away from Liese's games (which he actually found flattering when he would admit it to himself). It would be a book-buying trip. It was time he saw his sister and his nephews in Salt Lake City. On the way out he would stop by and see the ranch. Visit his parents' graves. And then there was this business with Kathleen and her attorney friend. He smiled inwardly. It would give him a certain perverse pleasure to show up on their doorstep, tell her in no uncertain terms what he thought, and then kick the attorney's ass up around his shoulders. His daughter was a teenager now, young, delicate. How much like her mother had she become? It was something he needed to know. It was time, he decided, that Elizabeth found out her father wasn't some ogre, some hippie living in a commune in Europe. It made him angry to think of the things Kathleen would be teaching her.

Marta would understand. It would give her a much-needed vacation.

Turning these thoughts over in his mind, McGarvey continued downtown, the city coming alive with the morning. Lausanne was a wonderful town, filled with contrasts of which the Swiss were inordinately proud but which tourists often found disconcerting. Rising from Lac Léman (here never Lake Geneva), the city hastened up into the hills in tiers on which the old and the new were situated in sharp defiance of any sort of convention. An eighteen-story modern skyscraper on a low tier might compete with a lovely Georgian cathedral perched on a hilltop. Old shops and homes, within rabbit warrens of narrow twisting streets and alleys, were being gutted in one section of the city to make way for the new, while all around the Notre Dame, the selfsame architectural style was being faithfully restored. It was a city of footpaths, of quaint bridges and overpasses, yet the din of heavy (at times even crazy) traffic was nearly constant.

He arrived at the busy Place Saint-Francois across from which his bookstore was located. As he did every morning, he stopped at the news kiosk and picked up a copy of the Paris edition of the *Herald-Tribune*. When he arrived here five years ago he had been a basket case. His nerves were shot to hell. Around every corner, in every doorway, under every overhang, in every shadow lurked some dark figure from his past. Perhaps friends of the Chilean general he had assassinated. They believed in vendettas. Perhaps the KGB, perhaps the Bulgarians who had been so active just recently, according to the newspapers. Perhaps any of dozens of people he had crossed could have come here to watch for him, to wait for the one moment of weakness, the moment when he would be vulnerable. As he had been doing since he had come here, McGarvey stood a few moments beneath the kiosk's awning, pretending to look at the headlines of the other papers on display while he scanned the large square and his approaches to the bookshop.

An exercise in futility, nothing more, he thought, although to adequately cover the square would require several teams, some of them stationary, at least one mobile. They'd stand out, especially here given the Swiss penchant for routine. He shook his head and started to turn. All a moot point. He himself had fallen into the bad practice of routine; up at the same time each morning, the walk along the same route, the newspaper, the quick scan, and then off to the store. Even an amateur could nail him after a few days' observation.

Out of the corner of his eye, he noticed a dark blue van pulling up across the square. A tall man in a dark overcoat materialized out of the crowd, hopped into the passenger side of the van, and a moment later another figure, this one dressed in a tan mackintosh and wearing a wide-brimmed hat, stepped away and walked off in the opposite direction. The van took off, merged with traffic, and disappeared around the corner toward the Regina. McGarvey held himself in check against the instinct to look directly across. Instead, he stuffed the newspaper in his sodden jacket pocket and headed around the square along his usual route.

There was no way of knowing for sure, of course, but he decided that he would bet his next six months' income that the two from the van were not Swiss. They did not have the look.

McGarvey had to hold up for a break in traffic before he was able to cross, and then he hurried, head bent low, apparently in deep concentration. The man in the tan mack was fifty yards beyond the bookstore pretending to take refuge from the rain in a shop doorway.

Across the square he spotted the van coming up from the lake. Two legmen, one van. They were amateurs. Lookers. No hit men here.

The tan mack looked directly his way, then stepped out of the doorway and hurried off in the opposite direction. The Ford van came around the square, and it headed again toward the Regina Hotel. As it passed, McGarvey saw the driver and the man in the dark overcoat riding shotgun, both studiously watching traffic. The plates were Swiss, but it was a rental.

Americans? He got the impression they might be. They had the look. But what did they want? Why the hell had they come after all these years? He was no threat. He wasn't writing a tell-all book like so many expatriate Company men had done . . . were doing. He had no ax to grind. Not now. He was merely trying to live his life here, out of the fray.

His store, International Booksellers, was a two-story yellow brick affair, rare books and the office on the top floor, the main body of the store on the first. It was nestled between a tobacconist and a perfume shop. McGarvey stepped across the sidewalk, dodging the heavy pedestrian traffic, and went into the shop. Several customers were browsing. Füelm, a short, scholarly-looking man with white hair and steel-rimmed glasses, was on his hands and knees, holding his glasses up with one hand as he myopically searched the spines of a row of books on the bottom shelf.

He looked up. "Good morning, Kirk, is it still raining?"

"Cats and dogs," McGarvey said, hurrying up the iron spiral stairs off to one side.

At the front window he looked down on the busy street for a minute or two, but the blue van did not make another swing, although he thought he saw the tan mack round the corner across the way.

Why had they come now? Marta would say he was imagining things. He knew better.

He turned away from the window and hurried back to his office where he closed and locked the door, then unlocked the big bottom drawer of his old oak desk. Reaching underneath he slipped the wooden stop and pulled the drawer all the way out, setting it aside. From beneath the main pedestal he withdrew a small bundle wrapped in oilcloth, which he quickly opened. Inside was a well-used, well-oiled

Walther PPK automatic, loaded, two extra clips with it. The compact weapon had been his companion in the old days. On more than one occasion it had saved his life, and at times he thought of it as an old friend. He handled it with great respect now, wiping off the excess oil with his handkerchief, then working the slide back and forth, pumping out several shells. He released the clip from the automatic's butt, reinserted the rounds, and reloaded the gun.

Possibly they were Americans, he thought, stuffing the gun and spare clips in his coat pocket. Possibly they were the opposition here with an ax to grind. He put the drawer back in his desk, locked it, then left his office and went downstairs.

Füelm was at the bottom of the stairs. "I was just coming up."

McGarvey hesitated on the bottom tread. Outside, the blue van passed on the street.

"Kirk?" Füelm said softly. "Are you feeling well this morning?"

"Just fine, Dortmund. What was it you needed?"

Füelm eyed his wet jacket. "Are you going back out?"

"An errand to run. Was there something you wanted to ask?"

"I can't quite seem to put my hands on the Oxford *Aquinas*."

"Upstairs on my desk. There's a hold on it for Herr Bergmann. He said he'd be in later this week for it."

"That explains the mystery," Füelm said, stepping aside to let McGarvey pass. "Everything is fine with you?"

McGarvey looked at him. "Marta telephoned?"

Füelm nodded. "She was worried."

McGarvey patted him on the arm. "It's all right,

believe me, Dortmund, it's all right. But just now I have to run."

"When will you be back . . .?" Füelm called, but McGarvey had spun on his heel and hurried to the back of the shop, into a tiny storeroom and book-repair area. He opened the alley door and looked outside. A delivery truck was parked near the east end, but in the opposite direction he was in time to see two young girls with the umbrella whom he had passed on the stairs below his apartment, coming up from the corner. They spotted him and immediately turned and disappeared back the way they had come.

There was more than one team! It meant they had been at his house. They had been watching him, without him detecting it. For how long? Long enough to have a handle on his routine.

He stepped out of the doorway and raced down the alley, the cobblestones slippery in the rain. He reached the narrow side street that led to the broad Avenue d'Ouchy. The girls were just crossing the street and he had to hurry not to lose them in the heavy traffic, nearly getting run over by a bus as he crossed.

He caught up with them as they waited for the light to change on the Avenue de la Gare across from the Victoria Hotel. He put his hand in his coat pocket, his fingers curling around the Walther's grip.

At a distance the girls had seemed very young. Close up he could see that they were at least in their late twenties. For a moment or two they just looked at him without saying a word. He felt silly. He was on a fool's errand. He was tired, hung over, and was still feeling a lot of guilt about what he had done last night to Marta. He was chasing after hobgoblins now.

He turned and looked the way he had come as the man in the tan mack came around the corner.

The van came up behind him and slowed down.

McGarvey turned back, suddenly angry. It had not been his imagination. The girls were staring at him. Across the avenue the man with the dark coat was watching them. His right hand was in his pocket.

"We mean you no harm, Mr. McGarvey," one of the girls said. Her face was round, her nose tiny, her eyes a pretty blue.

There were a lot of pedestrians around them, waiting for the light to change, indifferent to everything except the nasty weather and getting to where they were going.

"Please. We wanted contact with you, without alerting the Swiss authorities."

"For what purpose?" McGarvey asked. His adrenaline was pumping, he could feel his heightened awareness, the tensing of his muscles. The tan mack was holding back. The van passed through the intersection, then pulled into a parking space in front of the hotel.

"There is someone who wishes to speak with you. We have gone through great effort," the other girl said. The hair sticking out from beneath her scarf was red. Her eyes were wide, and there were freckles on her nose and cheeks. For some reason McGarvey thought of the German word for freckles . . . *sommersprossen.*

"I don't understand," he said. If they meant to harm him, he was cornered on three sides. But they had left him an escape route: east along the Avenue de la Gare. If they were driving him, the assassin would be waiting somewhere out ahead. The erratic behavior of a field man apparently on the run will tumble the best laid plans. Wasn't that the drill? But it had been a lot of years.

He glanced again at the tan mack. That'd be the direction. Through the back door.

"Please, sir," the blue-eyed girl said. "Just listen, that's all. It's Mr. Trotter. John Trotter. You were old friends."

A bus rattled by, exhaust fumes rising up into the cold drizzle. The freckled girl was getting nervous. Trotter, here? Why?

"We can't stand here like this," Freckles said.

"Mr. Trotter is waiting in the van in front of the hotel," the other girl said.

"Why didn't he telephone?"

"Your girlfriend is Swiss police, didn't you know?"

"He could have called at the store . . ." McGarvey started, but he had an idea what was coming next.

"Liese Füelm is also Swiss police, assigned to watch you."

Christ, he thought. He glanced across the avenue to where the van was parked. Someone in a light raincoat had gotten out. He was tall and very thin. He wore no hat. From here McGarvey could see the glasses, the very large nose. There was no mistaking who it was. But why here, like this? What did they want?

He was coming down, his anxiety that he was finally being flushed turning to anger. "I'm out of the business," he snapped.

"He would just like to talk to you, sir," the one with the freckles said.

The light was changing. McGarvey suddenly pivoted to the right and skipped across the street, traffic surging angrily behind him, momentarily cutting off the two girls and leaving the tan mack on the opposite side of the street.

Trotter raised his hand, as if in greeting, and McGarvey had the feeling he was back ten years. Trotter had been pretty good at what he did in operations, and although they had never worked directly with each other they had liaised from time to time.

McGarvey glanced back. The girls were gone, as were the tan mack and the man in the dark raincoat. He pulled up short.

"Hello, Kirk," Trotter said.

"What do you want?"

"We'll stop so that you can telephone the bookstore and Marta. I don't want them looking for you," Trotter said. He seemed somewhat agitated. "You'll be back in time for dinner."

Trotter had changed a lot. There was gray in his hair, and his glasses seemed thicker. He used to worry about losing his eyesight. But more than that was the change in his face. He was a different man. Older than his years. Worry. Stress. It was all there.

"Are you back with the Company?"

"The bureau. We need your help, Kirk."

McGarvey shook his head. "I'm out of the business, you know that. Coming here was a waste of your time."

"Just listen to us, it's all we want. No strings attached. I absolutely promise it. You have my word. On my honor."

"Who is the 'we'?"

"Someone from Justice, I don't know if you've heard of him. He wasn't much of a power when you were around. Name of Len Day. He's a deputy attorney general."

"Here in Switzerland to see me?"

Trotter nodded. "Honestly, Kirk, we do need your help. You can turn it down after you've listened, but at least give us that much."

"Who suggested me?"

"I did."

"Why?"

Trotter looked away, his eyes narrowed. He took off his glasses, which were dripping with rain, and rubbed his eyes. "It's getting strange out there, Kirk," he said, as if he were taking great care with his words. He put his glasses on and turned back. "I know you can be trusted. In fact, it's why you got the ax. You were too damned honest."

"That was then. How do you know what I've become in the meantime?" McGarvey asked. This was all so odd. He felt as if he were looking through the wrong end of a telescope at his life.

Trotter smiled. Shook his head. "Oh, no, Kirk, you haven't changed. Of that, at least, I am certain."

4

They had stopped at a gas station outside fashionable du Mont Blanc on the scenic route to Morges, so that McGarvey could telephone Füelm at the bookstore and Marta at the apartment. Füelm was understanding, but Marta was hurt that he wanted to go off by himself for the day. He could tell from her voice that she thought he was still angry from last night. But in the end she accepted his explanation that he simply wanted to be alone with his own thoughts, to work out his problem his own way without the pressure of the shop and so that he wouldn't be able to hurt her again. In any event, McGarvey thought, she was in no position to come after him. Short of turning out the federal police and issuing an all-points bulletin, what could she do? He and Trotter sat in the back of the van while the taciturn driver concentrated on traffic. Most of the others on Trotter's team would make their way down to the airport in Geneva. Now that McGarvey was in the bag, they were done and could return home. Trotter couldn't explain how he came to know Marta and Liese were Swiss police, and for a while McGarvey toyed with the idea that he was under arrest for the business in Chile. But something about his old friend didn't seem to gel, and he began to get the feeling that something was about to happen that he wasn't going to like.

"I never knew what happened to you," he said, lighting himself a cigarette. "After I left the Company, I was out of touch with the old crowd."

"They were pretty worried about you there for a while. Thought you would go sour on them."

"I'm surprised they didn't come after me. I've been watching for it."

Trotter laughed. "That was the Carter administration, remember, boy? You were bounced because you followed orders too well. They thought we were getting a bit too much like the Russkies. *Mokrie dela* . . . wet affairs . . . spilling of blood . . . Department Victor, and all that."

McGarvey remembered how it had been after he had returned from Santiago. Operations was in a shambles, field agents were streaming in from all over the place, and every day it seemed there was something in the *New York Times* naming one deep-cover operative or another in Portugal, in Mexico, in East Germany or Czechoslovakia. The Company was being reduced to satellite surveillance of target countries, and on a much broader scale, the Foreign Broadcast Information Service (which was administered directly by the deputy director of intelligence, to whose analysts the product was funneled) reigned supreme for a time. It was a huge, thankless task—listening to foreign broadcasts; reading foreign newspapers, magazines, and books; translating the material; and picking out the significant details. Every field station had its cadre of readers for translation, most of them locals, and in places such as Okinawa, Bangkok, the U.K., and Key West, receiving stations were manned around the clock to monitor broadcasts. It was a factory operation. The translated data was collated into a daily unanalyzed summary which was transmitted to Langley for the desk jocks to pick apart and put together in whatever the reigning pattern was.

"It's different now, you know," Trotter said.

"The press seems to be in love with the Company. Is Powers that good?"

"Absolute tops. I mean it. We worked together on the United Nations thing back in the mid-seventies. He was assistant DDO at the time, but he took the case under his wing. I tagged along as a legman. And I'm telling you, Kirk, the man is everything anyone has said about him and more. Absolutely brilliant. First class. A real force."

McGarvey had been cold; he was warm now, and he opened his coat. He had never actually worked with Powers. But he'd never met a man in the Company who had disliked him. Unanimously, Powers was considered the man with the right stuff. His appointment to DCI had surprised no one and had pleased a great many people.

"So what's the rub?"

"When you're in, you're solid. When you're out, you're cold. There's no real cooperation anymore. The CIA runs its show and we run ours, with very little contact in between."

"Sounds like sour grapes to me," McGarvey said, getting a bad feeling that they might be trying to catch him up in some interservice struggle.

"It's nothing like that, Kirk, believe me when I tell you this. We've done some work with the Company, of course. Passed a little information back and forth, but not much. Not enough and especially not lately. The lines of communication across the river are closing, and it's become . . . ominous."

"And now you're here in Switzerland, outside

your charter," McGarvey said, not wanting to get involved but curious nevertheless.

This was the sort of thing Marta was watching out for. He had visions of Trotter and the one from Justice asking him to use his connections to ferret out the Swiss bank account number of some nefarious character they were after. Only he didn't have any connections. Not here. They passed through the yachting town of Morges and the rain began to let up. Back toward Lausanne, the sun even tried to peek out from under the clouds.

"There's probably nothing I can do for you," McGarvey said.

"We just want you to listen, Kirk," Trotter said softly. "Nothing more. Afterward we'll talk. You'll see."

They passed through Saint Prex, Allaman, and Rolle, all little villages along the choppy, gray lake, finally turning inland up into the hills, the snow-covered slopes of Noirmont, ten miles away on the French border, wreathed in a halo of clouds. A large chalet rose at a sheer angle from the roadside; it had a short, narrow driveway to the garage on the ground floor. They turned in and stopped. The driver got out, opened the garage door, then came back and drove them inside.

Anonymous here in the hills above Lake Geneva, simply another lodge in a region of similar retreats; it was a safe house.

McGarvey followed Trotter up from the garage into a short corridor that opened into a large entryway. The house was gloomy, with polished dark woods and thick beams. The massive banisters in the stairhall were hand carved in ornate patterns, with intertwined stag horns and leaping fish in bas-relief. They passed through the hall into the living room,

which was a long, narrow chamber that ran the
length of the house and overlooked the road. Stained
glass windows flanked a massive, natural stone fireplace in which three very large birch logs were
burning. To the left, along the inner wall, were
bookcases looking down on a grand piano, on the
other side of which were a library table with a
Tiffany lamp and several chairs. To the right were
two huge, overstuffed sofas, several armchairs, and a
square oak coffee table that looked as if it weighed a
ton. The floors were highly polished wood covered in
two places by large oriental rugs. Paintings adorned
the walls. This was the chalet of a very wealthy
Swiss. Probably a banker who came here on weekends.

"Mr. McGarvey, I'm so glad that you could
come down here to talk with us," Oliver Leonard
Day, associate deputy attorney general for criminal
justice, said, bounding in from the hallway.

McGarvey didn't know Day, but he knew his
kind: career bureaucrat who had married the right
woman, ran in the right circles, and dined at the
right places. He was probably in his mid-to-late
fifties, but looked years younger. His eyes were baby
blue, his complexion tan, and his thinning hair
boyishly sun bleached. He was part of the California
health-nut crowd that had invaded Washington on
Reagan's coattails. Marta would probably have a lot
in common with him.

"I don't know if I'm going to be of any help,"
McGarvey said.

"John told you we only want you to listen," Day
boomed, eyeing McGarvey's long hair and beard.

McGarvey nodded.

"We want you to meet someone, listen to his
story."

Day seemed to be in constant motion. His eyes

darted back and forth; he spoke with his hands like an Italian, or like someone who was very nervous; and he had a habit of shifting his weight from one foot to the other as if he were a boxer ready to dodge any blow that might come his way.

"You don't know this person, Kirk," Trotter interjected. "It's not someone out of your past." He turned to Day. "I think Kirk may have gotten the impression that this was going to be some sort of an interagency squabble. Dredging up old issues from the past."

"Heavens, no," Day nearly exploded with sincerity. "Good grief, we can't have you thinking that. You can't possibly think we brought you here for that."

Trotter stepped into the breach. "You do agree at least to listen, don't you, Kirk?" he asked.

McGarvey nodded. They had gotten him this far, he might as well stay for the main attraction.

"No obligations, McGarvey. I want you to understand that right up front," Day said. He stopped his fidgeting and peered more closely at McGarvey, who got the impression that the man needed glasses but was too vain to wear them. "You do, don't you . . . understand?"

"No, I don't," McGarvey said pointedly. "I don't understand at all. But I'm here. I'll listen to whatever it is you're about to tell me, afterward we'll discuss whatever it is you want to discuss, and then I'll be back in Lausanne in time for dinner." He turned to Trotter. "That was the deal, wasn't it, John?"

"Absolutely."

They stood just inside the doorway. The room seemed peaceful, as if it didn't belong here, as if it belonged to another, less complicated time.

"Why don't we just have a seat," Day said,

motioning toward the couches, "while John fetches our other guest."

"Yes, sir," Trotter said. "Care for some coffee, Kirk?"

"Cognac would be better, I think, with the head I've got." He was starting to feel mean again.

Day sniffed his disapproval but said nothing. Trotter left the room. McGarvey could hear him going up the main stairs. He had absolutely no idea what to expect. But they had gone through a great deal of trouble to get him here, Trotter seemed on edge, and a high-ranking U.S. Justice Department bureaucrat had come along, presumably to lend his weight to the proceedings. That worried McGarvey the most. What was Trotter up to that he needed to legitimize his efforts?

"I understand you have lived here in Switzerland for five years now," Day said conversationally as they sat down, McGarvey in an easy chair beneath one of the windows.

"Since '82."

"Family back in the States?"

"An ex-wife in D.C., and a sister and a couple of nephews in Utah."

Day seemed distracted. He was watching the entryway. Upstairs they heard a door close, and seconds later someone was coming downstairs. There were two of them. Day sat straighter and looked at McGarvey.

"This will be hard for you to believe."

McGarvey managed a slight smile. "Do you believe it?"

Day started to shrug, but then he nodded. "Yes. Yes, I do, God help me."

Trotter appeared in the doorway with another man. Day jumped to his feet. "The staff is occupied?" he said.

"They'll leave us alone," Trotter said, coming the rest of the way into the room.

The other man was half a head shorter than Trotter and very slender. His complexion was olive, his hair jet black and shiny with hair lotion. He wore a long, thin mustache, and when he grinned McGarvey saw that two of his teeth were gold. McGarvey guessed him to be in his late forties, although he was dressed youthfully in baggy trousers with pleats in the front, a gaudy sport shirt open to the navel, and some sort of nearly collarless sportcoat, the sleeves of which had been pushed up to just below his elbows. His shoes were narrow and extremely pointed. He was a Latino. There was no mistaking it.

"You don't know each other?" Day asked McGarvey. "I'd like to establish that right off the bat."

"Never seen him before in my life."

"Good," Day said. "Francisco Artimé Basulto, most recently a guest of the Dade County Jail in Miami, before that a resident of Havana, and before that an employee of the Central Intelligence Agency."

The Cuban grinned, his gold teeth flashing as he came jauntily around the couch, sticking out his hand. His fingernails were long and well manicured. He smelled of bay rum and whatever lotion was on his greasy hair.

McGarvey didn't bother to stand, nor did he shake Basulto's hand. He had seen this type before. He could almost hear the story the little man was going to tell. It was going to be some sort of a shakedown, no doubt. McGarvey was surprised Trotter had fallen for it.

"I don't give a shit if you shake my hand, see?" Basulto spat, his accent heavy. "You think I care? As

long as you came to help, why give a shit?" He
swiveled on Trotter, who had taken on a suddenly
hard expression.

"Sit down," Trotter snapped.

Basulto stepped back, wounded, but then he sat
down with a flourish, crossed his legs, and lit a very
long, thin cigar.

"I'll get the cognac," Trotter said, and he left.
Day took his seat and Basulto stared defiantly across
at McGarvey.

It was a time for remembering. Twenty-five,
thirty years ago, at the end of Batista's Cuba. Trotter
brought them back and McGarvey had to wonder
what was so important about those days. Since then
we'd lived through the riots of the sixties, the Vietnam War, the horror of assassinations, Watergate.

Roger Harris, a CIA case officer working out of
the embassy in Havana as a third secretary for
economic affairs, was beating the bushes for recruits
when he came across Basulto, an angry young man
looking for a savior. Castro's name was on
everyone's lips, and had Harris come three months
later Basulto almost certainly would have taken to
the hills.

He was brought to Havana, and before he could
get himself into any trouble, he was flown up to
Miami where he spent two weeks in a southside safe
house learning the entire wealth of what the agency
had got from its OSS heritage and quite a few new
things it had invented on its own. Weapons, hand-to-
hand combat, radio communications, secret writing,
letter drops, tails—anything that would help keep
him alive and useful when he was returned.

Basulto was a natural back in Havana, running
with the high rollers down from the States. With his
flash and gift of gab, the agency training he had

received, and with Roger Harris running the plays in for him, he was a hit. He became the lapdog of the rich and famous who haunted such places as the Copa, the Lido, and the Paris Revu.

Through his rich American connections, Basulto was invited to the kind of parties attended by Batista's cabinet ministers and other high-ranking government and military leaders . . . along with their wives and girlfriends. For a couple of years, until Batista's fall, Basulto's product was said to have been the best they had ever seen.

At the end of 1958, when the government finally collapsed, Batista left the country, and Castro came triumphantly down from the hills, Basulto took off his glad rags and went home to the farm. The U.S. embassy was closed and sealed, our concerns in Cuba being looked after by the scanty American Affairs Interest Section in the Swiss embassy, and our agency operations severely curtailed.

"Our friend here would have been burned in any event, had the end not come when it did," Trotter said.

Basulto said nothing. He seemed to be waiting.

The wife of a certain colonel in Batista's defense planning establishment apparently lost her heart to Basulto. The colonel understood what was going on, but he actually encouraged it because Basulto was ostensibly supplying the Cubans with intelligence he supposedly gathered from his American contacts.

"And for all we know, he probably did give them hard intelligence," Trotter snapped.

Basulto sat forward, an angry glint in his eyes. "I never told those bastards anything except what Roger told me to tell them. I love the U.S.A., I swear to Christ!" He crossed himself and raised his right hand. There was a heavy gold chain on his wrist, a gold-cased Rolex on the other.

From what Trotter could gather, Harris did not leave when the other Americans left. He hung around for a time, laying very low of course, until things became too difficult, and he had to pull out. He was forced into it.

But an odd thing happened. Harris brought Basulto out of Cuba and pointed him in the direction of Mexico City. It was a definite no-no because Harris apparently was working on his own.

The name Roger Harris meant nothing to McGarvey, but he knew the type. They were almost a legend in the Company. The agency was fairly new at the time, and a lot of bright young case officers, many of them recently out of the military service, some of them transferred from the State Department, were trying their best to carve niches for themselves. The heights never loomed so brightly for the right young man as they had in those days.

"I loved that man," Basulto said softly. "I want you to know that Roger Harris was absolutely first rate in my book . . . the very tops . . . a real man."

5

"They left Cuba in early June of 1959," Trotter said. "Harris returned to Washington, but our friend here got a car and drove out to San Diego, where he entered Mexico at Tijuana."

"It wasn't so easy getting out of Havana," Basulto said. "Uncle Fidel hated Americans. He was telling everyone that Batista was an American puppet."

"Our friend here was on the hit list, of course," Trotter interjected. "He had supplied Batista with information."

"That was playacting."

"He couldn't have lasted very long. Perhaps Harris felt he owed it to him," Trotter said. He shook his head. "No way of knowing for sure. But Harris got back to the Latin American desk and our little scumbag here was on the loose."

"I don't have to take that!" Basulto cried. "Goddamnit, Mr. Day, I don't have to sit and listen to that kind of talk, do I?"

Day leaned his head back on the couch and closed his eyes. He crossed his legs. "Sorry we had to bother you like this, Mr. McGarvey," he said apologetically. "John, I want you to take Mr. McGarvey

back home, and then I want this scumbag on the very
next flight back to Dade County. I don't ever want to
see his miserable face again."

"Yes, sir," Trotter said.

"No," Basulto cried in real terror. "Goddamnit,
listen to me. I'm not kidding around here."

McGarvey admired the technique, but he wondered what it was for.

"Then stop your nonsense," Day said equably.

"I put my life on the line for this. They all think
I'm ratting about the coke train. They don't know.
My life is on the line if I go back."

"Your life is on the line here," Day replied.

Basulto's nostrils were flared, his eyes wild. He
was panting. "All right," he said, holding out his
hand. "I just don't like being called names. Especially when I'm with friends."

Everyone looked at him. The man was amazing.
Hope springs eternal, McGarvey thought, and sat
forward.

"Excuse me, may I ask a question here?"

Basulto eyed him warily, but Trotter nodded.

"When the end came, you went home. What
happened next? Did Harris drive down and pick you
up? Telephone you? What?"

"I had a wireless. He told me to come."

"He told you to come to him. Told you: 'Come
along to Havana, Artimé, I am taking you away from
all the bad things.' Is that it?" McGarvey asked.

Basulto seemed at a loss for words.

"I just want to get this early stuff straight. I want
to get the picture very clear." McGarvey could hear
the mean edge in his voice.

"There was a code word," Basulto said weakly.
"We had a regular schedule."

"Christ," McGarvey said, shaking his head.
"You lying bastard."

"Goddamn you, you sonofabitch," Basulto cried, jumping up, his fists clenched, his knuckles white.

"Sit down," Trotter shouted.

"You were going to burn Harris, weren't you," McGarvey continued calmly. "You were going to trade your case officer's safety for your own!"

"I loved that man!"

"I'm sure you did, once you were back in Miami with him," McGarvey said. "The wonder of it all is that Harris went along with you. If it had been me, I would have shot your miserable ass."

"I couldn't stay in San Luis . . . sonofabitch. They would have come after me. Any day. I was dead meat for sure. It was just a matter of time."

"You radioed Harris you wanted out?" McGarvey asked.

"I tried, but there was no answer," Basulto admitted. "He had apparently shut down the station. I buried my radio and went up to Havana."

"In June," Trotter interjected. "Is that right?"

Basulto nodded. "I knew where he was staying. I went to him. He was easy. Told him I wanted out. Told him I'd do anything for him. Anything."

McGarvey held his silence.

"We drove down to Matanzas that afternoon and flew out that night."

Day opened his eyes and sat up. "Why didn't Harris just leave him?"

Trotter explained it. "The bastard didn't have to say a thing to Harris, don't you see? He could act the innocent and get away with it. He knew he was being followed. Harris knew it as well. So he had to get them both out."

A car, moving very fast, passed outside on the road. They could hear the driver changing gears somewhere farther up the hill, and then it faded.

Basulto grinned, his sudden mood swing dramatic. He sat down with a flourish and crossed his legs. McGarvey had the urge to get up and smash out his teeth.

"I'll tell you, Roger was a good man. I did what I had to do. You would have done the same. I got no apologies to make. Without me you'd still be in the jungle with your pants down."

"He must have been an embarrassment to Harris," McGarvey said.

"He had a job for me," Basulto was saying. "Wanted me to go to Mexico City for him. I told him no problem, I would do anything for him. Anything!"

"I don't care," McGarvey said. He was tired. It was time to go. He started to get up.

"Wait," Trotter said sharply. "Please, Kirk, just let's finish this. Then you can decide."

"You can't believe this miserable bastard."

"Maybe not in all the details. But if we send him back he's dead, and he knows it. He'll tell the truth from now on."

"Absolutely—" Basulto started, but McGarvey cut him off.

"What'd Harris tell you in Miami?"

Basulto blinked. "He was mad at me. Said he had saved my ass, and now I was going to have to save his. I remember it as if it happened two days ago."

"What'd he hold over your head?"

"Nothing . . . I swear on my mother's grave!"

McGarvey just waited.

"There was this assignment," Basulto blurted. "There'd be money and girls and action. Mexico City is a big place."

"He gave you money? Bought you a car?"

Basulto nodded. "And papers, too. I was an American." ·

"In exchange for what?" McGarvey asked. "What exactly was it you were to do for him in Mexico City?"

"There was a place on Morelos Avenue called the Ateneo Español. I was to set up shop any way I wanted and just see what I could see."

"What was this place?"

Basulto shrugged. "I don't know for sure. There were a lot of Communists there."

"Cubans? Mexicans? What?"

"Them. And Russians, too."

"How were you supposed to report to Harris?"

"There was a café I was supposed to go to on Wednesdays at noon if I had anything. I could leave it in cipher with the waiter."

"If there was an emergency?"

"There was a number in San Antonio, Texas. I was to call long distance."

"Harris's sister," Trotter offered.

"He was working outside his charter?" McGarvey asked.

"Apparently."

Basulto set himself up in a small apartment just off the Plaza de la Constitución y Parroquia de San Agustin de le Cuevas, in an area called Tlalpan on the south side of Mexico City. The forboding walls of Morelos Prison were a couple of blocks away on the Avenida San Fernando, and even though it was no longer used as a lockup, it gave him the creeps.

"I could just see the place from my apartment. And it made me so goddamned nervous, I'm not ashamed to admit it."

"It made you think how you owed your freedom to Roger Harris," McGarvey suggested. He couldn't keep the sarcastic edge from his voice.

Basulto didn't bother to reply. He glanced at Day, who seemed indifferent.

"Let's just get on with it," Trotter said impatiently. "You told us you could see the Ateneo Español from your apartment."

"There was a lot of activity going on," the Cuban said. "People coming and going, you know. At night they would hold meetings on the second floor. The windows were open, and if you walked past you could hear them arguing like crazy people about the future of Latin America, about the people's revolution that would someday come to the U.S. But I didn't believe any of it."

McGarvey raised an eyebrow.

"It was all bullshit," Basulto argued. "It was a cover. The real work was going on somewhere else within the building."

"White noise," Trotter mumbled.

There was no big deal about Basulto's presence in Mexico City at the time. Strangers were coming and going all the time. One more was hardly noticeable. There was the café a block away where his contact worked, but after the first week he only went there to pass on his reports, figuring he'd probably be in the city for a long time and he was going to have to conserve his money. Of all the statements Basulto had made so far, that to McGarvey was the wildest.

He went fishing then, he said. Looking for a hook that might lead him to bigger things, just as he had been taught in Miami.

Basulto had taken a couple of dry runs past the building, which looked more like an ordinary cultural club than a hotbed of revolutionaries. Such places were very popular at the time. But in Miami, Harris had taught him that repetitious activity would almost certainly be noticed. Besides, he had been given the warning that whatever was happening down here was damned important, not only to Harris but to them all.

He purchased a set of powerful binoculars, which he taped to the top of an ordinary photographer's tripod, and set up the rig in the window of his living room so that he could see the front entrance to the Ateneo Español.

"I ate my meals and slept by that window," Basulto said with a touch of pride in his voice. "I'll tell you, I even dreamed by that window. Thought about everything right there. It was my salvation up there as I watched the world go by. Looking . . . always looking. Two o'clock in the morning a dozen people might show up, see. The lights would go on upstairs and the meeting would begin."

"What were you looking for?" McGarvey asked. "Harris must have given you some idea. You were watching for someone specific? Back in Miami he told you that he had saved your ass, and now it was your turn to save his."

A wild look came into Basulto's dark eyes. There was a sheen of sweat on his brow. He sat forward fast. "If he had been more honest with me, I could have saved his life!" he cried.

"Roger Harris was murdered?" McGarvey snapped.

Trotter nodded glumly. "But he's getting ahead of himself," he said.

"We're chasing a murder mystery, John?"

Trotter waved it off. "Nothing like that, Kirk, believe me. Just hear what this little bastard has to say."

"He didn't tell me anything," Basulto said defensively. "Goddamnit. He just sent me down there to watch and to report back to him."

"Every Wednesday at noon you were to give

your report, in cipher to the waiter at the café?"
McGarvey asked. "That was the drill?"

"Yes."

"He gave you the pad?"

Basulto shook his head. "We used a book, a
novela: *For Whom the Bell Tolls.* It was funny
because the guy was very big in Cuba."

McGarvey digested this for a moment. There
were so many loose ends. Why did he bother? Why
him, the thought hammered insistently in his head.

"That was for routine reporting. The San Antonio number was for emergencies."

Basulto nodded, but then realizing where
McGarvey was leading him, froze.

"Emergencies," McGarvey said sharply. "He
must have told you back in Miami what constituted
an emergency."

Again Basulto looked elsewhere for some assistance, some moral support. He was obviously a man
on the edge of a very dangerous precipice; he was
looking for help. But Day was suddenly quite aloof
from the proceedings.

"We told you that we would give you protection," Trotter said.

"I don't know him!" Basulto cried, barely glancing toward McGarvey.

"I do."

Basulto looked away for a long moment, then he
lit another cigar with shaking hands, inhaled deeply,
and let the smoke out through his nostrils. He
seemed to be calming himself; McGarvey had the
impression that it might be an act.

"He told me I would know an emergency when I
saw one."

"Get on with it," Trotter prompted.

"Nothing much happened in the first few
weeks," Basulto picked it up again. "I watched the

people come, I watched the people go. Really rough characters. But from where I was sitting they could have been anyone, you know. Mexicans, Cubans, Guatemalans . . . but all Latinos, all of them third-rate revolutionaries who preferred to stay behind and talk while Uncle Fidel went home and won the war."

After a while, Basulto said, he fell into a routine of catching catnaps during the daylight hours when there didn't seem to be as much activity. Around seven or eight in the evening, things usually stepped up at the Ateneo Español. Most of them came in by foot, a few of them had motorcycles, and very few came by car. It got to the point where he began to identify some of them. The midget, the fat man, the greaser who always wore dirty white shirts (he looked Panamanian), the two women who came hand-in-hand. They were an odd lot, and he began to make up stories for each of them. The midget was with the Peruvian circus. The fat one was a pimp. The girls, of course, were dykes, and the one he swore was Panamanian was a mad bomber who killed children.

One night in the fourth week, very late— probably around two or three in the morning—a large American car pulled up and parked just across the street from Basulto's apartment building. He had not been looking through the binoculars because no one had come to the Ateneo for the last hour, though there was quite a crowd over there that evening. It was very hot, and all the windows were open. He remembered hearing a lot of shouting and laughing and even a radio playing loud music. It was all background noise. All cover.

Two men got out of the car. (Basulto recalled thinking it was a Chevrolet or a Buick—long, with a lot of chrome and very big, flashy bumpers.) One of the men was short, on the husky side, with thick, dark hair. The other was tall, good-looking and very well dressed. Obviously an American. He stood out a mile. Together they walked down the street and entered the Ateneo, Basulto watching them all the way, now through the glasses.

"It was a change. It was something different. And it scared hell out of me. Here was an American and another man coming to the headquarters for Communist revolutionaries for all of Latin America. Something very big was going on."

"Did you know either of them?" McGarvey asked.

Basulto shook his head. "I watched the place all night, but it wasn't until morning—just about dawn —when they came out, walked back up the street, got in their car, and left."

"Who drove?"

"Not the American. The other one."

"Any sense of who he was? Another American?"

"No, he was no American. He was a Russian," Basulto said, positive. "A big man."

"How did you know he was Russian?" McGarvey said in wonder. He glanced at Trotter, whose eyes were bright.

Basulto wet his lips. "I didn't know at the time, see. But I could have known it. The way he dressed, the way he looked. I was used to dealing with them. They were all over the place in Havana."

"Did you get the license number? Did you try to follow them?"

"I didn't know what to do. Roger told me not to make waves. I was supposed to be the invisible man. His eyes and ears."

"Had he mentioned this American or the Russian to you in Miami?" McGarvey asked. "Were they your targets?"

"No," Basulto snapped, but then he corrected himself. "There were no targets at first. That came later."

For a moment no one said a thing.

"Get on with it," Trotter said. "What happened next?"

"I was goddamned scared, like I told you," Basulto said. "I took the bus downtown to the post office and telephoned the San Antonio number Roger gave me."

"He told Roger to come," Day said, sitting up. Like Trotter's, Day's eyes were bright. It seemed they were on the verge of something very big.

6

"I didn't know what to expect, but after the call I felt relieved, you know. Roger was coming and he'd know what to do. I was even afraid to go back to my apartment that morning. Revolutionaries are one thing, but a Russian and an American together, that was something else."

McGarvey was brought back in his mind to his old days in the field. To his own tradecraft, which had been considered very good. "After the San Antonio number answered, what'd you say? Were you given instructions?"

"No instructions, nothing like that," Basulto said. "We worked it all out ahead of time in Miami. I called the number he gave me and a woman answered. I told her I was alpha. That's all. Then she hung up."

"That was your emergency signal? Just alpha?"

Basulto nodded.

"Then Roger Harris must have had some idea of what you might run into. I mean, without any sense of your emergency, just on the strength of that one code word, he was going to drop everything and come to you? Was there a time limit on his arrival?"

"Twenty-four hours. He'd meet me at La Alameda, a park downtown on the south side. Juárez Avenue. At noon."

"He'd just be standing there, big as brass. No fallbacks?"

"If he was wearing a suit and tie, it would mean he was clean, and I was to walk around the park in a clockwise direction. He'd follow to make sure I hadn't been made."

"He thought there was a chance someone would be there watching him as well as you?" McGarvey asked. He was trying to make sense of this. "I mean, as early as Miami he set up these precautions?"

"I was just following his instructions!" Basulto shouted in frustration.

"But you liked it. This was exciting."

"I tell you it wasn't what I expected. Nothing was like I figured it would be in Mexico City. There were a lot of angry people there. Big things were happening."

"Yes," McGarvey said dryly. "Did you stay on the streets all night?"

"I went back to the apartment that afternoon. I figured I'd better lay low."

"What was going on at the Ateneo?"

"Nothing. Not a goddamned thing. It was spooky as hell. It looked as if the entire operation had been shut down. The American and the Russian show up and bang!—the very next day everything cools off. Nothing happened all that night. I know. I couldn't sleep. I was awake the whole night, watching. But there was nothing."

"Harris showed up on schedule?"

"Just like he said he would. He was wearing his suit and tie, and he looked goddamned beautiful to me. I practically ran around the park. He caught up with me in front of the Hotel del Prado, which was right on the corner. He told me to calm down and

took me upstairs to his room on the third floor. It
looked out onto the street. He told me to calm down,
and he was nervous and crazy. I thought he was on
something and I made a little joke, but he practically
exploded. 'This isn't some kind of a goddamned
game,' he shouted. He said it was my graduation
exercise. After this was done, I'd be able to write my
own ticket. We'd both be able to call the shots. This
was the Company talking, you know, Mr.
McGarvey. I mean, if it hadn't been for Roger I'd be
dog meat back home. He asked me to do something
for him, and I did it. We were going to have a long
association together. 'Profitable,' he kept saying.
And goddamnit, I believed him."

"But it didn't work out that way," McGarvey
said softly.

"It wasn't my fault, goddamnit. I mean, Christ,
how was I to know—"

"Roger Harris was evidently in over his head,"
Trotter interrupted. "As far as we can tell he made
no contact with the Mexico City chief of station.
He was working this on his own. It led to his downfall."

McGarvey glanced up. "That was July of
1959?"

"Closer to August," Trotter said.

"Roger sat me down and went through everything I had done, everything I had seen and heard,
step by step from the moment I had left him in
Miami. I told him about selling the car in Hermo-
sillo, and about my new identification in Guadala-
jara, and about my apartment. He was mad at first
that I hadn't done exactly what he told me to do,
but then when he thought about it, he admitted that
I had probably done the right thing. He was a good
man, I mean it. A big man. He could admit his mistakes. I don't think I liked him better than that
morning." Basulto looked from McGarvey to Trotter

and then to Day for emphasis. "I was just a kid then. What the hell did I know. Roger was everything."

"Harris, among other things, was his bank," Trotter said dryly. "If I know my man here, he probably held out for more money."

"That's a goddamned filthy lie!" Basulto cried. "We've gone over this ground already. I told you, I loved that man. I wouldn't have done a thing to hurt him."

Harris had probably been blind, McGarvey figured. He had seen it in others. The man was working way outside his charter. Looking for the big coup that would give him his battlefield commission.

"Don't be tiresome," Day said softly. "Your neck is still on the line here."

"I told Roger what I had seen the night before," Basulto plunged on. "I told him that the Ateneo had all but closed down. I had to go over and over it again, ten times for him. He wanted every single detail. The color and make of the car. What kind of clothes they were wearing. How they parted their hair, for Christ's sake. Were they clean shaven or not? I could see a lot through those glasses, but they weren't that good. So then he brought out the photographs. And there the Russian was. There was a picture of him getting out of the car. One of him standing in front of a hotel. One as he was coming from an airplane with a group of people. But there was no mistaking him. No mistake at all. It was in his eyes."

"As best as we can gather, they were surveillance photos probably taken right there in Mexico City two years earlier," Trotter said.

"KGB?" McGarvey asked.

Trotter nodded. "A very sharp individual. One of the very best, bar none. Name of Valentin Illen Baranov."

"How about the other one?"

"That came later. We're assuming—only assuming, mind you—that it was the American for whom Harris was looking. And he was probably the one who killed Harris."

"I know he was," Basulto said sullenly.

McGarvey jerked forward. "What—"

Trotter interrupted again. "We're getting ahead of ourselves here, Kirk. Believe me, I want you to hear the entire story in chronological order. It's essential that you understand the timing. I want you to be perfectly clear."

Nothing, of course, was ever perfectly clear for McGarvey. He had built a career in the Company on seeing beyond the obvious in supposedly "clear" operations. He had listened to the sages lecture at the Farm outside Williamsburg. They had called such things "anomalies." Look for the glitches in the fabric of any operation, and there you will find an anomaly that more often than not will lead to the core of the situation. To the truth.

Basulto was watching them with a strange, expectant look in his eyes, as if he were a condemned man, knowing the ax was going to fall and waiting for its coming.

"There was no photograph of the American?" McGarvey asked.

"No, but Roger had an idea who it was, I think," Basulto said.

"But he wasn't sure."

"No. He had a camera with a very long lens and high-speed film. He showed me how to use it, and the next time they showed up I was to take as many pictures as I could."

"And in the meantime?"

Basulto didn't catch McGarvey's meaning.

"You were to return to the apartment and take

some pictures. Meanwhile, what was Harris going to do? Come along with you? Stay there at the del Prado? Go home? What?"

"He was going to stay there for forty-eight hours. If something turned up, I was to come back to him. Eight, noon, then eight again at the park. First the east side, then the north, and finally the west."

"If nothing came up in that time?"

"It didn't. Nothing happened. The Ateneo was a closed shop. And Roger went home."

"You met with him a last time, though?"

"Sunday night at eight o'clock. We went back to his hotel, and I told him that no one had shown up."

"And how was Harris then? I mean, was he disappointed? What?"

"Nervous," Basulto said. "He told me that I would probably be pulled out of Mexico City before too long. He hinted that something very big was happening."

"But he wanted you to stick around at least a little while longer?"

Basulto nodded. "He said we still had a real shot at breaking this thing. If only I could get a clear photograph, we could write our own tickets. He kept saying that. It was a very big thing for him."

"But it scared him."

"Scared him silly, Mr. McGarvey."

"He never told you who you were after . . . I mean other than Baranov?"

Basulto shook his head. "He said the Russian was a very big cookie. He kept saying how Baranov was so young, and yet he was running the entire Soviet system of networks in the Caribbean. He took over everything that Oumansky set up in the forties."

"Constantine Oumansky," Trotter interjected. "He was the Soviet ambassador to Mexico. Killed in

1943 in a plane crash. He set up the entire Carib. network."

"Which was still going strong under this Baranov in the late fifties?" McGarvey asked.

"It's still going strong now, from what we gather," Trotter said.

"There is a connection . . . then to now? A bridge?" McGarvey asked incredulously.

"The Golden Gate," Day chirped.

They waited for Basulto to continue.

"I was to call the San Antonio number from different telephones around the city every day. When it was time to leave I would be given the word."

"And then where were you to go?" McGarvey said. "Back to Miami?"

"Guatemala City."

Again McGarvey was startled. It showed on his face because Trotter sat forward, his eyes bright.

"They were starting to train for the Bay of Pigs invasion. A camp had been set up on a coffee plantation at Helvetia."

"He must have been among the first to arrive."

"Harris was involved from the beginning because of his operations in Cuba under Batista. He pulled Basulto into it to provide them with the local knowledge they'd need," Trotter said.

7

The rain had finally stopped, and the sun had begun to peek out from under the clouds. From where he sat, McGarvey could look out the window, across the road at the trees growing up along the wall of the valley. The branches were dripping, the leaves glistening in the light. Marta would be at the apartment, worried about him. Or perhaps she had gone shopping. She would stop at the odd moment to cock her head (it was a characteristic gesture of hers that he found attractive) and think about him. Or at least he hoped that was the case. He hoped she wasn't looking for him. It would make it that much more difficult when he came home this afternoon.

Trotter had gone into the kitchen to get more coffee, and Day had jumped up and was grazing among the books on the shelves, leaving Basulto and McGarvey alone for just a moment.

"You weren't too unhappy about leaving Mexico City?" McGarvey asked softly.

Basulto poured some cognac into his cold coffee. He raised his head. "No, but I wasn't overjoyed at the prospect of going to Guatemala. They're a bunch of farmers down there. They don't know anything."

"About Mexico City. Did you ever get the feeling that someone was watching you? That someone down at the Ateneo knew what you were doing?"

Basulto smiled. "You could be Roger's twin, you know, Mr. McGarvey. He asked me the very same question. He was worried that I'd be tumbled sooner or later."

"But you weren't?"

"Worried?" Basulto laughed harshly. "I was worried the entire time I was there. Let me tell you, they were some desperate characters."

"How do you know that?"

Basulto's eyes narrowed. "You could see it just by looking at them. Roger told me to be very careful of this Russian. He said the man had eyes and ears everywhere."

"Did you believe him?"

"What's this?" Day said, bounding back across the room. "Getting acquainted, are we?'"

"Just waiting for the coffee so we can get on with it," McGarvey said.

Something flickered in Basulto's eyes. Cunning? Fear?

Day turned. "Trotter, for God's sake, let's speed it up here," he shouted.

Moments later Trotter appeared in the doorway with another carafe of coffee. He hurried in, poured more for Day, Basulto, and himself, and then settled down.

"Helvetia," he said, out of breath, starting them off again. "Harris was there waiting for his boy to show up. But there was no further debriefing. No words. Nothing about the Ateneo Español. It was taboo. Here was Basulto, one of Harris's experts from the Cuban days, down to help out with the big project."

"Didn't you find that odd?" McGarvey asked, directing his question to the Cuban. "In Mexico City he was excited. All of a sudden it's over?"

Basulto shrugged. "There was the American working hand-in-hand with Baranov. I figured him for a double. I didn't think Roger wanted that spread around. And I didn't know who to trust."

McGarvey was barely able to keep from making a sarcastic remark about *trust* coming from the lips of such a blatantly untrustworthy opportunist.

At first the remote training camp up in the Guatemalan mountains was nothing more than a collection of shacks at which a handful of Cuban radio operators were being trained. But throughout that year, and all through 1960, people kept streaming in. Eventually more than fourteen hundred recruits were in combat and infiltration training, and a big airstrip was carved out of the hillside. Basulto spent most of his time briefing the combat troops on the terrain and the waters around the *Bahía de Cochinos* (the Bay of Pigs) southeast of Havana. In the old days he had run a number of operations in the region for Harris, so he knew the bay fairly well.

"The best place on the entire base was the pilots' quarters," Basulto said. "Very nice, I'm telling you, at least by comparison to how the others lived. They used to call it the Hilton. They had their own showers, their own mess."

"Harris was there the entire time?"

"No. He would come and go. Sometimes he'd stay for a few days, but never any longer than that, until the very end."

"He was running the recruiting station in Miami at the time," Trotter said. "They had quite a setup. Doctors, nurses, the whole nine yards. It was an open secret."

"It was a big joke," Basulto said. "We used to laugh about it."

"Who was your boss when Harris wasn't around?" McGarvey asked.

"Pepe San Romàn was the top man, but Erneido Oliva was the deputy commander. If there were any problems, he was the one we went to first."

"But there were other Americans there, CIA people?"

"Coming and going all the time, especially after the runway was finished," Basulto said.

He stayed at the camp for a very long time, and every few months Basulto would get so frustrated with the isolation he would slip down to Guatemala City to raise a little serious hell. Sometimes he'd go alone, sometimes he'd take a few friends from the Hilton along for the ride. They'd start at one end of the town and work their way to the other, through all the bars and whorehouses, going strong twenty-four hours a day until they couldn't take any more. Sated, they'd head back to the base where they would get back to work.

"No one ever missed us, they were so disorganized," he said.

"Did you ever run into anyone in Guatemala City during your forays?" McGarvey asked.

"Sir?"

"Baranov or his crowd, or perhaps the American you'd seen him with in Mexico City."

Basulto shook his head.

After a short pause, McGarvey took another sip of his drink. "Then came the invasion."

"It got really crazy around there in the last couple of months. No one was allowed off base. They started to watch us pretty closely."

"What was your job to be? You were expected to go with them, back to Cuba, weren't you?"

"You bet, even though I didn't want to go back. I knew damned well it was going to fail. But Roger was there. He was coming along."

Green Beach was east, Red Beach was back up

into the bay at Playa Larga, and Blue Beach was just east of the town of Girón. Basulto came ashore at Blue Beach, along with Roger Harris and a heavy contingent of Cuban exile troops who had been trained in Helvetia. The fighting had already begun.

"It was a mess, let me tell you," Basulto said, lighting another thin cigar. His hand shook. "There was a lot of shooting, parachutes were coming down, aircraft buzzing all over the place. We heard later that at least two of our ships had been sunk . . . one right off our own beach and the other up the bay somewhere. One of our planes went down too, up by Jagüey Grande. We didn't know any of that at the time, of course. We were too damned busy trying not to be killed."

Basulto paused for a long moment. He turned and looked at the fire. His skin seemed to be stretched taut around his mouth and across his cheeks. Day had his legs crossed, his coffee cup balanced on one knee. Trotter sat forward. He was staring at Basulto.

"It was very strange, Mr. McGarvey, let me tell you," the Cuban picked it up without turning back. "All hell was breaking loose. A lot of our paratroopers were going down north of Girón, but there was nothing but swamps up there. Christ, if I told them once, I told them a thousand times, they would have to watch the wind. They'd have to pinpoint their landing. Someone was supposed to have gone out to the airstrip to lay out the signals, but they never showed up. Roger was mad as hell, but he kept saying he had a job to do, and we'd do our part."

They were called the brigade, and Basulto said their first operational headquarters were set up within the tiny town of Girón, several hundred yards inland from the resort cottages near the beaches. In town, but closer to the beach, a medical station was set up for the wounded, and directly across the street was the radio post.

"They were intercepting a lot of our traffic, but there wasn't a goddamned thing we could do about it. There wasn't a lot of time for coding and decoding. It was all happening so fast." Basulto turned back, a strange, haunted look in his eyes. "And then I saw him." He shook his head in wonder. "I turned around and there he was by the door of the radio shack. He was talking with Roger, just like they were long-lost friends. I mean, he was wearing battle fatigues, just like the rest of us, with a Thompson slung over his shoulder. He said he had just come down from the rotunda up on Red Beach. There was a lot of fighting going on. They were going to need some help."

"Just a minute," McGarvey said. "Who are you talking about here?"

"The American . . . the one from Mexico City who was pals with Baranov. Who the hell did you think I was talking about? What the hell do you think I've been talking about all fucking morning?"

"Easy now," Trotter cautioned.

"Harris knew him?" McGarvey asked.

"Presumably," Trotter replied.

"Did he know it was the one from Mexico City?"

"No, goddamnit," Basulto shouted. Then he shrugged. "At least I don't think so. He didn't act as if he knew it was the same one. But I was goddamned scared. Here he was, the double agent. It was real."

"You're sure it was the same one?"

"Damned sure, Mr. McGarvey. It's a face I'd never forget."

"Who was he?"

"I didn't know. I didn't know that until six months ago."

"Havana?" McGarvey asked, holding himself in check. It was coming now. The part they had brought him here to listen to was coming.

"Miami," Basulto said, looking at his hands.

"Wait up," Day interjected. "We're getting ahead of ourselves again."

"He killed Roger," Basulto said defiantly. "And there wasn't a thing I could do about it. Roger just took off with the bastard before I could say jack shit. Bam! He was gone."

"What happened then?" McGarvey asked carefully. "Did you follow them?"

"You're goddamned right I followed them, but it was too late," Basulto said, and in this it seemed as if he were appealing for their belief and support. "It was less than five minutes from the time Roger left with him until I found a jeep and took off. But it was too late."

Roger Harris was shot to death. At close range, two soft-nosed bullets into his face. Basulto found his body lying beside the jeep about ten miles north of Girón alongside the beach road.

"There was a lot of traffic all up and down the road. Aircraft overhead. It was a zoo, but no one stopped. No one gave a damn."

"You're sure it was Harris?" McGarvey asked. "You said his face was shot away. Could you be sure?"

Basulto threw up his hands. "What kind of a question is that? I knew it was Roger. I just knew it!"

"No sign of the other one?"

Basulto shook his head. "I was really scared then, you know. I figured if Roger could be taken in by the bastard, I wouldn't have a chance. There was no one I could trust. I mean, who was I supposed to take my story to? The so-called invasion was falling on its ass. And I'd be a sitting duck."

"So he ran," Trotter said.

"So, I got smart."

"Where? Where did you run?"

"Up to Santa Clara that night," Basulto said. "I took the jeep, stole some ID off a dead government soldier, and drove up there."

"In the American jeep?"

"They all had Cuban markings. Besides, I ditched it a few miles outside of town. I just got out of there on a bus down to Holguín, and from there to Santiago de Cuba."

"I thought you were dead meat in Cuba."

"I was dead meat anywhere," Basulto replied. "At least it was home. I knew my way around. I still had a lot of friends. Not everyone was in love with Uncle Fidel. Not then, not now."

McGarvey shook his head. There were holes a mile wide in his story. There was a hell of a lot more to it than Basulto was telling.

"I don't give a shit if you believe me or not, see!" the Cuban cried, clenching his fists. He was shaking. "The bastard killed Roger . . . the only good man I ever knew. And it was his own people who did it. I didn't know what to do except keep my ass down. I couldn't play their games any longer." Basulto pulled up short.

There was a longish silence then, in which Trotter and Day seemed literally to be holding their breath. Another car passed on the road, and from out in the hall a clock chimed the hour. It was one o'clock in the afternoon already.

"That was twenty-five years ago," McGarvey said, appealing directly to Trotter.

"Within a year he had a marijuana operation going, from what he tells us. They ran the stuff up into the Florida keys. By the time the Cuban authorities got around to him—remember, they had their hands full at the time—they decided he was doing them a service and left him alone."

It was too loose. There were too many unanswered questions. A man who had worked for the CIA, and who had participated in the Bay of Pigs invasion, suddenly makes a success of himself in the drug business in Castro's Cuba?

"He was arrested about seven months ago in Miami by a DEA team and was jailed pending trial," Trotter said. "That's when he began making noises."

"Darby Yarnell," Basulto blurted. "In jail, I saw him on the television. It nearly knocked me over."

McGarvey sat forward very fast. "What about him?" Yarnell was a power in Washington politics. Even from afar, McGarvey had heard the name.

"He was the one working with Baranov in Mexico City. He killed Roger Harris. He's a goddamned Russian agent."

8

Basulto was scheduled to leave with Day for the airport, but once there they'd separate, two of Trotter's babysitters picking up the burden of getting the Cuban back to Miami.

"We're keeping him on ice there. Less conspicuous," Trotter said. "The question is, will you be able to help us?"

"With what?" McGarvey snapped. He glanced at Basulto. "He's just trying to save his own ass with this story. You can't actually want me to run off half-cocked chasing goblins . . . twenty-five year old goblins."

A sudden intensity came to Trotter. "Kirk, we did the preliminary checks. Darby Yarnell worked for the CIA in the late fifties and early sixties. He was stationed in Mexico City at our embassy. He was involved in the Bay of Pigs business."

"Then send the Company after him. It's in their bailiwick."

Day and Trotter exchanged glances.

"Yarnell and Powers are . . . friends. They worked together in the old days. They still see each other occasionally, on a social level."

"What the hell are you trying to tell me, John?

Yarnell worked for this Russian. Are you saying Powers is a double as well?"

"Good God, no," Trotter blurted, rearing back as if what McGarvey had just said was blasphemy.

Basulto laughed out loud and rubbed his hands together. Day paled.

"If there is anyone in this mess who's clean, it is Donald Powers," Trotter went on. "And we want to keep it that way. The scandal . . . if it got out, would wreck the agency. Simply wreck it!"

"Powers has fought the Russians for his entire career, from what I understand," Day interjected. "He's hurt them too badly, too many times, for him to be suspect in this."

"Of that I can personally vouch," Trotter said. "I worked with him. We all know his reputation."

"Kim Philby had a wonderful reputation with the British, too."

"Come now, McGarvey, you can't possibly compare the two," Day said.

"No," McGarvey said, sitting back. "But what do we know about Yarnell?"

"That's just it, Kirk," Trotter said earnestly. "Superficially Yarnell's past is an open book. But on closer examination, the man is something of a mystery. One moment he is working as trade adviser out of the Mexican embassy, and the next he's in Helvetia training a contingent of the Cuban invasion force. In between, we suspect, he made a number of trips to Washington. For what? To see whom? There are no easy answers."

"If you can't unravel his past, how the hell do you expect me to do it?"

"We can't get too close to him," Trotter said. "Not without him finding out. He has his finger in nearly every Washington pot."

"Including the bureau, John?"

Trotter nodded. "Including the bureau. And the agency. If word got back to Powers that we were investigating his friend, he would naturally get involved himself."

"There cannot be a hint of scandal, I won't allow it," Day said.

"Which is why I went to see Leonard," Trotter said, nodding toward Day. "Personally."

McGarvey nodded toward the Cuban. "How about this one? How reliable is his story? How reliable is he?"

"Not at all," Trotter said. "But his life is on the line. All we have to do is throw him back on the streets and he's a dead man."

"I'm not shitting you here," Basulto cried. "I've got my own life to consider. It's a trade I'm offering you, see."

"What the hell are you talking about?" McGarvey snapped. "Trade for what?"

"He wants a new identity, a new track, new town, a job . . ." Trotter said.

"In trade for what?" McGarvey asked incredulously.

"Yarnell's head on a platter . . ."

"Hold on. All we have here is an accusation. Nothing more." McGarvey wasn't buying this at all. He looked at his watch. It was time to be getting back. Perhaps he'd take Marta out for dinner tonight. To make up for last night.

"We think there is sufficient evidence to proceed with an investigation," Trotter said softly.

"I'm convinced," Day added.

"On the strength of this . . ."

"Directly after the Bay of Pigs business, Yarnell was assigned to the embassy in Moscow."

"So what?"

"His product was said to be fantastic. Never been beat."

McGarvey held a sharp reply in check.

"Baranov, the Russian he was seen with in Mexico City, was reassigned back to the centre in Moscow at exactly the same time."

"Circumstantial."

"In the early seventies, when Yarnell was assistant DDO at Langley, the Company went into its slump. The lean years, remember? Then in 1978 Yarnell was elected senator from New York. That was your era, Kirk. Who do you suppose pulled the plug on Chile?"

"It was within the Company."

"Directed by the Senate Select Committee on Intelligence . . ."

"Of which Senator Darby Yarnell was a member," Day put in.

"It all fits, Kirk," Trotter said. "Circumstantial perhaps, but just because someone the likes of Basulto makes the accusation, if it turns out to be true it doesn't matter."

McGarvey turned back to the Cuban. "Why didn't you keep your mouth shut in Miami and take your fall like a good boy? The worst that could have happened was deportation to Cuba. You would have been back in business within a week or two."

"I was getting tired of it."

"Of making money?"

"He saw a better opportunity," Trotter said. "A chance for a new start in the States. Even with money, Cuba is no place to live."

"Sooner or later the big connections will get you. Make a little mistake and it's all over," Basulto said.

"He was losing his nerve," Trotter said.

It wasn't fitting, goddamnit. None of the pieces were in any kind of logical order. Too many holes. When this went sour—and McGarvey was certain it would—someone would be left holding the bag, and it wouldn't be pleasant.

Day had gotten to his feet, and he motioned for Basulto to get up. "We're leaving now, Mr. McGarvey. I sincerely hope you're with us."

"To do what?" McGarvey said, looking up.

"John will explain our thinking to you. Something will be set up for you in D.C., and this one here will be on call in Miami. Anytime you want him he's yours for the duration."

"Get the bastard," Basulto said with much feeling.

"Why, because he killed your case officer?"

Basulto grinned, his teeth perfectly white and straight. "Maybe you and I will become partners. We will become famous."

"Get that sonofabitch out of here," McGarvey growled.

The grin faded from the Cuban's face. "Goddamnit, you think I'm fooling around here, just trying to make a buck . . ."

"Yes, well . . ." Day said.

McGarvey got to his feet, and he and Day shook hands.

"As I said, I hope you are with us, Mr. McGarvey. I sincerely hope so," Day said. He and Trotter nodded to each other, and then he left with Basulto.

"Another cognac?" Trotter asked.

McGarvey shook his head. "I should be getting back." He listened and moments later heard the garage door swing open below; the van started up and left.

"As soon as they return, we'll get you back to

Lausanne. Shouldn't be more than an hour," Trotter said.

McGarvey didn't reply. He walked over to the window and looked down into the steep valley across the road. Switzerland was coming to an end for him. He knew it. He had known it for some time now. All the signs had been there for months: his interrupted sleep, his boredom, his sudden fits of anger, his drinking. This time he had hoped it wouldn't happen. Coming to Switzerland five years ago, he had sincerely hoped he'd be able to settle down.

The service is like a narcotic, someone once told him. Years ago it had been, and although he remembered the effect the words had had on him, for the life of him he could not remember who told them to him.

No matter. Perhaps it was time for another fix. But Christ, it was . . . what? Juvenile?

He turned back. "What exactly is it you want me to do for you, John?"

"Go after Yarnell. Prove that he worked for the Russians."

"Is it so important . . . all those years ago . . .?"

"Yarnell had lunch with the president last week. He was at a party at the German embassy with Donald Powers a couple of days ago."

"You think he's still active, then?"

"I don't see any reason for him not to be."

McGarvey thought about that for a moment. This was different now. He glanced toward the doorway. They had pulled Basulto out of here before coming up with this new tack.

"How about the Russian . . . Baranov?"

"We don't know where he is, for sure. Probably Moscow, but he could be anywhere."

"As Yarnell's case officer?"

Trotter shrugged. But there was something in

his eyes. Something that was causing him a lot of trouble.

"What is it, John? You want me to return to the States and find out if Yarnell is still active? Then what?"

Trotter turned away. He poured himself a stiff cognac, and drained the glass. When he looked back, his lower lip was trembling.

"There can't be a trial, Kirk," Trotter said. "It would be ten thousand times worse than Watergate. It would tear the country apart. The CIA would go down the tubes, and even the president would suffer. We'd be years recuperating. Perhaps we'd never fully recover."

"Then what, John? What's the alternative? Send him packing to Moscow? Why not go to the president with this?"

"That's the entire point, isn't it? It's why we decided to come to you."

"What am I missing here?"

"Yarnell almost certainly suspects he's being investigated."

"How do you know that?"

"We've had a tail on him. Routine surveillance. Twice he's ditched them. Naturally we had to back off."

"You told me no one else was in on this business except you and Day."

"I have my leg men, of course. I can't work in a vacuum. It was to be a routine background investigation."

"You botched it, and now you want me to pick up the pieces."

"You're the unknown element."

"Yarnell has already gone to Powers and to the president with this?"

Trotter nodded glumly. "I'm sure he hasn't

come right out and said he was being investigated as a spy. But he's almost certainly worked himself in solid with them. He'll begin digging in now. But, Kirk, listen to me, the man has his Achilles' heel. He has a weak side."

"Don't we all," McGarvey muttered.

"Yarnell was married back in the late fifties to a girl in Mexico. Very young, very pretty."

"I thought he was a bachelor."

"They divorced a long time ago. She's living in New York City these days. Her name is Evita Perez. She has a club. In SoHo, I think."

"Christ," McGarvey said softly.

Trotter suddenly turned away again. "We're asking a lot of you, Kirk. I know it; Leonard knows it."

The house grew very quiet. It was all coming to McGarvey now, and he felt very fragile, as if he were a delicate crystal vase that would shatter at the slightest vibration.

"There cannot be a trial; you can't or won't go to the president with this; he's Powers's friend; you're not sure of the bureau. So what, we send him back to Moscow? Is that it, John?"

Trotter shook his head.

"No, it would be another Kim Philby. They'd crow about it for years. The effect would be worse than a trial, wouldn't it?"

A lot of thoughts came tumbling, one over the other, into McGarvey's head. The business in Chile was uppermost in his mind. It was still an active file. He could still be prosecuted for murder. Were they holding that over him?

"We're talking about murder, here, John, aren't we? About the assassination of a former U.S. senator, one of the most influential men in Washington."

Trotter held himself very still.

"Does Leonard Day know about this? Has he approved this plan?"

"We didn't talk about it . . . not in so many words."

"But the implication was there between you, goddamnit, wasn't it?"

Trotter nodded.

God, he couldn't believe any of this. "What if I do kill him, John? What then? Where would that leave me? No official sanction from the agency, certainly none from the bureau or Justice. We just don't do those sorts of things, do we? What happens if I'm caught?" He couldn't believe any of this.

"You would have Leonard's personal help, as well as mine, all the way."

"You would take the fall with me if I was arrested?" McGarvey said. "Turn around, for Christ's sake, and look at me!"

Trotter turned. He was pale. Sweat lined his brow and his upper lip. "I've thought the possibility through. Believe me, I have. If that were to happen, we would go to Powers and to the president and lay it out for them by piece. Make them understand."

"If you are willing to do that *in extremis,* why not now? Go to them now!"

"We're not sure!" Trotter cried.

"I'm to make sure, first, is that it? I'm to suck after his ex-wife, dig through his dirty laundry. I'm to make sure and then kill the bastard. No trial. Nothing!" McGarvey wanted very much to hit something.

"We didn't know who else to turn to," Trotter said miserably.

"American justice has broken down," McGarvey said quietly. "Will I get a medal when it's over? Or will I be the next embarrassment? You have someone in the wings to put a bullet in the back of my head?"

Trotter's eyes went wide. "Good God, what do you take us for, Kirk?"

"We've already established that, John. Now it's just a question of degree. Nothing more."

The young girl with the *sommersprossen* drove McGarvey back up to Lausanne in the blue van while Trotter remained behind to close down the house. She knew nothing of the real reason for the Swiss trip or McGarvey's part in it, and he was of no mind to enlighten her. Instead he sank down within his own dark thoughts, quite oblivious to the lovely scenery, unaware that the day had become nice.

He could run. Paris. London, perhaps. Maybe the coast of Spain, or the Greek isles. But then, in the end, he would just be running away from himself. And that was impossible, wasn't it?

Like an old football injury, his sudden call to arms had come to him with a hurtful intensity. He became aware of his old wounds, both mental and physical; the cold fear that clutched at his gut whenever he was in the field rising strong.

Once a spy always a spy? But God in heaven he couldn't think of himself as a murderer. Not that. When they were married Kathleen used to tell him: "Plunge forward, it's the only direction." But she never had an inkling of exactly what it was that bothered him.

He had a very sharp vision of the man he killed in Chile. He had been close enough to see the look of fear in the general's face. The abject terror in the man's eyes. It was a vision that haunted him and would continue to haunt him for the rest of his life.

There had been others, too. Not many. Not in the numbers a combat soldier would experience, but for him they were a dark, dreadful legion.

"It is war," Alvin Stewart had told him in the old days. "Our survival or theirs. Simple."

War, yes. But it wasn't simple.

There are a million crossroads in our lives. At each intersection we have a choice that will forever determine the rest of our existence. How many wrong paths had he taken? Kathleen hadn't understood, neither had his sister, yet they both instinctively understood fear and how it worked its changes. They were experts at it, while it was his master.

Trotter had given him a Washington telephone number. Nothing else. It was the beginning.

9

The nondescript gray Mercedes 240D clattered up the switchback above the lake and finally pulled over just before the long flight of stairs that connected the terraced roadways. Marta Fredricks, wearing a white sweater, dark slacks, and a gray raincoat, sat on the passenger side. She felt as if she had been kicked in the gut by a friend; the pain was there but it was hard to believe.

Swiss Federal Police Supervisor Johann Mueller switched off the engine and turned to her. He was like a father to Marta. She had worked for him even before this assignment.

"He is a dangerous man, Mati," Mueller said.

Marta looked up sharply, almost resentful that he was using that name . . . now. "If he leaves Switzerland?"

"Then that would be the end of it as far as concerns us. But there are no guarantees. You knew that from the beginning. From the very beginning."

She turned away.

Mueller reached across her and, with his fingertips at her chin, gently turned her face back to him. "Listen to me now, young lady. If your father were alive, he would be proud of you."

"But it hurts," she cried.

"Yes, oh yes, I am sure it does. But do you think you are the only one who has ever made a sacrifice for Switzerland? I could tell you . . ."

She tossed her head and turned away from him again. The day had turned lovely, though the wind off the lake was still very cold. Oh, Kirk, she cried inside. She'd always known it would come. Eventually. But, God, she had not counted on the pain. Nothing at the school in Worb, outside of Bern, had prepared her for this. Not the confidence course. Not the tradecraft lectures, certainly nothing to do with the law, Swiss or international, had forewarned of this.

The surveillance had been spotted two days ago. Then this morning Kirk had been run down off the square. They had followed him to a house about an hour south.

He had taken his gun. It was the one damning bit of evidence against him.

"Men of his ilk don't rush for their guns unless they mean to use them," Mueller had said.

But she had been so proud of him, until his recent bout of restlessness. Liese had been trying to get him into bed for the past year and a half without results. Only just lately she had come to think . . . to dream that he loved her. That she could tell him everything and that they could run. But to where?

Marta could feel her eyes filling. It was still another thing they had not prepared her for at Worb. Big girls don't cry, that was how it went in the song, wasn't it?

"You either believe in your heritage or you don't," Mueller was saying gently.

He was like a Jew with his guilt. But she knew what was coming next.

"It should never have gone on this long. I should

never have let you talk me into continuing. I should have seen the signs." Mueller sighed, almost theatrically, although Marta knew it was for real. "If you can't do this, tell me. Other arrangements will be made."

A sudden panic rose in her breast. She spun around. "No!" she cried. "You don't understand."

"I think I do. Perhaps more than you want me to. But he must be neutralized. We cannot have an operation going on under our noses. He has a gun. He has been given his brief, apparently, and we must—Marta, I have to emphasize *must*—consider him a danger to Swiss law and order. To our peace."

If he meant by "a danger" that he was angry, then yes. Angry and dangerous. Kirk was all that and more. But dangerous to the precious Swiss law and order? No, she could not believe that, although there had definitely been something bothering him lately.

There had been a time, she thought, when they spent most of their waking hours together in bed. In fact, they used to share a joke: Why rent an apartment when all they needed is their bed and a closet large enough for their clothes? Then they'd laugh. Who needed clothes?

In the summer when it got warm, they wouldn't stop. Sometimes they'd crawl out of bed and look back at the outlines their bodies had left in sweat on the sheets after hours of lovemaking.

But it wasn't all sex, was it? Liese with her antics proved that. She certainly was a beautiful and desirable young woman, but Kirk had never once even hinted that he might want to take her up on her propositions.

"I know what you're doing," Mueller said sympathetically. "But you're a professional."

A young couple came up the stairway hand-in-hand and hiked off in the opposite direction. Marta watched them until they disappeared around the corner. Then she glanced up at the apartment she had shared with Kirk for nearly five years.

An entire period in her life was coming to an end now, and she didn't know if she was going to have the courage to see it through.

Mueller had suggested someone else handle it. Kirk could be arrested and then deported back to the States. But in his present state of mind, that would be a very dangerous operation. There was no telling what he might do. Marta was convinced that he would never surrender. He would run. She could see, in her mind's eye, what that might lead to. In that, at least, he was a danger to Swiss law and order.

"I'll do it," she said, looking back.

Mueller stared at her for a long time. "I'll be here for you," he said.

She shook her head. "It's all right, Johann. I can handle it."

"You'll need backup. I insist on it."

"No," she screeched. "Don't you understand what I am saying to you?"

"What are you saying to me?" Mueller asked softly.

"If he leaves Switzerland then it is over. You agreed to that."

"If his brief includes an operation here . . . ?"

"If he leaves Switzerland," she insisted.

"If he goes without a fuss, then there will be no problem as far as I am concerned."

"Very well," Marta said. She rubbed her eyes and wiped the tears from her cheeks.

Mueller reached in his pocket and withdrew a pistol. It was a snub-nosed .38 Smith & Wesson. He held it out to her, but she shrank away from it.

"Whatever you think or feel, Mati, we consider him dangerous. You will not go to him unarmed. I simply will not allow it."

"Do you honestly think I could use it against him?" she said, aghast.

"If your survival depended on it."

"What in God's name do you think he is?"

"We know that, Mati. Listen to me . . . he is an assassin."

"Was!" she cried. "He quit. He dropped out. He's done with it. It's over for him."

"Then why did he run for his gun this morning?"

Oh, Kirk, she cried again inside. She looked from Mueller's eyes to the gun and back again. He did not waver. She believed him. At last she reached out, took the weapon, and stuffed it in her purse.

"I want you away from here," she said. "Do that much for me. If he's spooked it might get difficult even for me."

Mueller looked at her critically. He nodded. "We'll listen on the monitors. But, Mati, at the first hint of trouble we're coming in."

Marta got out of the car and walked up the street without looking back. Before she got to the apartment she heard the Mercedes start up, turn around, and drive off. Only then did she look back. The street was empty.

McGarvey stood at the end of the Avenue d'Ouchy, looking up toward the Place Saint-Francois, only now the familiar scene seemed somehow strange to him. Disjointed. Alien. It could have been the first time he had ever been to this city, though he watched the traffic with a practiced eye. It was all coming back to him; the precautions and the adrenaline that gave him an edge, the tradecraft. It was as if he had never left the service. But there was nothing untoward going on here. He had expected police, perhaps some of Trotter's team to make sure he did the right thing. Marta might have sent someone, he told himself as he crossed with the light and headed up to the bookstore. But if they were here, watching, they were well hidden. If that were the case, it would not matter what he did or didn't do.

Darby Yarnell, according to the Cuban slime-ball, had been and possibly still was a spy for the Soviet Union. He had murdered a CIA agent back in the sixties. He had been married to a young Mexican woman. And his Soviet case officer was a brilliant star named Valentin Illen Baranov.

Yarnell's intelligence product was said to be fantastic.

It all fit, according to Trotter. Leonard Day was on his side. The big guns were lined up. There was enough evidence, circumstantial and otherwise, to make at least a prima facie argument. But there were so goddamned many holes.

McGarvey continued around the square, an almost preternatural awareness coming to him. A catalog developed in his mind of cars and vans and trucks; of an antenna half-bent, a Mercedes limousine, a window down, two kids on motorbikes, a bus. No repeats, no passenger switches, no studiously indifferent faces, no dark, mysterious figures.

At the corner he crossed with traffic and walked back to the bookstore. Through the front windows he could see Füelm speaking with an older, white-haired man. Two women were in the art section, browsing among the Degas and Rembrandt books, and a stocky, youngish woman clutched a thin book to her breasts as if it were a baby.

Inside, Füelm looked up. "Ah, Kirk. Are you back now, for the day?"

"Only just for a moment. Can you close up this afternoon?"

"Of course," Füelm said after the briefest of hesitations.

McGarvey took the spiral stairs up to his office and stopped a moment just inside the door to let his eyes roam critically around the room. Nothing had been touched since he had been here this morning. No one had come up searching. Looking.

He crossed the small, book-lined room to the windows and looked down on the alley. No one was there. No watchers. No lookers this time. No young girls arm-in-arm. None of Trotter's people, nor the Swiss. He wondered where Liese was this afternoon. He hoped she would be genuinely disappointed when he was gone. She thought too much of herself.

From a small lockbox in a desk drawer, McGarvey retrieved his battered, well-used passport and an envelope containing five thousand American. His escape mechanism. His return-trip ticket. Along with the Walther, it was his only guarantee of safety.

For a minute or two he stood behind his desk looking across the room at the door, staring at nothing, smelling the musty familiar odors, hearing the familiar traffic sounds outside on the street. From below he heard the tinkle of the front door bell. Someone coming, someone leaving. Füelm could handle it.

Much depended on Marta now. She was Swiss police after all. That one little delusion of his—the one in which he had given her the benefit of the doubt—had been shattered casually by Trotter's people. If Marta and Liese were searching for him now, if they had sent out the alarm, run up the balloon, if they were getting nervous, then the fiction was finished in any event. With luck they would let him walk away clean. Easiest that way, he tried to tell himself. Don't look back, you can never tell what might be gaining on you. Your heart?

That was it then. It came down to a simple yes or no. Did he love her or didn't he? There'd be no

coming back from this one. No knocking about in
the field for a week or a month or two, and then
settling back into the bookstore, into the old, comfortable routines. The Swiss were far too sophisticated to let that happen. Marta, he suspected, was
too fragile. And, like a strip of metal that has been
bent back and forth too many times, he himself was
feeling the signs of fatigue. Before long he would
bend once too many times and he would break.

McGarvey picked up the telephone, started to
dial his apartment, but then changed his mind and
hung up. She was there or she wasn't. Calling her
would neither drive her away, nor conjure her up. He
wondered what he really wanted.

Before he left, he looked one last time around
his office. Five years of his life was coming to an end.
Easier than he thought it would be.

Füelm looked up when McGarvey came down.
The young girl with the small book was gone. The
other customers were still in the shop.

"Are you leaving now?" the older man asked.

McGarvey nodded. "You will be all right this
afternoon?"

"This afternoon . . . yes."

Of course Füelm would be in on it with his
daughter and Marta. How much did they really
know? McGarvey glanced up the stairs to his office
door. They'd probably taken the place apart. They
would know about the money, about the passport
and the gun.

"*Auf Wiedersehen,*" McGarvey said.

"*Ja, geht mit Gott, Kirk,*" Füelm replied gently.

Somehow the simple act of walking out of the
shop became difficult. But McGarvey forced himself
not to look back. He crossed the square at the news
kiosk, then hurried up the hill, his hands stuffed
deeply in his pockets, his thoughts black.

Füelm was bad enough. But Marta was going to be many times more difficult.

On the way up the hill McGarvey avoided the issue of good-byes by working out his first steps once he got clear of Switzerland. Trotter and Day had both assured him that his track would be clean. Entering the States would create no notice—not by the Company and certainly not by Yarnell. Trotter did suggest, however, that McGarvey limit his visibility as much as possible when he got to D.C. There were still a lot of people around who remembered him. And Washington was not such a large metropolis that a chance meeting of some old crony was out of the question. Nothing would probably come of such a meeting, but why tempt fate? Why spit in the face of the gods? Trotter had muttered.

Evita Perez, Yarnell's ex-wife who lived in New York City, would be his first, most obvious target. But there were other issues he wanted to address; issues that were none of Trotter's or Day's business . . . at least not for the moment.

One of the old hands in the Company in the early days when there seemed to be genuine purpose to most things (or was McGarvey just younger then?) had talked earnestly about excess baggage. Not the kind carried through airports, but the kind all of us carried in the form of relationships—wives, friends, associates. The man who comes up clean of baggage, is the man you'll most likely see alive at the end. Entanglements can be fatal. Travel light.

Sound advice, wasn't it? Hurtful at times, but then so was the amputation of a gangrenous leg in order to save the body.

They're all enemies, don't kid yourself. Just as if they held a gun to your head . . . wives, lovers.

But he had already seen it was time to leave,

hadn't he? He'd already made that decision, even before he had seen and spoken with Trotter.

He went to the end of the terraced street and turned the corner, climbing up to the next row of houses perched on the side of the hill so that he could avoid the stairs to his place. From the top he could look down at his building, as well as at the road, the stairs, and even a portion of the street below.

Nothing moved. No cars were staked out. No one waited around the corners, under the eaves, in doorways. He considered turning away and simply leaving. He would buy a few things in Geneva before his plane left. Get away clean. Paris first. Then New York. Paris would be his buffer zone. By the time they realized he had skipped, it would be too late for them to do anything about it. But Marta was one of *them*. It made him angry, this vacillation. A lack of commitment, his sister would say. She was right. Bucking up his shoulders, he tossed away the cigarette he'd been smoking and trudged back down the hill and around the corner to his place. On the stairs he suddenly could hear the radio playing above, and he could smell Marta's perfume, a clean, lilac odor. His stomach felt hollow. The door opened. She stood there in a pretty skirt and blouse. She had been crying.

"You didn't think to pick up some bread, did you?" she asked. "We're almost out."

"No. Sorry," McGarvey said. At the head of the stairs, she stepped aside for him. He hesitated for just a moment but then went in, taking off his coat and laying it on the side of the couch. Now he felt like a stranger here with her.

"Are you hungry? Did you have lunch?" she asked, coming in and closing the door.

"I'm going away, Marta," he said. "I came back to get some things."

"Away? A long time? A long distance?"

"Out of Switzerland."

Marta sagged a little with relief. "Back to the United States? Has something happened? Can I help? Kirk?"

McGarvey had gone to the bedroom door. He felt terrible. He turned back. "Listen, Marta, I know."

She nodded.

"I know that you and Liese work for the federal police."

"How long?" she asked.

McGarvey shrugged. "I guess I always suspected. I always knew that you were here with me because you were ordered to be here. Because I was a CIA . . . operative." He'd almost said killer.

"At first, Kirk," she said queerly. "I swear it was only at first. Not later." Her eyes begin to fill again.

"Don't . . ."

"I love you, Kirk. I have for a long time now. Don't you know that, too?"

"Don't do this to yourself."

"I'll come with you."

McGarvey shook his head. "It's not possible."

She took a step closer. "You were followed, you know, from the square to the store, where you picked up your gun, and then to the safe house above the lake."

McGarvey wasn't really surprised about that. "Have you been ordered now to stop me, Marta?"

"No one cares, darling, so long as whatever it is you've been given to do does not occur on Swiss soil."

"I'm leaving the country. Tonight."

"Take me with you."

"No."

"Then I will wait for you. When this thing you

are going to do is finished, I will come to you. Wherever you are."

"But not back here."

She shook her head. "They won't let you return."

McGarvey looked at her. It had been a mistake coming back. He hadn't counted on it being this hard. He wanted now to take her into his arms and hold her close. Make love. The hell with Trotter and Day and their problems. The hell with Yarnell and the Cuban slimeball. The hell with it all. But he simply could not do it. Something deep inside of him, in some little dark corner, anchored his soul as if by a chain wrapped around a bloody great rock. If it ever broke loose, he suspected he would founder and drown.

He turned and went into the bathroom where he got a pair of scissors and his disused shaving things. The photograph in his passport showed a clean-shaven man.

"It must mean something to you, these five years," Marta said at the doorway. "Us."

"I can't change," McGarvey said looking at her reflection in the mirror over the sink. "You can't. None of us can."

"I know what you do . . . what you did. I don't care."

"It's over, Marta. You know it."

She sighed. "Ah . . . Kirk. It hurts, damnit. It bloody well hurts. Do you know that?"

McGarvey nodded, but Marta turned and left. He could hear her in the kitchen putting on the tea water. He paused with the scissors before he began to cut his beard. It wasn't too late, he told himself. Or was it?

Marta stayed in the kitchen while he finished shaving and trimming his hair. In the bedroom he changed into a pair of slacks, a clean shirt, and a sport coat, then packed a single suitcase and a leather overnight bag. When he was ready he telephoned a taxi service to bring him to the bus station. A direct service was operated between Lausanne and the Geneva airport. He brought his bags downstairs to the outside door, then went back up to the apartment. Marta sat at the kitchen table, a cup of tea cradled between her hands, a bottle of cognac open in front of her. A snub-nosed .38 revolver lay on the table. He'd never seen the gun before. He looked at her eyes. She had stopped crying. She seemed distant. For a moment or two, McGarvey stood in the doorway watching her; he thought just at that moment that she looked very brave and strong and wonderful. He waited until she looked up at him, but her eyes were the eyes of a stranger, so he turned and left the apartment.

At Cointrin Airport, he bought a one-way ticket to Paris on the early evening flight, then sat at the bar in the Plein Ciel drinking a whiskey, smoking a cigarette, and trying to fix in his mind exactly how Marta had looked. The restaurant was very busy, and more than once he imagined that the Swiss police had stationed someone here to make sure he actually left. He had disassembled his gun and packed it with his toilet kit in his checked-through luggage so that there would be no problem with airport security. Customs could be a problem, but if he ran into trouble he could call the Washington number Trotter had given him.

Yarnell was assistant DDO at Langley when the Company went into its slump. The lean years, remember? . . . That was your era, Kirk. Who do you suppose pulled the plug on Chile?

10

McGarvey arrived in New York City after his five year hiatus with little or no fanfare. It was early afternoon on a chilly spring Friday. He took a cab into Manhattan, watching from the back seat as the great city showed itself from across the river. He had forgotten just how big and dirty and exciting New York was. He had forgotten about the billboards, about the derelict cars along the sides of the roads, not even worth the scrap. He had forgotten about the traffic and the city smells and the feeling of tense excitement here. Out of habit he took a room in a Forty-second Street hotel just around the corner from the United Nations, had a quick shower, retrieved his gun from his luggage, and then went for a walk. The city was alive in a different way than were cities in Europe. There was a roughness here that seemed to exist side-by-side with elegance very easily. Street people competed with limousines for the right of way. What was uniquely American, in McGarvey's view, was that both belonged, both had the same right to be wherever they wanted to be, and no one seemed to notice, let alone dispute the fact. As a young man growing up on the plains of the Midwest, New York had been his Mecca. His escape from a humdrum existence. His salvation. Yet Washington had snagged him, and anyway he had actually spent more years in Europe and in South America than here in the States. So it was good to be back. If there was one spot in the world that was uniquely American—large, brash, contradictory, free—it had to be New York City, and he reveled in the fact that he had come home, no matter the reason.

After a dozen or so blocks he found that he had circled around to the United Nations complex. He crossed First Avenue, trudged up the few steps past the guards, and walked the broad footpath down to the East River overlook where he leaned on the broad rail. The wind was cool here, but he didn't mind. After Chile, Kathleen had come up here to straighten herself out (while she was seeing her attorney friend). They had met right here for the last time out of court, and she had told him that she was through with him. It had been spring then, too. She looked more beautiful than he had ever seen her, though she had already begun to hold herself differently; prim, proper, a little disdain showing. She couldn't go on like this any longer, she said. The uncertainty and fear had become debilitating. For a moment there he thought she was worried sick out of love for him. But she dashed that hope. Her life was no longer hers to control; too many sleepless nights, mistrustful friends (what few she still had), and ugly rumors she was having a hard time keeping from their daughter. Just what was it, after all, that he did do for a living? Could he just tell her that once and for all? They could not go on.

McGarvey looked up from his thoughts. He would have quit for her then and there. The Company fired him a few weeks later in any event. But already it was too late for them. Too late for him.

He had an early lunch at the Howard Johnson's across from Grand Central Station (he was still on Swiss time), then entered the Grand Hyatt Hotel, where he used a public phone to call the Washington number Trotter had given him. It was his first request for assistance and thus the signal that he had accepted his assignment and had actually begun. When he was finished he felt dirty. He went back to his hotel, stripped, and stayed in the shower for a very long time.

The day of the starving artist or writer was all but finished in SoHo and Greenwich Village. St. Christopher's was a large, exclusive, four-story nightclub-cum-salon with apartments above on Broome Street, which never had (in its new life, at least) nor ever would see anyone starving. Tucked between an art gallery and an antique shop, it once had been a sweatshop factory of some sort. On its facade a plaster shield near the roofline was carved with lions and the date 1907. The windows had once been bricked over. They were open now and looked stainless steel and new. It was just past nine-thirty. From inside came the sounds of music and laughter. McGarvey went to the doorman, as he had been instructed to do, and gave his name as Peter Glynn. He was let inside and into a small vestibule where he paid a twenty-five-dollar cover charge to a lovely young woman wearing a colorful off-the-shoulder peasant dress. A big bullfight poster from Mexico City was framed on one wall. Hung on another was an Aztec sun calendar. Now he could hear that the music was Mexican; several guitars competed with a flat trumpet. He signed the guest register.

"Welcome to St. Christopher's, Mr. Glynn," the young woman said, glancing at what he had written. "Have you been here before?"

"No. This is my first time."

"I'm sure you will enjoy yourself."

"I was told Ms. Perez might be here this evening."

"Yes, of course. Shall I say who is asking for her?"

"Tell her an old friend," McGarvey said. "From Mexico City. In the old days."

"Certainly," the young woman said, inclining her head. She picked up her telephone as McGarvey went through the frosted glass doors into a large, crowded room that had been designed to look as if it were a Mexican village on the edge of a lagoon across from which a large volcano spewed smoke and fire. A mariachi band played on a tiny stage at the base of the volcano.

A young woman, scantily dressed in what appeared to be nothing more than crepe paper, escorted him to a small table off to one side, where she took his drink order of bourbon and water, and then left. Across the room on a slightly raised platform couples crowded around a long bar; some also sat at tables on the main floor. He thought he recognized a few of the faces from television or movies. At one large table, half a dozen older men (with the unmistakable look of politicians) were seated with six young, very good-looking women (with the unmistakable look of high-priced call girls).

His waitress came back with his drink as he was lighting a cigarette. "Will you be dining with us this evening?"

"Perhaps later," McGarvey said, looking up.

"Do you wish to be alone . . . for the evening, Mr. Glynn?" The girl was smooth, but very young.

McGarvey smiled. "It is being taken care of, thanks."

"Of course."

It was fitting, he supposed. Yarnell was selling himself to the Russians. The man's ex-wife was apparently selling herself to everyone else. McGarvey leaned back, then forward, as if he were a weary traveler stretching his back. He reached beneath the table and with his fingertips explored the base of the support. He felt a tiny loop of wire which emerged from the tabletop and disappeared into the base. It explained why the girl had used his name; for identification on the tape recording.

More people kept coming in, but no one was leaving. There was a lot of smoke from the volcano and from people's cigarettes. When the band stopped playing between sets McGarvey could hear the sounds of running water even over the babble of dozens of simultaneous conversations. Then the ragged trumpet would blare, the guitars would take up the beat, and the noise would begin to echo off the walls.

The voice on the telephone had not been Trotter's. McGarvey had not been surprised by that fact, but he had been irritated, not only by the man himself, but by his insinuating tone. In addition to Trotter and Day—and the Cuban—knowing that McGarvey was involved, now there was Trotter's buffer service. It was necessary, at least for the moment, for his old friend to keep him at arm's length, but it was beginning to gall McGarvey that too many people over whom he had no control knew of his interest in Yarnell. Even if the mesh is fine, the bigger the sieve, the more that leaks out.

The music died again, the house lights dimmed, and a spot illuminated the tiny stage as the trumpet player stepped up to the microphone with a flourish. "Ladies and gentlemen," he cried in a comic Mexican accent. "Miss Evita Perez!"

Applause swelled, the bandleader stepped back, a drum rolled, and a slender woman with midback-length shimmering black hair bounced out onto the stage, her arms akimbo, her hips and shoulders in constant motion, her breasts nearly bursting from her low-cut sequined gown, which was slit all the way up to her hip. She was laughing and trilling. The band picked it up as she began to sing "La Paloma," sensuously coo-cooing into the microphone as she continued to move around the stage.

McGarvey was too far away to be able to tell much about her except that she had a great deal of energy, a modicum of talent, and that she could have been anywhere from twenty-five to fifty depending on the skill of her makeup artist. He figured that she would have to be at least in her early forties to have been married to Yarnell in the early sixties, but she looked good from where he sat.

Her audience loved her. Between songs she called out names and joked with them, telling little supposedly intimate stories that she wasn't supposed to be telling and then pretending coquettishly to be the naughty little girl who kissed and told.

As he watched her, McGarvey began to get glimpses of a great sadness in her; and of fear that she was being laughed *at* and not laughed *with*. At times she became too strident, too shrill, and sensing this fault in herself, she pulled back from the brink . . . of what he wondered. At other moments she was cool and sophisticated, a talented woman very much in charge not only of herself but of the room. This was her command performance. She had the crowd eating out of her hand.

Near the end of her forty-five-minute show, her age began to show on her. McGarvey sat forward. The spots were skillfully softened, yet it was obvious that Evita was wearing down. Her dancing became a little forced, as did her stories and, in the end, even her singing. Sweat glistened on her face and upper chest, ruining her makeup, but if anything the audience loved her even more for this effort. She went above and beyond the normal role of the performer. But it was sad; as if she were a marionette doomed to dance as long as her audience demanded; or as if she were the street dancer, holding out her tin cup for spare change.

Then it was over and she was bowing deeply to thunderous applause, catcalls, and whistles. McGarvey lit a cigarette, and moments after Evita had left the stage his waitress came back to his table.

"Mr. Glynn, Miss Perez will see you now."

McGarvey rose and followed the young woman across the floor as the guitarist in the band on stage began a sad, haunting classical melody. The nightclub became hushed. It was a change of pace, a breather, and the audience was appreciative.

"Just up the stairs, sir," the waitress said.

Evita Perez's apartment occupied most of the second floor. The salon itself, where she apparently held her parties, was huge, with a sunken conversation area, a large area for dancing, extremely long, plushly upholstered couches, and broad rugs of white fur. A fake fire burned in a Mexican tiled fireplace in the center of the room. Sculptures in wood, stone, and metal were scattered around the place as if it were a museum. The indirect lighting was soft, lending a curiously intimate effect to the large, open spaces. Evita, dressed in a short terry cloth robe, her hair up in a towel and her feet bare, breezed into the room. She stopped when she saw McGarvey, a sudden puzzled look coming to her narrow, sharply defined features. He decided she looked a lot better without all the garish makeup.

"Well," she said. "You're a hell of a lot younger than I pictured you." Her Mexican accent was all but gone.

McGarvey smiled. "You don't look so bad yourself."

She returned the smile. "I think you and I are going to get along just fine," she said. She motioned him to the couch in front of the fireplace. "What are you drinking?"

"Bourbon and water."

She mixed his drink at a buffet near one of the windows, then poured herself some white wine in a long-stemmed glass. "Have you got a cigarette?" she asked, returning. She sat down next to him, her feet tucked up under her.

McGarvey lit one for her. This close, he could see a few flecks of gray in the loose strands of hair that escaped from beneath the towel. She had crow's feet around the corners of her eyes and they were starting at the base of her nose. Her olive skin was beginning to go slack beneath and around her tiny jaw. She was definitely in her forties.

"So, what brings you to see me, Mr. Glynn . . . or whoever the hell you are?".

"I'm trying to get some information about a couple of people. Richard Harris and Artimé Basulto," McGarvey said.

"Never heard of them. Should I have?"

"I thought you might've."

Evita held her silence for a long time before she spoke again. She stared at McGarvey, who noticed that her eyes were circled with tiny green specks. It made her look like a cat or some other night animal.

"Are you a cop?"

"No," McGarvey said.

"CIA?" she asked softly.

"I used to be. Now I work on my own. I listen, I

watch, I ask a few questions here and there. You know how it is."

"What are you doing here?"

"I thought you might have heard of them. Harris was an agency man in the old days. Basulto worked for him."

"So what?" Evita asked defensively. "What does this have to do with me?" The ash from her cigarette dropped on the front of her robe. She didn't notice.

"Artimé has gotten himself in a bit of a jam with the DEA down in Florida. Something about running coke with the help of the Cuban government."

"You said you were looking for him."

"I am, in a way."

"What the hell are you talking about?" Evita said. "You are a cop. So what are you doing here? What do you want from me?"

"I wondered if you had ever heard of Artimé Basulto. He might lead me back to Harris."

She shook her head, her eyes narrow. "And then what?"

This time McGarvey took his time answering. The delay made Evita nervous. The room was warm. McGarvey sipped his bourbon. He felt like a heel with her. She was obviously in a fragile state for all of her bravado and energy on stage. He decided that Yarnell had probably hurt her very badly at one time, and she still hadn't recovered.

"It has to do with a long time ago, actually," he said. "Mexico City in the old days. The late fifties, early sixties."

"I was just a little girl then," she said wistfully. "What can any of this possibly have to do with me? Please, I am very busy tonight. I have another act to do in less than an hour, and afterward there will be a lot of people up here. Already I'm tired."

"They were doing some very important work for the agency in Mexico City," McGarvey said.

"I don't know . . ."

"Harris is dead. Someone killed him. I want to know who, and more important, why."

Evita reached forward with a shaking hand and stubbed out her cigarette. She got to her feet, drained her wineglass, looked at McGarvey for a long second, then went to the buffet where she poured herself another glass. She stared out the window down at the street, her back to McGarvey.

"Why did you come here like this, Mr. Glynn?" she asked. "Why tonight?"

"You were born and raised in Mexico City."

She laughed. "So were a lot of people."

"You were there in those years."

"It is a big place, I assure you."

"Your husband worked for the Company. He was stationed there."

McGarvey could see her reflection in the dark glass. She had closed her eyes.

"Was this Harris working out of the embassy?" she asked. "If he was I never knew it."

"You remember some of the others, then?"

She turned around. She was frightened. "It was a long time ago. I was just a young girl, barely out of my teens. What did I know about anything? Ask yourself that, Mr. Glynn. What did I know? My eyes were filled with wedding veils."

"I came to help," McGarvey said softly.

At first it didn't seem as if she had heard him. She looked toward the fireplace, her shoulders sagging. Idly she reached up with one hand, undid the towel around her head, and let it drop to the floor. She shook out her long, glistening black hair, then focused on McGarvey.

"Help with what?" she asked, her voice husky.

"What are you doing here? Who was this Harris to you?"

"Harris was nothing to me. Just a name. But whoever killed him is now after Basulto and will be coming after anyone who knew what happened in those days."

"Those days . . ." She shook her head. "What *are* you talking about?"

"The Ateneo Español. Does that mean anything to you?"

Her eyes widened just a bit. He could see her fighting for control. If she hadn't heard about Harris or Basulto, she certainly had heard of the Ateneo Español.

"You have been to this place?" she asked, holding herself together.

"No."

"It is not there any longer, I don't think."

"It was important when Harris and Basulto were there. I think you know it now, and I think you knew it at the time."

Her lips parted. "And what do you expect me to tell you? I'm no spy, all right? It is dirty work. My hands are clean. I don't want anything to do with it. All of it, everything, is finished."

McGarvey held his silence. What the hell was she telling him now?

Evita leaned back against the buffet and looked up toward the ceiling. "Virgin mother," she whispered. "Someone is filling your head with stories. This Harris you say is dead. So who sent you to me? This drug runner friend of yours?"

"Just Company files."

She looked at him. "What?"

"I went through the agency's files to see who was stationed in Mexico City during those years. I wanted to find out who was active."

"Then why are you here? Why don't you talk to Darby?"

"He won't talk to me," McGarvey said, holding his triumph in check. She had admitted she knew her ex-husband was active.

She laughed. "He's a real prima donna, that one."

"A prima donna?"

"My ex-husband has always been an important man. Sometimes a little more important in his own eyes than for the rest of the world. But he has always done big things."

"You were active in Mexico City?"

"That is a filthy lie," she snapped. "Who told you such a thing?"

"How often does he come up here to see you?" McGarvey asked.

Her face turned pale. She dropped her wineglass on the fur carpet, then reached back to the buffet for support. "What are you talking about?"

"Your husband." He wanted to keep her off balance. "Has he been up here to see you? Do you have any contact with each other?"

She was shaking her head as if she didn't understand a word he had said.

"Evita?" he said softly. Something was drastically wrong, but he did not want to break her delicate mood. She wanted to tell him something.

"You don't know . . ."

"I don't know what?" he prompted softly.

She shook her head. She seemed puzzled. "Get away from here," she said. "Please, just get away from here. I don't want to think about . . ."

"About what?"

"Go!" she screeched. "Mother of Christ, go! Get out of here you sonofabitch!"

"I have to know, Evita . . ."

Suddenly she snapped. She reached behind her, grabbed a half-full wine bottle from the buffet, and threw it toward McGarvey. Her aim was very bad and the bottle crashed against the side of the fireplace. Her robe came open, exposing her large, perfectly formed breasts, her slightly rounded stomach, and the narrow swatch of dark hair at her pubis.

McGarvey got to his feet as she snatched up another bottle. He reached her before she could throw it, and he took it out of her hand. She came after him then like an insane woman, biting and scratching and kicking, all the while screaming obscenities. For a few intense moments McGarvey had all he could do to keep from getting injured. She was very quick and strong despite her slight frame.

He got her away from the buffet and up against the wall where he pressed his body against her, immobilizing her as he held both her wrists over her head.

Her face was screwed up in rage, her eyes narrow with hate, her nostrils flared, bright red blotches on her cheeks and forehead.

"You bastard! You bastard," she cried.

"I didn't come here to hurt you. Evita, listen to me! I came here to help." McGarvey was conscious of the press of her breasts against his chest. It was oddly disturbing.

Very slowly the fight began to drain out of her. She began to loosen up beneath him. He relaxed his grip and stepped back.

For a long time she remained against the wall, her robe open, her legs slightly spread, her eyes locked into McGarvey's. Finally she looked down at herself. She pulled her robe tightly closed and shivered.

"Just go away now, Mr. Glynn. Please."

"Harris was a good man."

She looked up. She was on the verge of tears. "They were all good men. Young. Not so smart as now. Pretty boys."

"Who?"

"All of them."

"At the embassy?"

"Them, too," Evita said. "The ones who came and went."

They could hear music from downstairs now as the mariachi band started up again. Evita cocked her head as if to listen to it.

"Can't we sit down and talk? I need your help," McGarvey said gently.

She looked at him again. "It's been a terribly long road. I'm finished with all of that now."

"You could be arrested."

She smiled wanly. "That would never happen, Mr. Glynn. Don't you know that?"

"You won't help?"

"I don't think so," she said. She stepped around the buffet, crossed the room and, without looking back, disappeared through the rear door.

McGarvey stared at the door for a very long time. In a way he was sorry he had come here. She was a sad lady. Nothing good was going to come from this business, he decided. Nothing good at all.

He walked over to Lafayette Street and headed north, catching a cab around Astor Place. It was a long time before he got to sleep. When he woke in the morning, the television set was still on and he felt a ravenous hunger not only for food, but for the real world. On the way out to the airport, though, he began to get the terrible feeling that he would never know such a world. His sister had warned him when he sold the ranch that he was forfeiting his heritage. Maybe she'd been right.

11

Georgetown is a lovely section of pretty streets, beautiful old wood-beam and brick homes, the university, and numerous parks. Dumbarton Oaks and Montrose Park that morning were deserted of all but a few tourists and the occasional nanny pushing a baby carriage. Lovers Lane, a pleasantly broad walkway, separated the two, opening at its south end onto R Street.

McGarvey had come directly from the Holiday Inn accross from the Naval Observatory, sure that no one had noticed his arrival in town. It had felt strange to be back in New York, but Washington seemed somehow even more distant for him. He felt as if he were looking through the wrong end of a telescope; it was all so familiar to him, yet everything was out of kilter. He could have been looking at a model of the city, instead of the real thing.

This was Yarnell's city, McGarvey thought, looking out from the park exit up toward 31st and 32nd streets with their fancy houses, many of which had limousines parked in front of them. The man had worked as deputy director of operations out of headquarters at Langley. He had served as a U.S. senator from New York, working out of the Capitol. Now he directed Yarnell, Pearson & Darien, one of the largest, most prestigious lobbying firms in the city. Among his friends he counted the president, congressmen, the heads of the CIA, the FBI, and the NSA, the Joint Chiefs, journalists . . . the power base of the entire country. It was frightening to think not only of the power he had, but of the inroads to sensitive information he possessed.

McGarvey crossed R Street and started up toward 32nd. Yarnell's house was at the end of a narrow lane that led back into a mew. Trotter had described the place as a fortress; impossible to approach without being seen. The man could stop you in your tracks before you got within a hundred feet of his front door. He has to feel safe back there, McGarvey thought. Protected in his little cocoon. Perhaps safe enough to be lulled into a false sense of security? Perhaps safe enough to get careless?

In the park he had strolled at a leisurely pace. Here he walked faster so as not to attract attention. It was midmorning on a weekday. People were supposed to be in a hurry. Busy. A delivery van rumbled by, followed closely by a Mercedes limo driven by a clearly impatient uniformed chauffeur. The car's windows were dark so it was impossible for McGarvey to see if anyone was in the backseat. But the limo had to belong to someone important. The car passed through the intersection at 31st Street and kept going. Perhaps to the White House. Maybe the Pentagon.

McGarvey had to think back to why he ever left. Why he had run to the imagined safety of Switzerland. It was because of the Yarnells of the world, wasn't it? At least he used to tell himself that. Now he was back again, and the same old gut-wrenching fear was beginning to climb up from his bowels; the same old quickness of breath, the supersensitivity to anything and everything around him.

If you're not careful, you'll think that you can

see and understand everything. Every car, every truck or bus, every person standing on a street corner, every window up or down, every bit of trash lying in an alley, every chalk mark on every fence post. You can't, of course, know everything. Drive yourself crazy trying to. So you damned well better learn to be selective if you want to survive.

He crossed with the light at 31st Street and continued up to 32nd, where he turned away from the park and started past Scott Place, on which Yarnell's citadel was situated. There was a smell of flowers and cut grass and trees from the park, made more noticeable now that he was away from it. This was definitely not the lower end of Georgetown's socioeconomic scale. Even the street was swept and washed, the cars parked along it all polished, chrome gleaming.

A second, narrower lane led left off Scott Place. McGarvey stopped a moment with his foot up on a fire hydrant to tie his shoelaces. Yarnell's home was behind a tall brick wall, so that the first floor windows couldn't be seen. It was a large, three-story European-looking house with several chimneys, dormers across the front, and a steeply pitched roof. It sat at an angle to 32nd Street. A window in what would probably be the attic was open. It caught McGarvey's eye. The room behind it was dark, but he got the curious impression that someone was there, watching. As he straightened up, he glanced over his shoulder, back the way he had come, following a line from the window back out to R Street. He looked up again. From that window an observer could see the entire neighborhood, north-to-south, along 32nd Street as well as both parks. It would be difficult if not nearly impossible to mount any sort of a serious surveillance operation, at least from this side. Assuming Yarnell had the usual equipment up there—microwave, audio dishes, infrared, electronic monitoring—this side would not provide a safe vantage point.

A small Toyota Celica came out of the lane as McGarvey reached Q Street. He had to wait for it to pass before he could cross. He got a momentary glimpse of a good-looking young woman, with dark hair and an olive complexion, well dressed, alone. She had seemed very intent, as if she were in a big hurry to get someplace important. Again out of old habit he looked at the license plate. It was a D.C. tag. He memorized the number, murmuring a mnemonic as he crossed.

Just around the corner, another narrow lane led back at an oblique angle toward the park. McGarvey stepped down the cobblestoned path, and within fifty feet he could see the back of Yarnell's house, protected as in front by a tall brick wall. The twin of the front attic window was open, affording a view of Wisconsin Avenue and the other east-to-west approaches.

Yarnell was paranoid, McGarvey told himself backing off. Paranoid men were wont to make mistakes. But more importantly, paranoid men in this business usually had something very concrete about which to feel paranoid. An Achilles' heel, as Trotter had described Evita Perez. Yarnell had made a dreadful mistake marrying her. What other mistakes had he made? What mistakes might he be making right at this moment? The thought was intriguing.

Once again on the corner, McGarvey could look down the narrow lane as well as down 32nd Street as they diverged. This one spot, and fifty feet or so up either leg of the angle, constituted a blind spot in Yarnell's surveillance. It was not much, he decided, but it was something.

He walked up to Wisconsin Avenue, which was

busy with traffic, and got a taxi within a few minutes, telling the driver the Holiday Inn, which was less than ten blocks away.

It was time for him to get to work now. If he was going to do this thing for Trotter and Day, he would need more information and he would have to start taking some precautions.

McGarvey had lunch in his hotel, then went into town to do the sights. With the weather warming and the cherry blossoms starting to bloom, Washington was filling with tourists. Traffic was terrible, though it still wasn't quite as bad as Lausanne in the summer. The cabbie left him off at the end of Bacon Drive between the Vietnam Veterans Memorial, and the Lincoln Memorial. He dawdled for more than an hour looking at the long, polished black stone tablets on which were engraved the names of those who died in the Vietnam War, stopping and starting, hanging his head as if he were in deep sorrow . . . which in a way he was. It was impossible not to feel something standing in front of such an overwhelmingly tragic reminder of a world somehow gone wrong. As his heart overflowed, his motions naturally became erratic. Twice he thought he might have picked out someone. A pink sweater in the crowd. A torn field jacket across the walkway. But then they were gone, in opposite directions, one by bus, the other on foot. He strolled up to the Lincoln Memorial, where he circled the building with its thirty-six columns, then headed on foot at a brisk pace back up to Constitution Avenue.

He was wearing his tweed sport coat, and a shirt and tie; Washington was warm after Switzerland, and he was sweating. He took a bus to Union Station, where he mingled with the crowds inside for a while; buying a newspaper at a stand, making a phone call to his room at the hotel, getting a cup of coffee in a styrofoam cup and drinking it while he read the newspaper as he had his shoes shined.

It was nearly four in the afternoon by the time McGarvey emerged from the station. He was moving fast now. If anyone had tailed him to this point, he decided they were damned good. He hadn't spotted a thing. But he had to give it one last chance. He took a cab out to National Airport on the river south of the Pentagon, rented a plain Chevrolet Caprice, and headed north along the parkway, sometimes going ten miles per hour faster than the flow of traffic, sometimes ten miles per hour slower.

By five-thirty he was a long way up into the Maryland countryside, but he was finally satisfied that no one could possibly be behind him. Extraordinary lengths, they might say at the Farm in Williamsburg. But when your life depended on it, you'd go to any lengths . . . to the moon if need be.

He turned and headed south again, back across the river into Virginia; Annendale Acres with its Pine Crest Golf Club, A&P Supermarkets, Ace Hardware, green rolling hills and curving streets with cute names along which were mile after mile of contemporary houses, some in brick, some with shake roofs, some with split-rail fences, but all of them depressingly neat and similar. The neighborhood was twenty years old, and showed it.

It was dark by the time McGarvey finally parked across the street from a split-level ranch with attached garage and a lot of new trees and bushes. It had been a long time for him. Nothing much had changed. The garage door was up. Two cars were parked inside; one older and a little beat up, the other a new Ford station wagon. A basketball hoop and backboard were centered over the open door. The house was lit up. He went up the walk, hesitated a moment, then rang the doorbell. He could hear it chime inside. A dog barked. Someone shouted . . . one of the kids? And the porch light came on. A woman wearing blue jeans and a gray sweatshirt, the sleeves pushed up to her elbows, opened the door. Behind her, carpeted stairs led up to the living room and down to the finished basement.

"Pat? It's me. Kirk," he said.

She looked at him for a very long time, a range of emotions playing across her broad, pleasant features; surprise, disbelief, uncertainty and sadness, and then just a little fear.

"Good Lord, where did you come from?" she asked softly.

"Is Janos here?"

She hesitated for a fraction of a second, then shook her head. "He's out. They sent him up to New York. . . ."

"Like the old days?"

"Yeah, like the old days. . . ."

A big shaggy dog appeared on the stairs from the basement, its tail wagging, Janos right behind it.

"Pat? Who's at the door?"

"No one," she said wryly, looking into McGarvey's eyes.

The dog sniffed at McGarvey's shoes. He reached down and scratched behind the animal's ears. Janos had stopped halfway up the stairs.

"Hello, Janos," McGarvey said. "Long time no see."

Janos Plónski, majordomo of all things recorded in the archives at the CIA's Langley headquarters, was a big, barrel-chested bear of a man with a face so ugly that even a mother would have a hard time warming up to him. When he was little he lost his hair to scarlet fever and one year later had a severe case of chicken pox that left permanent scars. He didn't care, and his wife and two children, Barney and Elizabeth, all adored him. He was born in Oświęcim, forty miles west of Kraków, Poland, in 1935, and lived there through the war and concentration-camp days (Auschwitz was just outside of town), while his father collaborated with the Nazis. Just before the war's end, his mother shot his father to death and managed to make her way completely across Europe, all the way to England, with her ten-year-old son in tow. She joined a Polish émigré group that during the war had fought Nazis and afterward fought Communists. By the time he was twenty, Janos had completed his college studies at Oxford (he was something of a hero because of his mother), immigrated to the United States, and joined the army as a translator and intelligence analyst. His career afterward was spectacular. He was dropped into Poland on at least half a dozen occasions; he did work in East Germany, Hungary, Yugoslavia, and Rumania, and then he gave it all up when his young wife became pregnant with their first child.

"Running the show in the basement may not be the most exciting job in the world, Kirk," he once told McGarvey. "But it makes Pat happy, and me, too. This way I can be at home in bed with her every night. And I like her cooking."

Janos pulled McGarvey inside, and they sat on stools in front of a long workbench in the basement. Pat brought them beers and then shooed the children away from the stairs, shutting the basement door. No one had asked him to stay for supper, though he could smell it cooking upstairs. Of course he was out, Janos was in. The association would have to be considered dangerous, no matter the closeness of the friendship.

"So, Kirk, my old friend, what has brought you back? It was my understanding you were tucked away somewhere . . . Switzerland?"

"Lausanne. I had a little bookstore there. An apartment. Not much."

Janos smiled appreciatively. He was very proud of what he had in the way not only of material possessions, but of his position with the Company as well as within the community.

"You're here for a visit? Is that it?"

McGarvey looked at him for a moment. He was glad Pat had gone upstairs. She'd always been the tough negotiator. She was English. Cockney. She understood real poverty even more than Janos did. And she didn't want to go back.

"Not really," McGarvey answered softly. He took a swallow of his beer. "I'm doing a job, actually."

Janos seemed pained. He sat forward. "For who, Kirk? Who are you working for? Not the Company; I would have heard."

The implication was obvious. By answering it, McGarvey would be dropping to Janos's level. But then it had always been that way. Despite his experience, Janos was one of the most naïve, direct men he'd ever known. Once, at a party, Pat confessed it was that very innocence that caused her to fall in love with him in the first place.

"I came all this way, Janos, to be practically turned away at the door, and then to be insulted by my friend?"

Janos sat back, his beer between his big paws. "I'm sorry, Kirk, really I am."

"How have Pat and the kids been?"

"Very good, actually. The tops. We're a happy family here, you know that. At least in that, nothing has changed."

"I thought about you a lot over the years."

Janos shrugged. "We missed you, too, Kirk. You and Kathleen."

"It's over between us. You knew that."

Again Janos shrugged. "Yes, we both knew it. And it saddened us. But she is still Elizabeth's godmother. Will she ever come back to us?"

"I doubt it," McGarvey said. He felt like hell. She was only in Alexandria. Christ, it seemed like a million miles.

Janos sensed something of that. "Does she know you're back?"

"No," McGarvey said softly. "How are things in the Company these days?"

Janos brightened cautiously. "A lot better, Kirk. Believe me, under Reagan and Powers there is no comparison to the old days."

"Danielle is running ops now?"

"He's doing a good job, Kirk, even if he is a little mouse. We have a lot of respect now, you know. It didn't used to be that way. Of course cross-Atlantic operations have shifted from Eastern Europe to the Eastern Med. But even I am getting used to it."

"You don't miss the field?"

Janos started to shake his head, but then he laughed self-deprecatingly. "I could never lie to you. Yes, of course I miss it. But only sometimes. It is like smoking, Kirk. When you first give it up, it's hell. But then the urge finally begins to go away. It doesn't ever disappear, sometimes it gets very bad, even for me, but by then you know that you have it licked. I'm just fine."

"I'm glad to hear that. Sincerely, my friend."

Janos nodded solemnly. "You have come as a very large surprise."

"Pleasant, I hope."

"Pat is frightened."

"I'm sorry."

"Barney and Elizabeth will want to see you before you go." Janos stopped. "Are you back in Washington for good?"

"I don't know. Probably not."

"No," Janos said. "But you did not tell me who has engaged you. It is important."

"I can't, Janos. It's very sensitive," McGarvey looked into his eyes. "But it's legitimate. In this you must believe me."

"I do."

McGarvey leaned forward. "I'm going to need your help."

"My charter—"

"I don't care about your charter," McGarvey interrupted sharply. Janos had to be handled this way sometimes. "Your mother never cared about charters. No one does. Just listen and then if your heart tells you no, you can walk away with a clear conscience."

"You are a friend, but I have my position here!" Janos said, raising his voice. "I signed the Secrets Act. For me it is a very important thing. They could easily send me back to England. And from there you know where—straight back to Poland."

"I signed the same act. And there is no way in hell they'd send you back to Poland unless you shot the president or something."

The color drained from Plónski's face. "Don't even joke like that, Kirk. For God's sake."

"I need help, Janos. Some information out of your machines. Nothing terrible or bad. Nothing about anyone who makes any difference in this world."

Janos looked down at his beer. "We all make a difference. I don't think you ever understood that."

"His name is Artimé Basulto. Used to work for

us in the very early days. Fifties, early sixties."

"Cuban?"

"He worked out of Havana watching Batista. Got in on the Bay of Pigs thing, then dropped out."

"He'd be in the old records down in Lynchburg. Army. But what about him, Kirk? Is this an old vendetta? Are you writing a book?"

"He's been running cocaine out of Matanzas."

Janos brightened. "You're working for the DEA?"

"I didn't say that," McGarvey replied quickly.

Janos chuckled. "You want his track?"

"I want to know everything."

"Of course."

"No, Janos, listen to me. I want to know *everything*. From day one. What he did, how much he was paid for it, his day sheets, who he worked for. Everything, do you understand?"

"I understand, Kirk," Janos said, happy now that he believed McGarvey was working on a legitimate operation. "But this could have come through channels."

McGarvey put his beer down. He looked at his old friend. "Listen very carefully this time. Very closely. I want you to pay real close attention. This Cuban we're talking about worked for the Company a long time ago. He might still be working for the Company."

Janos sat back as if he had been slapped. "For who?"

"I don't know. But open inquiries might cause trouble, if you see what I mean."

"Oh, I understand," Janos said.

"I'm sure you do, Janos."

"I love this country, Kirk. I want you to know that."

12

If Janos Plónski wasn't particularly proud of his job
as deputy director of records at Langley, he was at
least proud of his own past record, and of the
renewed strength the Company was enjoying since
its emasculation by the Carter administration. Of
the old hands he was one of the very few to have
come out of that dark era unscathed. His wife, Pat,
understood his moods of depression when he sometimes thought about the old friends who died in
Eastern European operations, or were scalped like
McGarvey. But Janos had kept his nose clean, hadn't
he? And that counted for something in this day and
age. That, and his wife and children, for whom he
would do anything, were his world.

Janos had become the star of archives. Who
better than an operations type—an ex-field hound
—to understand the practical side of an intelligence
service's record-keeping system? The college grads
were mainly interested in the historical perspective.
The computer whiz kids tinkered with their machines. Administration had always been, and always
would be, dedicated to following the financial trail of
all operations . . . fitting each little budget line into
the whole picture. And the bookworms, who were a

class all to themselves, gave a damn only about order versus chaos. Janos knew better. The only reason for the existence of an archives in this business was to provide operations planners and field men with the accurate and timely information they needed when and as they needed it. No excuses about perspective or downed data links or administrative holds on jackets. Somewhere in the great bloody pile of facts and figures is the needed bit, get it now, Janos.

He was, in nearly everyone's eyes upstairs, a magician. Operations was pleased with his work, but so were administration and personnel and intelligence. "How do you do it, Janos, old boy? Must be a juggling game down there, keeping everyone going all at the same time. Like wagging both ends of the tail at the same time."

His somewhat spartan office was at the rear of the exposed basement, with one large window that overlooked the construction of the new section of the building. He had spent the first hour of the morning in a staff meeting upstairs, in which the effects of the recent budget cuts were hotly debated. Everything but Central American and Libyan operations would have to bear the burden of the cuts. He told the bad news to his chief of computers, who had for the third year in a row pleaded for an updating of peripherals. Then he informed his secretary that he would be leaving his office for the entire day. At ten, having cleared the last of the morning's business off his desk, he telephoned Ft. McGillis Army Depot outside Lynchburg and asked for Captain Leonard Treitman, Special Records Section.

"Good morning, Leonard, this is Janos."

"Hello, Janos. I was just on my way out. Staff meeting. What can I do for you?"

"I'm driving down. Be there a little after lunchtime."

"Damn. I won't be here. Sam wants me at the Pentagon at two. Can yours hold till tomorrow?"

Janos looked at his watch. He was beginning to feel tight. "No, actually I'll be tied up for the rest of the week. It's routine anyway, unless you're locking the doors."

Treitman chuckled. "Sounds like another inspection to me."

"I'd like to run a few tracks. The budget reared its ugly head again this morning. Next thing they'll be down here fussing about our efficiency."

"I'll tell Charlie and the others that you're on your way down . . ."

"No, don't do that, Leonard," Janos said a little too quickly. He covered himself, though. "I want this as routine as possible. I just called you as a courtesy. It really doesn't matter if you're there or not."

"I see," Treitman said, a bit of disappointment in his voice. He was one of the bookworms who didn't care for someone else playing amongst the bits and pieces in his inner sanctum. "Do me the courtesy of a follow-up report."

"Of course, Leonard. It goes without saying."

"I know, but do it anyway."

On the way out, Charlene, his secretary, chalked him out on the status board for an inspection visit to the Lynchburg facility. She was new from the pool. "Shall I transfer your calls down there, sir?" she asked.

"Unless the Russians invade Poland, make my excuses until morning," Janos said. It had been his standard joke for years. She didn't crack a smile. McGarvey had told him to watch himself. Not to trust anyone. Anyone at all. They'd be working under the old rules on this one. Janos figured Charlene was high on his list of those not to trust.

* * *

He got his car from the parking lot, drove off the agency's grounds, then took the George Washington Parkway over to the Beltway and down to Interstate 66. The day was pleasant. He rolled down his window, lit a cigarette, and turned the car radio up. They were playing Tchaikovsky, one of the few things Russian Janos could honestly enjoy, though over the past few years even that passion had begun to abate. To say it was Russian wasn't to make it automatically bad in his mind.

He thought about Pat. She said they were becoming comfortable. He agreed with her, though for him it wasn't a point of pride, as it was for her. She liked McGarvey, but this morning before Janos left the house she had come out to the garage in her robe and slippers to face him eye-to-eye. "Janos, tell me you are not going back into the field for Kirk, or for anyone else." He had lied to his wife, the thought lingered on the long trip south, but as he entered Ft. McGillis the old feelings of excitement and self-preservation had begun to sharpen his wits. He was glad to be back in the field.

"Oh shit," the officer of the day, Lieutenant Charles Guthrie, said, jumping up as Janos walked in. "Captain Treitman isn't here this afternoon, Mr. Plónski."

"I know, but that doesn't really matter, does it." On the way down Janos had mentally prepared for his inspection tour. The safest place to conceal a snowflake, after all, is in a blizzard. "We'll just do a few line items, and then I'll get out of your hair."

"Yes, sir," the young lieutenant groaned.

The entire small post was nestled in a heavily wooded area of rolling hills. Lynchburg itself was a few miles to the south, and Appomattox Court House, where Lee surrendered to Grant to end the Civil War, was not too far to the east. Most of the installation's buildings were constructed of red

brick with white Colonial wood trim. From the
standpoint of a record-keeping facility, the post was
inefficient. The records themselves were kept in a
dozen warehouse-type buildings in cardboard bins
on steel shelving that rose almost twenty feet toward
the very high ceilings. Here, there was no such thing
as electronic retrieval. It was thought that the files, as
sensitive as they still might be, had aged sufficiently
so that their rapid retrieval wasn't necessary. Since
Janos became director of records, that had changed.
Now, unlike the old days when a few antiquated
clerks ran the entire post, there were a dozen young
administration types who were constantly being
drilled to keep on their toes. The solution, of course,
was to reduce the material to computer memory. But
the amount of data was so vast, so complicated, and
so sensitive that no one dared suggest such an
undertaking. Some things were better left undone.
The funds that such a project would drain were
better spent elsewhere. The main administration
building contained a couple of offices; incoming-
records processing, in which arriving cartons of
material were opened, sorted, graded, and cataloged
according to their national security sensitivity and
classification, given a retrieval code, and finally
placed on the appropriate shelf in the appropriate
warehouse; and the reading room, which contained
the brains of the system.

Janos followed the lieutenant down the corridor
that opened onto the reading room, which stretched
across the entire rear of the building. Fully half the
large room was taken up by rows of chest-high oak
cabinets in which were contained the heart of the
retrieval and cross-referencing systems. Laid out
much like a library's card catalog, the filed information was given a number akin to a Dewey decimal
system classification in which each document or file

was located by building, shelf, and slot, and was also referenced to dates, subjects, and case officers. A few chairs and tables were grouped at one end of the room, and at the back was a short counter from which the runners were dispatched to the various warehouses.

It was fairly quiet this afternoon. Only a couple of tables were occupied. Case officers doing their homework for the DDO, who was a stickler for details during planning. Janos knew neither of them, though he'd seen them around. He knew the type. They were the same as him . . . or at least the same as he used to be. One of them looked up and nodded as he passed, the other was buried in his files.

"Is there something specific you'll be wanting this afternoon, sir?" Guthrie asked.

They had come to an empty table. Janos put down his briefcase. He smiled as Mary Prentiss, the chief duty clerk, came from behind the counter. She was one of four capable civilians Janos had hired. He'd got her from the staff of an angry U.S. senator.

"I'm going to pick out a few random case histories for your people to track down," he said to Guthrie. "Nothing important."

"What nasty tricks have you got up your sleeve today?" Mary said, smiling. She was in her thirties, somewhat too athletically built to be pretty, and was married, though no one had actually ever seen her husband.

"Leonard is gone for the day . . . " Guthrie started.

"Well, I think we can manage for Mr. Plónski," Mary said, ignoring him. "Is there anything specific you need, Janos, to make you come all the way down here?"

In many ways she reminded Janos of his own wife. They both were capable women who sometimes displayed a hard edge. He'd learned early on to relax around them, let them do the work, not fight them. In the end he usually got what he wanted.

"I like to watch you work, Mary," he said, shrugging. "Maybe we'll look at a few case histories. Maybe we'll see how well you've taken care of the jackets. Maybe we'll see how fast your crew can perform for you."

"You won't be needing me, then, sir?" the lieutenant asked hopefully.

"No," Mary said to him before Janos had a chance to reply. "We'll handle it."

The lieutenant went back to the front office. Treitman didn't like civilians messing around on his turf. He'd get a full report from Guthrie.

"He's okay as long as he's shuffling army forms around. Back here he's a disaster," Mary said.

At least, Janos thought, the lieutenant didn't actually believe he *owned* the base, as Treitman did, or the records, as Mary did. She was good, but she was worse than the bookworms; she felt she had a proprietary interest in every scrap of paper here. She would be behind the same counter twenty years from now, he figured. A fixture.

"Let's get started, then," Janos said, opening his briefcase. He took out a legal-size tablet and a pen, but before he closed the lid he made sure she had gotten a good look inside at the several fat case files he had purposely brought with him. Two of them were marked with a diagonal orange stripe, indicating they contained secret material.

"Anything for me in there?" she asked.

Janos looked up. "No." He locked his briefcase, then moved directly across to the first row of the card catalogs under Case Officers, A–C.

Mary came up next to him as he opened the first drawer and at random picked out a card for Albright,

Edward J. Three terse lines gave a clinical history of his life; date of birth, place of birth, education, service record, employment covers, and finally date of death, in this case April 19, 1959. The body of the card contained the code names of the operations in which Albright had been involved, followed by a three-digit building number, a three-digit row number, and a two-letter three-digit address for each particular jacket. The card was nearly filled on both sides. Albright, it seemed, had been a very busy man.

Janos jotted down three of the file numbers, then looked over his shoulder at Mary, who was hovering just behind him. "Do you want to bring me some pink slips?"

"I'll do them for you, Janos," she said. "It'll speed things up."

She went back to her counter as Janos moved to another drawer, this time selecting the card of Aumann, Dieter K., born in 1909 in Hamburg, Germany, ending his career, it seemed, with the BND (the West German intelligence service) in 1957. He jotted down a pair of addresses.

Mary returned with a bundle of pink retrieval slips. Each was supposed to be filled out with the name or subject of the requested file and its archives address, as well as the date and time and the name of the requesting officer, whose signature was also required.

"What have you come up with here?" she asked.

Janos tore off the top sheet of his tablet and gave it to her. "I'm going in for misfiles. Dig these up by address alone. When they come in I'll match them against name and operation."

"You won't find any in there," she said.

"None?" Janos chided.

She grinned. "Not one."

As she began filling out the slips, Janos quickly

moved to the Bs, where he found Basulto's name in the second drawer. He glanced at Mary, who was still busy writing, then back at Basulto's card. There were only three reference files under his name. One was listed as Operation Sweep, another Operation Box Cars, and the last was Operation White Out. McGarvey had worried that there would be no references to Basulto in the files, or at least none under his own name. The alternate source would have been Roger Harris. After that it could have been anyone's guess. Only they had gotten lucky on the first try. Janos jotted down the three addresses and then as Mary came toward him he closed the drawer and tore off the paper for her. She gave him a half a dozen pink slips to date and sign. As he was signing them he was conscious that she was studying him. He looked up when he was finished.

"How many more?" she asked.

"I don't know. A few more maybe."

"I'll just get started with these."

Janos pulled out a stopwatch, made a show of setting it to zero, then clicked the start button. "You're off, then," he said, stepping around her and moving over to the next row.

McGarvey had been a surprise last night. Not so pleasant for Pat, though she had finally asked him to stay for dinner. The children loved him. He was Uncle Kirk, Daddy's best friend. Only five years ago when the witch-hunters had been in full stride, daddy hadn't done much to help his friend. His mother told him once that people do most things out of guilt. It was easy to see in others, but not so easy in yourself. Today part was guilt, but another part was . . . what? Larceny? McGarvey's warning that Basulto could still be working for someone within the Company rang in his ears. In a way the old adrenaline felt good.

In ten minutes Janos had picked out a dozen more files, as the first of the runners came back. He set himself up at one of the tables, his briefcase unlocked and open beside him, his stopwatch beside him, a fresh tablet and several sharp pencils at the ready. Mary brought him the first of the jackets, and then a coffee, black, as he started to work.

The case histories themselves were contained in thick buff-colored envelopes with accordion bottoms and tie flaps. He opened the first of the Albright cases marked with its address and, in gray type, CONFIDENTIAL: OPERATION HAT RACK. All case files were the same. Just inside was a slip on which was marked the date of each withdrawal and the initials of the withdrawing officer. On the first page of the main body of the file was a summary of the jacket's contents: work sheets, budget items, justification data, authorization documents, planning and analysis, actual details of the operation, follow-up analysis, and references, if any, to other files. Hat Rack was an operation that had taken place in East Berlin in January of 1948. Albright, along with a half-dozen Americans and some British agents, were to organize as many cells as possible of unhappy East Germans who would be willing to conduct a rumor campaign of an impending Russian drive to round up petty criminals and low-ranking Nazis for work in the mines in Poland. The operation had apparently meant to stir up unrest in the Russian sector. There was a lot of that sort of thing going around in those days. The Russians to this day maintained it was just because of that kind of Western operation that they were forced into building the Berlin Wall.

During his reading Janos made a great fuss of making frequent references to the various files he carried in his briefcase. After half an hour, when the remainder of the jackets had been brought to him, his files were intermingled with the ones from Archives. It would be no problem switching the contents of the Basulto jackets to three of his own.

For a while he stayed away from the Basulto files. Twice he went to the card catalogs where he pretended to make reference to the files, and after a short time his paper shuffling and trips back and forth became so commonplace that not even Mary paid much attention to him.

At one point he sat back, stretched his legs under the table, and sighed deeply as if he were a man weary from his labors. Actually his chest had begun to feel tight, his mouth dry, and the old heartburn had returned. It was a part of the business. It burned out a lot of agents, but he had been weaned on such feelings.

Mary turned away as he pulled the first of Basulto's files to him and looked at the slip on the inside cover. The file had been signed out three times in 1959, seven times in 1960, three in 1961, and then once in 1964. It had not been signed out since then. The first times the withdrawing officer's initials were R.H.—probably McGarvey's Roger Harris. Whoever had signed out the file in 1964, however, had signed his or her initials in a tiny, illegible scrawl. Impossible to make out.

Turning next to the contents, Janos pulled out the first page. For a long moment he simply stared at it uncomprehendingly. It was nothing. Just a page from an encyclopedia. *Euphrates* to *Euripides.* The first page should have been the summary. But this was nothing. Someone had tampered with the bloody file. Janos could feel the tightness building in his chest. McGarvey had warned him. He glanced up toward the counter. Mary was still talking with one of the clerks. He took the rest of the thick sheath of papers and documents out of the jacket and began thumbing through them. They were nothing. It was almost too incredible for him to believe. Here in Archives! Basulto's file—at least this one— contained nothing more than encyclopedia pages, telephone directory pages, and some blank papers. Nothing of any significance. No underlined messages. Nothing with a date such as a newspaper or magazine page.

In 1964, this file was still up at Langley. Nothing had been moved down here yet. Almost anyone could have had access. But Christ, why? he asked himself.

Mary was looking at him. He forced himself to smile. Lean forward. Casually, Janos, he told himself. After a moment or two, Mary went back to her work.

He pulled the second Basulto file over, this one marked SECRET: OPERATION BOX CARS. Inside, the withdrawal slip showed some activity in the late fifties and early sixties with the last action coming on the same date in 1964. For a few terrible seconds Janos could not bring himself to look through the jacket. He knew what he was going to find, but he did not want it to be so. He could feel himself being drawn into McGarvey's operation against his will. He should have listened to Pat. She had known. She had seen it in Kirk's eyes.

He glanced again at the withdrawal slip, June 14, 1964. Then he thumbed through the main body of the file, which like the first contained nothing but book pages, telephone directory pages, some blank pages, a few ruled sheets, also blank. The third file, titled OPERATION: WHITE OUT, was the same.

Slowly he retied the jackets and stacked them with the others ready to be sent back. Someone had concealed Basulto's activities back in 1964, in anticipation that he would be under a drug investigation twenty-three years later? Or, he asked himself, had the files been tampered with more recently than that and simply not been signed for?

Each question raised a dozen more. Each possibility admitted a thousand dark avenues down any one of which was some unknown danger.

I want you to pay real close attention. This Cuban we're talking about worked for the Company a long time ago. He might still be working for the Company.

For whom, Kirk? he wanted to ask. The back door was wide open, and no one was there covering it for him. The next time he was going to get more information before he went off half-cocked.

For the next half hour he made himself work through the remainder of the files he had requested, going through all the motions of checking them against the card catalog. When he was finished, he bundled up his own files and put them back in his briefcase along with his tablets and pencils. Mary came over from the counter.

"Well, how'd we do this time, Janos?" she asked. She did not seemed worried, nor did it seem to him that she could see he was upset.

"You were a little slow on 201," he said casually. "But it was within limits. I'm not a hardass here, Mary." He got up. His legs felt a little weak. It was from sitting in the car, and then here at the table.

She laughed. "Oh, I don't know about that." She glanced at her watch: "Are we done here? Can I get these back to the roost?"

"Sure. You did a good job here, Mary, as usual. All of you did." He locked his briefcase and hefted it.

"Are you heading back to Langley?" she asked.

"Why?"

"I thought I'd buy you a drink at the club. Something I'd like to talk to you about."

He looked guiltily down at the files. Had she found him out? She was sharp. Christ, she could have looked in each jacket before bringing them over to him. She could have seen what Basulto's contained. Now she wanted to find out from him why he hadn't said anything about it. And that was the least of it. At this moment there should have been a four-alarm fire beneath the tail of every man, woman, and child on this post. Or, she could be working for whoever was still running the Cuban.

"Janos?"

"Another time, Mary," he blurted. Careful, Janos he cautioned himself. "I've really got to get back."

Disappointment showed on her face. "How about later this week, then? I could drive up to your office. I'd really like to talk to you."

"About what?"

"Maybe I'd like to apply for another position."

"What?" he asked stupidly. He felt dense.

"At Langley. In computers."

Then he understood, and he laughed in relief. "Sure," he said. "Sure thing, Mary. But I've got to go now. Call me later this week. Better yet, next week. I need a . . . I'm busy this week. Next week we'll talk."

"Thanks," Mary said.

In the front office, Lieutenant Guthrie had stepped out. Janos signed himself out, then headed north again, sweat making his shirt stick to his back. This time he had no stomach for music, Russian or otherwise. He could only think what a disappointment McGarvey had been. He was an old friend and yet he hadn't warned Janos—at least, he hadn't made his warning clear enough. Be careful, Janos, he could have said. I mean be really careful, Janos. I don't want you to get hurt. You are a good friend. I

want to protect you. Right now there could be a lot
of trouble coming down—for all of them. It was all
right for Kirk, the man had resilience; he was like a
rubber ball. When he was knocked down, he always
seemed to come back up with just as much strength
as before. But for Janos, who felt as if he were a man
out on a very long, shaky, and dangerous limb, it
wasn't all right.

Ten miles north of Charlottesville, he pulled off
at a Mobil station, where from a pay phone near the
men's room, he telephoned a number McGarvey had
given him. It was answered on the second ring by a
gruff male voice. "Yeah?"

Janos could hear a lot of talking and laughter in
the background. It sounded like a bar.

"Is Mack Kirtland there?" he asked.

"Who's calling?" the man demanded.

"His mother," Janos snapped. The man
laughed. Janos glanced out at his car. The attendant
was washing the windows.

"Hello, mother," McGarvey came on the line.

"Three jackets. Nothing in any of them. Someone was there first."

"Easy now," McGarvey said soothingly.
"You're calling from a secure phone?"

"Absolutely, Kirk. I swear it." Trucks were
rumbling by on the highway.

"Tell me what happened, then, Janos. Everything."

Janos told him everything he had found and
exactly how he had gone about it. He also share his
speculation that the files could have been cleaned out
at any time after the date in June 1964, and before
the archives had been moved down to McGillis.

"But I'm mad, Kirk, that you didn't give me a
better warning."

"Nothing has happened yet, Janos," McGarvey

said. "But if it's any consolation, I had no idea someone would have wiped out his files. There wasn't a thing?"

"Nothing, Kirk. Now what happens?"

The line was silent for a second or so. When McGarvey came back his voice sounded strange. "Go home, Janos. Just go home, now, and forget about it."

"What's going on?"

McGarvey hung up.

A dark blue Mercedes had come into the gas station, and two men got out as Janos hung up the telephone. He stood by the telephone for a moment or two as one of them came across from the island.

"Through with the telephone, sir?" the man said.

Janos looked at him. He was short, thin beneath a well-tailored blue pinstriped suit. But there was something about his eyes, something dark and cruel, something Janos had seen before.

The man suddenly had a large handgun in his right hand. It was an automatic, but it was silenced. In a fleeting instant before he was shot and killed, Janos realized that he not only recognized the gun, he understood exactly what was happening. He never heard the shots that killed him.

13

Until this day McGarvey had had a fairly clear sense of his own past and at least some idea what possibilities the future might hold. He was not proud of his past, nor did he hold much real hope for the future. But they were his, nonetheless. He'd always thought, for instance, that despite his previous bad luck with women he would eventually settle down with a good one. He could see himself at a ripe old age, finally understood. Now he wasn't so sure.

Up to this point he had not really committed himself to Trotter and Day. Oh, he'd gone through the motions all right. He had left Switzerland, hadn't he? No matter. The end there had been inevitable. And once back he had gone to see Yarnell's ex-wife, though how much of that had been out of idle curiosity and not his duty was a moot point. And he had come here to Washington to take a run past Yarnell and a brief look see down Basulto's track. He wanted to do his preliminary sums before he got himself totally committed. A lot of what they had told him in the mountain safe house an age ago didn't seem to make sense; the twos and fours were coming out nines and thirteens. "After the Bay of Pigs business, Yarnell was assigned to the embassy in

146

Moscow," was how Trotter had begun to build his case. After that he became assistant DDO, then a U.S. senator, and now he was one of the most influential men in Washington. This morning McGarvey had driven over to Yarnell's house, where he waited around the corner up on Wisconsin Avenue out of sight of the attic windows, and at ten when Yarnell had emerged, he had followed him over to an office building on 16th, a couple of blocks from the Sheraton-Carlton. The entire day had been a waste. Yarnell had not moved. Once in the first hour, twice in the second, and six times every hour after that, McGarvey had said the hell with it and had started away. Each time something drew him back. Like iron filings to a magnet, or more like a hungry bear to a cache of tender meat, McGarvey returned. At four Yarnell went on the move, and by 4:20 McGarvey had gotten his reward.

He telephoned from a booth in the International Visitors Information Center across the street from Lafayette Park and within sight of the White House entrance. "I need to talk to Trotter," he said.

"I'm sorry, but that's not possible," the same voice from before replied calmly. "If you would give me your message . . ."

"Listen, you sonofabitch, I want Trotter. I'll call again in five minutes. He'd better be there or I'll run down to the Washington Post and tell them everything. Loudly."

McGarvey hung up and went outside where he lit a cigarette, then crossed the street into the park. From where he strolled he could see through the Pennsylvania Avenue fence to the north portico of the White House where Yarnell's car was parked. He'd shown the guards a pass, McGarvey had seen that. And he'd been met at the door. The man was there as a friend of the president's.

Someone in uniform came out of the White House, got behind the wheel, and drove off with Yarnell's car. McGarvey watched until the car disappeared around the back. He threw his cigarette down, turned and went back across the park, crossed the street, and entered the Visitors Center. The five minutes were up. He dialed the number.

Trotter answered it on the first ring. "Yes."

"It's me."

"Where are you?" Trotter demanded. He sounded all out of breath.

"Across the street from the White House."

"What the hell are you doing there? You must leave immediately. But not back to your hotel. Check into another one and then call me here."

"Wait a minute," McGarvey snapped. A clerk was looking at him. He smiled, then turned away and lowered his voice. "Yarnell just drove up. He's in the bloody White House right this moment. But he didn't come alone. He's with a young, good looking woman. I saw her coming from his house yesterday."

"Probably his daughter. But don't worry about her. You must get away from there now, Kirk. It's very important."

McGarvey realized the urgency in Trotter's voice. "What's happened, John?"

"Everything has changed. We're going to have to meet with Leonard. Now. Tonight."

"What's happened?"

"Maybe nothing, maybe everything. I just don't know any longer, Kirk, in this you must believe me. I am holding nothing back. Nothing. But it's . . . simply too coincidental. Everything is. Believe me, you must get out of there, we'll talk tonight."

"Don't hang up on me, goddamnit. I want to know."

The line was quiet. McGarvey tried to hear any

stray noises from the other end, anything that might give him a clue where the number was located. But there was nothing.

"This may be simply a coincidence, Kirk. Believe me, I hope it is. I just received word that an agency officer was killed somewhere in Virginia. At some gas station along the highway."

McGarvey was cold. He looked toward the window that overlooked the park. He was just able to see a portion of busy Pennsylvania Avenue and the edge of the gate house past which Yarnell had driven. "Anyone we know, John?" he asked softly. "Anyone I would know?"

"You knew him from the old days . . ." Trotter started, but then he stopped. "Kirk? Christ. It was Janos. Janos Plónski. Was he doing something for you? Did you make contact with him?"

"How did it happen?" McGarvey asked, his voice choked. It wasn't possible. It had happened far too fast. He had the terrible urge to throw down the telephone, race across to the White House and put a bullet in Yarnell's brain. No mercy. No more questions. How in God's name was he going to face Pat and the children? He should have provided Janos with a backup. It was the least he could have done for an old friend. But then he hadn't believed any of this nonsense until now; he hadn't believed Basulto, he hadn't believed Day or even Trotter. None of it.

"He was calling on the telephone and they shot him. No one saw it, no one saw a thing, Kirk. His prints were lifted off the phone. An attendant found his body in the men's room. I repeat, Kirk, was he doing something for you?"

"He was working for me. Yes," McGarvey said. "He was looking down Basulto's track. The records must have been flagged or something. Maybe they followed him down, I don't know. But I'll call you within the next two hours. Set up a meeting with Day, I need some answers."

"You had no authorization to approach anyone at the Company, Kirk. Why the hell did you do it. . . ?"

McGarvey hung up and left. A lot of people had been trusting him lately, and it was getting to be dangerous.

14

McGarvey took his time driving out of the city. Cherry blossoms seemed to have appeared overnight; they were everywhere, along with the blossoming tourist traffic. Washington had become somehow garish since he had last been here. Or had he gotten used to a different standard? There seemed to be more people in smaller spaces and more buildings rising vertically in dozens of contrasting and certainly not complimentary architectural styles. He had crossed the district line into Maryland on Rhode Island Avenue and then headed up through Riverdale toward the University of Maryland's College Park. In distance it wasn't very far. But in style it was forever.

"We'll meet at Leonard Day's house on Lake Artemesia. It's near College Park. Do you know it?" Trotter had said excitedly on the telephone. "Seven o'clock. But for heaven's sake, make sure you're not followed."

"Anything further about Janos?"

"Leonard is upset. And I can't say as I blame him, Kirk. You may have jeopardized this entire project. Or, at least you could have."

"What?"

"It may not have had a thing to do with . . . you after all," Trotter said softly. "A Polish activist group has been operating here in the area for the past few months. We've been watching them. Apparently they think they'd like to settle some old scores, though they'd all have to be in their fifties or sixties in order to have any memories at all. It's possible they may have killed him."

"I don't understand, John."

"It was his mother. I don't know if you knew it. She was an activist during the war and then afterward in England."

"It's been years."

"What can I say? There are fanatics out there. You wouldn't believe . . ."

"There certainly are," McGarvey said, letting out his breath.

"What the hell is that supposed to mean?"

"Nothing," McGarvey said tiredly. He was looking out the window of his hotel at Yarnell's office building. He had checked in to a hotel this close to it as a joke. It was beginning to pale now for him. "I'll be there at seven sharp. And, John . . . ?"

"Yes?" Trotter replied hesitantly.

"My ass is now on the line for sure. I'll be wanting some answers."

"Remember who hired whom, Kirk."

"I think you're running scared, John. You and Day. I think you need me now more than ever before. Janos was killed because of this. Don't kid yourself into believing otherwise. And you know what I think?"

"What?"

"There's more going on here than even you or Day can guess. I won't be followed, just make damned sure you aren't."

The sun was low over the rolling green hills of

the university and reflected as a blood red ball in the waters of the tiny lake around which were a few lovely English- and Colonial-style homes that were not quite large enough to be considered mansions but were certainly much too large to belong simply to the upper-middle class. Two men in an aluminum fishing boat were in the middle of the lake just across from the stone entrance to Day's property. In the distance McGarvey could make out the high roof, dormers, and chimneys above the darkening line of trees. The house disappeared into the woods as he drove up, then suddenly appeared across a broad lawn so well tended it looked as if it were a giant putting green on a championship golf course. It made McGarvey think about croquet in Kansas as a child.

McGarvey parked behind two other cars near a side entrance under a broad overhang. By the time he had shut off the ignition, got out, and mounted the two stairs, Trotter had already come to the door. He was still in a business suit, but his tie was loose and his collar undone. He looked frazzled.

"Were you followed, Kirk?" he asked, stepping aside.

"If I was it's certainly too late now, don't you think?" McGarvey said, brushing past him. He was beginning to feel mean again. He was lashing out because of Janos and because of his own mistakes.

"Christ," Trotter swore, hanging by the door a second longer; then he closed it and motioned McGarvey through the mudroom, down a broad corridor, and across the front hall into a huge study with floor-to-ceiling bookcases around which an oak ladder ran on a track. Dominating the far wall was a huge cherrywood desk, to the left of which was a teak buffet and to the right of which was a grouping of

mahogany-and-leather furniture. The combination
of woods and styles was worse than downtown
Washington.

"Leonard will be with us in just a moment,"
Trotter said. "Care for a drink?"

"Bourbon," McGarvey said, crossing the room.
"Who else is here?"

Trotter was pouring drinks at the buffet.
"What?"

"There was a second car out there. Besides
yours."

"I didn't notice."

McGarvey went to the tall windows. He pulled
back the drapes and looked outside. From here he
could see the front driveway and the road down to
the lake. He knew that Trotter was watching him; he
could feel the man's eyes on his back. Who spies on
the spy? the old adage went. It was odd though, being
here like this; even odder that he hadn't had as great
a reaction to Janos's murder as he thought he should
have.

"Did you really go see him last night?" Trotter
asked. "Here's your drink."

"Do you suppose Yarnell had him killed?"
McGarvey asked, remaining at the window. It was
pretty here.

"If he was looking down Basulto's track, it's a
possibility."

"That would mean he has people within the
Company. At least in records. But the timing would
have been tight. It bothers me."

"You could have been followed, you know."

"I don't think so, John," McGarvey said. He
heard a door slam somewhere in the house, and then
he heard a car starting.

"Come away from that window."

McGarvey didn't move. "Yarnell is at the White

House. He has a pass. They even parked his car for him."

"He's a powerful man."

The blue Chevrolet sedan—one of the two cars parked at the side of the house—came around from the back and headed quickly down the long road to the lake. It had flashed by, but not so quickly that McGarvey hadn't gotten a good look at the man behind the wheel. He watched the car disappear into the trees as the road dipped into a valley and curved left.

"What is so fascinating out there?" Trotter complained.

McGarvey let the drapes fall back into place, then turned and accepted the drink from Trotter. They sat down in leather chairs across a massive mahogany coffee table from each other. Trotter had lost some weight even since Lausanne. His nose seemed more prominent, hawkish. His complexion seemed pale. It was obvious he was under a great strain.

"You owe us an explanation, you know," Trotter said, breaking the uneasy silence between them.

"And you owe me the truth, John. At least that."

"I don't know what you mean."

McGarvey looked at the door. It opened a moment later and Leonard Day appeared, out of breath, but fresh looking in a sport coat, open-collared shirt, and tan slacks that just touched his boating shoes. He looked as if he had just stepped off the set of a commercial for after-shave.

"Kirk's just arrived," Trotter said unnecessarily.

"Yes, I can see that. And I think we have a lot to get straightened out between us," Day said, fairly bounding across the room to the buffet. He poured himself a drink. "Anyone for bumps?"

"I'm sorry that Lawrence couldn't stay," McGarvey said softly.

"Lawrence?" Day piped without turning around.

"Danielle. I just saw him leaving. Anything to do with our little plot?"

"Whatever gave you such an idea?" Day asked, turning at last. "We're old friends. He came for a visit."

Day's voice had changed. The difference was subtle, but it was there. He was disturbed. "You have some explaining to do, mister. You are in town barely a day and the killing begins. A little extreme I'd say."

"Do you think I killed him?"

"Heavens no!" Trotter blurted.

"It isn't a coincidence, despite what John has to say about it." Day came across the room and flopped down on the edge of the couch. His movements were studied, McGarvey thought.

"Yarnell was at the White House this afternoon," Trotter volunteered.

"The president is having an impromptu meeting with the Senate Foreign Relations Committee. Powers will be there, I suspect. I'm not surprised our little spy wrangled an invitation as well, the bastard!"

"He's not working alone," McGarvey said. He thought he was at a sideshow here.

"Of course not. He has his control officer. Baranov, perhaps. Who knows? They're like a cancer. Cut them out, ruthlessly. It's the only answer."

"I meant here in the States. Most likely in the Company. Maybe in the bureau. Maybe even in Justice."

At this last suggestion, Day flinched, but he

didn't move from his perch on the arm of the couch, nor did his outward manner or expression change. But the barb had hit home; McGarvey could see it in the way Day held himself.

"Because of this Polish DP who ran the agency's archives?"

"The Polish activists didn't kill him."

"Oh?" Day said, his right eyebrow rising. "I see. Who did then, Yarnell himself?"

"I think there is a lot here you haven't told me. I'm out in the cold." McGarvey decided in midstride that he did not like nor trust Day. The man wanted to be president. It was written all over him. Next there'd be Secret Service bodyguards crawling all over the place. He expected Day to put out his hand at any moment for him to shake.

"I think you're forgetting your place, Mr. McGarvey."

"This isn't helping anything," Trotter tried to interject.

"We found you rotting away in some Swiss bookstore. Remember? We should have left you there."

"Yes, you should have. But now that I'm here, how about cutting the bullshit and telling me what's really going on."

"We're not getting anywhere this way, Kirk," Trotter said a little more forcefully. "Please. This is counterproductive."

McGarvey's eyes had not left Day's. "Just what is it you want from me, Mr. Day?"

Day slowly stood. He looked across at McGarvey for a long time, then he threw back his drink. Not a sideshow, McGarvey thought, more like a bloody circus or a B movie.

"You are an assassin, Mr. McGarvey. We have

hired you to assassinate Darby Yarnell."

McGarvey grinned and sat back with his drink. He hadn't thought Day would actually commit himself like that. "You don't want an investigation, then?"

Trotter jumped up too. "Good God, what are you trying to imply, Kirk? What do you take us for?"

"You've already asked that question once, John. But Mr. Day hasn't answered mine."

Day stared through hooded eyes. He must have to jog at least five miles a day to look so fit at his age. Probably around the lake every morning before a breakfast of whole-wheat toast, guava juice, and wheat germ on everything.

"Yes, an investigation, but not at the expense of innocent people." Day could have been lecturing. "It is the innocent who must be protected. That's why we are in business. Too often the little man gets in the way and instead of our kind making the proper considerations, he gets steamrollered."

From his chair Trotter voiced his agreement. "Poor Janos Plónski, case in point."

"Then you are convinced he is guilty. No trial. The man is a spy. I'm simply to walk up to him some dark evening and put a bullet into his brain. That it?"

"Don't be tiresome, McGarvey. I don't care about the details. It must be done. He's murdered one of your own, by your own account. What more do you want?"

"The truth."

"What do you mean by that?" Day asked indignantly. He played the role well. "Exactly."

"Who else is Yarnell working with, besides the Russians? You?"

A dangerous silence came over the study. Even Trotter was moved to keep his peace, apparently because of the monstrousness of the question. Chile had taught McGarvey a painful lesson: Nothing is ever the way it seems, especially not in this business. Connections within connections, plots within plots, there never were any simple or rational answers. Janos's world as a field man had been relatively simple by comparison. Kill or be killed. The real perfidy was at the upper echelons of the business. That treachery had gotten Janos killed in the end; McGarvey's sloppiness after five years of inactivity was a contributing factor. Knowing this didn't make him feel particularly secure.

"Perhaps you don't fully appreciate the measure of Darby Yarnell," Day said at last. He was wounded. He was letting them all know now that he was too big a man to let such a snipe stop him cold, but that he was sensitive enough to be hurt. He went back to the buffet, where he poured himself a second drink. "Besides friends," he said over his shoulder, "he has quite an extensive organization of his own."

"His firm?"

"More than that. You've seen his house; it's Fortress Yarnell. He has similar bastions elsewhere: Paris, Monaco, Austria, I'm told, though I don't actually know for a fact about that last. He has cooks and house staff at each place, of course. He has his drivers, his bodyguards. He has his secretaries, even a Learjet for God's sake, complete with a full-time crew, though I'm told he's a pretty fair pilot in his own right."

"An accomplished man."

Day turned back, his right eyebrow arching. "Indeed." He came back with his drink. "He does have his friends, as you say, within the bureau, certainly within the Company, Powers included, and no doubt he has his crowd even within my bailiwick. Unwitting helpers, I'd say. Pass the innocent bit of information back and forth. Good heavens, the man is a friend of the president himself. Doesn't make him an accomplice, now does it?"

Day looked to Trotter for confirmation. "Of course not."

"Enough friends for him to know by now that I am here?" McGarvey asked softly. "Why I am here?"

"That's the point, isn't it?" Day replied. "If it wasn't the Polacks who did in your friend, and it was Darby Yarnell's gang, the implications are somewhat sticky."

"If Darby Yarnell were to meet with an accident, what would become of his organization?" McGarvey said, trying a new tack.

"I don't catch your drift," Day said. His expressions were sophomoric.

"Pearson and Darien, his partners in the firm. Mightn't they take over the spy business if their boss departs?"

Day turned again to Trotter. "That's your turf, John. Anything on them?"

"They're clean as far as we can tell."

"Doesn't that strike you as odd," McGarvey said.

Trotter shrugged. "If he has help, they'll dry up once he's gone."

"All on the say-so of a Cuban drug dealer," McGarvey said, half to himself. "That's what I meant, you know."

Day wanted to pace. A muscle twitched beneath his left eye. "We've gone over all of that. Don't be tedious."

"I haven't begun to get tedious, believe me. We have a long ways to go."

"What exactly is it you want?" Day snapped irritably.

"Your signatures on a piece of paper."

Day laughed out loud. Trotter reared back until he, too, realized it had only been a joke. He didn't seem amused by it.

"Access to bureau and Justice files," McGarvey said. "For a start."

"Only on matters pertaining to this business," Day said. He glanced at Trotter. "John?" Trotter nodded.

"Now that I no longer have Janos Plónski, I'll need someone with the Company. Lawrence Danielle, for instance."

Day laughed again. "I'll work on it."

"I don't want a direct link with him; in fact, it would be better if I dealt exclusively through you."

"Whatever." Day shrugged.

"What was he doing here today?"

"I've already told you—"

"The truth this time."

A strand of hair had boyishly fallen down on Day's forehead. He brushed it aside. "If I were to promise you that Lawrence's visit here had absolutely nothing to do with why you are here, would that be enough?"

McGarvey was thinking ahead. He nodded and then sat forward. "If at some later date I discover you have lied to me on this point, Mr. Day, held back on me, thus making my position over the coming days more dangerous or difficult, you'll regret it."

"I don't take kindly to threats," Day said evenly.

"Not a threat. I am merely telling you that if I find I've been lied to, all bets are off. I'll go to the *Post* as well as the *New York Times* with the entire story. Names, dates, and exactly what I was hired to do."

Trotter started to protest, but Day held him off with a gesture. "Fair enough. What else?"

"I'll need a safe house somewhere in the city. Close to Yarnell without being obvious."

"I can arrange that," Trotter volunteered.

"I'll need four or five of your top legmen assigned to me, John. Someone who knows electronics and will bring along the entire kit. Computers. Cameras. Second-story people. No one squeamish."

"What are you planning?" Day demanded.

"Getting away with my own skin intact."

"They cannot be involved in the . . . actual operation," Trotter said. "Even so it will be difficult breaking them loose from the bureau. Questions will be asked."

"Have you someone in mind?"

Trotter nodded.

"They'll have to be told the truth. All of it. And they'll be working directly for me. No middleman, not even yourself. If I find monitoring devices or tapes or any kind of bugs of our surveillance, the deal is off."

"When would you need them?" Trotter asked.

"Immediately."

Again Trotter looked to Day, who nodded his sage approval. "All right, Kirk, we'll do as you say."

Day leaned forward. "Now, we would like something from you in return. Only fair, wouldn't you say?"

McGarvey inclined his head. Trotter had come a long way down since they'd last known and worked with each other, he thought. Now he took orders not only from the director of the bureau, but apparently he took orders from a tinhorn bureaucrat as well.

"I would like you to check in with us through the telephone number John provided you. Every six hours, I think."

McGarvey had to smile. Day was a wheeler-dealer. "Forty-eight."

"Twelve," Day said.

"Thirty-six."

"Eighteen."

"That's reasonable, Kirk," Trotter interjected. He was worried.

"Twenty-four," McGarvey said. He got to his feet. "With a twenty-four hour fallback."

"Fallback? What's this? I'm not familiar with the term."

"I'll check in every twenty-four hours unless I'm tied up, in which case I don't want you doing a thing—nothing—for another twenty-four hours."

Day laughed. "You got your forty-eight hours in any event. Agreed."

Yes he had, McGarvey thought. But he wondered if in the end it would be enough for him, or for anyone else for that matter.

Donald Suthland Powers's Cadillac limousine was passed immediately through the east gate of the White House grounds, where it was met by a uniformed guard. Only a handful of men within the government had instant access, day or night, to the president; among them was the DCI. It was a privilege Powers had never abused.

Powers felt no sense of victory knowing he had predicted this day nearly six months ago. He had been watching the happenings to the south, had personally studied the KH-10 satellite photos, and had felt a mounting sense of frustation and finally fear with what he understood was probably happening at half a dozen places along our southern border.

The Mexican ambassador had been making his president's warning clear over the past months, not only here in Washington but through their delegation to the United Nations. A new relationship had to be negotiated between the United States and Mexico. Now. Falling oil prices, unjust drug accusations against Mexican government officials, immigration disputes, another Mexico City earthquake, and a failing economy were contributing to a general malaise among his people. Hunger had finally become a major political issue; with it, socialism of the Soviet Russian variety was rearing its ugly head.

For the first time in a very long time, Powers was frightened; not merely concerned, but deeply and utterly convinced that unless something was done—immediately and decisively—a shooting war was about to begin.

He took the stairs up to the office in the West Wing. The president was meeting with some members of the Senate and a few other people in his study down the hall. He promised to return in five minutes.

Powers opened his briefcase and began spreading computer-enhanced satellite photographs on the desk. The president came in. He was alone, though Powers caught a glimpse of his press secretary outside.

"What's got you so het up, Donald?" the president said, his voice betraying a deep weariness.

"These, Mr. President. Something has to be done."

The president looked at Powers, then bent over the photos laid out on his desk. He studied them, one at a time, for a long time before he finally straightened up. He leaned back, his hands at the small of his back.

"Well, are you going to tell me what I'm looking at, or am I going to have to guess."

"Those are photographs of six regions of Mexico, some of them within twenty-five miles of our border . . ."

"Yes?"

"I think the Mexican government, with the help of the Soviet Union, is constructing bases for the launching of nuclear missiles."

"Christ," the president swore. "Oh Christ."

PART TWO

15

For forty-eight hours, while Trotter assembled the team and found a suitable safe house, McGarvey would have languished at the Sheraton-Carlton within sight of the White House and Yarnell's office building but for a single occupation. Before their meeting had broken up he had requested from Day excerpts from the staff directories for each of the years Yarnell had been active in the Company. It was a tall order, but one with which Day nevertheless said he would be happy to comply, and did within the first eighteen hours, having the bundle delivered to the hotel by courier.

As he waited for the assembly of his army and a fortress from which he would wage his battle, McGarvey began the first steps of his oblique look down Yarnell's path.

As he explained much later to a mystified Trotter, it wasn't as if he were having doubts about Yarnell. On the contrary, by then he was fairly well convinced the man was a spy . . . or had at least been a spy. But he wanted two things: the first was proof that Yarnell had spied; and the second was the name or names of his contacts here in Washington — his non-Russian contacts, that is.

Also, during these hours when McGarvey did not leave his room, he let a certain amount of guilt wash over him. First about Janos's death; next about his daughter and ex-wife, who were within a stone's throw of him; and finally about Marta, whom he missed. Twice he had picked up his telephone and nearly called her in Lausanne. Each time, however, he thought better of it and hung up before he had finished dialing.

He watched television sporadically, especially the news broadcasts and news-magazine shows. In his Swiss life he had kept himself relatively isolated from world events. The country was geared to this state of isolation; in Switzerland if you didn't want to hear what the superpowers were up to, you merely ignored Swiss Television One and any foreign newspaper. You weren't considered odd, at least no odder than the average Swiss, for whom neutrality was not only a badge of long-standing honor but one of smug indifference to the other four billion inhabitants of the planet. (The only oddity in Switzerland was the man who didn't read the financial section!) The isolation had spawned in him a hunger for hard news of the American television variety, even if the networks' editorial positions were blatantly espoused. U.S.–Mexican relations were troubled again. Coincidence, he wondered as he watched the news, or was this part of some larger picture that somehow included Yarnell, the man's ex-wife, and Baranov, the Russian everyone seemed so respectful of?

By then, however, he had developed what he called his "short list of rogue's rogues" and Trotter had telephoned with the setup. Finally it was time for his duty call.

The address was in Chevy Chase, on a curving street that just looked over the south side of the

country club. Half dozen white pillars fronted the
big Colonial house that sat well back on half an acre
of manicured lawn. A powder blue Mercedes 450SL
convertible was parked in the driveway, and
McGarvey nearly drove past, his courage flagging at
the last moment. Kathleen had always wanted just
this sort of house. A proper place to raise a daughter,
she said. She'd be a member of the country club,
which probably was where she'd met her attorney
friend; there'd be bridge, debutante balls, and the
dozen or so black-tie parties each year. She'd gotten
a healthy part of the ranch money, but even that
probably wouldn't have been enough to support this
life-style. But then she'd always been an opportunist.
It was one of the reasons they'd married—he was an
up-and-comer. And of course in the end they had
divorced over it when he turned out to be not so
much of an up-and-comer after all. He parked behind the Mercedes and got out of his rental car,
hesitating only a moment before he went up the walk
and rang the bell. A basket of spring flowers hung at
eye level. He reached out to pick one when he heard
footsteps and withdrew his hand. The door swung
inward.

She was standing there—suddenly, it seemed
—with one hand on the edge of the door, the other
up as if in greeting. It struck McGarvey that she had
not aged; in fact, if anything she had somehow
learned the secret of eternal youth and become
younger. She was dressed in a silk lounging suit, high
heels on her feet, her hair done up, wearing only the
slightest bit of makeup and a thin gold chain around
her long, slender neck. She smelled of lilac; clean and
fresh and new. He hadn't remembered that her eyes
were so green.

"Hello, Kathleen," he said, finally finding his
voice.

"You should have called," she replied, her voice smoother than he remembered, well modulated, cultured. She'd definitely changed over the past five or six years. For the better.

"I'm sorry. I can come back. I was nearby . . ."

"You never were much on timing," she said wryly. She looked beyond him to his car. "You'd better come in, then."

"I can only stay for a minute," he said, stepping past her into a large hall.

"Yes. I was just leaving. If you'd come five minutes later you would have missed me."

She led the way into a large living room, extremely well furnished with Queen Anne furniture. A harpsichord, its sound-box lid propped open, its finish an antique lacquer, dominated one end of the room. A large oil painting of Kathleen and Elizabeth hung over a natural-stone fireplace. McGarvey walked over to it.

"Elizabeth is away at school. I'd rather you not bother her there."

McGarvey couldn't tear his eyes away from the portrait. His daughter was a beautiful young woman; not the little girl in braces he had left, but a young woman with straight, fine features, long lovely hair, and graceful limbs. How much like her mother had she become? The spitting image, he hoped. Yet couldn't he see a spark of rebellion in his daughter's eyes?

"She is a lot like you, Kirk," Kathleen said. "I suppose I should be grateful. She'll probably grow up to do great things. They absolutely adore her at school. And Phillip thinks the world of her. But she is tiresome at times."

McGarvey turned. Kathleen hadn't changed after all. "She is beautiful. Like you."

The compliment was her due. She barely ac-

knowledged it. "When did you return from Switzerland?"

"A few days ago."

"Business?"

"In a manner of speaking, yes. I also wanted to
see you."

"If it's about Phillip's letter, the alimony . . ."
she asked.

He shook his head. "No."

She was actually embarrassed by her own crude
comment. "No," she said. "It wouldn't be that,
would it. But you are back in the States for good?"

"I don't know, Kathleen. I doubt it."

"Then what?" she asked softly. He'd known her
for a couple of years before they were married, and
they were married for twelve years; they'd been
separated now half that long. Yet he was conscious
that this was probably the very first time he had ever
seen her for what she really was; merely a woman,
like others, trying to find her way. He could see her
now not blinded by love, nor confused by hatred.
And in a small measure he felt sorry for her
loneliness—though he also felt a great deal of pride
that this self-sufficient, classy, and certainly tough
woman had once been his to love, had once been in
love with him. He could see her now through more
objective eyes, however. He saw that she had indeed
aged, but that the process had not been unkind to
her. She'd matured, advanced along with the times;
she was a modern woman in makeup, dress, life-
style, and certainly in attitudes. There was no lag-
ging for her. He saw also that she was frightened of
him. Frightened that he would somehow disrupt her
carefully constructed life. But perhaps also frightened that she was still vulnerable to him.

For the very first time he felt no need or desire to
find out.

"I never knew what to say to you," he said. "Is Elizabeth the same? Does she hate me?"

She softened. "I haven't taught her that, Kirk. I promise you. She doesn't hate you."

He wondered why he had come here. He looked back up at the portrait over the fireplace.

"I wanted to make sure," he said. He turned back.

"We were on a different plane, Kirk. We still are, for that matter. Nothing has changed . . . or if it has, it's changed for the worse." Her eyes glistened. "The odd part is that I never stopped loving you, Kirk. It's just that I can't live with you."

She took out a handkerchief and daubed her eyes with it. She came across the room and took his arm. Her touch shocked him with its sudden tenderness. Together they looked up at the painting of their child. Theirs. The artist had only rendered what they had created with their love, with their bodies. At this moment looking at their creation, they were both proud. They could feel their pride in each other. It was something at least.

"Phillip is a good man, Kirk," she said. "Elizabeth has a lot of respect for him."

Of all the statements she had made that one hurt the most. "Will you marry him?"

"It's possible. He hasn't asked yet." She looked into his eyes. "I plan to say yes when he does. Happiness is out there for some of us, you know."

"He writes a nasty letter."

She laughed. "You didn't take it that seriously, I hope. Good Lord, Kirk, you haven't changed that much have you? Even I might get to like you if you had, you know."

They no longer knew each other. Maybe they never had, he thought.

He drove away wondering again why he had

come out to see her. Elizabeth was away at school.
He knew that, yet he had come out anyway. It was a
beautiful spring day, quite different from a lot of
the days he had had in Lausanne. He'd never really
given Marta a chance. Another of his mistakes. She
had put up with a lot of his uncertainties, which had
caused him to do a lot of lashing out. At first it had
been duty, she tried to tell him. "I swear it was only
duty at first. Not later. I love you, Kirk." She had
pleaded with him. "I have loved you for a long time.
Didn't you know that, too?" They used to read
Elizabeth Barrett Browning to each other:

> *When no song of mine comes near thee,*
> *Will its memory fail to soften?*

The Boynton Tower apartments on the corner of
R and 31st streets in Georgetown, overlooked
Dumbarton Oaks Park to the north and Yarnell's
fortress to the south across 32nd Street in its own
little mews. McGarvey adjusted the the focus on his
powerful binoculars, and the roof and top two floors
of the house came into sharp focus. The attic window was dark, though as he watched a man in short
sleeves, his tie loose, appeared momentarily and
then disappeared. He looked bored to McGarvey.
Bored but professional and very dangerous. He had
seen the type before.

"Do you know him?" Trotter asked, standing at
his elbow.

McGarvey looked up from the binoculars. Trotter was worn out, though here he was in his element.
It was like the old days.

"No. Do you?" McGarvey asked.

"There's another up there, too. Shorter. Black, I
think. Maybe a Mexican. God only knows. We'll run
photos on them both."

McGarvey nodded. "In two hours? By yourself?" Trotter had held the others back for just a moment or so. He wanted to get a few things straight with McGarvey first.

"They're watching, all right. But I don't think they're expecting anyone, Kirk. They're sloppy. Our advantage."

Trotter had found them a top-floor apartment in the eight-story building; it was just tall enough for them to have a clear line of sight to Yarnell's house and Wisconsin Avenue beyond, yet it wasn't so far away that they couldn't make out a reasonable amount of detail with optics. The only disadvantage was that they had no clear view of the garage behind the house where the cars were kept. The first they would know that Yarnell or anyone else was on the move would be when a car came around the corner of the house and emerged from the gate directly onto Scott Place and then 32nd Street. But by then the angle would be all wrong for them to see inside the car. Yarnell could come and go as he pleased unless they permanently stationed a man down on the street, which at best was dangerous, no matter how lax Yarnell's people seemed to be. But if anyone showed up they would know it. And they had a clear view into at least six rooms of the house.

"We couldn't get much closer, in all good conscience, Kirk," Trotter explained. "I don't want his people picking us out. He'd go to ground immediately."

McGarvey straightened up and lit a cigarette. From here they would begin their surveillance of Yarnell. For better or worse, whether the man picked them out of the crowd or not (and McGarvey suspected he would), he wanted to see what Yarnell was up to, what his routine was. He wanted a measure of the man's daily habits; his comings and goings; the time the electric meter reader came by; the time the postman delivered the mail; the grocery runs, the emergencies, if any. McGarvey wanted it all. Once a base had been built, then they would find the weak link in the man's armor.

"Have you got good people for me, John? Anyone I know? Experts?"

Trotter had to smile. "You know two of them from Lausanne. They're professionals, believe me. They'll do the job for you."

McGarvey glanced again out the window toward Yarnell's fortress. Yes, he thought, there was a job to be done here. But that was only a part of it. He himself had watched Yarnell while poor Janos was being shot to death at some service station beside the highway, his body stuffed unceremoniously in a men's room. Yarnell had his army. But was he the king . . . or was he merely a general?

The apartment was large and well furnished. It contained two bedrooms, an efficiency kitchen, two bathrooms, and a long living room–dining room combination in which the surveillance equipment had been set up.

"They'll be back within the hour," Trotter said. "I sent them away for the afternoon. I wanted to have a little chat with you before they got started. Ground rules."

McGarvey didn't feel like showing his old friend much mercy. "You want me to kill Yarnell for you, but you don't want your crew to know about it."

Trotter's jaw tightened. "We've gone a long way for you, Kirk. We've bent over backward to accommodate your needs. Don't push us too far."

"Then I'll quit and return to Switzerland."

This time Trotter did not react the way he had before. This time McGarvey had Janos's murder on his conscience. It was a psychological weapon Trotter was going to be using regularly from now on. McGarvey could see the entire plan, and it saddened him in a way. Nothing had changed, it seemed, in the five years he'd been out of the fold. There was no honor here, as someone at the Farm had once told him about the spy business. "We're dealing in what is fundamentally one of the most dishonest occupations in the world; that of inducing perfectly ordinary people to betray their country, to go back on their principles and ideals. Don't expect any honorable men in the profession," he'd been told. "And don't expect to keep your honor intact for very long, not if you want to be very good at your job." But then, assassins were not to be treated with honor in any event; respect, of course, but not honor.

"Build the case for them, Kirk. Tell them all the little bits you want—of course, they already understand that a surveillance operation on our Mr. Yarnell has been ordered. Tell them, if you'd like, how you were recruited, or why, and that you've been brought in as an outsider to prove Yarnell's guilt. But leave out the part about the prosecution, will you? It's all we're asking. Not much."

"If I don't?"

"They will be withdrawn."

"By then it would be too late. If they know what might happen and it actually does, they will come forward during the investigation that will follow."

"No they won't, Kirk."

Again McGarvey glanced out the window. "I won't take that risk, John."

"Under the circumstances I don't think you have much choice."

McGarvey turned back. There was an odd light in Trotter's eyes. "What circumstances?"

Trotter puffed up a little. "We had to have our

insurance, too. You must understand that. You would not be welcomed back in Switzerland, that part of your life is over with. There is simply nothing left there for you to go back to. And, from what I understand, Kathleen will probably marry Phillip Brent."

"What are you getting at?" McGarvey asked softly.

"Do you know this man? Have you heard of him?"

"He wants to sue me for an increase in Kathleen's alimony. Harassment . . ." Another chilling thought suddenly struck McGarvey. "Who is he, John? What does he have to do with this?"

"It wasn't up to me," Trotter said. "I mean, I knew nothing about it until after the fact."

"What the hell are you talking about?"

"I'm surprised you didn't catch it. But then you were out of the country so long that the name couldn't have meant anything to you. And these past couple of days have been hectic at best . . . confusing."

McGarvey was having a very bad premonition about this.

"Phillip Brent is one of Darby Yarnell's closest friends and associates. They do a lot of business together. In fact, Kathleen and Elizabeth have been frequent houseguests—"

"Oh, Jesus Christ," McGarvey swore softly. "Down there?" he demanded, pointing toward Yarnell's fortress.

"There. Yes."

A wave of anger and disbelief washed over McGarvey. That and fear, not only for what was and had been happening, but fear for what he might do.

"How long has it been going on?" he asked.

Trotter said nothing.

"How long, John?"

"A year. Maybe a little longer."

"My ex-wife and daughter and Phillip Brent have been pals with Darby Yarnell for more than a year?"

Trotter nodded.

McGarvey could feel his blood pressure rising. The old meanness was coming back. Only this time he felt dangerous. "Not only didn't you mention this in Lausanne, it was the very reason you came to me in the first place, wasn't it? Whose idea was it, yours or Leonard Day's? The joke was on me the whole time, wasn't it? You must have had quite a few laughs."

"No one is laughing about this, Kirk. On that you must believe me. Yarnell was and is a very dangerous man—"

"Who is involved with my ex-wife and daughter!"

"He must be eliminated."

"And I am the only man for the job, is that it? Can't miss with Kirk. He has a personal stake in this."

"If you warn her and she suddenly withdraws, Yarnell will become suspicious. It would be extremely dangerous for her, Kirk. Surely you can see that."

"You don't involve families, John. Don't you remember the old score?" McGarvey was sick at heart. He realized now that he knew absolutely nothing about dishonor. He'd never really known about it.

"It's bigger than families, can't you understand that?" Trotter's eyes were wide behind his glasses. He looked like a fanatical revolutionary. "The man is friends with the director of Central Intelligence, for God's sake. He is on a first-name basis with the president of the United States. Let's put it in perspective!"

Trotter's team showed up later in the afternoon, all bright and full of cautious enthusiasm. Among them were Lewis Sheets, the tan mack from Lausanne, and Lorraine Hawkins, the girl with the *sommersprossen*. Bill Porter, the bureau's resident electronics expert, and a Mexican second-story man, Emiliano Gonzales, rounded out the little group. McGarvey behaved himself, but he would forever remember having the feeling that they all were playacting and everyone knew it. The deception was part of the new regime. They'd watch Yarnell on his home turf. Meanwhile, the ball of string saved up all these years had to be unwound, and McGarvey thought he knew where the starting bit might be.

16

He watched from the window of the Long Island Airways Piper Navajo as they came up from the southeast, parallel to the beaches of Long Island. It was nearly noon, and after the strain of Washington and the hustle-bustle of LaGuardia Airport, the barrier islands, broad beaches, and tree-studded communities below seemed peaceful, idyllic. Ahead just off Highway 27 lay the airport in East Hampton, the hills and sand dunes flattened at this altitude, the big Atlantic combers breaking all the way from Ireland, tame. Even the vast ocean distances were softened by the haze that obscured the horizon. He'd not been around these parts in years, not since Elizabeth was a little girl. The Hamptons in those days had been Kathleen's idea of "arrived." She met a lot of people, made a lot of friends up here. For a time she even attempted to affect a Hampton accent. Their house back in Alexandria in those days was filled with Long Island bric-a-brac, as if they were tourists back from Mexico or Morocco, somewhere where the vendors were as thick as flies and one *had* to buy souvenirs. But then, he was using his memories as a shield against his bleak thoughts about John Trotter, Oliver Leonard Day, and all that they *hadn't* told him—which was a legion.

He'd driven up to the Baltimore-Washington International Airport to pick up his flight to New York, watching behind him for anyone from the bureau's team on his tail. But he'd come away clean as far as he had been able to determine. Of course, again at LaGuardia he had gone through the switchbacks, the feints, the over-the-shoulder routines, and in the end, climbing aboard the tiny prop-driven executive aircraft out to Long Island, he'd even looked to the observation platform, half expecting someone to be up there even then, watching him, reporting back. By then Trotter would have been able to put two and two together and would have figured out who he was coming to see. But there'd been no one.

The cab, which was an old Chevrolet station wagon, took him to the house, which was located on the beach three-quarters of a mile north of town. The road wound down through dunes and tall grasses that were permanently bent toward the land because of the nearly constant sea wind. They drove past an old storm fence that was half-buried in the sand, a No Soliciting sign knocked down. It hadn't taken much to find the place from the files Day had sent over. A couple of telephone calls to a folksy local tax assessor and he'd had his directions. The house was a lot larger than he had expected it would be. Tall dormers, a widow's walk, weather-beaten shingles, a broad screened porch that looked out to sea, a large stone chimney—which was smoking a little now because it was chilly and old men were almost always cold, especially in the spring—were all punctuated by dark, unblinking windows. On a sand hummock below the front steps a picnic table with one leg broken leaned forlornly into the salt breeze. Big rolls of brownish foam scudded along the beach beneath an overcast sky. Way out to sea a large container ship headed south.

He'd brought a leather shoulder bag packed with a few last-minute things. After the cabbie left, he shouldered the bag, walked up the sand path, mounted the steps, and let himself onto the screened porch. The place smelled musty and dead and very old. He knocked on the door with the heel of his right hand, the entire front wall of the house shivering under the blows. The house would be considered a disgrace in the Hamptons, he mused. Raze the place and don't look back, Kathleen would have said. But then there never had been too many rich spies and almost never any *old* rich spies.

The door opened and a very old man with watery, pale green eyes, wispy white hair, and a few days' growth of white whiskers on his chin stood looking out. He was dressed in a thick wool sweater with the tall collar turned up, steel gray wool slacks, and thick carpet slippers. His skin seemed parchment thin, and his lips, his bony cheeks, and the arches above his eyes were blue-white and veined. His right hand, raised as if in greeting, shook slightly from a palsy.

"Mr. Owens?" McGarvey asked. He didn't know if he should shout. "Darrel Owens?"

"Who the hell are you?" the old man asked, looking beyond McGarvey down toward the driveway. His voice was soft, precise, and cultured. McGarvey felt just a little like an idiot. He smiled.

"Kirk McGarvey, sir," He held out his hand.

"Is something funny, for Christ's sake?" the old man demanded looking McGarvey in the eye.

"No, sir."

"What do you want?"

"I'd like to ask you some questions."

"About what?"

According to his jacket Owens had had a reputation for being a tough bastard. McGarvey had little doubt this old man was him. He'd cut his teeth during the Second World War in the OSS, and had been one of the shakers and movers when the agency was established in 1947. His name, along with Donovan's, Bill Casey's, and a very few others were a legend. He was seventy.

"Darby Yarnell," McGarvey said with just a little trepidation. After all, Owens had been Yarnell's boss for much of the man's career in the CIA. "Just a few questions. I won't take up much of your time."

"You don't look Russian. And your name does seem to ring a bell in the distance."

"Russian?" McGarvey asked.

This time Owens chuckled. "We've all got our enemies, what? Russians. You've heard of them? They're supposed to be the bad guys."

"Maybe I shouldn't have come," McGarvey said, softening his tone even further.

The old man lowered his head and looked up at McGarvey as if through the tops of bifocals. "I'm not senile, you sonofabitch. Old, but I've still got most of my marbles. You came to ask about Darby Yarnell. We called him a prick, do you know why?"

McGarvey shook his head, not knowing what to expect.

Owens laughed. "Because he had such a perfect head."

"I don't know . . ."

"You have questions, son? I've at least got the time, if not all the answers." Owens stepped back into the house. He beckoned. "I always figured Yarnell was too big for his britches. What's the sonofabitch supposed to have done?"

"I don't know if he's done anything. But that's just it." McGarvey came into the house and closed the door. He dropped his bag in the vestibule and followed the old man back into the hall, which smelled of must and age, of medicine and faintly of backed-up toilets, over all of which was the odor of

wood burning in a fireplace. Masculine odors. Together, not so terribly unpleasant.

A very large, very old dog raised its head from
where it lay in front of the fireplace and looked up at
McGarvey. It wagged just the tip of its tail, yawned
deeply, and then laid its head back down. The
remnants of lunch—soup, some bread, and a bottle
of beer—remained on a broad oak coffee table.
Photographs of dozens of foreign places, each with
Owens and sometimes others in them, adorned the
walls. The room was dimly lit and very warm from
the fire. McGarvey suspected that Owens lived alone
here.

"You with the Company, then?" the old man
asked. "One of the new regime? A Powers man? Hear
he's doing good things. About time, I suspect,
what?"

"Ex-Company. I was fired a few years ago."

Owens stared at him through eyes suddenly
shrewd. "Knew I'd remembered the name. You're
the hit man who got canned over the Chile thing. A
Carter regime casualty."

McGarvey nodded.

"Who are you working for now? What are you
doing here?"

"Looking for answers."

"You going to kill him? Is that it? Is this an old
vendetta? Are you settling an old score? You're on
intimate terms with the bad guys, then?" McGarvey
had the feeling that the old man was enjoying this,
even though he was skeptical and mistrustful. It
probably got very lonely out here on the beach.
Especially in the winter when the winds blew the
weather in. With spring came hope. He could see it
written on the man's face.

"I hadn't planned on it."

"He hadn't planned on it," the old man hooted.

He turned to the dog who looked up again from its sleep. "Hear that, he hadn't planned on it. Maybe it'll just happen, then. Moscow Center rules and all? I suppose he's packing a piece. Probably a Makarov . . . light, accurate, reliable. Maybe even a Graz Buyra, the heavyweight. Do the job right. Final."

"Are you familiar with Oliver Leonard Day?"

Owens's eyes narrowed. "Justice?"

"He would accept a telephone call from you. If you needed any kind of a confirmation he would make it, though he wouldn't necessarily like it. I can give you his number if you have a phone out here."

"I'm capable of looking up a telephone number," the old man said. He shook his head. "I'm truly sorry you are here, you know, though I suspected someone like you would be showing up on my doorstep sooner or later. Part of the business, I guess. Though one could always hope." Again he shook his head. "Justice."

McGarvey didn't know if he was referring to Justice the department, or justice the noun.

Owens stacked the dishes on his tray and picked it up. "Would you like something to eat?"

"No thanks."

"A beer?"

"If it's not so cold," McGarvey said off-handedly.

Owens grinned. "Been in Europe for a while, then. Make yourself comfortable." He left the room.

McGarvey took off his jacket and dropped it over the back of the chair. The crackle of the fireplace was real. Nothing else seemed to be. On a table was a stack of magazines: *Central Intelligence Retirees Association Newsletter*. They went back a number of years. Over the mantle were photographs showing Owens with Truman, Eisenhower, Kennedy, Johnson, Nixon, and finally Ford. All of them

were signed best wishes or with similar sentiments
except for Kennedy's, which made mention of Cuba:
Cuba libre—next year, Darrel. The date on the
photograph was more startling, however. It was
November 21, 1963—the day before Kennedy was
assassinated in Dallas.

"Washington was called Camelot in those days,
remember?" Owens said coming in from the hall.
He'd brought a couple of beers.

"I was in the service, stationed in Germany. I
remember the day Kennedy was shot perfectly,"
McGarvey said.

"Everyone remembers that day." Owens
handed McGarvey his beer. It was cellar-cool. "I was
convinced a shooting war was imminent. After the
Bay of Pigs, and the missile crisis, there wasn't much
left except for an all out exchange of ICBMs." Owens
looked up at the photograph, his eyes moist. "He
wasn't such a hot president, you know. But he
cleaned up nice, and his wife was a looker. Our
country was young—we weren't even two hundred
yet—and so was our president. Hell, we could lick
the world, or at least show them the way into the
twenty-first century. We were going to the moon!"

A ways off they could hear the horn of some very
large ship, the sound blown onto the shore by the
breeze. Then it faded as the breeze momentarily
died.

"Will you trust the memory of an old man?"
Owens asked softly. He hadn't taken his eyes off the
Kennedy photograph. "Could be faulty."

"As long as no one has tampered with it, such as
is done with paper records, I'll be satisfied."

Now Owens looked at McGarvey. "You've got a
bone in your teeth, haven't you, lad," he said.
"You've got the look about you. Oh, boy, have you
ever got the look."

Owens was married for forty years. His wife had

been dead now for nearly ten. McGarvey figured the man could write the book on loneliness.

"Yarnell played double for the Bay of Pigs," Owens began with no preamble. "It was his first real field assignment. We knew the Russians were getting themselves involved in a big way down there, so we decided to throw Yarnell into the equation. We wanted to see if we couldn't hold them off. Provide a little diversion, if you catch my drift. Misdirect them. By then it was too little, too late. It was one of the few projects at which Darby Yarnell ever failed. But then, it wasn't his fault. The conception was all wrong."

McGarvey hadn't thought the man would begin with an apologia for Yarnell, but then it was Owens's story and he'd tell it in his own fashion. Only if he got off the track, McGarvey decided, only if the old man wandered too far afield, as old men are wont to do, would he bring him back. McGarvey settled down with his beer to listen and listen closely, because if there was one lesson he'd learned well from the early days, it was that more than half of any story was *between* the lines. So pay attention, boyo, and you just might learn something.

In those days, Owens explained, the agency was very young. They were still learning their lessons from the NKVD straight out of Moscow and still trying to assimilate everything their own OSS had taught them. *Overlap* as a conceptual term became the bane of their existence. The organizational chart had gaps a mile wide in some places, and even worse, crossovers wider. Too many chiefs and not enough Indians was the watch phrase. Their pariah was the man who tried to play both ends against the middle, and they were loaded with the type. It gave just a hint of the troubles they were having and would continue to have in the years to come.

"In the midst of all this came Darby Yarnell, the bright young MBA directly out of Harvard. Oh, what a force he was in those days. But how ready we were for him. Let me tell you," Owens said.

He was recruited in the spring of his senior year right there at the school. It was before the Vietnam era when the mention of an agency recruitment team on a campus was cause for a major riot. In the late fifties there was still a lot of idealism around. The recruiting teams consisted mostly of a grade-one clerk, a regional desk officer, and as often as possible a field man home for debriefings. The clerk covered the entry-level possibilities, the desk jock talked about the advancement, the good pay, and the intellectual challenges of the Company, and of course the field man bespoke the James Bond romance of the job.

"I don't remember who we sent up there that year, but the young Yarnell nearly talked every one of them out of the Company, convincing them that they were wasting their time, that theirs was an immoral task, and furthermore, that someday they'd be remembered by their children as no better than Gestapo thugs, mindless wretches for whom *1984* had already become reality."

Of course, Yarnell had overwhelmed them with his intelligence, his breeding, and the sheer force of his personality. Who could resist such a combination in those days? Who could resist such a combination in any age? Pharaohs and czars had fallen for less. The man was possessed of that rare combination: charm *and* intelligence.

"Our team came back with their tails between their legs, ready to give up on everything they'd ever learned. We didn't have the Farm down in Williamsburg like we do now. No place really to send them to get their heads back on straight. Yarnell did it for us. He came traipsing down to Washington, innocent as all get out, ready, willing, and able to give his all for the cause. Gabriel couldn't have done better with his horn."

Owens chuckled with the memory.

"He must have been the wunderkind," McGarvey suggested.

"Oh, yes, the wunderkind," Owens hooted. "Someone's exact words, I'm sure. I was working the Latin American desk in those days, and I saw Yarnell as the perfect catch. He'd not only learned Spanish —and learned it well—in college, he'd spent time in Spain and he actually understood the bastards. Not simply their language, mind you. Any high school kid can master Spanish in a few semesters. I'm talking their souls. Their *esencia.* Yarnell knew what he was talking about, no question about it. He was exactly what we thought we needed at the time."

Yarnell went through his training at the speed of light, soaking up information sometimes faster than the instructors could feed it to him, which started his prowling days.

"We weren't so compartmentalized then, you know. Should have been though. The *Abwehr* had taught us a big lesson . . . I mean, Canaris did pay the ultimate price for knowing too much, having too many feelings. . . . And the NKVD was years ahead of us, too, but then we'd never had a Dzerzhinsky or a Beria. Still . . ."

Owens was starting to wander, so McGarvey brought him back on track. "Prowling days? I don't understand."

"He became an alley cat. Any handout was welcome, didn't care which hand fed him. Went from office to office, section to section, finding out what was up. Often as not he'd drop in with a bottle of French brandy or a box of Cuban cigars, and by the time he'd left they'd all be on a first-name basis and he'd have made three suggestions in seven different directions as to how they could improve their operation."

Again Owens stopped a moment to think back.

"The damndest thing about him, though—and this part I remember directly—was that no one ever took offense with Yarnell's meddling because, quite simply, it wasn't *meddling*. You always got the feeling in those days that he was genuinely interested in helping you out. He was sincerely concerned that the CIA should become the very best intelligence agency the world had ever seen. He wanted breeding in the service. Knowledge. Sensibilities for the arts. Spying to the music of Bach, Beethoven, and Brahms."

"So he went to Mexico?" McGarvey asked.

Owens looked up. "After his training, after a stint with me overseeing him on the Latin American desk, we sent him down to our embassy in Mexico City."

"Mexico was our southern neighbor and in many ways our ally, but the Russians ruled supreme in the diplomatic and intelligence circles in Mexico City. They'd adopted our philosophy there from day one: If you want to run the show, throw a lot of money into it. And they did. Their embassy was bigger and better equipped than ours. They cultivated more people within and outside of the Mexican government than we did. They threw more parties, offered more clandestine aid to almost any cause in the bush, and had consulates in more outback cities than we thought was necessary.

"For forty miles beyond our border along Texas, New Mexico, Arizona, and California we were king. Beyond that there was—and still is from what I'm told—a definite Russian presence. The proletarian uprising may not have gained any kind of a foothold in the desert hinterland, but democratic capitalism certainly doesn't hold sway either. In that, rural Mexico is very much like rural Spain; the poor are concerned with their government only in as much as it has the capability of feeding their families.

"Yarnell understood all of this long before any of the rest of us did. Some of it instinctually, some of it intellectually, and the remainder experientially. He was a very fast learner."

"It was '57 when he went down there?"

"No, more like late '58, maybe even the spring of '59. I remember that he hadn't been down there very long before we began gearing up for the Bay of Pigs invasion, and then of course he got married in the midst of the CESTA investigation and the whole ball game with the *Junta de Liberación Latinoamericana*. You know, revolution was coming to Latin America once and for all, and look out Western Hemisphere because the downfall wasn't going to be exactly pretty."

As Owens went on talking, McGarvey could begin to envision a young, arrogant, well-educated Yarnell first taking over the fledgling CIA and then transferring his efforts and considerable talents to the Russian presence in Mexico City. God, how it must have galled mere mortals like Basulto's case officer, Roger Harris. How much, he wondered, of Harris's pushing was simple paranoia? Harris had wanted to be king, or at least in the top ten. He had to work for it, whereas a man like Yarnell could simply snap his fingers and the service, collectively, would come running. Men like Yarnell became presidents or senators or at least DCIs. Men like Harris had to work for every single scrap that came their way, and they often resented those for whom success seemed to come so naturally. Maybe he was chasing after a very old vendetta after all, McGarvey thought.

Yarnell took over our embassy in Mexico City just as he had taken over the agency itself back home. The State Department, which even in those days raised objections about the CIA, never said an unkind word about Yarnell, but their universal sentiment was that he was wasted in the agency; he'd fit in so much better at State. He would have become an ambassador. It was a foregone conclusion. He had the feel for the job. He had the look, the flair. But for Yarnell in those days there was nothing but the agency.

"Operation Limelight, it was called," Owens continued telling his story. "From the beginning it was Yarnell's brainchild. In fact, it was he who suggested the program in the first place."

"Program?" McGarvey asked. It was an odd choice of terminology, he thought.

"It was more than a project. Yarnell figured to put a permanent mechanism in place that would counteract the inroads the CESTA network had made. The Russians certainly would never quit the region so it was up to us to neutralize their effect." Owens was remembering everything now. "CESTA was more than simply Russians, of course. There were East Germans, Hungarians, Czechs, Bulgarians, and naturally the odd lot of Spanish Communists. Their product was said to be the best, though there was a lot of natural animosity between the Mexicans and the true Spaniards. But then a lot of money was being spent down there. Nothing was too good for CESTA. Nothing was too good for the cause; the best equipment, the cream of the crop from NKVD's Intelligence School One outside of Moscow, the old Eastern European hands. And above all, one of the most sophisticated banking systems anywhere in the world."

"He must have had the help of the Mexicans themselves," McGarvey suggested. He could envision Yarnell as a force, but even a superman doesn't work in a vacuum.

"He could have been president of Mexico, for all I know," Owens said, cross that his story had been interrupted. "He arrived in Mexico and promptly took over the capital. In those days he didn't spend much time at the embassy. Of course it was exactly what we wanted, but no one figured that Yarnell was so dedicated to the cause that he'd actually go out and get married to a native just to ingratiate himself to the country."

Yarnell had had his detractors in those days, too, Owens stopped a moment to explain. There were a few early voices who thought he was too big for his britches, that he was going too far too fast, and that when the fall came Yarnell, for all his youthful enthusiasm and foolishness, would take a lot of good people with him. When he married this young girl, a member of a good family, his critics claimed he had finally gone too far. The girl was just a baby, still in her teens! What could he be thinking?

"But then none of us really knew Yarnell's measure then, not yet, and none of us had met Evita. If Darby Yarnell was a force to be reckoned with, if he was the sun, then Evita Yarnell was a super nova. All of Mexico City was at their feet."

CESTA was pals with bureaucrats at every level of the Mexican government. Yarnell's Operation Limelight was the counteraction; our answer to something that had been in place since the forties. Not so easy a task. His first step was to gain the love and respect of the Mexican people, which had been hurried along by his marriage, and then he could come in with his sweeping gestures to capture the hearts of the men who ran the country.

Owens was a natural storyteller, but he was an old, lonely man who was happy for the company and meant to string out every little detail for as long as he could get away with it. McGarvey had no real objections, for often the kernel of truth you were looking for came in the offhand remarks of some garrulous storyteller. But he wanted the man to at least stay within the main framework of the story—Yarnell's life.

"I still don't get a sense of what Yarnell's program was all about," McGarvey said. "I understand *what* he was trying to do, and I certainly understand *why,* but I'm not quite sure I see the *how.*"

"Yarnell has always had money. He was raised by his grandparents, as I recall, and they died when he was quite young, leaving him a bundle in trust, which came under his sole control when he turned twenty-five. He hasn't lost money, from what I heard."

Yarnell bought himself a house on the outskirts of Mexico City . . . possibly one of the largest, finest palaces in the capital. He staffed it with a lot of his friends—God knows how he got them so quickly, but he was always surrounded by them—and he began to throw parties.

"I saw the house only once," Owens said, smiling at the memory. "Let me tell you, McGarvey, the place was a palace. He had one of everything there and perhaps two of some things."

"Who were his targets in those days? I mean, how were they picked out of the crowd?" McGarvey asked.

"He had a governmental directory, of course. He went through it with a red pencil for everyone he figured was committed to CESTA, and a blue pencil for everyone committed to us. In those days the reds outnumbered the blues two to one."

"He invited the unmarked . . . uncommitted ones to his house?"

"To his house, to a hunting lodge he rented, to a little retreat on the ocean. He bought them presents, gave them weekends with beautiful women if need be, but mostly he gave himself; his free, helpful advice on how to solve any problem they might have, from love to engineering, from business to bureaucracy. He became their banker as well as their father confessor. For the entire government."

"CESTA had more money than Yarnell," McGarvey said. "Even rich Americans couldn't possibly compete with an entire governmental network. . . . From what you're telling me CESTA was the entire Warsaw Pact's organization."

"Of course there was no competition, at least not for money. But CESTA was indiscriminate. They went in for quantity, while Darby Yarnell went for quality. CESTA, for example, might manage to turn five out of the six men running the water utility for Mexico City. But Yarnell would pick the one man on whom the department was most dependent. The one indispensable man. He'd put that man into the limelight so that the entire world could see that he was numero uno, that he loved Mexico above all other nations, that his loyalty could never come into question, and that there would never be another man half as good as he for the job.

"Yarnell knew how to make a man feel good about himself, but he also knew how to make everyone else feel the same way about that man. It was an art.

"But then the Bay of Pigs fiasco came along, Yarnell was assigned to the planning team in Guatemala City, and when it all fell apart he was lucky to get off the beach alive."

17

Houses seemed to take on the personality of those who lived in them, McGarvey had always heard. He wondered, mightn't it also work the other way around? After lunch Owens said it was his custom to walk along the beach every afternoon. Kept his mind fresh, he explained, his juices flowing, and demon constipation, the absolute bane of an old man's existence, from rearing its ugly head. Looking back now as they walked at water's edge, McGarvey could see that the house was a lot like its master; old, a bit on the worn side, but with a grace and wisdom that pressed you to come back again and again. That part, McGarvey suspected, Owens had inherited from the building, which was comforting in a Victorian way, yet demanding of nearly constant attention and care lest the entire fabric of its structure unravel because of careless handling. Clouds had begun to form out to sea, but they didn't look very threatening although McGarvey could tell there was wind in them because already the surf was up from when he had first arrived. Owens wore an old navy pea coat, its broad round collar up around his blue-tinged ears, and a woolen watch cap on the back of his head, a few strands of wispy white hair sticking out in back. His hands were stuffed deeply in his pockets as they walked, and from time to time he would spit into the water. They headed up the beach at a fairly good pace. No one else was in sight in either direction.

"Does the name Roger Harris ring any bells with you, Mr. Owens?" McGarvey asked, keeping up.

"Maybe. Maybe not."

"He was stationed in Havana until Castro took over. In the fifties."

"He might have been one of them in charge of the recruitment medical exams down in Miami. If he's the same one."

"Was he a medical doctor?"

"No, just another idiot with ambitions like the rest of us." Owens looked back without breaking stride. "Wasn't he one of the ones who bought it in Girón?"

"Yes, sir," McGarvey said. "And I think there is a very real possibility that Darby Yarnell murdered him."

This time Owens did stop. He studied McGarvey's face. "Are you trying to pull my goddamned leg, or what?"

"No."

"Where the hell did you come up with such a notion as that? Did someone feed you that line of crap? Is that why you're here? Was Harris something to you, then?" Owens came a little closer. "That was a long time ago, mister. I suspect you weren't even out of college by then."

"High school."

Owens laughed. "I don't think you know shit-from-Shineola. You're guessing."

"But you're not. It's why I came here like this."

"For what? For whom?"

"I wanted to know about Yarnell. You called him a prick; you couldn't have liked him."

"I've got no ax to grind," Owens said. He turned as if to continue up the beach but then came back. "People could get themselves dead, dredging up old business. It's happened before, it'll happen again. You should know." He looked out to sea. "Dark clouds on the horizon," he muttered. "When the grim reaper is standing next to you, it makes you want to think out your next moves pretty carefully, if you catch my drift."

"Maybe he keeps doing it. Maybe—"

"I watch the television. I read the newspapers," Owens interrupted. "I have a question for you, McGarvey. Does the name Plónski ring a chime with you? Janos Plónski."

"A very old friend," McGarvey replied softly.

"Did you kill him?"

The question was startling. McGarvey hadn't known quite what to expect, but he had not expected that. Owens was looking at his eyes.

"He was working for me," McGarvey said. "Doing me a favor. I should have warned him. Watched him. Anything."

"Who killed him?"

"I don't know. Yet."

"Yarnell?"

"Not him, at least not him directly. I was watching him when it happened."

"Yarnell always had his followers, his entourage, wherever he went. Not always visible all of the time, mind you, but they were never far. His mob, he used to call them. Different ones all the time, but after a while all the faces seemed to be the same one. Do you know what I mean?"

McGarvey nodded.

"Maybe I'm one of his mob, had you considered that?"

"No, at least not seriously," McGarvey said.

Owens blew air out of his mouth all at once, as if he had just run a mile. He looked back toward the house. "You're an arrogant sonofabitch, too. But, what the hell, it makes the world go round." Again he looked into McGarvey's eyes. "At one time I would have called you a liar and a damned fool. Yarnell was tops in my book, and in the books of a great many people who counted. But that was then."

They started again up the beach, this time walking at a much more leisurely pace. The fight, or more accurately the spunk, seemed to have diminished in Owens. McGarvey was sorry for it, but he couldn't stop now.

"What made you change your mind about him?"

"I don't know if I ever changed my mind about him," Owens said over his shoulder. "Maybe not until this very minute, you know. But I'd always had my doubts. Then, which one of us doesn't have his doubts about his fellow man? 'Everyone is crazed 'cept thee and me, and sometimes I wonder about thee.' Bastardized Shakespeare, maybe, but pretty valid on the whole, I'd say. From day one you had to wonder just what the kid was trying to prove, scrambling the brains of the very people we had sent up there to recruit him. It wasn't just a little joke, though a lot of people did take it that way. Nor was Mexico City such a light and easy lot. Real people's lives were in the balance, and Yarnell was in many ways the fulcrum and the motivator all at the same time. By the time he brought his bride up to Washington she was starting to fall apart at the seams, and it wasn't a very pretty sight. Of course, we all thought that once Darby finished down south he'd come

home and put her back together. He had that power.
But he never did. From that day on, Yarnell became
a possessed man, a driven spirit."

It was thought that the shock of the failure of the
Bay of Pigs had set Yarnell over the edge. He had put
his all into the project. Once he had his wife settled
in Washington (settled in the sense that he had an
adequate house and staff for her), he returned to
Mexico City where he began feeding the Russians all
sorts of wild stories about Cuba. At least once a week
he would fly down to Guatemala City, though he
never did spend the amount of time there at the
training base that everyone thought he should.
But they were confusing times. Americans were just
learning to flex their muscles, and no one was very
sophisticated about it.

"He was at the Bay of Pigs? He went ashore?"
McGarvey asked. He wanted absolutely no mistake
about it.

"Yes, he was there. At Girón. But so were a lot of
others, including a lot of angry Cuban regular army
who were shooting at our people. Anyone could have
killed your Roger Harris."

They walked for a long time in silence. It was a
couple of miles up the beach to the Marine Museum
at Amagansett. For a bit McGarvey figured they were
going to walk all the way, which was fine with him.
Owens had told him a lot, but McGarvey figured he
had much more to tell. In fact, the important parts
were yet to come, and although he wanted to keep
the old man on track, he did not want to push him
out of his cooperative mood. He didn't think the
chance would come again. It was just a feeling.

After a while Owens stopped and looked back as
if he had suddenly awakened to realize he had gone a
lot farther than he had intended. He glanced up at
McGarvey.

"Let's go back," he said.

"Sure."

Evita Perez Yarnell could have been the hit of Washington, Owens said. But she kept pretty much to herself, with her staff. A sister came up for a time, and of course her mother visited whenever possible. But Evita was not the same woman she had been in Mexico City. Whether Yarnell had taken her spirit from her, or she was just out of her element in Washington, no one knew at the time. Everyone felt sorry for her, but no one knew what to do about it. In the meantime Yarnell's product coming out of Mexico City was fabulous. The sun and the moon wouldn't have been enough payment for what Yarnell was sending back. Not only was he gathering intelligence about the Mexicans, but about the entire CESTA network as well. Yarnell had managed to turn some of the CESTA agents as doubles. It was his moment of glory.

But it didn't last forever, of course. Nothing ever does. It was in the late spring of '62 that Yarnell came home in triumph.

"He could have had anything he wanted. Any assignment. Practically any job. All of Washington was kissing his ass, and I was one of them. I was right there standing in line with everyone else. The only thing that bothered me at the time was how that wife of his was turning out. But then it takes two to tango. No such thing as a one-sided argument—like clapping only one hand."

"He moved back in with her, I assume," McGarvey said, but he didn't know why. Yarnell's marital status really had no bearing on whether or not he was a traitor. But after having met her, he was curious.

"Sure he did. And nine months later she had Juanita, their only child. A very pretty girl. Had her mother's beauty and her father's brains."

McGarvey thought it was likely she was the one he had seen leaving Yarnell's house. "She's living with her father?"

"That's what I heard," Owens said dryly.

By that time Owens had been bumped up to assistant deputy director of intelligence, they had moved into the newly constructed building across the river in Langley on what was called the Bureau of Public Roads Research Station, and Yarnell contented himself to take over the Latin American desk, running the entire Caribbean Basin show. "And he was nothing short of brilliant, let me tell you. I had been nothing but a technician during my tenure in that hot seat, whereas Yarnell was the concert master." Owens smiled wanly with recollection now that the story was becoming more personal to him. "It also marked the beginning of the period when Darby and I worked with each other on the same turf. Even though I was right there all along, I could never quite figure out exactly how he did what he did. It was like witchcraft following in his footsteps, legerdemain. But damn, he was good."

On the way back McGarvey was on the seaward side, where the sand was packed a little more tightly and the going was much easier. Owens had slowed way down. McGarvey wanted to reach out a hand for him, but he didn't think the old man would have accepted it. He was too proud. Little by little as the story progressed McGarvey began to build up a picture in his mind of the relationship that had existed between Yarnell and Owens in those days. Owens was in awe of Yarnell, or had been, and yet he had also felt a small measure of resentment for the cavalier way in which the younger man dealt with the world in general, with the co-workers around him on a day-to-day basis, and in particular with his wife.

"I used to see him around town with his women," Owens said, a little bitterness creeping into his voice. "They were nothing more than a part of his mob scene, he used to tell me. Mostly they were the wives and mistresses of the foreign diplomats assigned to the missions in town. He got a lot of gossip that way, but it was tough on his marriage."

Owens was a puritan. He had married his high school sweetheart and had never strayed, not once, though he admitted he had been tempted plenty. In this day and age he was a refreshing anachronism, and McGarvey found that he had a lot of respect and admiration for the man.

"Of course he made his mistakes. Rarely, but the construction of missile bases in Cuba escaped his people until six hours *after* the first photos were brought in from our U-2 overflights. The first conclusive photos. Yarnell was in a rage for months afterward. He drove his people mercilessly. We had a pretty high attrition rate there for a while because of it. But Yarnell wanted only the best around him. He wasn't going to let something like that happen again."

"Then the president was assassinated," McGarvey said softly.

Owens looked up at him, his lips compressed. He nodded. "The bastards killed Jack Kennedy. I'll never forget that day, not as long as I live. None of us will. We all thought it was the end of Yarnell, he took it so badly. He blamed himself."

The remark was startling. "How so?"

"He was convinced that it was Castro's people who arranged it. Something about the Mafia being paid off by Cuban Intelligence to do it. Twenty-five million dollars. For six months he tried to prove it. He should have known, he should have forseen it, he kept saying. But it never happened for him, and following so closely on the heels of the missile thing, he figured he was done on the Latin American desk. Said he wanted no part of it any longer. He wanted to work on something else, something more civilized, anything that did not involve spics. He started drinking, too, and he moved out. Took an apartment in town and left his wife to herself. She finally went back to Mexico City for a couple of years, but even her home had been ruined for her. She felt like an outcast, so she came back to the States, put the child in a boarding school, and moved to New York."

Something very large dropped into place for McGarvey, who had been listening to Owens's narrative and picking up an extra beat between the lines. Owens knew and was disturbed by Evita Perez Yarnell, yet he was in love with his own wife. There was only one other possibility for his depth of knowledge and obvious emotional attachment.

"Darby Yarnell was your protégé."

"Wasn't so terribly difficult to guess, was it?" Owens said sadly.

"Did you tell him that you were disappointed in the way he was treating his wife?"

"Not my place."

"He was turning out badly . . ."

Owens flared. "Just listen here, his product always had been, and at that point still was, without reproach. The very best. The way I figured it, if his home life wasn't going exactly the way it could have, or even should have, who was I, or anyone else for that matter, to say anything? I wasn't a preacher, and we weren't running a Sunday school down there. This is the big, grown-up world in which nuclear missiles are aimed at you from ninety miles away, and where presidents get shot down. This is a crazy, goddamned world, McGarvey. If a man isn't exactly as devoted to his wife as he's supposed to be, then we know that he's just like everyone else—not perfect."

"But it hurt," McGarvey suggested gently.

"He was so goddamned good it was a crying shame. A lot of us looked up to that kid."

Including your wife, McGarvey wanted to say, but he could not. It would have been too cruel, true or not. He had a strong suspicion, though, that Yarnell was a man who never left anything to chance.

They walked on for a time in silence. Clouds continued to build out to sea, and the surf continued to rise. A salt mist drifted on the air so that a hundred yards down the beach it seemed as if the fog was coming in. The air smelled wonderful though. It brought McGarvey back again to the Hamptons with Kathleen and Elizabeth. It struck him as odd that he had not known a single soul who had escaped at least one such emotional disaster in their lives. Even his sister's marriage was rocky at times. Christ, where were the devoted people? Where was sincerity and openness? Perhaps Owens was the only one in the world who had had a good marriage. But then it had ended tragically with her death long before his.

"We were doing a lot of building in those days. The intelligence directorate, for instance, consisted of only half a dozen departments. But within the next few years that number was doubled: operations, strategic research, the U.S. Information Bureau, the Intelligence Requirements Service, central reference, the Foreign Broadcast Information Service, imagery analysis, the National Photographic Interpretation Center. The list went on and on. Every day it seemed as if we were being asked to provide another type of product to a host of new customers."

"You were busy."

"Yes," Owens said dryly. "Too busy to give a damn about another man's problems." He looked over at McGarvey. "I had my own bad luck there for a year or so, too. I was working twelve and eighteen hours a day. Some nights I wouldn't even go home. My marriage nearly went on the rocks. It was never quite the same afterward."

McGarvey didn't want to hear it. Not that. "Did Yarnell get off the Latin American desk?"

Owens blinked. "Right into operations the first part of '64. Worked for the deputy director until he started up the new Missions and Programs section. Pulled half a dozen of our very best people right out of the field, put them in a think-tank environment, and told them they were to come up with a world-wide missions and programs plan that was based on their direct experience." Owens grinned at the memory. "All hell broke loose there for a bit. Yarnell had apparently emasculated our foreign intelligence operation. But in the end the seventh floor recognized the wisdom of his action and gave him the gold star. An A for effort."

"Funny they didn't give him operations."

"He was offered the assistant deputy director-ship, but he turned it down from what I heard."

"He had something else in mind?"

"Oh yes, and so did I, though I didn't know it at the time."

"Within operations?"

"Foreign intelligence," Owens said. "He sent himself out to help replace the people he had pulled in. He said he needed the field experience. So long away from Mexico, it was time for him to put his hand back in. None of us was getting any younger, and he was always worried that time was passing him by much faster than it was for other people. In a way I suppose it was. He seemed always to be living his life on half a dozen different levels all at the same time, and all at breakneck speed. He was like a flame in pure oxygen, someone said. A lot of people in the

Company thought he'd burn himself out one day soon. In the meantime, though, he was the brightest star in the sky."

"Where did they send him?"

"Why, Moscow, of course. Right into the heart of the lion's den."

McGarvey wasn't surprised. Of course he had known some of this already from the background Trotter and Day had given him. But it was the timing that he found so fascinating now.

"That was in what year?"

"The summer of 1965."

"They sent him out as chief of the Moscow station?"

"Assistant chief of station," Owens said. "He was very good, the best, but he was still pretty young. Besides, there is something you have to understand about Darby Yarnell. He never gave a damn about titles. He was more interested in getting the product, analyzing it, and then satisfying our customers with it. 'The end results are what counts,' he used to say. 'We're in the business to provide enough information that our political leaders can make the very best of choices for us, Darrel,' he would say. It was his pet philosophy."

"Who was chief of station during his tenure, then?"

Owens laughed. "I was given the job exactly one month after Yarnell was sent over. We worked together in Moscow for twenty-eight months, until the Russians finally kicked him out."

They reached the house, but before they went in, Owens took a cigarette from McGarvey and they sat on the porch steps, smoking and looking into the wind at a cold sea filled with white horses. McGarvey, of course, had seen Yarnell in a different light than Owens. If Yarnell had been a Soviet agent he might have known about the missile bases on Cuba, and only when they had been discovered by another section within the agency did he "discover" them himself. To throw suspicion off himself, he drove his people hard, probably causing the best of his field men to quit in disgust, while secretly rewarding the inept operatives. Yarnell's little stunt of pulling some of the Company's best field men into head up a missions and planning department was nothing short of brilliant. He *had* emasculated our foreign intelligence service, evidently just as it was about to make some major discovery harmful to the Soviets. And pulling Owens with him out to Moscow was a stroke of genius. With his mentor running the operation, Yarnell would have had a totally free hand to do whatever he wanted. It made McGarvey sick to think how Yarnell had used Owens, and even sicker to think how wide open our embassy had to have been in those days.

But then, he thought, it was the nature of the business.

18

"Why did the Russians kick him out of Moscow?" McGarvey asked. "Seems to me he would have charmed them just as well as he had the Mexicans, unless the Russians were sore at him for his successes against CESTA."

They'd gone inside where Owens had straightened out the kitchen and opened them each another beer before they settled back in the living room. The fire had died down a bit so the room wasn't as hot as it had been before. The dog had not moved from its spot on the rug. McGarvey wondered if it was dead.

"He killed a man," Owens said holding his beer bottle in both hands. His cheeks were rosy from the wind and chill air outside.

"In Moscow?" McGarvey asked, startled.

"In Moscow. He was one of ours. Darby just gunned him down. It wasn't very pretty."

"So the Russians kicked him out."

Owens nodded. "I left a few months later."

"In disgrace?"

"What?"

"I mean because of what Yarnell had done. You were his mentor, his chief of station."

Owens laughed. "I don't think you understand,

McGarvey. Killing the kid was the culmination of a first-rate operation. Darby went home a hero and so did I. The only reason I stuck around was to pick up the few loose ends. And let me tell you, there were damned few of those. Darby ran a tight ship."

McGarvey was amazed. He didn't quite know what to say. "Yarnell was in his element."

"You can say that again. He hadn't been there thirty days when I arrived, and already he had developed half a dozen stringers, was having dinner and weekends on a regular basis with a couple of generals and a deputy on the Presidium staff, and he and our ambassador were on a first-name basis."

"You would have been disappointed with anything less," McGarvey suggested mildly.

"But it never ceased to amaze me. Remember, I'd been reading Darby's field reports from Mexico all along, but this was the very first time I had ever been in the field with him. It's one thing to read about it, it's an entirely different matter to actually see it."

McGarvey lit them both another cigarette. Owens seemed grateful for it. He started off in another direction.

"Those twenty-eight months we were together went by quicker than any two years plus I've spent, before or since. I was chief of station, but it was as if I were in school, at the feet of a master. Our product was brilliant. Beyond compare, that's how they described our dailies in Langley. And I got most of the credit."

True to form, Yarnell took a nice apartment near Moscow University, in a section of the city called Lenin Hills, though how he managed to get approval from the Soviet authorities to move up there was beyond most of the embassy staff. (To McGarvey's question at this point as to why no one had become suspicious of Yarnell, Owens not only couldn't provide an answer, he had no idea what McGarvey had implied.) There were a lot of comings and goings from his apartment at all hours of the day and night. Russians are great ones for having very late dinners, and then staying up half the night drinking spiced vodka and eating snacks and listening to music or poetry or dancing, or just talking. This was Yarnell's sort of life, exactly, because he was a highly social animal. He was in his glory. Living life to the hilt.

Then came Operation *Hellgate*, which right from the beginning everyone realized was a horse of an entirely different stripe. This time Yarnell seemed somehow vicious. Mean. It was as if he were trying to get back at someone for something very terrible.

The business was something new, something disturbing, according to Owens. "Up to this point, Darby Yarnell had been the sort of a man who was able to clearly see both sides of any issue no matter its emotional content. He was a man who understood the little foibles and failings we're all loaded with. But this time, McGarvey, it was different."

In those days any major operation had to be first outlined in some detail and then sent to Langley for approval. Of course Yarnell's projects always went through without a hitch.

"With Operation *Hellgate*, I sent him back to Washington to present his side of the issue in person," Owens said.

"You were against it?"

Owens nodded.

"But in your estimation it was important."

Owens looked up. "It was that—" He stopped a moment, apparently at a loss for the correct word. "It was that *indecent*."

McGarvey was surprised at the choice. "He got his approval from Langley, I take it."

"He was back within the week. And yes, he was

given the green light. It was the only time I ever disagreed with him about a project. But I was overruled." Owens shook his head sadly at the memory. "We talked about the operation, at least we did at first, until it actually got underway. Then we were very busy. He said that he agreed with me that it was a bad business, but that we hadn't made the choice. It wasn't either of us who was the traitor. But since it was staring us in the face—'An opportunity of tarnished gold,' he called it—we would be remiss in our duty if we didn't go ahead. It was the basis on which, I suppose, Langley went along with him."

Classified communications were taken care of by the air force and the National Security Agency, which loaned the embassy the operators and technicians and the cryptographic equipment. This was before the days when satellite communications were common. All long line, then. Classified information was sent via encrypted teletype to Washington. The Russians could and did intercept our encrypted messages all day long, but with the equipment we were using then, the codes were literally impossible to break. (It still held true today.) The days of the one-time cipher pad for anything other than confidential material were all but gone. An electronically-produced, totally random signal was mixed with the text, producing a signal that had no rhythm or meter, hidden or otherwise. Only a receiver in perfect synchronization with the transmitter could possibly reproduce the clear text. The system was called KW-26.

The equipment was foolproof, but its operators and technicians were not; they were only human after all. "Yarnell fingered one of the technicians, Staff Sergeant Barry Innes, as being on the KGB's payroll. To this day I don't know how he got his information, but the proof was there."

Yarnell prepared several dummy messages out

to Langley that consisted of information of potentially great interest to the Soviet Union's delegation to the UN in New York. Within days of the transmission of the messages—transmissions done only during the time when Innes was on duty—the information was showing up on the Security Council in New York.

"We had a traitor in the embassy. A kid in the air force, clean shaven, wife and a small child living somewhere in California. I wanted to arrest him, send him home. He was young enough, I figured, he might have gotten out of prison with time enough left for some sort of a life."

Innes, along with the other air force operators and technicians, as well as the marine guards, had quarters within the embassy itself. The rule was that single men and women resided automatically in the embassy—that is, military people, of course, not civilians—while married personnel had a choice. If they brought their spouses with them to Moscow, the assignment was for three years and they lived in town. If they came alone, leaving their mates at home, or if they were unmarried, Moscow was a remote assignment for only eighteen months, and they lived in the embassy. Innes came alone.

Within three months of his arrival, Yarnell had him cold, Owens said.

It was around Christmas that Yarnell proposed *Hellgate*, and he got back to Moscow a day before the twenty-fifth, leaving his wife all alone back in the States. By then, of course, she wasn't quite as big an issue as she had been earlier. Too many other much greater things were happening in Moscow and elsewhere around the world for them to worry about someone's wife, who, after all, was living a life of relative splendor and luxury at home. Who could feel sorry for a poor little rich girl?

"So you had your traitor cold," McGarvey said.

"Why wasn't he arrested and sent home for trial? Operation *Hellgate* was a success."

"You don't understand," Owens said. "Just proving that the kid was a traitor wasn't what Darby had proposed. Not at all. Operation *Hellgate* was a hell of a lot more than that."

"What then?"

"The Russians had turned one of our people; Darby wanted to get back at them. He wanted to send it back to them in spades. He wanted to send them a great big bomb that they'd take into their midst and that would blow up in their faces, causing them not only the maximum damage, but the greatest embarrassment as well."

"Innes was the key."

"He was our carrier," Owens said. "And from day one it was Darby's baby. No one—and I do mean no one, not even the ambassador—got in his way."

The idea in conception was rather simple, as all good ideas are, but in execution it was damned difficult, according to Owens. The notion was that if the Russians had successfully turned Innes, and if our knowledge of it could be kept secret, Innes could prove to be of inestimable value to us. Yarnell's plan was to give Innes a promotion to technical sergeant, put him in charge of CIA communications, and then begin pumping him with information so stunning that when he passed it over to his Soviet control officer, the man would be mesmerized, he would take whatever we wanted to give him. He would be ours.

"We set about to make poor sergeant Innes a superstar," Owens said. "Within a month he was working directly for Darby, and within a few weeks we were pumping him with information."

There were two classes of data fed to Innes, Owens explained. The first class was absolutely true things useful to the Russians. We had to mix the good with the bad in order to present a convincing front. The second, of course, was disinformation. On Mondays the select committee at the embassy—me as chief of station, Darby as Innes's control officer, the chargé d'affaires, usually an analyst or two, and at least the Military attaché—would get together to work up the product we would force-feed the kid. During the remainder of the week, Yarnell would give it to Innes. Worked like a charm."

"So Sergeant Innes actually passed good information across?"

"Yes."

"A lot of information? Damaging information?"

"A big volume, yes. But most of it was pretty mild by comparison."

"By comparison with what?" McGarvey asked.

"By comparison with some of the other stuff we fed him, as well as all the bogus shit Darby was coming up with. And some of that was very wild, believe me."

"So, no matter what happened or didn't happen, Sergeant Innes actually did pass along some valid intelligence to the KGB."

"Only on Langley's specific approval."

McGarvey could understand at least the first part of the operation, and he could appreciate its boldness. He was, however, having a little trouble visualizing the actual method. He asked Owens about it.

"For the most part that was Darby's province," Owens admitted. "Sergeant Innes worked directly for Darby, so most of his briefings were done in private. It built up a barrier of trust. A barrier in the sense that Innes had eyes and ears only for Yarnell. It was the old charm all over again. Yarnell had totally taken over the kid, whom he began to refer to as 'the Zombie' during our Monday jam sessions."

"You didn't much like that?" McGarvey asked.

"It was enough that we were using the kid without calling him names behind his back."

"How long did this go on?"

"Months."

"Three months?" McGarvey asked. "Six? Seven?"

"Maybe a year. It was a long time. Darby wanted everything to be just right. He wanted the complete trust not only of Sergeant Innes, but of Innes's Russian control officer as well. He wanted them eating out of his hand."

"And they did?"

"They did."

"How did Yarnell know this? I mean, did he give it twelve months exactly, and then after that time had passed he said now we make our move? What?"

"It was easier than that," Owens said. "Yarnell figured he would have them by the balls on the day Innes came back with a specific question."

"A question from his control officer?"

"Presumably."

"Did he ask you, or did he ask Yarnell?"

"Darby was handling it on a personal basis, I've already told you that," Owens flared.

"Then you don't know what this important question might have been?"

"Goddamnit, I don't know what the hell you're getting at, McGarvey. Of course I knew."

"How?"

"Darby told me, of course . . ." Owens suddenly trailed off, realizing what he was saying, at long last understanding what it was McGarvey had been getting at all along. "It was documented . . . I mean a lot of what we were feeding the kid was showing up . . ."

"You went on Yarnell's word alone?" McGarvey asked as gently as he could, though the question itself belied any gentleness.

"He was a friend," Owens replied. "Darby *was* the CIA in Moscow. I'd sooner have questioned the president."

"What was the question?"

Owens took a moment to reply. He focused on McGarvey, then shook his head. "Hell, I don't remember. It seemed important at the time. Something about satellites, I suppose, but for the life of me I can't remember it now."

"But it was Yarnell's signal that the first phase of his operation was done."

Owens averted his eyes. "After that it began to get nasty. Sergeant Innes, as well as his control officer, had bought the program, hook, line, and sinker—"

"According to Yarnell," McGarvey interjected.

"According to Darby, all right."

"So the question was asked, and presumably Yarnell gave him an answer to take back to his control officer. What then? Did it continue? I mean, did you give them more and more?"

"No," Owens said. "It was time for the change."

"For the next phase?" McGarvey prompted after a moment. Owens suddenly seemed less than eager to continue now that they had gotten this far. McGarvey lit them both another cigarette and then went into the kitchen, where he opened them each another beer. When he came back into the living room, the old man was sitting back in his overstuffed chair, his eyes closed. McGarvey stopped just inside the doorway and stared at the man. He could not see Owens's chest rising or falling. For a terrible moment or so, he thought Owens was dead. But then the old man opened his eyes and looked over.

"I usually take a nap this time of the afternoon," he apologized. "The beer and all makes me sleepy."

"Go ahead," McGarvey said, coming the rest of the way in and setting the beer down on the big oak coffee table. "I have plenty of time."

Owens shook his head. "I'd just as soon go on. Get it over with."

McGarvey figured what the old man meant was he wanted to finish the story so McGarvey would get the hell out of his house and leave him alone. It was just as well. McGarvey sat down and put his feet up.

"The next phase of the operation?" he prompted again.

"Darby wanted everything to be one hundred percent," Owens picked it up. "He figured that the kid, no matter how good he and his control officer had become as a team, could not have passed over more than twenty-five or thirty percent of the material he had been given. It left a hell of a lot of fantastic misinformation rattling around in Innes's head. Darby was crazy to get the entire bundle across. It was like fishing, he told me. 'Getting nibbles is fun and all, watching the bobber going up and down gets the blood pumping, but I want the big strike, I want the bloody marlin, the sailfish, a whale.' He changed his tactics from that point on. Sergeant Innes had been his pal, and now Darby set out to manufacture an enemy instead. It was something to watch how Darby used the same old charm, only now in reverse, to get the sergeant to understand that he was no longer trusted. It was subtle at first. So subtle, in fact, I don't think Innes had any inkling for the first few weeks. But then we started to see it on the kid's face, in the way he acted, in the things he said. Or didn't say. I suspect he lost a lot of sleep in those days. I don't think I could have taken it as long or as well as he did."

"How did Yarnell manage to accomplish this, exactly?" McGarvey asked.

Owens shrugged. "It was nothing obvious at first. Darby just stopped sending some of the agency's traffic through Innes. He began using some of the other operators. A few here and there at first, more and more as time went on."

"He was counting on the other operators to mention it to Innes, I imagine. Make him think about it, worry about it."

"Exactly," Owens said. "And of course it worked. We all watched as Sergeant Innes disintegrated. That in itself wasn't such a pretty sight."

"But there was more."

"Much more," Owens said tiredly. "The most important parts were yet to come."

The wind had started to blow in earnest now. McGarvey wondered if the return flight scheduled for eight that evening would be able to take off. Of course, if it did not, he could rent a car and drive back down to the city or stay in a motel here. Actually it did not matter one way or the other to him if he rested up here at this end or back in Washington. He had a feeling he knew what was coming in Owens's story and what he would have to do about it ultimately, yet he wanted to stay to hear it to the end. And afterward, he wondered as he listened to the wind howl around the eaves . . . well, afterward he would just have to see.

"Did Sergeant Innes ever come to you or anyone other than Yarnell for advice or help?" McGarvey asked. "Did he ever once question why he was being cut off from the job he had been trained for and promoted to? For a year the kid was a superstar, now all of a sudden he'd developed a social disease."

"He never said a word."

"What about his mail to his wife? Was it monitored?"

"We opened his mail," Owens said. "But he never mentioned a single thing about his work. Mostly he wrote about Moscow, the people, the weather, and the food—and about how much he missed her."

"Not traitor talk," McGarvey suggested gently, looking at his shoes.

"He was a cool customer. He was playing it close. I'd have done the same thing had I been in his place. At least I would have tried."

McGarvey thought about himself and Kathleen in the early days. He'd never told his wife any secrets, of course, and yet a lot of his job had come home with him, had seeped into his relationship (enough to cause the divorce), seeped into his telephone calls when he was away, and into his letters, some of which had to be voluntarily censored. He was a professional. Sergeant Innes had supposedly begun as an amateur and had learned his tradecraft on the run from his Russian case officer. It did not make a lot of sense to McGarvey, the kid's sudden professionalism, unless he was a cold fish after all, a young man with nerves of steel or without a conscience. But even then, when things apparently began to go sour at the embassy, he would have mentioned something in his letters, let some clue drop; at the very least he might hint to his wife that he no longer enjoyed Moscow, that he was homesick, that he was counting the days until he came home. An eighteen month assignment, Owens had said. By that time Sergeant Innes was getting to be a shorttimer. He said as much to Owens.

"Oh sure, by then Innes only had a few months

to go. We discussed that very thing during our
Monday planning sessions. It came down to two
choices: either we could extend Innes, tack some
extra time onto his assignment—which we figured
would have made him and his case officer skittish—
or we could push him into doing what Yarnell
wanted from the beginning."

"Which was?"

"For the kid to jump," Owens said.

"Why?"

"To legitimize him, for one, and so that he
would bring the rest of his disinformation over with
him."

They had their timetable then; it was some
eighty-five or eighty-six days before Innes was to ship
out. So Yarnell stepped up his efforts to convince the
kid that his arrest was not only possible, but was
indeed likely and imminent. More and more, Innes
was isolated from the cryptographic section on little
errands around the embassy. For two weeks he
worked in the consular section processing visa appli-
cations. For nearly a month he worked keeping track
of visiting American tourists of the VIP variety.
Boring work for Innes.

The coup de grace came when Innes had barely
a month to go. "Darby had made up this message to
the DDO back at Langley. It was supposedly sent out
over my signature. The flimsy was sitting on Darby's
desk when young Innes was brought upstairs. Darby
contrived to have himself called out for a moment,
leaving Innes plenty of time to go snooping and find
the thing laying there out in the open. And we made
sure he took the bait. Darby was watching from the
next office through a peephole. He wasn't going to go
back in there until Innes read it. But it didn't take
very long, let me tell you. Of course, by that time
Innes was getting pretty gun-shy. He was trying to

cover his ass seven ways to Sunday. He picked up on that message within ten seconds of the moment Yarnell stepped out."

"So he jumped," McGarvey said.

"That night. I don't know exactly how he did it on such short notice. Might have simply taken a bus over to the Lubyanka and knocked on the door. He may have had an emergency setup with his control officer. But by morning when he didn't show up for work we knew he had gone over."

"You mean to tell me after all of that you didn't follow him to make sure?"

"Of course not, McGarvey. We were trying to legitimize him. If there had been so much as a hint of a tail on him, that night of all nights, and his Russian control officer had gotten wind of it, the jig would have been up. They would have shot him themselves."

"What was your posture at the embassy?" McGarvey asked. "How was this handled, in the open I mean?"

"We went through all the moves, if that's what you mean. Conducted our own little search, of course. Then we contacted the Moscow city militia, the police, and told them one of our people was missing, and that we suspected foul play. We had to go through the maneuvers. We had to make it seem as if we were worried about him and that his disappearance had come out of the blue."

"What did that produce?"

"Nothing, not a damned thing," Owens said. He was looking inward, his thoughts traveling backward in time. "It struck me as a little odd, though. That one aspect." He looked up. "If the kid was going over, I would have thought he'd have asked for political asylum. The Russians would have made a big hoopla. They would have crowed about it. Shown him off on television. But there wasn't a damned thing."

"Maybe they weren't so sure of him themselves."

Owens nodded. "Darby suggested the same thing. Said we would have to continue making some noises, but that for the most part we were going to have to keep our mouths shut. He wanted us to go on an emergency footing, call in our field people across the entire Eastern Bloc because as soon as Innes started to talk in detail, the Russians would expect it of us."

"Did we pull our people in?"

"No. Langley overruled that."

"Was Yarnell angry?"

"Not angry, worried. He didn't care who got the credit when something went right, or who got the blame if things fell apart, he just didn't want to see any blood shed." Owens saw the sudden intense look of incredulity on McGarvey's face. "He didn't want to see any *innocent* blood shed."

"Was there?"

"No more than normal attrition. Innes only had bogus information for the most part."

"What happened next?" McGarvey asked. Owens was beginning to wind down. McGarvey suspected that the story was nearly finished.

"We spent a few days looking as if we were licking our wounds, and then we began making serious noises about getting him back."

"How?"

Owens chuckled. "I picked up the telephone and called the centre. Lubyanka. Identified myself and told them we wanted Sergeant Innes returned or we were going to make a very large stink. Kidnapping, since Innes had not yet asked for political asylum."

"You didn't get through to anyone, did you?"

"No one important. But our message had been received. Their incomings, just like ours, are automatically taped. And the telephone numbers are no great secret. We figured by then that the Russians might be getting skeptical of the kid's information. We wanted to make absolutely sure they believed him. If we treated him as if he were real, it would go a long way toward convincing them."

"Did it work?"

"Not right off the bat. It did eventually, of course. We made enough noises so that the Russians finally agreed to a trade. Sergeant Innes for Yuri Suslev, a spy we had nicked in Washington four months earlier." Owens seemed a little pale. The flush from the wind had faded. He got to his feet, stretched, and went to a window where he looked outside across the porch toward the rising waves pounding the beach below. There was a wistful set to his shoulders, as if he had gone as far with his story as he wanted to go because the telling had drawn him back to an earlier age when he was active. He had come face-to-face, via an unpleasant memory, with his own age.

McGarvey got to his feet, too, and threw another log on the fire, poking the dying flames to life. "Who was Innes's control officer, did you ever find that out?"

"A young man, coincidentally the same one who had run CESTA," Owens said.

McGarvey turned away from the fire to look at the old man. The atmosphere in the room had suddenly gotten a little thin. "Baranov?" he asked.

Owens turned. "As a matter of fact, yes, that's the one. A real sharp cookie. I suppose there was some kind of a vendetta between him and Yarnell for Mexico City. So Innes became a special case for both of them."

19

It was nearly time to leave. There was little or no doubt in McGarvey's mind what was coming next. Owens had come back to his chair so that he could be nearer to the fire. The wind in the flue sounded cold; it made the room a little smoky.

"Did you ever meet him? Baranov?" McGarvey asked.

"I saw photographs of him. Never actually came face-to-face with the man, though."

"Had Yarnell?"

Owens looked up. "I couldn't tell you. I don't know. I suppose he might have in Mexico City."

"But not in Moscow?"

"I don't know."

"They were enemies though?"

"What the hell do you mean by that?" Owens flared. "Of course they were enemies."

"Yet the Russians let Yarnell come to Moscow. They knew he was a spy. They knew he had worked wonders in Mexico. They even knew that he had been involved in the Bay of Pigs, and in at least some measure with the Cuban missile crisis, yet they let him accept an assignment in Moscow."

"That's not so unusual. You should know that.

If you have a good operative spotted, you can do one of two things; bar him from your country, in which case he might drop out of sight and then God only knows what mischief he'll get himself into, or you can keep him out in the open, in plain sight, where you can watch him. KGB has a sophisticated setup in Moscow, as you might suspect."

McGarvey offered a nod of understanding. "Yuri Suslev was brought to Moscow for the trade?"

"No. He was being held in Maryland. The plan was to bring him to Washington, where we would hand him over to representatives from the Soviet embassy. They could provide him with his transportation home. Meanwhile, KGB would be handing Sergeant Innes over to us on our front doorstep."

"Where?"

"In front of our embassy."

"During the day?"

"No. Everyone agreed that would be too risky. No one wanted any publicity about this. Suslev had been a damned effective spy—"

"Whose brains we had picked clean," McGarvey interrupted.

"Naturally," Owens said. "They picked Innes clean."

"Of disinformation."

"Suslev didn't fall into our hands with any guarantees. It's a game. You know about it."

"What were the safety signals?" McGarvey asked. "I mean, how were we to know in Washington, for instance, when exactly to turn Suslev over to his people?"

"We set up a radio link. Actually it was pretty sophisticated. Both ends of Tchaikovsky Street within a block of the embassy had been blocked off all day for construction. The switch was to take place at four in the morning, our time. In Washington it was eight in the evening, so the switch took place in the parking lot of the Marriott Twin Bridges. Our people brought Suslev over by car, and the Russians brought Innes to us the same way. The embassies were in communication with the drivers and bodyguards in both places and with each other on trans-Atlantic links."

"Yarnell was in on the switch? I mean, he was actually down there on the street in front of our embassy?"

"Yes," Owens said. "Our people got out of the car with Suslev, and the message was radioed to us and to the Russians on Tchaikovsky Street. Two of them got out of their limo with Innes between them. I was watching through binoculars. The sergeant looked pretty rough. He'd apparently had a hard time of it."

"Drugged?"

"As it turns out, yes. At the time it was hard to tell at that distance and in that light, but he didn't look like himself. He looked as if he had aged a couple of hundred years."

"Then what?" McGarvey asked, envisioning the early morning scene.

"We let Suslev go. Our people simply got back into their car, and Suslev started to walk toward his people. Again a radio message was sent, and Sergeant Innes's guards climbed back into their car. Innes just stood there for the longest time. I still remember it. 'Come on, kid,' I said out loud. I thought one of us was going to have to go to him and help him back. But I think one of the Russians said something to him, because he looked back and a moment later started for us."

"What about Yarnell?"

"He got out of the car on the opposite side from me so I didn't really see what he was doing. Not until it was too late. I got out when the sergeant was about halfway, and as soon as he saw me, he stopped.

'Sergeant Innes,' I called to him. 'Barry,' I said. 'Come on. We're waiting for you.' But he just stood there. Close up he looked like a zombie. He was dirty, bruised. I remember thinking that we were probably giving them Suslev in a hell of a lot better condition."

"Then?" McGarvey prompted.

"Innes turned around and started back, Darby stepped around from the side of the car and fired four shots, every one of them hitting the kid in the back, one of them taking off half his head. And that was the end of that. The Russians turned around in the middle of the street and drove off, leaving us to pick up the pieces."

"Did he give you any explanation?"

Owens looked away from the fire. "Darby? None was needed. It was obviously a double cross. The kid had lured us into exchanging him for Suslev, and once he figured Suslev was safe, he tried to make it back to his pals. I didn't agree with how it had been set up, but Darby did the only thing possible under the circumstances. Operation *Hellgate* absolutely depended on it. You have to realize that we gave Innes a lot of important bogus material, along with the good. Material we wanted the Russians to swallow. Innes had to be legitimized. And he was."

What would you have done under the circumstances? Owens wanted to know, but McGarvey had no comment. He was listening to the wind, to the sound of the crackling fire, to the sounds of the house and the surf on the beach; and he was listening to some inner voice that was telling him to proceed with care. There was something else here. Something else was going on.

When they stepped out it was cold on the porch. The clouds had come and rain was beginning to fall

in fits and starts. Lightning flashed in the distance
out to sea. It wouldn't be long, McGarvey figured,
before the full brunt of the storm came ashore. He
had called a cab. It would be along soon. He didn't
want to hold the old man out here very long. He had
gotten most of what he needed in any event. There
were only a couple of things he was still curious
about. Among them, Owens's attitude at the beginning of their conversation.

"I'm a little confused."

"Aren't we all, McGarvey, aren't we all?"

"When we started, you said that Yarnell was too
big for his britches. You asked me what the sonofabitch had done."

"He could have killed your Roger Harris. But
that's a long time ago. *Could* have is a whole hell of a
long ways from *did*."

"You spoke of Yarnell as your friend."

Owens had been looking down at the waves. He
turned to McGarvey. "Let me put it this way, I had a
lot of admiration for the man. It started out at nearly
one hundred percent, but as time went on it became
less and less. Sort of got eaten away, if you know
what I mean."

"Because of how he treated his wife?"

"That and some other things. Little day-to-day
piss ant things that didn't amount to a hill of beans
by themselves but taken together were arrogant. The
company he kept, the presumptions he made going
in and out of everyone's lives and work."

"And then Moscow?"

"Yeah," Owens said, nodding. "Then Moscow.
Hellgate had all the numbers, you know, all the right
moves, all the right results."

"But it was too expensive for your tastes,"
McGarvey put in, taking a guess. He'd hit the mark.
He saw it in Owens's eyes.

"Sergeant Innes was just a young kid who had gotten himself off the track somehow."

McGarvey thought it was very likely that Sergeant Innes had been completely innocent. He had been nothing more than Yarnell's dupe, a stooge whom Yarnell had used to pass along *real* information to his own Soviet control officer, Baranov. And when the operation was over with, he had gunned the kid down.

"He should have been sent home," McGarvey suggested.

"He shouldn't have been killed. It didn't have to get to that point," Owens said. But there was even more that bothered him. "It was the look on his face," he said, turning away, unable for the moment to face McGarvey.

"Innes? I thought you said he was walking away from you when he got shot."

"I'm talking about Darby. The look on *his* face. I was just across the hood of the car from him. The light was right. I could see everything." Owens hesitated even then. He shook his head again. "Darby enjoyed it. He actually enjoyed killing the kid. The sonofabitch was smiling. He looked at me and he was proud. I didn't know him, finally. I just didn't know him any longer."

The telephone rang in the house. Owens looked over his shoulder.

"I won't keep you, Mr. Owens," McGarvey said. "Thank you for your help."

The phone rang again.

"I hope it was a help," Owens said.

"What happened after that? After Yarnell went home and you finally went back to the States?"

"Darby got out of the agency. Became a U.S. Senator."

The telephone rang a third time.

"Did you and he have any contact afterward?"

"None."

"Never?"

"Come to think of it, I did run into him once, several years later . . ." The phone rang a fourth time. "Hang on," he said, and he hurried back into the house.

McGarvey heard him catch it on the fifth ring, and he could hear him talking, though he could not hear what was being said. A couple of seconds later Owens was back.

"Must have been a wrong number," he said, irritated. "I was having lunch at the Rive Gauche on Wisconsin Avenue when Darby walked in with Anne Sutton on his arm. God, what a vision. She was more beautiful in person than on the screen. Stopped the place dead."

"The movie actress?"

"Marilyn Monroe's pal. One of the crowd that hung around the Kennedy fringes, at least that's what I heard. He spotted me and came over to my table, introduced her, and told me that I was looking good."

"Was he?"

"Like a million bucks. He was tan, and this was in the middle of winter, so I figured he and the Sutton woman had been off somewhere. Probably the Caribbean."

"Seen him since?"

"Not in person," Owens said, regretfully. "On the television, in the newspapers. But do you think you can prove he killed this Roger Harris in Cuba? Prove it so that it'll stick?"

McGarvey shrugged.

"Are you going to kill him, McGarvey? Is that why you came to me? For ammunition?"

The cab came down the road and beeped its

horn twice. It was the same one as before. McGarvey could see the old driver waiting impatiently.

He smiled, and offered his hand. Owens took it. "Thank you for your help."

"Just be careful, McGarvey. I'm telling you. Yarnell was a sharp operator. I don't think anything has happened to change anything. On the contrary, he's probably a lot wiser and sharper, and from what I hear out here he still surrounds himself with a mob wherever he goes."

"Thanks for the tip. I'll keep it in mind," McGarvey said. He stepped down off the porch into the wind, bent low, and hurried up to the waiting cab. Before he got in he looked back, but Owens was gone. A moment later sparks came out of the stone chimney.

Because it was the off-season, the nearest comfortable motel was a Best Western at Riverhead, nearly twenty-five miles down the island. The evening flights had been canceled and in the end McGarvey hadn't felt much like renting a car and driving all the way down to LaGuardia just to catch a late plane back to Washington. Morning would be soon enough. He took a shower and changed clothes, then had an early dinner in the motel's adequate dining room. Afterward he went back up to his room where he ordered a bottle of brandy from room service. When it came he poured himself a stiff drink and sat by the window, the room lights out, watching the wind and the rain kicking up whitecaps on an inlet of Great Peconic Bay.

There was very little doubt left in his mind that Yarnell had been a traitor to his country, and probably still was one. Nor was there much doubt that the Russian called Baranov was his control officer. McGarvey's only concern now was the possibility that Yarnell had not worked alone—was still not working alone—that he had had, either then or now, one or more Americans on his payroll. His specialty in Mexico had been turning Mexicans, there was no reason to suspect he hadn't done the same thing with his own countrymen.

He thought back to his own years in the Company, to the things he had done in the name of loyalty, to the projects he'd seen other case officers do, and he remembered that almost any single act in the business could be construed seventeen different ways. It was such an inherently clandestine business that no one could have all the answers all of the time, not even the DCI himself.

Sipping his drink, he found himself thinking about the earliest days he had spent at the Farm outside Williamsburg. Where had the idealism gone, he wondered. It had been bled away by a dozen assignments in which the entire truth would never be known; it had been sapped by thousands of lies told by hundreds of liars; it had been drained by the uncounted double crosses by the legion of men without honor; and in the end, for him, it had been destroyed by assassination. With the first man he had murdered had gone something indefinable within him. It was something, some force, some emotion, he supposed, that became invisible if he tried to examine it too closely, but became a bright, even hurtful beacon when he caught a glimpse of it out of the corner of his eye.

He had been different after that. Changed. Frightened. It had marked the beginning of the end of his marriage, and, he supposed, the long slide down the far side of his career. When assassination becomes a necessary expedient, it was wise to put the very best man into it. But afterward the taint on him would be terrible: oh, the stain makes it impossible to get very near such a man. Use him, then, for as long as he can be stomached and then get rid of him. It's the only way. At times like this, McGarvey was truly surprised that they hadn't simply put a bullet through the back of his head. It would have been so much easier for them in the long run—though the problem would have been technical; reduced to the question of who kills the killer? He'd given a lot for his country, he thought morosely; his livelihood, his self-respect, his marriage, and in the end his honor. All the while he had never questioned if it was worth it. He'd always thought so, of course. But now he wasn't so sure. He could not change, could he? None of us could in the end.

Yarnell would feel nothing, he suspected, turning his thoughts to the other concern. Men such as him never did. They accomplished their given tasks, lived their lives, married their women, had their children, even endured their divorces, all barely ruffling a feather. The Yarnells of the world were the self-assured ones. You could pick them out of a crowd, standing head and shoulders above the competition. (Actually there was little competition for men such as Yarnell, except for the projects they were involved with, and the manner in which they worked their particular magic.) The Einsteins ran the sciences, the Barrymores the stage and screen, and the Yarnells the world of the spy.

At ten he got up from his chair, stiff from sitting so long, his throat raw from too many cigarettes, but his mind clear despite his lack of rest and the brandy he had drunk. He'd been missing something all along. It had bothered him during the afternoon he had spent with Owens, and it had nagged at him tonight. It was something he had meant to ask out there but had not. Owens would know. He had been there at the end, back to the States after Moscow. McGarvey wanted to know why Yarnell had quit the CIA. What excuse had he given? What projects had he left behind? And even more importantly, who had he left behind to fill his spot? In a broader sense, McGarvey wanted to know who Yarnell had worked with and for in Mexico and back in the States besides Owens himself. Who was their boss? Who had been next up the chain of command? Especially at the end. He knew that he could have it looked up for him, but Owens had been there. He wanted to hear it from the man's lips.

Owens had made no attempt to hide his presence on Long Island from anyone. His name was listed in the telephone book. McGarvey got an outside line and dialed the number. It was likely that Owens would be in bed asleep by now and would resent being awakened to answer even more questions. Couldn't it have waited until morning, Owens would ask.

The connection was made, and the telephone in Owens's ramshackle beach house began to ring. McGarvey leaned back against the nightstand as he listened to the burr of the distant instrument. He counted the rings as he stared out the window at the still rising wind and rain, an uneasiness mounting. After ten rings he broke the connection and tried again with the same results. He dialed for the operator and had her try. Still there was no answer.

"I'm sorry, sir, the line does seem to be in order, but there is no answer."

The town's three off-season cabs had quit running for the night. It took McGarvey less than fifteen minutes to get dressed and then convince a startled night clerk to rent out his car for a couple of hours. Driving as fast as he possibly dared on unfamiliar roads, wind and rain blowing in long, spiteful gusts, McGarvey kept telling himself that Owens was hard of hearing, he was asleep in his bed and he had simply not heard the telephone. Or at night he shut off his telephone so that he would not be disturbed by damn fool callers and wrong numbers.

It was this last that bothered him the most on the drive out. Wrong numbers. Who was it who had telephoned as he was leaving? A legitimate wrong number, or someone calling to check that Owens was there? Alone.

At another time he might have missed the turnoff in the darkness and rain, but not this night. Despite the storm he could see the flames rising from Owens's house more than a mile away. Whipped by the wind into long, ragged plumes, sparks shot a hundred feet or more into the sky. Closer he could see flashing red lights of the emergency vehicles along the unpaved track in the sand. There was little left of Owens's house. Nor, McGarvey suspected, driving past without stopping, would there be anything left of Owens.

20

Warren Nicols crossed the Texas border at Big Bend National Park and entered Mexico a few minutes after ten in the evening. He had no problem fording the shallow Rio Grande, which here barely came up to his chest. Pushing the dirt bike on its inflated raft was a snap. On the far side he deflated the bag, buried it in the sand, shouldered his MAC-10 machine pistol and kit bag—containing a Handie-Talkie capable of transmitting and receiving via the CIA's communications satellite, his night-vision spotting binoculars and high-speed camera, and his provisions—and headed away from the river.

There were no roads here. The nearest paved highway was more than twenty miles to the east, across the low Sierra de la Encantada mountains. Overhead the stars shone as brilliant, hard points in the crystal clear desert air. Nicols concentrated on driving without lights. To have a serious spill here on the open desert would almost certainly mean death. He would not be listed as missing for a full seventy-two hours, though his first transmission via satellite to Langley was scheduled in barely six hours.

He had spent the past four days camped in the park with a Boy Scout troop from Joliet, Illinois.

They were background noise. No one would *officially* miss him for the next three days. Nor would anyone from the campsite miss him until breakfast in the morning. By then, however, if everything went as planned, he would be back.

The 75-cc dirt bike with long-range tanks, a specially designed engine shroud and hi-tech muffler to minimize noise, and a highly sophisticated satellite-navigation system by which he could pinpoint his location anywhere on earth within ten meters, was capable of open-road speeds in excess of seventy miles per hour and nearly the same across open country provided the track was reasonably smooth and the driver had the guts and stamina to hang on. Nicols had both.

He followed a general line along the base of the mountains, which according to the analysts and planners would make him hard to spot either from direct surveillance or from the ground scatter radar the Russians probably employed in the region. If he painted at all, he might look like a wind devil, a fast-moving desert hare or perhaps even a low-flying bird.

Nicols was a large man, over six feet tall without boots and two hundred pounds. He had returned three months ago from Afghanistan, where he had distinguished himself in the field not only because of his strength, stamina, and courage, but because of his intelligence and understanding. At forty he wasn't a spring chicken, but what he might lack in youthful zeal he more than made up for in experience and reliability. He was married and had three children who all adored him because he was a kind and gentle man.

He had spent the past two weeks at the Farm outside Williamsburg preparing for this assignment. Nothing the instructors or planners had come up with, they had finally decided, could work effectively for him as a cover story. Americans armed with equipment such as he had simply had no business in the Mexican desert—except to spy. At the last they had allowed him to pick whatever weapon he wanted. The MAC-10 seemed correct. It was light, reliable, and deadly. In addition, he carried a World War II bayonet in a sheath taped to his chest beneath his shirt. It had been his father's. He was an expert with it.

For the first few miles he ran on underinflated tires because of the loose sand and sand dunes which rose and fell like swells on the open ocean. Farther away, however, the desert smoothed out to a hard-pan. He stopped long enough to inflate the dirt bike's tires and then continued, pushing harder, driving at times at an almost reckless forty miles per hour, yet in the next instant having to slow to a bare crawl because of rocks, in a few places ancient lava flows, and in eight places in one mile washouts from desert flash floods.

In one long stretch of at least five miles, the going was comparatively easy and Nicols was able to engage in the luxury of thinking. As had been the case over the past few weeks, his thoughts automatically went to the briefing he had been given by the DCI himself.

"The Soviets have armed Siberia to threaten our northernmost borders. They tried in the south to arm Cuba with offensive weapons and failed, and now we think they are trying again in northern Mexico."

Nicols had been stunned. It wasn't possible. Mexico was our friend. He was born and raised in San Antonio, Texas. In addition to being fluent in Russian and Chinese (from college), he was also fluent in the romance languages (from his boyhood chums)—Spanish, French, and Italian. It was a facility of his, languages.

"But we are not sure, Warren. Not one hundred percent certain," Powers had admitted. They were alone, seated across a coffee table from each other in the DCI's office.

"What can I do, Mr. Director?" he'd asked.

"Someone has to go across the border and see them firsthand. Take some photographs from the ground."

"Of the installation?" Nicols said naïvely.

"Of the installation, yes, that too. Ideally we'd like to have photographs of the missiles themselves. Their serial numbers."

Nicols had smiled. He suddenly saw the entire operation and beyond, like a long, clear highway out to the horizon. "We can invent a satellite-surveillance photograph, but not a serial number, sir."

Powers laughed out loud, but then he suddenly sat forward, an intense look in his eyes. "I don't want you to get yourself shot up or captured, Warren. If someone—I don't care who—should happen to get in your way, it'll be too bad for them. Whatever happens, whatever you do, you will have my personal backing. Is that perfectly clear?"

It had been perfectly clear then, and it was clear now. The situation was not the fault of the Mexicans. They'd been taken in just as so many other poor nations had been. Soviet influence was like quicksand he'd been told over and over again by the Afghan rebel leaders. Get your leg caught in it and you have troubles. Jump in or slip in with both feet—no matter which—and you're dead.

As he drove he began to think about what would happen within the next few hours. He began to hope that he would run into someone. A guard. An engineer. An officer. His fingers tightened on the handle grips.

He slowly picked his way across a dry riverbed

and on the other side maneuvered the bike to the top of a rise, where he stopped a moment to check his position. Far to the south he thought he caught a glimpse of a light, but then he wasn't sure. It had to be over the horizon from him, at least fifteen miles away. The SatNav gave his position in grid coordinates. He opened the panel, flipped a couple of switches, then compared the readings with a plasticized chart he carried in a leg pocket of his black coveralls. The suspected Soviet-built missile installation was directly south of him, about eighteen miles away.

The land flattened out on the other side of the rise, and as far as he could tell no one had come this way for a very long time. There were no tracks anywhere. He had studied the satellite surveillance photographs that had been overlaid onto a topographical map of the region. The missile installation, which was still under construction but apparently nearing completion, was nestled between parallel ridges in the mountains, the rises about three miles apart. The land in between was perfectly flat, forming a natural amphitheater with good protection on three sides, open only to the southwest toward the open desert. The construction was meant to look as if a large oil exploration project was underway. It had not fooled the agency's analysts, nor would it fool anyone who came for a closer look, except perhaps for the farmers in the area. But they would be of no bother. They were very poor. A few pesos would guarantee their complete cooperation.

He covered two-thirds of the distance in less than twenty minutes before he stopped again. This time he shut off the bike's engine, took out his night-vision binoculars, and trained them on the hills rising to the east, beyond which lay the construction site. At first he saw nothing. He looked specifically for lights, any kind of lights, as well as for fences, movements such as patrols might make in jeeps, on horseback, or on foot, or any kind of a track in the sand.

A thin white light flashed in the sky just above a cut in the hills, probably an arroyo. For a second he thought it might have been a spotlight of some kind, but then the light bounced into the sky again, and he realized what he was seeing. The light had moved from right to left. A couple of seconds later he saw a much smaller red light wink on, then off, and then there was a pair of them. Taillights, he thought. A patrol vehicle was working its way along the ridge, which offered views down the one side into the valley where the missile base lay, and down the other across the open desert to where Nicols crouched beside his dirt bike.

They were obviously expecting intruders, or at the very least they were prepared for such a possibility. Let them be Russians, Nicols told himself mounting his bike and starting it. Not Mexicans. Let them be Russians, please God. After Afghanistan he had a few old scores to settle.

He cut straight across the desert now, directly for the northern edge of the arroyo, the last place he had seen the lights of the patrol vehicle. Whatever their schedule might be, he did not think they would be making a pass by any one spot more than once or twice each night. He would be relatively safe up to that point for the next few hours, he figured. From there he would descend into the valley on the other side, make his way onto the base, take his photographs, and then get the hell out. God help the man who got in his way. Especially if he was Russian. Here on this continent! Christ, it made his blood boil.

The desert dipped down toward the base of the first hills, then rose on an alluvial fan that spread out beneath the broad cut above. Leaning into the pitch of the hill, Nicols gunned the little bike, rocks and sand spitting out behind him and clattering down the hill as he spurted up. He was making too much noise, and he knew it. But he wanted to gain the first rise in the series of hills below the main crest. He figured he would find a spot to conceal the bike somewhere there and then make it the rest of the way on foot. If he was lucky the patrol vehicle he had seen earlier would be a long distance off by now. He did not think they would have installed any other kind of short-range surveillance equipment out here; heat sensors, motion detectors, pressure grids buried just beneath the surface. At least he hoped they hadn't.

His luck ran out just at the top of the lower ridge. The headlights of at least half a dozen jeeps suddenly came on, catching him in a blinding glare. He tried to spin the bike around so that he could take off back down the hill the way he had come, but the rear wheel got away from him on the loose sand and gravel and he went down.

Moving purely on instinct, Nicols rolled left, away from the still sliding bike as he grabbed his MAC-10, yanked the bolt back, thumbed off the safety, and came around on his belly into a shooting position.

He fired one short burst at the nearest jeep to his left, and as the headlights suddenly were extinguished and a man cried out, he rolled left again.

A split instant before a withering rain of automatic weapons fire slammed into Nicols's body, he heard someone shouting "Left! He has gone left!" at the top of his lungs. In Russian. They were the last words he ever heard.

It was two in the morning, a time that Donald Suthland Powers had always found the most enchanting, the most mysterious, a time when things always seemed to go bad. If you could somehow get past three A.M., the rest would naturally fall into place. Or at least anything that might happen afterward would be manageable. Like many of his predecessors, Powers had developed the habit of staying at his office during crucial operations when lives were on the line; lives of men and women he had personally sent out into the field. It was a part of the business that he had never become accustomed to. Here in his office on the seventh floor of the headquarters building at Langley, he felt more secure than he did at home, more in control, as if he were a direct part of whatever operation was in progress. As if his mere presence here would lend strength to the battles on distant fields. There was no one at his home in any event. Sissy was away at school, the housekeeper had taken the week off, and how many years had it been since Janet? More than he cared to count. It was at times like these he missed her the most. The nest was empty. This was home.

Danielle, his DDO, felt the same way although for different reasons. He sat across the desk from Powers, and they both looked up as they heard someone running up the corridor outside the open door. Stuart Flagler, Powers's bodyguard, was sitting in the anteroom. He jumped up, his hand automatically reaching for his weapon.

Powers stiffened. He had had a premonition of disaster since this afternoon. Was this it, then? he wondered. "Stuart, see who that is," he called.

"Yes, sir," Flagler answered over his shoulder as he stepped to the outer door.

Danielle got to his feet as Tom Josten, one of his young staffers out of operations, appeared, out of breath.

"Mr. Danielle," he called past Flagler.

"It's all right, Stuart," Powers said.

The big bodyguard stepped aside and the young man rushed in. He brought with him a half a dozen computer-enhanced and printed photographs from their surveillance satellite. They were infrared tracings. "There's trouble with Banyan Tree, sir," Josten said, spreading the photos on Powers's desk. Banyan Tree was the code name of Warren Nicols's operation.

"What have we got here, son?" Powers asked, bending over the stark photographs.

"These were sent down from Big Bird Four at 0517 Zulu—that would have been 1117 central time last night. I have the grid coordinates here. . . ."

"Banyan Base?" Danielle asked.

"Just outside it, sir. About four miles to the west. We overlaid it on the topo. It would have put the action at the first ridge just below the west wall." Josten pointed to the first two prints, which showed a ragged red streak about three inches long. "This would be the exhaust-heat trace from Nicols's bike. He was going up the hill at a pretty good clip." Josten pointed to the next several prints, which showed a U-shaped ring of lights, and a fifth and sixth print showing pinpoints of light that bloomed into long red streaks. "They were waiting for him. Looks like headlights to Scotty downstairs. I'd have to agree. We'll know once spectral analysis is done."

"And these are gun bursts," Danielle said.

"Yes, sir. A lot of them."

Powers had picked up a magnifying glass, he bent low over one of the photos and looked at a series of pinpricks, and several streaks facing inward, toward the headlights. He looked up. "Nicols got off a few shots?"

Josten smiled unhappily. "Yes, sir. It would appear so. But we don't think it did him much good. We counted at least twenty-three separate weapons locations, every one of them trained on and just to the left of where Nicols had fired. He didn't have a chance in hell, sir. Not a chance."

Powers put down his magnifying glass and exchanged glances with Danielle. "Nothing from him? No emergency signal?"

"No, sir."

"I want his frequency monitored for the next seventy-two hours, no matter what this may look like."

"Yes, sir."

"We're not giving up on him. Not yet."

"Yes, sir," Josten said.

Powers sighed deeply. He was tired. He nodded. "Thanks for coming up here, but let's not give in so easily. Let's give him the benefit of the doubt. Can we do that?"

"Of course, sir," Josten said glumly. He nodded, then turned and left the office. They watched him go. In the anteroom, Flagler settled back to his magazine.

Powers came around his desk, crossed his huge office, and from a sideboard behind a bookcase, he poured two stiff shots of brandy.

"A little water in mine, Mr. Director," Danielle said.

Powers poured water in both and brought them back to his desk. They looked at each other as they drank. Powers put down his glass and went back behind his desk.

"I think we should call the president," Danielle said softly.

Powers nodded. He leaned his weight into his fists, which were bunched up on the desktop. "Nicols is scheduled to transmit his first status report in an hour or so."

"Give it up. You can't believe he survived that." Danielle gestured at the infrared satellite photos.

"We've been in this business long enough, Lawrence, to know not to jump at the obvious. This could have been a snoopy rancher straying someplace he didn't belong. A drug runner looking for someplace to stash a future load. It would be a perfect place for a drug operation; close to our border, flat ground for a landing strip, the protection of the mountains, almost no population center anywhere nearby."

"You're clutching at straws, if you permit me to say so."

Powers thrust his hands into his pockets, as if the action would stay him from picking up the telephone. The pieces were beginning to fall into some kind of a pattern, though he still could not recognize it. This had the earmarks of a Baranov operation. That much he did recognize. It had begun last October with the hijacking of the Aeromexico flight out of Miami and the assassination of Jules and Asher on the taxiway at Havana. They had been on their way into place in Mexico, and it was very possible they would have uncovered the incoming Soviet construction equipment and missile-base supplies, which would have alerted us to the situation when there could have been time for a political solution. Baranov had known. He was smart. And he was back in Mexico. Powers could feel the man's presence as a powerful, electromagnetic force that caused his hair to stand on end.

"We're not going to have time to send another man down there," Danielle was saying. "And this time is different from Cuba. Back then we had time for a blockade. This time all six of their installations are nearly operational."

"I should have seen it," Powers mumbled, his mind still on Baranov, the charmer; Baranov, the magic man, the Houdini.

"You're talking about Jules and Asher last year?

We've gone over it before, but I just don't see the connection. It's too farfetched. He'd have to have someone here. Someone either within the agency or certainly here in Washington with top-level sources." Danielle had said it all before. "Trotter found nothing in the hijacking to suggest a larger plan. And he's a damned good man. One of the best. Something would have shown up. We would have gotten at least a glimmer in Mexico City."

That in itself was the most surprising, Powers thought. An operation this big would have had some fallout somewhere. Too many people would have to be involved for no leaks to occur. But where were they? No one had yet invented an airtight operation. But there'd been nothing. Not so much as a hint except for Jules and Asher. And except for the fact that eighteen months ago Baranov had allowed himself to be seen. Just once, in public. And Powers thought of it as "allowed" because Baranov never made mistakes. He was incapable of that kind of error. No, something else was missing. Powers could feel it. The battle was mounting, but he still had no idea what the final weapons might be, or even where the battlefield would be located except that an ugly dark cloud seemed to be rising in the south. Christ, Baranov had never, not ever, been as obvious as he was being now. There was more. But what did he want?

"Donald?" Danielle said gently.

Powers looked up and nodded. "I'll see the president first thing in the morning. I want to get past Nicols's broadcast schedule and then I want to see what the KH-10 picks up at dawn before I rush off half-cocked."

"We know what will show up."

"Yes, we do, Lawrence. And I'm afraid it's going to get a lot worse than even we can imagine."

21

Washington seemed empty and somehow very dangerous now to McGarvey. Dangerous for himself, dangerous for his ex-wife and daughter, dangerous in fact for anyone connected with this business. It was midafternoon by the time he arrived, rented a car at National Airport, and then fetched his few things from the Sheraton-Carlton Hotel in the lee of Yarnell's office building. Driving back across the river he could see the Capitol on the hill in his rearview mirror. The buildings, he thought, were fine and sturdy, but the institution—despite the fact it had survived for more than two hundred years—was in fact nearly as fragile as its weakest link. The thought gave him very little confidence about what might be coming. But, he tried to console himself, we had survived the Kennedy years, the Bay of Pigs, and the Cuban missile crisis; we'd even survived Nixon's downfall.

He checked into the huge Marriott Hotel directly across from the Pentagon, where he took a shower, changed his clothes, and had a quick meal in the dining room. He kept seeing Owens's palsied, thin hands, kept hearing the old man's voice, kept smelling the rising sea wind; and finally he could see clearly in his mind's eye the flames and sparks rising into the night sky.

Plónski and Owens were dead. Who would be next? And why? There was someone else involved here in Washington other than Yarnell. McGarvey could feel it. A sixth sense, a premonition, whatever.

The night was dark. A chill rain was falling. He had taken a taxi down to Arlington and had walked from St. Mary's Academy in Monticello Park, watching over his shoulder, making absolutely certain that he was not being tailed. Since Long Island he had become very jumpy. There was absolutely no pedestrian traffic tonight on these streets which made him somewhat conspicuous. But so, too, would be a follower.

Reaching a curved avenue in Braddock Heights, he stayed well away from the streetlights, keeping as far into the shadows of the tall shrubberies and thick trees as possible. A car came up the street and turned into a driveway halfway up the block, the garage doors opening silently. He hung back until the car was inside and the garage doors closed before he continued. He heard a television playing in one of the houses and voices raised in anger. A window was open, or perhaps a door was ajar; he couldn't see in the darkness.

A carriage light illuminated the driveway to number 224. It was a large, two-story brick house set well back from the street, and most of the ground-floor windows were lit up. McGarvey stopped a moment to make sure he wasn't being observed, then he crossed the lawn and pushed open a gate in the tall wooden fence, following a walkway that led around back. Once inside he felt a lot safer. It wasn't likely he'd be seen back here. The patio was bricked, the rear door was Dutch, with curtained windows in the upper half. He pushed the bell. From inside he could hear a chime. A moment later the patio lights came on.

The door opened and Trotter stood there peering out into the night. McGarvey stepped back a little, directly under the light so that there would be absolutely no mistaking who it was. He thought about double agents, about traitors, about murders, and liars, but Trotter, he thought, was the one person in the world he felt he could trust. Completely. At times the man was a fool, but he was honest.

"Kirk," he said, opening the door wide and moving back. "What in heaven's name are you doing here? Has something gone wrong?"

McGarvey stepped inside, and Trotter closed and locked the door.

Trotter was still wearing his tie. He'd exchanged his suit coat for a shawl-collared sweater, however, and his shoes for slippers. He smelled of brandy. From the front of the house music was playing; it sounded like Mahler to McGarvey, who was feeling jumpy. The kitchen was large and very modern. Trotter and his wife had been famous in the Washington area for their dinner parties here in this house. The spotless kitchen somehow seemed like a mausoleum.

"What's wrong, Kirk?" Trotter asked again. "What are you doing here? Is it still raining out there? You look as if you've walked five miles."

"Are you alone tonight, John?"

Trotter sucked a deep breath all at once as if he'd just had a very sharp pain. He let it out slowly. "I'm alone."

"There's been another killing. And you're next . . . or me, or Leonard Day. It won't stop."

"Goddamn you," Trotter said softly. His lips were red. Beads of perspiration formed on his forehead. McGarvey thought the man's eyes were suddenly larger than normal. It made his old friend seem vulnerable somehow.

McGarvey unbuttoned his sodden overcoat and took it off. He looked for a place to hang it, then laid it on top of one of the tiled counters. Trotter was watching him as if he were from Mars. He didn't want to become contaminated by some outer-space bug.

"Who was it this time?"

"Darrel Owens."

"Yarnell's supervisor from the old days?" Trotter asked. "Retired to upstate New York somewhere. Maybe Long Island. We looked at him, of course. But he was clean as far as we could tell."

"I went to see him. Asked him about Yarnell. Told him I thought Yarnell had killed Roger Harris and was probably working for the Russians."

"Bloody hell."

"He wasn't shocked. Called Yarnell a prick, in fact. And now he's dead."

"Did you see it, Kirk? Were you actually there? Did you see the body?"

"His house burned down." McGarvey once again saw Owens standing at the door, walking up the beach, stopping and turning back, his eyes wide, his slight frame bent as if against a terrible wind. McGarvey wondered what he himself would look like at seventy, if he lived that long.

"You're sure he was in the house? You're absolutely sure he didn't get out?"

"Yarnell is not working alone here."

"The arrogant bastard."

"He has help, John. Here in Washington. He knows too much. He's too many places all at the same time, without moving from his spot."

"What are you saying to me? Just what is it you're trying to tell me?"

"He knows about me. He knew I'd gone up to see Owens."

"He has his army here, Kirk, you know that," Trotter said quietly. "You were warned."

"I wasn't followed."

"Can you be so certain?"

McGarvey nodded.

"How then? Even I didn't know where you had gone off to. Leonard didn't either. We're not following you, Kirk. We're not watching you. You have my word on it."

"I know, John. It's why I came to you like this. But you and Day both know what it is I'm after. Who else knows?"

Trotter drew himself up. "What are you getting at? Exactly, now."

"Who else is in on this besides you, Day, and whoever you have manning your emergency switchboard?"

"He doesn't know anything."

"Who else, then? The bureau's director? Do you report to him?"

"No one in the bureau."

"What about Day? Who is he reporting to?"

"I don't know. But even if he was reporting everything to the attorney general, and I'm not saying he is, Kirk, remember that; but even if he was, no one knew you were going to see Owens. We keep coming back to that."

"If it had gotten back to the Company, someone there could have put it together." McGarvey had figured it out on the flight down. "If anyone inside knew that I was going after Yarnell, and had an idea why, they could be second guessing me all the way, keeping an eye on my likely targets. Owens, as Yarnell's boss from the old days, would have been one of the logical choices."

Trotter saw it, too. It was written in his eyes. "And Plónski," he said, as if he were afraid of the name. "Another logical choice." He turned away. "But that would mean . . ."

"It means someone is working with Yarnell here in Washington. Someone besides Baranov, his Soviet control officer. Someone active within the CIA."

"It would have to be someone high up. At least within operations."

"Someone with an unlimited, unquestioned access to records, as well as operational plans and programs."

Trotter finally turned back. His eyes were round and moist. He took off his glasses and cleaned them with a handkerchief. He looked naked. "I'd have no idea who to trust over there, Kirk. Everyone I know, everyone I work with, is at high levels and therefore suspect." Another thought struck him. "Christ, he might even have the ear of Powers himself."

"Day is the conduit."

"He's not a spy, for God's sake, Kirk. Not Day."

"An unwitting source. This whole thing has him scared shitless. It's only logical he'd be trying to cover his own ass."

"So what can we do?"

"Lock him out. This is between you and me from this moment on, until I get my operation lined up."

Trotter put on his glasses and peered myopically at McGarvey. He was shook. "You're ready to . . . move?" His reticence just then was boyish.

"Not quite. But listen to me; when it comes, it may not be quite what you thought it would be."

Trotter nodded his understanding. "You're going after Yarnell's source within the CIA as well."

"That too."

"What do you mean?"

"There's more here, John. Something else is going on, too. I have a feeling that whatever is happening at the moment with Yarnell and his Company source is part of an operation that we've either stumbled onto or that was set up just for our benefit."

"What makes you say that? Christ, Kirk." This was getting to be too much even for Trotter, but then he'd been thinking about Yarnell's assassination; McGarvey was thinking about something else.

"Yarnell is still active, you know that."

"It's obvious . . ."

"But he hasn't come after me. Just Janos, and then Owens. Nor is my ex-wife's involvement simply happenstance."

"That's been going on for more than a year," Trotter protested.

McGarvey nodded, a sour knot in his stomach. "Makes you wonder, doesn't it, just how deeply they planned this thing. Whose idea was it, John, to hire me?"

"Mine."

"Yours alone? Day had no say in it?"

Trotter was about to reply, but he held himself off. Thinking back to his conversations with Day. He shook his head after a moment. "Leonard suggested an outsider, but someone who knew the business intimately. Someone who wouldn't be afraid to act. Someone we could trust."

"So my name came up."

"I brought it up, Kirk."

"But Day approved your choice."

"Yes," Trotter said glumly. "Wholeheartedly."

"Keep him insulated, John," McGarvey said grabbing his coat.

"Where will you be?"

"Around. I'll let you know when I have everything set up." At the door McGarvey turned back. "One last thing. Have you any idea where Yarnell's control officer, Baranov, is keeping himself these days? Moscow, perhaps?"

"I don't know."

"Could you find out for me without making waves, and without going through Day?"

"I'll try, Kirk. But, Christ, be careful. This entire thing could blow up in our faces. I don't want you jumping at shadows."

"CESTA is no shadow."

An odd expression came across Trotter's features. "CESTA?" he asked.

"Baranov's old network. Used to run it out of Mexico City. It's where he and Yarnell presumably first met."

Trotter nodded.

"Anyway, shadows don't kill people, John."

"No," Trotter said absently. "No, I suppose they don't."

22

A low overcast sky hung over Manhattan, threatening a cold rain at any time; traffic was frantic even for a weekday. This was McGarvey's third trip back to New York since he'd returned from Switzerland, and this time he had even fewer illusions in his sparse kit after talking with Owens and then Trotter. He had taken a cab directly in from La Guardia Airport, crossing beneath the East River through the Midtown Tunnel and taking the FDR Drive down to Houston Street before heading across town. It was much quieter in the Village. Two young men wearing unlaced combat boots, dirty blue jeans, and leather jackets, their hair cut extremely short, walked arm-in-arm along Houston toward Broadway. He had spent a restless night at the Marriott Twin Bridges and then had taken the shuttle up. Before he left he had called Trotter at his office without giving his name. Trotter had not been happy, but he had understood what McGarvey wanted. "Mexico City," he said, and McGarvey hung up, pleased with the fast work. Evidently he'd finally gotten to his old friend; Trotter finally was beginning to understand the real problem. Yarnell had been a Soviet agent in Mexico City in the old days. There was little doubt of it. And he had probably murdered Roger Harris in Cuba. There wasn't much doubt about that either. But Trotter had begun to understand that Yarnell was most likely still active, and that besides his control officer, Baranov, who now apparently had returned to the helm of CESTA in Mexico City, Yarnell had someone else working with him in the States. Most likely in Washington. Merely killing him would do little more than ruffle a few feathers in Moscow; it certainly would not end the network.

Broome Street was quiet. McGarvey paid the cabbie when they got to West Broadway and Grand, and walked back. He'd brought his shoulder bag, which he had checked through on the flight so that he could take his pistol. On the way in the cab he had taken it out of his bag. It felt heavy, but comforting now. A greengrocer's truck was parked in front of St. Christopher's. A thick-chested man chewing a cigar and wearing a long dirty apron was loading boxes of lettuce and tomatoes for the club onto a hand truck. The front door was propped open. McGarvey hesitated a moment across the street. The club looked very quiet. No one was around except for the delivery man. Upstairs in Evita's salon, the curtains were open, but he could see nothing of the inside. He crossed the street and entered the club. The vestibule was open, but no one was around. From within, though, he thought he heard someone talking, a second later a piano started up. It took a moment before he recognized the tune, *Stardust*. Whoever was playing was very good and played with a lot of emotion and sadness. He went through the frosted-glass doors into the cabaret. Two women sat at the bar; they were eating something. A maintenance man was atop a very tall stepladder doing something to one of the big ceiling fans. He climbed down. Evita Perez, dressed in a pair of baggy shorts, an old sweatshirt, no shoes on her feet, was on the tiny·stage playing the piano. Owens had thought she had a lot of talent. Evidently he had meant it literally as well as figuratively.

No one paid any attention to him as he crossed the main floor, dropped his bag on one of the chairs, and perched on the edge of a table just below the stage. He lit a cigarette while she finished playing. She looked pretty good even in the daylight, he decided. Her hair was up, exposing her long, delicate neck. A few lines marked the sides of her cheeks and she had developed just a hint of a double chin, but her arms and legs were still very slim and her feet were surprisingly small and nicely formed. A glass of champagne was sitting on the piano, and the half-empty bottle was next to it.

"Hello, Evita," he called softly to her when she was finished.

She turned to him. Her eyes were very large, but there was no surprise in them. "What are you doing here?" she asked quietly.

"I wanted to finish our talk while you had the time for it," he said. "There were a lot of things I wanted to ask you. A lot of ground to cover. I wasn't sure about some of what you told me."

"There is no time for you here. I can telephone the police, or I can call for Harry. He's a man you wouldn't want to know."

"I need your help."

She nodded. "So do the starving kids in Ethiopia. Nothing I can do for them, or for you."

"Maybe if you'd listen to what I have to say, you'd change your mind."

"I don't think so. Get the hell out of here, would you? Now."

"An old man by the name of Owens was murdered two nights ago. He was Darby's old boss."

Evita was holding onto the edge of the piano bench so tightly her knuckles were turning white.

"I talked to him. He told me about Mexico City and about you. And he told me about Darby's days afterward, in Washington and then in Moscow. He was afraid of your husband. I think Darby was sleeping with his wife."

"Christ," Evita swore in disgust. She jumped up. "Harry!" she shouted. "Harry!"

McGarvey glanced over his shoulder just as a huge black man, his shoulders bursting out of a white T-shirt, stepped around from behind the bar. The two women had turned and were looking over.

"Yo," he called out in a deep baritone voice.

McGarvey tried his last card. He didn't want a fight with Harry, who looked as if he could tear down a large house with his bare hands. "Did you know that Baranov is back in Mexico City?" he asked Evita. "I have that for a fact." He glanced again toward the bar. The big man was clenching his fists. He looked like a small Sherman tank painted chocolate brown.

Evita was suddenly trembling as if she had just stepped out of a very cold bath directly in front of an open window.

"A lot of innocent people have already been hurt," McGarvey said.

She looked down at him, her lips pursed. She shook her head. "There are no innocent people, don't you know that?" She looked up. "Hold my calls, Harry," she shouted. "I'm going to be in conference for the rest of the morning."

"You got it," her bouncer said. He went back behind the bar. The two women went back to their breakfast.

Evita came down from the stage. "Where did you hear this, about Baranov?"

"I have my sources. But it's true."

She studied his eyes for a long time, then turned away as if she were resigning herself to some very bad news. "I knew he was going back down there. I saw him. Here, in New York, you know. Maybe nine or ten months ago."

McGarvey suppressed his excitement. He had inadvertently stumbled onto another aspect of this business; her relationship with the Russian. Yarnell was at the center of this mess, of course, and he apparently had help at high levels in Washington, but Baranov was the key; at least he was as far as concerned Evita Perez. His was more than the name of a Russian spymaster to her. He could see her involvement written all over her face, in her eyes, in the set of her shoulders, in the way she held herself as if she were reliving the pain of a very old, very deep injury.

"We'd better go upstairs," she said at length.

McGarvey picked up his overnight bag, followed her across the cabaret floor, and went up the stairs to her apartment-salon. At the top she closed and locked the door.

"Fix yourself a drink," she said. "I'll take champagne." She turned and disappeared into the back.

McGarvey dropped his bag at the end of one of the couches, took off his overcoat, laying it aside, and went to the bar. He mixed himself a bourbon and water, and found a split of Mumms for her, which he uncorked and poured. When she came back she had changed into a thin yellow cotton dress, let her hair down, and put on a little makeup. The change was startling. She looked almost beautiful and certainly very seductive. He could clearly see the shape of her nipples through the material of the dress. She sat down on the couch in front of the fireplace, tucked her legs up beneath her, and accepted the glass of champagne. There was some expectation in her eyes, but he could see that she had girded herself for a difficult time ahead. Difficult but necessary.

"You're out to get Hizzoner, Darby," Evita said.

"I think your husband was and is a spy," McGarvey said.

"Ex-husband, let's keep that part straight right from the beginning, shall we?"

"His Soviet control officer has been and still is Valentin Baranov."

Evita laughed disparagingly. "You think you know so fucking much. You don't know a thing. Nothing."

"I've come to you for help," McGarvey said, quite calmly. "I'd hate like hell, you know, to see you deported back to Mexico. Baranov is there. He'd take over."

"Who are you trying to kid?"

McGarvey measured his next words. He watched her carefully, especially her eyes and her hands as they gripped the champagne glass. He was looking for her vulnerable spot.

"You'd probably never see your daughter again if you were sent away," he said. "I saw her in Washington a few days ago. She's living with her father. Quite a beautiful young woman. A lot like you."

"You sonofabitch," Evita swore. "You bastard."

She wanted to speak Spanish. McGarvey could hear it in the way she chopped her words. English was far too slow for her, yet she must have figured Spanish would be lost on him.

"I came here trying to avoid all of this," McGarvey said sitting forward. "Believe me. I think Darby has used every person he's ever come in contact with. Including you. Including your daughter."

It was a heavy thought for her. The weight of it seemed to press down upon her, causing her shoulders to sag, her back to bend a little; even the weight of the champagne glass became too much for her and she rested it on her lap.

"Is she a pretty girl, do you think? I haven't seen her in so long. She doesn't know me any longer. Whatever Darby tells her is true. She has stars in her eyes." Evita shook her head, looking inward. "Who wouldn't? I don't know anyone who could resist him. His charm. He's so damned self-assured, no matter what he says you have to believe him. You know?"

"Is he still working for the Russians?" McGarvey asked gently. "For Baranov?"

Evita looked up. "Have you met my . . . have you met Darby? Have you come face-to-face with him? Have you spent a few minutes listening to him?"

"No."

"I thought not. You don't talk as if you were one of his initiates." She drank her champagne nervously. "I don't know what you're doing here."

"When is the last time you saw him?"

"A long time ago. Not long enough . . ."

"You mentioned that Baranov had come here. You saw him? You met with him?"

"How can you think you know Darby without meeting him?" Evita asked. "I want to know that. I don't think you know a goddamned thing about him, see. I think you're guessing."

"I'm guessing, you're right about that much. But I think he killed a very good friend of mine. Or at least I think he *had* my friend killed. I don't suspect there is a lot more that I want to know about him, except for his relationship with Baranov."

"You really think Darby is a spy?"

"Yes."

"You think he is a murderer? You think he was working for Valentin?"

"Yes. I think he's still working for him."

She laughed again. "Listen to me. Darby doesn't have, nor has he ever had, enough dedication to anything or anyone other than himself to become a spy," she explained. "You say he worked for Valentin? It's true, you know, in the old days. But it was also true that he turned in absolutely top-rate intelligence to his own people. To your people, you know. The agency. The Company. Our Father who art in Langley . . ."

"But he worked for Baranov."

"He was in love with Valentin. We all were."

"Still?"

"What do you want?"

"You told me downstairs that Baranov had come here nine or ten months ago. What did he want?"

"Old times . . ."

"What'd he want?" McGarvey insisted. "You were in love with him, too. Did he come here to . . ."

"Yes!" she asked defiantly, her head up.

"Did you and he make love? For old times' sake?"

"What kind of a fucked up question is that?" Evita jumped up, flinging her champagne glass toward the fireplace. "What did you come here for? What do you want? I don't care what you think, you know. Darby gave himself and then he gave me. But that's all there is to it. There's where you don't understand anything. He never gave a damn about anything or anyone. Not about me, not really about Baranov, not about his bosses in Langley. None of it. It was nothing more than a big game to him. He was playing chess, only it was with real people. But he didn't care."

McGarvey understood what frightened her now, and the sudden understanding did nothing for his dour mood, nor for his satisfaction.

"Get out of here," she said, turning away from him. She went to the window, where the bar was set up on a sideboard. She looked outside, but he didn't think she was really seeing anything. She was looking inward again. "Just . . . just go away," she said.

"Baranov came here ten months ago looking for something, Ms. Perez," McGarvey said softly. "Now you think it's a real possibility that Darby is going to give him your daughter."

Evita said something very fast in Spanish, but the only word McGarvey caught was *amor,* which means love, and she hung her head and began to weep, her back bent, her head bowed, big racking sobs shaking her narrow shoulders. There was nothing he could do for her; he supposed she was crying not only for her daughter but for her own lost youth, and for the golden days, as Owens had described them, when she and Darby Yarnell were the hottest item in Mexico City. But that was ten thousand years ago, and now she probably thought of herself as an old lady. Her daughter was apparently next on the sacrificial altar Darby had built with the blood and tears of those nearest to him. McGarvey could not leave now, though. He'd come this far, and so had Evita. They would have to share the entire story, for better or for worse.

Evita had come back to the couch. She sat erect, her knees primly together as if she were a schoolgirl prepared to recite her lessons. The room was quiet and McGarvey could hear the vagrant noises of the building: an elevator rising, someone laughing in the distance, a door slamming. Ordinary sounds that punctuated an extraordinary situation. As she talked, she watched the flames in the fireplace.

"I was just twenty, and he was the finest man I had ever seen or even imagined could exist," she said. "My parents loved him, my friends were jealous of me—they secretly adored him—and we had dinner at the President's Palace at least once a month. It was a dream."

"You were much younger than he."

She smiled in remembrance. "In Mexico in those days that did not matter." The x in Mexico was silent. As she continued she began to revert more and more into Spanish pronunciations.

It was a traditional courtship, she said. Darby had never tried to rush it, although she got the feeling at the time that she was racing headlong down a slick but wonderful toy slide. They were the feted guests wherever they appeared; he knew more people in Mexico than did her parents: Her mother was the third daughter of the governor of the State of Hidalgo, northwest of Mexico City, and her father was the assistant secretary of finance for the federal government. After their honeymoon, though, they seldom spent a quiet evening at home together. Either they went out or there was a crowd at their palatial home outside the city. Sometimes they went to the mountains, sometimes to the seaside, but wherever they went after that there was always a crowd around them. Darby, she said, called them his mob.

"One month later Baranov came into our lives," Evita said. "But I think he and Darby were already old friends by that time."

If her husband was a charming man, she said, Valentin Illen Baranov was a simply bewitching human being. He was short and powerfully built, with a thick, square head and dark, bushy eyebrows. But after five minutes of conversation with the man you would forget his physical person and seem to see through to his soul. He was a power, a force, an adrenaline in even the most casual of encounters.

"When was that, exactly?" McGarvey asked. "Late '59? Maybe 1960."

"I don't know, but it was in the winter, I think. Around Christmas. I came into Darby's study and they were having drinks together. Filthy vodka. 'A peasant's drink,' Valentin called it." She raised her eyes, a small smile on her moist lips. "He always said he was a peasant, and when it was time for him to retire, if he lived that long, he would go back to the land. Somewhere in the Urals. He made it sound lovely."

Darby was a little put out that she had barged in, she said. But Baranov was a charmer; jumping up, bowing, kissing her hand. "Oh, yes, Darby, you do have a lovely wife indeed," he'd said. The words were sticky sweet, but Evita said she always got the impression he meant everything he said. Every single word. He insisted that she stay. It was nothing more than the conversation of two old friends getting to know each other a little better. He wouldn't let Evita drink vodka, though, or any other hard liquor for that matter. Champagne was her drink. Sweet for in the morning, a little dryer for afternoon, and the Sahara Desert of champagnes—as only the French truly know how to make them—for the evenings.

They all went out that evening. Baranov insisted on showing them off. He'd heard a lot of good things about Evita, of course, and now that he had seen for his own eyes that what he'd heard was not an exaggeration, he wanted a little of her glitter to rub off on him.

"We always had a lot of friends in those days," Evita said. "Mostly Mexican government officials at first. But shortly after Valentin's first visit, we started chumming around with other couples from our own embassy."

"Other CIA?"

"I guess so," she said. "Though at the time I didn't know it. I didn't even know that Darby worked for the Company. That didn't come until later."

"How did you find out?"

"Valentin told me."

"What did he tell you?"

"That Darby worked for the CIA, and that he also worked for . . . KGB."

"And that they worked together?"

She nodded. "That too."

"Did he mention anyone else? Another American working with them both?"

"Not that I can remember. But he was proud of himself. Proud of the relationship. He wasn't any older than Darby, or at least not much, but he was more like a father to him than a friend. A father confessor, his priest."

"And for you, Evita?" McGarvey asked gently.

She looked at him, her eyes wide, but she said nothing.

"What was Baranov to you? What did he become to you?"

"My husband's friend."

"That's it?"

"What do you want?" she flared, but it wasn't very convincing. Her emotions were by now rubbed beyond the point of simply raw. She was overloaded. The majority of the hurt might have happened more than twenty years ago, but the pain was still very fresh and very real to her.

"What was your husband's reaction to this?" McGarvey asked.

"To what?"

"To your knowledge that he was working for the KGB as well as the CIA?"

"He said it wasn't true. . . ."

"But he admitted that Baranov was KGB?"

"Of course. But he told me that not everything was as it seemed. There was more in this world than simple black and white. He kept talking about geopolitics and balances of power. We were on a teeterboard; Western democracy on the one side, and Russian Communism on the other, with nuclear weapons in the middle."

McGarvey had heard the argument before. The Soviet Union and her satellite states were balanced by the Western European nations. It was important that the United States and Canada be balanced by Cuba and others in the Western Hemisphere. Only in this way could nuclear war be safely avoided. It was why the Russians had called the Cuban missiles "peace missiles."

"Did you believe him?"

"What did I know? I told you I was a little girl with stars in my eyes. But already Darby was beginning to change, you know. He was busy. He was gone a lot those days. If I was at our town house, he might spend a weekend in the mountains, leaving me behind. Business, he said. Or if I was at the mountains, he might go to the seashore for a week, sometimes even longer."

Baranov began coming around, then. He took her out to dinner once, and afterward to the Ateneo Español, but the place frightened her. They were real revolutionaries, radicals who talked endlessly about shooting and burning and tearing down the establishments. They all had a great deal of respect for

Valentin in that place, but he promised never to take her back. He was sensitive to her needs. McGarvey suspected he had been digging a deeper hole into which Evita would eventually be dropped once she realized what was and had been happening around her.

Everything else seemed to change then for Evita. She'd become an American, her parents told her. And her father died within ten months of the wedding. Darby was sent out of town at that exact moment; exactly when she needed him more than she'd ever needed anyone in her life. Her final lesson came the very evening of the funeral.

Valentin was there at the house, Evita said. It was late, her sisters had stayed with their mother, and she had gotten the feeling that they didn't really want her there with them, that her place was at home waiting for her husband as any good wife should. Her father was dead, her husband was gone, and the rest of the family was beginning to ostracize her.

He was waiting in the conservatory, Evita's favorite room in the house. He had dismissed the staff for the evening. He knew that she would be coming back, and he even knew in which room she would bury herself when she did return, so he had set it up for her return with champagne and flowers. She asked him what he was doing there like that, at that hour, but she was secretly glad he had come, whatever the reason. The champagne was Mumms, the very driest, he said. He poured her a glass and watched her drink, even held her hand for a time while she cried. He talked then about dying; about the old moving aside to make room for the young and how it was the responsibility of the young therefore to make a difference in the world, to make life just a little nicer, a little safer, so that when it was time to hand things over to the next generation we could be proud to do so. As her father must have been proud to do for her, in the end.

"I don't know what I would have done that night without him there," Evita told McGarvey, her eyes glistening.

McGarvey lit a cigarette and handed it to her. She accepted it gratefully. The gesture made him think of Owens. The two of them—Evita and Owens—had a lot in common; both of them had been badly abused by Darby Yarnell, and in the end by Baranov.

It wouldn't be easy, Valentin had told her, keeping up appearances, keeping a stiff upper lip, keeping up with their work. She was one of them now, and even if her father could not have known what great services she would perform, Valentin did, and he was very proud of her. Then he had a glass of wine with her, and somehow, ridiculously, she was in his strong, wonderfully gentle arms. He smelled clean of soap and of cologne, and of wool and leather. (Which was odd, McGarvey thought, for a Russian. But then Baranov, by all accounts, was not an ordinary Russian.)

"He told me that I should just let go. That if I needed strength he had plenty for me, and for Darby, too. I thought he had enough strength then for the entire world. 'Trust in me, Evita,' he said to me. 'I will always be there for you. No matter where. No matter why.' Goddamnit, I believed him, you know." Tears welled up in her eyes. "I believed in him all the way."

And still did, at least in some measure, McGarvey thought.

Baranov took her to the big bedroom that looked toward the glittering city in the distance where he gently undressed her, telling her all the while that he was proud of her, that Darby would understand, that all of us needed to gain strength

from someone else from time to time, there was no
dishonor in it for either of them. He, too, needed
strength. And he was so different from Darby, the
only other man who had ever touched her. She had
such a terribly infinite need that there was a fire in
her head that would have been impossible to quench
in any other way, even with Darby himself, had he
been there. They made love, or rather, she said,
Valentin made love to her. She was like a puppet
beneath him; he pulled every string, and he knew
exactly which strings to pull, and his touch was
perfection.

She stopped in midsentence and looked up
again, realizing perhaps for the first time who she
was talking to and just what she'd been saying.

"Goddamnit to hell," she said without anger.

"He is a very bad man, Evita," McGarvey
suggested. "What happened was not your fault."

"But I loved it, don't you see? I even loved the
danger. But it wasn't enough in the end. I wasn't
nearly enough for them. But then they had each
other."

23

Evita got up and put on some music. It was Spanish classical guitar, very good, very sad, very distant. They sat across from each other, smoking cigarettes, drinking, listening to the music, allowing the music to soothe, in a measure, the embarrassment she'd felt by her admission of faithlessness not only to her husband, but to the new system she'd embraced with her marriage: the U.S.A.

"It wasn't all so black and white," Evita explained. "You don't live your life, ordinarily, thinking how history will judge you. It happens hour by hour, sometimes second by second. Am I going to be prosecuted for it after all these years? Are you a real cop after all? Are you going to try to arrest me?"

"I don't think so."

"But you are after Darby."

"Yes," McGarvey said.

"And Valentin?"

"Him too."

"You might have said him especially. He is the devil. But I don't think it will happen. He's too smart, and he has too many friends. He told me an old Russian saying once: 'Before a fight two men are boasting; afterward only one.' It will be him in the end who will do the boasting. You'll see."

"Not if you help me," McGarvey said earnestly, sitting forward.

She laughed. "What, a disenfranchised cop and me, a drug addict?"

McGarvey listened to her in utter amazement. She did not know his real name, she did not know who he worked for or what he was after, she did not know a thing about his background, he was just a face professing to know something about her past, and yet she'd called him a "disenfranchised cop."

Had she been waiting for him, or someone like him, to show up all this time? Had Baranov predicted he, or someone like him, would come sniffing around her as if she were a bitch in heat. Did Yarnell attract that type? Or had the remark simply been coincidental? Was he jumping at straws? Christ, how did one know in this business; everyone lied about practically everything, to practically everyone. A great depression seemed to settle on him. He thought about all the women in his life. His mother, his sister, his ex-wife, his Swiss girlfriend, and now Evita Perez. There wasn't one of them in the bunch who'd liked him for what he was, or who had told him the complete truth about anything.

McGarvey sat back, his feet propped up on a white lacquered coffee table, willing himself to remain calm.

"That shocks you, I see," Evita said, moistening her lips. She stood up and got a small silver box from the mantel. She brought it back and opened it, taking out a tiny mirror, a razor blade, a tiny golden straw, and a small vial. She smiled. "There are worse habits," she said. She opened the vial, carefully tamped out a tiny bit of cocaine on the surface of the mirror, then closed the vial and replaced it in the silver box. Her movements were very slow, very deliberate, very precise; she was a chemist working with a precious substance in an important experiment. She was overcoming her guilt and paranoia with a certain belligerence. She cut three lines of coke and quickly bent down sniffing a line up her right nostril with a practiced hand. She waited a moment, then sniffed the second line up her left nostril and immediately the third up her right again. She sat back with a long, languorous sigh. Her eyes were shining.

She put the paraphernalia back in the box, and then took her time about replacing the box on the mantel. She'd done something fine. She was becoming cocky. She even swaggered a little. "What else do you want to know, Glynn, or whoever you really are?"

"Darby came home eventually. He must have known that something had happened," McGarvey said. "What did he say to you?"

"What happened after that, you want to know." She came back and sat down on the couch, pulling her dress above her knees so that she could sit cross-legged. "Valentin was a much better lover than Darby. And Darby was damned good, you know. It was grand for a while. When Darby was in town Valentin got scarce. But when Darby was gone, Valentin was there. Sometimes Darby would hardly be out of the driveway and Valentin would be coming up in his big, flashy Buick with all the chrome. Never saw it dirty. Must have had a boy or someone polish it every day. Wouldn't let me smoke in that car. He was proud of his cigarette lighter. It had never been used. You could see it was new. He'd pull it out and show it off."

"What did you do for him?" McGarvey asked. With her legs spread he could see everything. She wore no panties. He averted his eyes. She laughed.

"For Valentin? Nothing much. Attended a few meetings. Waited once in his car for him outside the Ateneo Español. He said he wanted to talk to someone. But mostly we went dancing, and sometimes we went to parties."

"Just you and Valentin?"

"Sometimes Darby and I would go to a party. But if I was with Valentin it meant Darby was gone. He was seeing other women, of course, Darby was. He's always had his women on the side, so I didn't feel so goddamned bad."

"Who was at these parties that you went to with Baranov, then? Americans? Mexicans? Russians?"

"Yes. And Bulgarians and Spaniards and a few Cubans from time to time. I met Uncle Fidel when he was just a piss ant lawyer. He was nothing big in those days."

"Americans?" he asked again.

"Some."

"CIA?"

Evita shrugged. "I never asked. They were good times. Everyone was having a lot of fun. Sometimes we'd fly over to Acapulco . . . that was before it became really big. Sometimes we'd fly over to Cancun on the Gulf Coast. One night we had a picnic, a bunch of us, in front of a Mayan pyramid. We went up to the top, just Valentin and me, and we made love there. I was an offering to the gods. That's what he told me."

"Did you love him?" McGarvey asked gently.

She smiled dreamily and leaned her head back, her eyes toward the ceiling, her lips parted, her hands on her lap as if she were in some yoga position. "Maybe if you explained what that word means . . ." She drifted. "I used to know, but then it seemed to change. Every time I thought I had it, it would change again. Damndest thing, you know. There weren't any answers anywhere . . . not even in the Mayan temple. Even the old ones didn't know. So who was I, a lesser mortal, to figure it out? Darby wanted me sometimes. I understood that. Valentin wanted me at other times. I understood that, too. But it didn't last very long."

She'd been a little girl looking for love and security, McGarvey thought. What she'd gotten instead were lies and manipulation. Owens had seen the confusion and unhappiness in the girl, and it had made him angry at his student, at his superstar. Life was filled with disappointments, though. He didn't know anyone who was guiltless, or anyone who had never suffered.

After the revolution came to Cuba and Castro installed himself in office, Mexico City cooled down for a time. Baranov stopped bringing her past the Ateneo Español to wait for him while he talked with friends. Even the nightlife seemed subdued compared to what it had once been. People had become more serious, Evita said. She had been flying high, and she began to come down. A week, or sometimes two, might pass during which she would see neither her husband nor Baranov. She had no idea where either of them were getting themselves off to in those days (later she learned that Baranov was bouncing back and forth between Mexico and Moscow, while Darby was commuting on a weekly basis between Mexico and Washington, D.C.). She did know that they were very busy. When they were together, she said, they seemed preoccupied, distant, as if only a part of them had returned to her. Big things were in the wind, she knew at least that much. And a year later, when the Bay of Pigs story broke in all the newspapers, she'd known what her husband and Baranov had been up to all that time, but by then, of course, she had been installed in their Washington house, and she became pregnant with Juanita. After that she rarely saw her husband, and only once in that first year, shortly after her daughter was born, did she see Baranov.

"I was a widow, but I was too dumb to realize it at the time," she told McGarvey, sitting up. Already she was starting to come down from her coke high. Her tolerance was up. McGarvey figured she probably had a pretty heavy habit for it to work off so fast. She'd probably be on crack before too long. The cycle was common from what he'd read about it.

What about the three houses in Mexico? The town house that Owens had called a palace, the mountain house, the beach house? She had never gotten herself involved with the finances of their marriage. Darby was a more than adequate provider. She never wanted for anything. The bills were always paid, their house staff in Mexico City and again in Washington, operated a household account which took care of their physical needs, and five thousand dollars was automatically deposited into her own checking account each month. If she'd wanted more, even twice that amount, she knew that Darby would have given it to her, no questions asked. Not once in the years they were together had she ever balanced her checkbook, or even noted a check in the register. There simply was no need for it. Such work, when she first came to New York, was so alien to her, so outside the realm of her ordinary knowledge, that she immediately hired an accountant who did it all for her, and who was still doing things with numbers to keep her afloat. She was even quite prosperous in her own right, she'd been told a couple of years ago. But money meant nothing to her. It never had meant anything to her. She had wanted a relationship, plain and simple. It's all she'd ever wanted, really.

"There were a lot of years there when I was alone, raising Juanita. And I didn't mind being alone. Not really. Mexico City had been fun, but now I was a mother. That to me was a million times more important than all the little intrigues and schemes we'd played. I don't think I even read a newspaper or looked at a news show for five years. I had my own little world raising my daughter, and I was content in it."

"No friends?" McGarvey asked.

"I didn't need any. Darby would breeze in every now and then. We'd get dressed up and make the rounds of the Washington parties. But it never lasted very long. A weekend, sometimes a little longer. Never more than a week. Which was fine with me. I'm telling you, I was done with that life. Completely done with it." Her eyes glistened.

"But you still loved him. Your husband."

"I wanted to, believe me, I wanted nothing more than to be in love with my husband and him with me."

"And Valentin Baranov?"

"Sure," she said noncommittally, glancing toward the silver box on the mantel. "Him too."

McGarvey got up and poured Evita a fresh glass of champagne and himself another bourbon and water. It was still morning down on the street. He felt as if he'd actually lived through those twenty years with her since he'd come up here. But then it was an occupational hazard. He'd been a specialist at attaching himself to other people's lives; listening to them, watching them, reading their mail and their personal notes, their diaries, even their shopping lists. Seeing where they had been, what they were up to now and in which directions they were likely to go in the future. He knew their schedules and routines, their habits and pet complaints. He got to know some people so well that like any competent biographer, he could lay out his subject's life better than the subject could. Along with this occupational hazard or vice or whatever came another gift; he could tell when people were lying to him by commission, but especially if they lied by omission. Evita had left a gap a mile and a half wide back there sometime between the preparations for the Bay of Pigs invasion and her move to Washington, D.C. Something had happened in Mexico City, something terrible, something that irrevocably changed her life, transformed her overnight from a still-naïve little girl to a hardened woman for whom isolation in a large city in a foreign land without her husband or any other emotional support was no particular strain. In fact, like a fallen princess who seeks the convent for solace, she had gotten along quite well in her solitude. She was content, she'd said, to remain alone in Washington raising her daughter without friends, without worries, without concerns. But it didn't last.

"I sent Juanita away to boarding school when she was thirteen," Evita explained.

"Why?"

"I went through a bad period there. She was growing up without a father. There was a lot I didn't know. A lot I couldn't give her. I knew that much."

"Did you get to see her very much in those days?"

"Oh, sure," she said, pushing her hair back away from her eyes. A car horn honked outside, startling her. She glanced toward the window then looked away guiltily. "But not enough. She was starting to ask questions that I couldn't answer. . . ."

They drank their drinks. The band had started to practice downstairs. They could hear the hard thumps of the drums and the harsh notes of the trumpet.

McGarvey had come this far and had only got half the story. He wasn't going to leave without the rest of it. But there was something from her past, something from Mexico City that had shamed her, that had frightened her and had made her grown up all at once. He suspected she'd been trying to bury it all these years.

"Something happened to you in Mexico City, Evita," he said. "Before you moved up to Washington. Before you got pregnant with Juanita. I think it's important."

"I don't know what you're talking about," she flared.

She was crashing from her coke high, and already she'd gone too far with him, answered too many of his questions, revealed too much of her past to him for her to stop now. Her resistance had very nearly totally collapsed.

It was a strange year during which she had tried to ingratiate herself with her family, she said. She spent a lot of time with her mother and with her sister. But it wasn't the same any longer, and she'd known at the time that she had crossed some invisible bridge, not only because she had married an American, but because of her infidelity. Her mother had looked into her eyes and had seen as clearly as if it was written there. It was a thing she was incapable of hiding from someone who had known her so well. Her sister knew or suspected, too, that something was amiss. She became terribly busy that year, too busy with her own family for Evita, which added still another burden in a load that was rapidly becoming impossible to hold up let alone carry. "Get on your knees and ask forgiveness from God," her mother told her. But by then she figured it was already too late for her. She was a spy and an adultress. How could there be any forgiveness for her? For a time she traveled, moving from their city house to their mountain chalet, where she would stay for a month or a week or sometimes for just a day. Then she would pack a few things in her sports car and drive recklessly fast down to their house on the sea, where she would isolate herself even from the house staff, sometimes remaining in her room for days on end, eating only a small meal every second or third day so that she lost a lot of weight. She began to be sick all the time. Her movements became erratic. She traveled all over Mexico. Sometimes staying at their homes, sometimes in luxury hotels, sometimes in terrible, dirty, bug-infested village inns from which she would come away even sicker than before. She was trying to find herself. Trying to make some sense out of her life. And not doing a very good job of it.

McGarvey didn't know how he could help her. He wanted to reach out and take her into his arms and hold her close and tell her that those times were long past, that memories alone could not hurt her, not really. But he suspected she was beyond even that sort of comfort.

Evita was staring past him into the fireplace, her eyes filling, tears running slowly down her cheeks as she relived the personal hell she'd been subjected to. She could have been alone in the room for all that she was aware of his presence.

"Evita?" he said gently.

She blinked and nodded.

"I was no longer a mexicana, don't you see?" she said. "I had lost my country, but I hadn't found a new home. Not yet. I was alone. Drifting. Darby and Valentin had both left me, though I hadn't realized it yet." She closed her eyes.

"What happened to you down there?"

"I got my education, didn't you hear?" she whispered. "I saw my family and my country as a gringo would see them, as a foreigner would see them, and what I found wasn't very pretty. Especially the part where everyone was looking back at me. I had become a stranger in my own land, and my own people looked at me like I was a foreigner. I'd been to the north and to the south. I'd been west to the

Pacific and to the ancient East. But there was nothing left for me. Nothing at all." She held out her glass. "I'd like more champagne."

"Don't you have a show tonight?" McGarvey asked.

"More."

McGarvey poured her another glass of wine and brought it back to her. He lit her a cigarette. He was getting a little worried about her. Between the wine and the cocaine she was very strung out.

"What happened, Evita?" he asked. "What did they do to you down there?"

"I walked in on Valentin and Darby," she said. "They were together in my bed making love to each other."

McGarvey had expected almost anything except that, but although he was startled he did not allow it to show on his face. Baranov was a powerful man. He'd heard it a dozen different ways now, and still he had not begun to suspect just how powerful and dedicated a man the Russian was until now. Baranov had got Yarnell to spy for him and had then cemented the relationship by seducing first his wife and then Yarnell himself. He had ruined them both as a couple and both, ultimately, as individuals. Yarnell the superstar had met his match, and Evita the naïve little Mexican princess had succumbed simply as a matter of course. Her turning had to have been ridiculously easy. Hardly a challenge for the likes of Yarnell or Baranov. Yet they had taken the time and effort to do it. Why? Yarnell because he wanted an image during his tenure in Mexico. But why Baranov? What more could he have hoped to have gained by seducing first the wife and then the husband . . . unless Yarnell had made a desperate attempt to control the situation instead of himself being controlled? If that had been his battle, he had lost. Yet later, in Washington and then in Moscow, Yarnell had comported himself as the perfect spy. He hardly faltered. By then Baranov's control had probably been so utterly complete that Yarnell was no longer even thinking for himself. And poor little Evita had been left behind in the dust. So why pick on her again? She'd said Baranov had been here less than a year ago.

"He wanted Darby and me to get back together," she said. "Because we both needed each other, we both were drifting and there was more to life than that. He came here in the middle of the night and let himself in. The first I knew he was here was when I woke up with him in bed beside me. And we made love. He still knows me. Knows my body, which buttons to push, which chains to rattle. And I enjoyed it, do you understand? It was wonderful. Had he asked me, I would have run off with him anywhere. Even to Moscow."

"But he didn't ask."

"No."

"What then, Evita? Why did he come here? What did he want?"

She looked away.

"What did he say to you?"

"He told me about you."

"By name?"

"No. He said that someone who had once been in the Company would be coming around asking questions about him and about Darby. He was specific in that you no longer worked for the Company. You don't, do you?"

"No," McGarvey said.

"He told me that I should tell you everything. That I should be completely honest with you."

"Except about his visit."

She closed her eyes. "He never knew that I saw him and Darby together. He knows everything except for that. It's been my own secret."

She was getting back at Baranov. Now, after all these years, she had finally struck a blow at the man who in her estimation had ruined her marriage. It was the real reason she had talked to McGarvey. Or at least one of the reasons. There was another. Fear.

"Now he wants Juanita, doesn't he?"

Evita opened her eyes. "You bastard!" she said with a lot of feeling. "You sonofabitch! You're all alike."

"Darby will give her up to save his own position and you know it."

"She's all that's left, don't you see? Darby went up to school and charmed her. She fell under his spell, and she never comes here anymore, never calls, never writes."

"Then we'll have to stop them both. You'll help me."

"It's impossible. They're old pros, both of them. What chance would I have? What chance did I ever have?"

"None, unless you try."

"Try," she said disdainfully. Her lower lip was quivering again. "You don't know what you're talking about. You don't know them. Darby alone could have held the Alamo. With Valentin's help they're impossible to beat. They know everything. They've each got their armies. Impossible."

McGarvey could hear again Darrel Owens's words about his young protégé, bitter words that had still, after all that had gone on, after all the years, been tinged with open admiration. It was the same now with Evita. After everything that had been done to her, she'd still made love quite willingly with Baranov, and she still had a great deal of awe, fear, and respect for her ex-husband. Darby Yarnell was simply the very best there ever was, Owens had said. No one could resist his charm. What a powerful weapon he'd been and continued to be in Baranov's arsenal. And now Yarnell had the ear of the director of Central Intelligence and the president of the United States. It was frightening. Such men did not fall easily.

"There can't be a trial, Kirk," Trotter had said in Switzerland. "It would be ten thousand times worse than Watergate. It would tear the country apart. The CIA would go down the tubes, and even the president would suffer. We'd be years recuperating. Perhaps we'd never fully recover."

"We're talking about murder, here, John, aren't we?" McGarvey had said. "About the assassination of a former U.S. senator. One of the most influential men in Washington." It had only been a notion then, now it was becoming a dreadful reality.

The band was still practicing downstairs, and Evita got unsteadily to her feet and went to the sideboard as she sang a few off-key words to the song. She poured herself another glass of champagne and then stood looking out the window at the street below.

"I think it is enough now," she said without turning. "I'd like you to go. There's nothing to be done. Nothing I can help you with."

But there was one last thing McGarvey had to know. Baranov was Yarnell's Soviet control officer, but Yarnell had someone here in Washington. He'd had someone in Washington all along. Someone within the CIA. At the upper echelons. Someone like Lawrence Danielle, who would have access to Operations, and who would also have a direct pipeline down to Archives. Someone who had been betraying his country all these years just as Yarnell had, or had perhaps unwittingly been a betrayer if he had simply been outmaneuvered as Darrel Owens had been. "There was someone else in Mexico City, Evita.

Another American. Someone Baranov had cultivated just as he had cultivated Darby."

"There were many of them," she said softly.

"This one in particular would have been young.
Another whiz kid like Darby, perhaps. Someone for
whom Valentin might have had a great deal of
respect."

She turned around. Her tears had stopped, but
her eyes were red and her complexion wan.

"Maybe he was in Mexico City for a short time.
Darby would have known him, or known of him. He
would have respected the man. And Baranov would
have treated him as a special case. Does that ring a
bell, Evita? Was there anyone like that in those days
that you can remember? Someone you met, perhaps,
at a party or a reception? Someone Baranov may
have mentioned, just in passing?"

She was remembering. He could see it in her
eyes, in the set of her shoulders. It was coming back
to her. She was returning to those days and nights in
Mexico, when her life at the start, to hear her tell it,
had been a long fairy-tale dream that in the end
turned into a nightmare. But for a while all of
Mexico was at her and Darby's feet.

"There was someone else," she said. "Just once.
It was very early on. Darby and I had just gotten
married, and we'd just opened our beach house
north of Acapulco. There was a party."

Her voice was soft. He had to strain to hear her.
She came back to the couch and sat down. He lit her
a cigarette, and she pulled the smoke deeply into her
lungs, exhaling slowly. Her cocaine high had completely left her, and her eyes had grown dull.

"There were a lot of people at this party?" he
prompted.

"A lot of Valentin's friends. Most of them I'd
never seen. And there were girls, too. Always girls."

"Girls?" McGarvey asked. "What girls?"

"Whores from Mexico City. High-priced call girls. Prime beef. The very best. Nothing was too good for Valentin's friends. Nothing. The best of everything."

"Did this always happen? The girls at the parties?"

"Not always. But sometimes Valentin or Darby wanted to impress someone so they'd bring the women. At the time I was very naïve about it. I thought they were models or movie actresses or something like that. I didn't know they'd been paid to go to bed with Valentin's friends."

It had been the proverbial honey trap. In those days the Russians used it all the time. If they wanted to turn a man they'd arrange for him to be seduced (Americans seemed the easiest to burn), during which time they'd take photographs and make audio tapes of course. Outwardly, morality ran high in the States in those days, so that trap worked very well.

"And there was one American in particular that night?" McGarvey asked. "You met him? You were introduced? Perhaps you can remember a name, even a first name, or his face? Anything?"

But she had not actually seen the man, though she had heard his voice. It was late, probably after one in the morning when Darby, who had been talking with Valentin in the corner for nearly an hour, broke away and came over to her. The lights were low, the music soft and already a lot of the men had paired off with the whores, some of whom had gone out to the changing house by the pool, while others had simply wandered off into the gardens or down to the beach. The guest house in back was reserved always for special guests. The entire cottage was set up with the photographic and recording equipment, all of it evidently state of the art at the time. Anything that went on inside the cottage, even in the bathrooms, no matter the light conditions, would be picked up. It was the perfect setup. "I saw some of the photographs that came out of that place, and let me tell you they left nothing for the imagination, nothing at all." They'd burned a lot of people there, and they were proud of their accomplishment. "But I wasn't. I thought what they were doing was despicable. Of course, that was later, you understand. At the time we're talking about I had no idea what was going on. Darby just broke away from Valentin, came over to me, and we started dancing. He was holding me close, whispering in my ear, kissing my neck. It didn't take very long and we were upstairs on the balcony making love."

"What about the American?" McGarvey asked. "Did he arrive afterward? Or had he been there all along? What? I don't understand, Evita."

Their bedroom was on a balcony that was open to the large living room below. The bed, however, was set far enough back so that no one from below could see up, nor could she see down. But from the window she did see the flash of a car's headlights on the beach road that led down from the highway. When she tried to get up to see who was arriving, Darby pulled her back down onto the bed. By then it had quieted down quite a bit so she heard Baranov welcoming their new guest. But without names, Evita answered McGarvey's question before he could ask it. "We never used names in those days. Everyone thought it for the best." But their voices were very plain, and Darby didn't seem to mind that she was listening, he just didn't want her to go down there. Baranov was respectful toward the American, that much she could tell from what he was saying, and how he was saying it. By then she'd known him well enough to pick that out. And the American sounded young and eager, but she had thought at the time that he was probably hiding something. He was being too polite, she figured. Here he was at one or two o'clock in the morning, at a party with beautiful girls, booze, and music, and he was being terribly proper, formal. It didn't seem to fit.

The music started again after that, and she could hear the others talking softly as they danced, the tinkle of ice cubes in glasses, laughter. Still Darby kept her upstairs, and before long they were making love again. He had an amazing capacity in those days, she said, and so did she.

"We were all a lot younger, Mr. Glynn. And foolish and uncertain about what we were supposed to do with our lives. In a way life was a lot easier then; there didn't seem to be so much to worry about as now. It's this American who showed up at the party that you're after too, isn't it? I can tell. Valentin came up later and I heard him tell Darby that their friend had gone over to the cottage, and that everything was set. It didn't mean all that much to me at the time, though later I figured out that they were probably going to blackmail the poor bastard."

"No idea who he was? Did he work at the embassy? Was he a visiting businessman, a doctor? What?"

"I only knew he was an American from his accent," Evita said.

McGarvey held himself in check. "Accent?" he asked.

"He was a gringo."

"From the South, this American? Maybe from Texas? Maybe from Georgia or Alabama? That South? Did it occur to you at the time?"

She shrugged. "Not the South, more to the Northeast, I think. Maybe Massachusetts. Maybe Connecticut or Maine. A funny accent, but not that strong. It was there, though."

"Cultured?"

"You mean like Darby?"

"Yes."

"Maybe," Evita said. "I don't know. I didn't hear all that much, and I had my mind on other things at the time."

"He was gone in the morning?"

"I didn't get up until noon, and by then he was gone. Darby or Valentin never mentioned him again. And the only reason I still remember it is that I'd never heard Valentin so respectful of another man as he was of that American that night. It struck me as odd, that's all. I figured the American had to have been someone important."

Or someone who would someday become important, McGarvey thought.

"And that's all of it," Evita said tiredly. She finished her champagne. "That's all I know. You'll never beat them. Like I said, they've been at it far too long for you to do anything about it. Give it up. You'll lose. We all will."

She laid her head back and closed her eyes. She had come a long way, and the journey had inflicted a terrible weariness on her.

The band had taken up a new tune. Watching her resting, McGarvey was struck by how Evita's life had been so irrevocably ruined by Darby Yarnell and Valentin Baranov. But there'd been a purpose, of course. And he suspected it had gone beyond a simple legitimization of Yarnell in Mexico City at the time. He had come to suspect that Baranov had been, and still was, a man gifted with a far-sighted vision of things to come. He was a planner and mover who apparently deeply understood basic human motivations. Whatever he had set in motion more than twenty years ago was now finally coming to fruition. He had laid his plans, had gathered and trained his troops, and now the real battle was just beginning. In spite of everything he had learned though, McGarvey felt as if he were operating mostly in the dark. If Baranov's gift was clarity of vision, and Yarnell's was dedication to a purpose, McGarvey's failing would be a basic lack of understanding of the big picture. There was so much more going on that he felt as if he were a blind man preparing to cross a very dangerous mountain range.

"Valentin's in Mexico City again," McGarvey said softly.

Evita dragged her eyes open. "You've already said that."

"Something is going to happen very soon. Something he has been planning since the late fifties. It's why he came back here to you. He wants to use Juanita merely as a motivator. He wants you to do something for him. You and Darby. Just like the old times."

"What do you want me to do?" she asked, her voice slurred.

"I need your help."

"To do what?"

"To prove that Darby was and still is a spy. To expose whoever is working with him in Washington these days—the man from that night in your beach house. To defeat Baranov. And to protect your daughter."

"Impossible—"

"Not if you help me, Evita. I promise you."

Evita looked at him for a very long time, and when she finally nodded her assent, the motion was barely perceptible. She got unsteadily to her feet, looked again at him, and then turned and left the room. He heard the bathwater running a minute later, and he let himself out.

At LaGuardia he had to wait until five for a flight, and while he waited he worried about her, worried that she would end up like Owens and Janos Plónksi, whom he now suspected had only been the tip of an iceberg that threatened to sink them all.

24

McGarvey arrived in Miami a few minutes after eight, retrieved his single bag from the carousel, and rented a car, which he drove into the sprawling city. The night felt warm and humid after New York. He passed some sort of Cuban demonstration in which an effigy of Castro was being burned at the stake. City police were directing traffic around the distur-bance, which had spilled out from a rat warren of streets and up onto the expressway. He found a place to park the car then checked into a small hotel just off Biscayne Boulevard, directly across the bay from the towers of Miami Beach. He walked to a pay phone five blocks away where he telephoned the number Trotter had given him. He was taking no chances that something would go wrong. If Trotter's contact man was the conduit back to the agency, he'd know that McGarvey was in Miami, of course, but they would not be able to find him so fast. It would take time. He did not intend remaining here that long. The city was just coming alive with the night. Traffic was endless and the lights from the big hotels shimmered across the black water. Some-where a big boat horn tooted mournfully, and down the street he could hear the raucous sounds of steel drums. Always there were sirens in the distance.

He'd heard that Miami today was like Havana of the fifties; a big, wide open melting pot of Caribbean humanity in which the rich lived in garish contrast to the miserable poor; where every human depravity imaginable went on day and night at breakneck speed. He'd never known either city, not really. He'd been too young for Havana, and his assignments had never taken him here. But he could well imagine what Havana must have been like. And he figured this was Basulto's kind of city. It must have been like coming home for him to be here.

The same voice as before answered on the first ring. "Yes?"

"I want to see Basulto," McGarvey said. "I'm going in, sixty minutes from now. Tell them to expect me."

"We'll need more time."

"Sixty minutes. Talk to Trotter."

"He's not here."

"Call him."

"That will take time."

"Where is he being kept?"

"Can you hold?"

"I'm at a pay phone," McGarvey said. The line went immediately dead. He held the telephone between his shoulder and cheek as he lit a cigarette. He looked at his watch. It was a couple minutes past nine-thirty. He thought about Evita alone and frightened for all of these years. And he could practically feel Baranov's presence, watching him, knowing his every move. It had become clear to him that all of this had been carefully engineered by the Russian as early as ten months ago when he had gone to Evita in New York to tell her that an ex-CIA agent would be coming to her for information. The implications were staggering. And for the first time since Trotter had come to him in Switzerland, McGarvey was beginning to have some doubts in his own abilities.

"He's at a residential motel in Hialeah, near the race track," the Washington man said. He gave McGarvey the address. "Make certain that you are not followed."

McGarvey hung up. He went to his car and drove immediately over to the address although they weren't expecting him for an hour. He wanted to see who else might show up. The only way to survive, he figured, was to understand the possibility that Baranov had ears everywhere.

The Surfside Motel was a full five miles from any of the beaches and looked as if it had been neglected for a lot of years. It was located six blocks from the racetrack on a broad street that specialized in car dealerships and fast food restaurants, but was tucked behind a low cement block fence that was further screened by a mostly unkempt line of bamboo. There was a sad, dirty, little outdoor pool between the fence and the driveway that McGarvey could just see through the brush. A few plastic chaise lounges and two rusting patio tables flanked the pool. McGarvey pulled into a MacDonald's just across the street and went inside where he got a cup of coffee and took a seat by the window. He could see the motel office beneath the canopy down the short driveway, as well as the line of second floor units, barely a third of which seemed to be occupied. There was no movement. McGarvey checked his watch. It hadn't yet been fifteen minutes since he'd telephoned Washington. They were not expecting him for another three quarters of an hour. It would have taken more than fifteen minutes for even Baranov to arrange something. He was fairly confident that if anyone was going to show up here tonight, he'd beat them. But then we were never certain, were we? It was part and parcel of the business. It had been a long time for him, this over the shoulder feeling, this sustained watchfulness, the edge that made the difference between survival and failure. Christ, it galled him to think that he'd been so easily sucked back into the morass. "Once it's in your blood there's no going back," he'd been told once, but for the life of him he could not think who'd said it. His trouble now was that he had begun to have difficulty distinguishing between what was good and real and what was not, between what was truth and what were lies. Who to trust, who to love, where to run, where to hide. He thought again about Evita and about Darby Yarnell. They both were under Baranov's spell. They were the man's strength, but they also were his weakness.

Traffic was light. No one had entered or left the motel. McGarvey went out to his car and drove at a normal speed twice around the block, watching his rearview mirror, watching the other cars, watching the few pedestrians. But there was no one there. No one watching. No one had come.

He pulled into the motel's driveway, passed the office, and parked at the far end of the building. He switched off the headlights and the engine and sat in the darkness for a few moments, watching, listening, waiting for someone to come, for a curtain to part. But the motel could have been a haven for the dead or the deaf. He took out his gun, checked to make sure it was ready to fire, then got out of his car and climbed the stairs to the second-floor balcony, where he stopped in the shadows. The light in the exit sign was burned out. The place smelled of garbage and of sulphur water and urine and something else, something spicy and exotic. He slipped the Walther's safety catch off and moved quietly along the balcony on the balls of his feet. Now he could hear music from one of the rooms, and conversation, perhaps from a television, from another. Basulto was being kept in 224, which was four rooms from the end. When McGarvey reached the door he paused before knocking. No light came from behind the curtains, nor could he hear any sounds from within.

He knocked. Softly.

"It's open," someone inside said.

McGarvey flattened himself against the cement block wall, brought his gun up, and with his left hand eased the door open a couple of inches.

The room stank of stale beer and cigarettes. It was dark.

"It's me, Artimé. From the house in Switzerland. Do you recognize my voice?"

"It's him," Basulto said cautiously after a second or two.

"Are you sure?" someone else asked.

"Yeah," Basulto said. "It's okay, Mr. McGarvey. Just a minute, we'll have a light."

McGarvey remained against the wall as the light came on. He could see into the room. The double beds were unmade. Dirty laundry lay everywhere, along with empty beer cans and liquor bottles. Ashtrays were overflowing, the bureau and a small table were piled with MacDonald's bags and wrappers, the remnants of a large pizza still in its flat cardboard box, and several potato chip bags. Basulto, wearing nothing more than baggy trousers and a dirty tank T-shirt, stood by the bathroom door. A husky man with thick dark hair stood next to him. His weapon was drawn.

"I'm alone," McGarvey said, making a show of lowering his gun as he stepped around the corner into the room.

"You'd better be," the agent across the room said.

The second man stood in the corner at the

window, his gun out, his eyes wide. He wore a jacket. McGarvey got the impression he might have just come in.

"I'm here to talk. Nothing more."

The two agents looked at each other, and then they lowered their weapons, uncocking the hammers. "You're five minutes late," the one by the window snapped. He was nervous.

McGarvey closed the door, then pushed the window curtain aside so that he could look out. Nothing moved below. No one had come. No one was out there, and yet he could not shake the feeling that someone was looking over his shoulder. That Baranov, or whoever, knew that he was here and was watching him.

"Is this it?" Basulto asked. "Are we ready to get that bastard, Mr. McGarvey? You and me?"

He turned back.

"I hope to Christ you came in clean," the one by Basulto said, gruffly. "It's one thing being cooped up in this pigsty, but it would be another defending this little prick."

"See?" Basulto cried. "See what I have to put up with here."

"Why don't you two take a walk. Give yourself a break." McGarvey looked at Basulto. "I'd like half an hour with my friend here."

Again the agents exchanged glances. "What the hell." The bigger one shrugged. "They said cooperate, so we'll cooperate."

"I'll take full responsibility," McGarvey said.

"You're goddamned right you will," the big one said. He grabbed a jacket and he and his partner left without bothering to look back.

McGarvey locked and chained the door. Alone, Basulto seemed a little more sure of himself than with Trotter's two men. He didn't seem so tense, though there still was a wariness about him. His life, at least, according to what he had told them in Switzerland, was on the line. Which meant he would cooperate so long as it would benefit him, but only as far as he felt was necessary and no farther. McGarvey swept the debris off the table with a clatter, sat down, put his feet up, and lit a cigarette. Basulto wasn't impressed, but McGarvey knew he had his attention.

"There've been some killings," McGarvey said.

"What killings? Where? Nobody's told me a thing down here. I just sit and wait and sweat in this stink hole. What are you talking about?"

McGarvey loosened his tie. "He was a friend of mine, Artimé. A very good friend. I had him make a few inquiries for me, and he was shot to death for his trouble. Left a wife and children."

"I told you, goddamnit. I sat there and told you over and over again. But nobody would believe me. Called me a slimeball. Well, maybe now you believe me."

"He'll probably be coming after you next."

A momentary look of alarm crossed Basulto's face. McGarvey got the impression that it might have been a put on. But then Basulto was an unusual man and hard to read.

"Then we'd better get the bastard."

"That's what I'm here for."

"Have you got a plan?" Basulto asked eagerly.

"I'm going to need your help, Artimé," McGarvey said, patiently. He took a drag on his cigarette. He wanted to be almost anyplace except here.

Beside the dresser was a large paper bag. Basulto pulled a couple of beers out of the bag, opened them, and brought them over to the table. A peace offering.

He hadn't shaved in a couple of days, and his complexion was red and splotchy. He'd probably been boozing it pretty hard, cooped up here like this. He smelled ripe.

"Anything," he said eagerly. "I'm a pretty good trigger man. Christ, Mr. McGarvey, I don't give a shit, see. As long as you guys hold up your end of the bargain, I'll do my part. Anything."

"We appreciate it, believe me," McGarvey said, accepting a beer. He motioned for the Cuban to sit down.

"Anything, Mr. McGarvey," Basulto said sitting across the table. "I mean anything. Goddamnit, I love this country. You could be Roger Harris's twin, you know."

"He was quite a guy."

"Yes, he was . . ."

"Ambitious, from what I gather," McGarvey said. He took a deep drink of the warm beer, then raised the can to Basulto; two conspirators gathered to share a little secret.

"You talked to someone else about him," Basulto said. "You looked up his record. Found out about him. All right, so what are you doing here? What do you want from me? I told you I'd give you anything."

"The truth, Artimé," McGarvey said.

Basulto drank his beer with a nervous energy, as if he were a man just off the desert who'd suddenly found himself in the midst of a grand party; he didn't know which way to look or how to behave.

"Okay. What do you want? Just ask me," he said defiantly. "I've gone over this so many times, not only with them, but in my own mind, that I'm not sure of anything. Do you know what I'm saying? You *capice*?"

He'd internationalized his act, but it was no

more convincing than it had been in Switzerland.

"Just a couple of minor points, nothing terribly important. Just something I have to get straight in my mind before we fly off the handle. Lives are at stake here, you know."

"Yeah, mine for one."

"Back to Miami. I'm interested in that period," McGarvey said softly. "After Roger Harris had recruited you and you'd been sent up here for training. I'd like to know about that. You never really did cover those days in any detail."

Basulto just looked at him, his eyes unblinking.

"I'd like to know about the team that trained you. Their names if you can remember them. Maybe their methods. What sorts of things they were filling your head with in those days. What kind of a place they put you up in."

"A dump," Basulto said, and he took another drink of his beer. "Not far from here. But it's all gone by now. Torn down. Progress."

McGarvey handed him a cigarette and held a light for him.

"Who was it got wasted?" he asked. "Anyone I know?"

"There were two of them."

Basulto's hand shook.

"One of them was looking up your records, and the other was Darby Yarnell's old boss."

"Christ," Basulto swore softly. "Christ." He glanced at the door. "Were you followed down here?"

"He knows I'm here, Artimé. And there's a good chance he knows you're here, too."

"Oh, well, that's just goddamned fine now, isn't it. Why didn't you take out a full page ad in the newspapers? Send the bastard a printed invitation."

"We're running out of time."

"No shit."

"I'm going to need your help. The truth now, it's the only thing that's going to save your ass. We're going to have to burn Yarnell, and whoever he's working with. But in order for me to do that, I need to know everything."

"It's his army, isn't it? His mob."

McGarvey looked at the man in amazement. "Where'd you hear that?" he asked softly.

Basulto hadn't heard or understood the question. He was sweating now, nervously tapping the cigarette against the edge of the ashtray until the ash fell off. "I don't know how the hell we're going to nail him now. You were supposed to be the best. What a joke."

"You mentioned Yarnell's mob. Where'd you hear about that?"

"I don't know," Basulto said absently, his mind still on his own troubles. He looked up. "Mr. Trotter mentioned that we were going to have to be very careful. He was talking with Mr. Day and some of the others. They said Yarnell had his own private army."

"A mob?" McGarvey asked again, wondering why it was that sometimes the little things bothered him more than the bigger issues.

"Mob. Army. Crowd. Christ, I don't know. Crucify me for a choice of words." Basulto was becoming agitated again. "If he sends his army down here after us, we won't have a chance in hell."

"What makes you think that?"

Basulto shook his head. "The sonofabitch has managed to survive this long, hasn't he?"

"But we know about him now."

"So what are you going to do about it? Are you going to talk him to death?"

"Do you think it would work?"

"Not fucking likely!" Basulto snapped. "You're going to have to blow him away. It's the only way. He's too smart for you. Roger Harris got in his way, and he got wasted for his stupidity. Don't you be next, because this time my ass is really on the line. I got no place else to go."

"He's working with someone, Artimé."

"Yeah, his army."

"He's a spy. He has a control officer. Someone who calls the shots. Someone he reports to. He's got his own Roger Harris."

"The Russian from Mexico City."

"Perhaps. But that was a long time ago." McGarvey was watching the Cuban's eyes. There was no clear-cut reaction.

"Maybe he's still around."

"It's possible. But Yarnell has someone else he's working with, or for. Someone in Washington."

Now Basulto's eyes narrowed. "Who?"

"I don't know. Not yet."

Again Basulto glanced toward the door. "Mr. Trotter? Could it be him? He's trying to burn us both and keep his hands clean? It sounds like something Yarnell might have done."

"Had you ever met him before they brought you to Switzerland?"

"No."

"How about Mr. Day?"

"No, never saw either of them until they showed up down here."

"Yarnell never made an appearance during your training here in Miami?"

"I would have recognized him in Mexico City. We went through all this before. He never came here. Neither did Roger, for that matter. I was sent up here for my training, and when I was finished they shipped me back to Havana."

"So how many people were here in Miami for you, Artimé? Two? Three? A dozen?"

"Two of them, mostly. And don't ask because I can't remember their names, except for the communications expert. He was the third man. Showed up for a couple of days then left. He was called Scotty. Had just gotten out of the army."

"How is it you remembered his name and not the others?"

"I don't know. It's just one of those things, you know. He was nice, knew what he was talking about, didn't have an ax to grind. Leastways not with me."

"The others did?"

"They didn't really give a shit. I was just another piece of dog meat as far as they were concerned."

"Anyone else stop by?" McGarvey asked. "Just pop in for a visit or a look-see? Anyone introduce themselves?"

Basulto shrugged. "There were a few. I couldn't tell you about any of them though. I was pretty young, and my eyes were filled with stars. This was the big time for me. I was going to be a spy."

Just then Basulto's words reminded McGarvey of Evita's. When she'd been turned in Mexico City she too had been young, with stars in her eyes. It almost sounded like a well-used script.

"Were they all Americans? Can you remember that, Artimé?"

"All Americans. WASPs, they were."

"Young? Old? Remember anything on that score?"

"They were older than me. I was just a kid. But I suppose they all were in their twenties, early thirties. Ex-military, I think. I remember they sometimes ran the place like boot camp."

"Not a foreign accent in the lot?"

"No."

"Southerners, some of them, do you suppose?"

"You mean like Alabama or Mississippi?"

"Or Texas?"

"There might have been."

"East Coast, Artimé? Intellectuals. Maybe some young kid with a holier-than-thou attitude? Silver spoon in the mouth?"

"They were all intellectuals."

McGarvey looked at him. "It's important."

"Why do you keep asking about it?" Basulto asked, his voice going a bit soft.

"I didn't know I had."

"What the hell is so important about an East Coast snob anyway? Who gives a shit. It doesn't make any difference. Yarnell wasn't there, otherwise we would have nailed him then . . . me and Roger Harris."

There it was again, McGarvey thought. Basulto, for all his isolation, knew too much. Yarnell's mob. And now the fact there might have been an East Coast snob. Someone important. Someone such as the man Evita told him about for whom Baranov had had a great deal of respect. It was beginning to come together now for him.

"Did Roger Harris have a name for him?"

"For who? What are you talking about?"

"The East Coast snob?"

"What the hell *are* you talking about?"

"The man Roger Harris hired you to find for him, Artimé, who did you think I was talking about?"

"I haven't got a clue," Basulto said, but this time McGarvey could see that the Cuban was lying. His eyes were wide, and a small bead of perspiration had formed on his upper lip.

McGarvey got slowly to his feet, lit another cigarette, and stood at the window looking down into the night again. If anything, it was quieter on the street now than when he had arrived. Hialeah was holding its breath. He had underestimated Roger Harris. As early as the late fifties Harris had known about Baranov and had suspected that the Russian was running at least one American. He apparently had not suspected Yarnell but had targeted someone else. The same one, possibly, who had shown up at the party in Mexico, and the same one who might have stopped by the training house here in Miami to see how young Basulto's indoctrination was coming. Harris had figured on using Basulto as his eyes and ears. First here in Miami, next in Havana, and finally in Mexico, where Baranov kept his headquarters. Sooner or later, Harris figured, his suspect should have shown up and Basulto would finger him.

Basulto had not moved from the table. He was looking up at McGarvey.

"I didn't understand until now, Artimé," McGarvey said, sitting down again. "I'm out of practice, or something."

"Understand what?" Basulto asked warily.

"What Roger Harris really wanted from you."

Basulto didn't speak.

"It didn't make any sense to me, your emergency signal for Mexico City. You were supposed to telephone Roger Harris's sister in San Antonio, Texas, with the single word *alpha.*"

"In case of an emergency."

"Right. But what emergency, Artimé? I mean, what constituted the emergency that Roger Harris prenamed alpha? An earthquake? A tornado? A riot? The appearance of Baranov with an American?"

"I was supposed to watch the Ateneo Español. . . ."

"For who?" McGarvey asked. "Did he give you a name?"

Basulto was cornered. "No name."

"A description?"

"No."

"What then?"

"We're getting into an area here that I don't want to get into," Basulto cried desperately.

McGarvey sat forward, slamming his palm on the tabletop, the noise like a pistol shot. "You little sonofabitch!"

"There's no call for that," Basulto squeaked.

McGarvey was feeling mean again, to the point where he was almost frightened of himself. Yet a great clarity seemed to come over him, as if he could see everything and everyone, all the relationships in this business, all the truths and the lies from the fifties all the way to this moment. He'd asked if there was a bridge between then and now; Day had called it the "Golden Gate." He pulled out his gun, pulled the hammer back, and pointed it across the table into Basulto's face. The Cuban went white.

"What did alpha mean? Who was alpha?"

"I don't know. I swear to God. Cristo!"

"Talk to me, Artimé." McGarvey began to squeeze the trigger.

"It was a voice," Basulto blurted. "Nothing more."

"What voice?"

"An East Coast voice. Connecticut or something. An intellectual."

"I'm listening."

"Back in Washington Roger overheard a telephone conversation between a Russian and this American."

"Baranov?"

"Yes, Baranov and this American."

"Where?"

"At CIA headquarters."

"The American was CIA?"

"Yes. Roger thought so."

"He was talking with Baranov from a telephone within the building?"

"Yes."

"So he sent you to Mexico City to watch for Baranov and an American? Any American?"

"Yes."

"If you saw an American you were to call with the code word *alpha*. But what about the voice?"

Basulto said nothing.

"The voice, Artimé? How were you to recognize the voice unless you were near enough to hear it, which you could not have done from your room overlooking the Ateneo."

"I was a member," Basulto said softly.

"Of the Ateneo Español?"

"Yes."

McGarvey lowered the gun. It had become too heavy for him; his trigger finger had begun to shake. "You didn't see Baranov and Yarnell from the window. You saw them inside. You were down there with them, then."

Basulto nodded. "But it wasn't him. His voice was different."

"The voice Roger Harris was looking for wasn't Yarnell's."

"No," Basulto said, hanging his head.

"Then why did you call San Antonio? Why did you use alpha?"

"I was frightened. Roger knew about one of them, but there was someone else working with Baranov. I thought he would want to know."

McGarvey holstered his gun and got to his feet. He looked down at Basulto for a long time. There were still many questions, many holes in the man's story, but for the most part he had got what he had come looking for; confirmation that Yarnell wasn't Baranov's only conquest. That there was indeed someone else in the equation.

"I'll come back for you. In a few days."

"We're going to burn Yarnell?"

McGarvey nodded. "Him and the other one." At the door he hesitated a moment. "At the Ateneo, did Baranov see you? Does he know your face?"

"Yes," Basulto said. "God help me, yes."

"Well, we're going to burn him, too, Artimé."

25

The lake near Leonard Day's house was calm, not the slightest breeze rippled the water. There were no fishermen this morning, nor was there any traffic on the road that led back through Indian Creek Park to Kenilworth Avenue. It was Tuesday; everyone was at work in the city by now. McGarvey had caught Day and Trotter before they'd left for work, and they'd agreed to meet with him. At McGarvey's suggestion they talked outside as they walked around the lake. Trotter was highly charged, he half walked and half ran along the footpath. Day, on the other hand, seemed contemplative, as if he were deeply troubled but by something else. He seemed distracted. They made an odd trio, McGarvey thought; the bureaucrat, the cop, and the spy.

"When John first came to me with this problem, and mentioned your name in conjunction with it, I was frankly skeptical," Day said. His hands were stuffed in the pockets of his maroon jogging suit. He wore a sweatband around his head, making him look boyish. "I'm still skeptical."

"Good heavens, Kirk, even you have to see that what you're saying is hard to swallow," Trotter piped up, looking back. He was nervous around Day after what McGarvey had told him two days ago.

"But we're stuck with it," McGarvey said. He'd expected the objections, but he wanted to see how Day would react.

"We can hardly turn from it. Not at this stage of the game, especially not now."

"Yarnell is almost certainly still actively working for the Russians, and he almost certainly has a contact man in the CIA."

"Who?"

"I don't know. But it's someone at high levels."

"What makes you believe that?"

"The quality of his information."

"Such as?"

"He knew that I would see Darrel Owens, his old boss. He also knew that I'd sent Janos Plónski searching after Basulto's files."

"Which means, of course, that he knows you're coming after him," Trotter said.

"Then why hasn't he had you eliminated?" Day asked sharply. "I'd do it."

It was the one question for which McGarvey had found no satisfactory answer, but he gave voice to the only possibility that even seemed plausible. "Because something else is happening, or is about to happen, and I'm an important source for him."

Day pulled up short, a dangerous glint in his eyes. "I don't understand."

"It's a two-way street. I check on him, and in the process he finds out about me."

Trotter had stopped a few feet farther along the path, and he was looking back now, his eyes wide behind his thick glasses.

"What else?" Day demanded.

McGarvey took out a cigarette and lit it. He gazed across the lake. "John knows why I was called back to the States, and so do you. Who else?"

"Basulto," Trotter said.

"He's isolated," McGarvey replied, his eyes never leaving Day's. "Who else?"

"No one," Day said evenly. The morning air seemed to have gotten thin.

"There's my team," Trotter chirped.

"Do they have contact with the agency?"

"No."

"I do," Day said. "But I have discussed this situation with no one."

"Have you made notes? Left them on your desk?"

"Nothing has been committed to paper. Not by me."

"Mentioned it to Powers, or the president?"

"No."

"Discussed it on the telephone with John?"

"My telephone, along with John's, is swept."

"That's right, Kirk," Trotter said. "Absolutely. There simply are no leaks."

"Yes there are," McGarvey said softly. "We just haven't found them yet."

"Perhaps it's you," Day suggested. "His people could have spotted you from day one."

"He would have to have been tipped off as to why I came back." McGarvey was thinking about his ex-wife and her lawyer boyfriend. It was not coincidence that they were friends of Yarnell's. But that had been going on for more than a year now. Where was the logic?

"Could be Yarnell's ex-wife," Trotter said. "You went to see her. What'd you two talk about?"

McGarvey turned to him. "About the fact that Yarnell was working for the Russians as early as the late fifties in Mexico City. It's one of the reasons he married her. For cover."

"Mexico City?" Day asked.

"He was stationed out of our embassy until after the Bay of Pigs thing. Then he moved to Washington and finally out to Moscow. Each time his control officer went with him."

"You know this man?"

"Valentin Illen Baranov," McGarvey said. "Now he's back in Mexico City, running what's called the CESTA network."

"Good Lord," Trotter said. He and Day exchanged glances.

"What is it?" McGarvey asked.

"How certain are you of Yarnell's connection with this Baranov and CESTA?"

"Very."

Trotter had been holding his breath. He blew it out all at once as if he were a racer trying to clear his lungs of carbon dioxide. He needed oxygen and he wasn't getting it.

"That's it, then," Day said. "I'll have to go to Powers and the president with this now. I'm putting you on hold."

"What the hell are you talking about?" McGarvey asked, trying to keep his temper in check.

"It's CESTA, Kirk," Trotter stepped into the breach.

Day shot him a warning glance.

"It's gone too far, Leonard. We never suspected this connection. Not really. And it's simply gone too far now. His life is on the line."

McGarvey waited. He understood at that moment that he had been lied to all along; not lies of commission, rather lies of omission. He had a feeling that what he had not been told was legion compared to what he had.

Day looked away momentarily in disgust, as if he were being forced into a decision he had wanted to avoid at all costs. When he turned back he nodded.

"Seven months ago an Aeromexico flight out of Miami was hijacked and diverted to Havana," Trotter said. Day was watching him, his eyes big and bright. "The two hijackers got off the plane with two hostages. Before they got ten yards from the plane, all four of them were shot and killed by the Cuban militia."

"Who were they, John?"

"The hostages had been on their way to Mexico City. Agency for International Development."

"CIA?"

"Right."

"Why were they grabbed?"

"We didn't know at the time. Except that Lawrence Danielle worked with us on the preliminary investigation. He told me that the weapons the hijackers had used had been supplied to them by CESTA."

"CESTA presumably knew who they were, arranged for the hijacking, and further arranged for their assassination," Day said.

"Why?" McGarvey asked. He thought about Baranov coming to see Evita ten months ago. It had been barely weeks before the incident.

"I didn't know about this until two days ago," Trotter said. "I promise you, Kirk."

"John came to me with Baranov's name. Said you thought he was connected with the Yarnell thing."

"I didn't believe it at the time. It was impossible—"

Day interrupted. "This is classified top secret, McGarvey. No matter what has happened before this moment, if you release what I'm about to tell you, I will personally see that you are prosecuted under the Secrets Act. To the full extent of the law."

The man was a pompous ass. "Talk to me," McGarvey said.

Again Day and Trotter exchanged glances.

"The Russians are apparently building six

missile-launching facilities in the Mexican desert barely forty miles south of our border," Trotter blurted.

McGarvey had come to believe, over the years, that he was sufficiently inured to bad news that his tolerance for shock was high. He could never become nonplussed. At this moment, however, he was truly frightened. He did not know what to say. He could feel it as a weakness in his legs, a hollowness in his gut, and a tightening in his chest.

"CESTA?" he said.

"They're almost certainly involved," Day agreed.

"Baranov, who runs CESTA, is Yarnell's control officer."

Day nodded.

"Yarnell has a man in the CIA. He fingered the two AID officers on the plane."

"It would go a long way toward explaining everything," Day said heavily.

Another thought struck McGarvey. "How do you know about this?"

For the first time Day suddenly seemed unsure of himself. He hesitated. McGarvey was having a bad feeling.

"Donald Powers is a personal friend of mine," Day said.

"And Yarnell?"

Again Day hesitated. He nodded. "Darby and I go back a lot of years together."

McGarvey realized he was shaking. Day stepped back a pace. "I swear to God that I didn't tell anyone about you. Not even Powers."

"If I ever find out you lied to me, I'll kill you," McGarvey said softly.

"For heaven's sake, Kirk," Trotter said.

Day straightened up a little, a determined look coming back into his eyes. "I'm going to Powers and the president with this. No one else. They must be informed. In the meantime you're to make no move, no move whatsoever, without first clearing it through me." He said it as an order, but then he softened his tone. "You do understand what's at stake here. It's no longer simply a case of proving Darby Yarnell is a spy who works for the Russians. Now it's a matter of another missile crisis. This one a hell of a lot closer to our border than Cuba."

"A crisis made impossible for us to win because the CIA is an open book to Baranov."

"The bastard," Day said with much feeling.

Driving back into the city, McGarvey tried to put a name to exactly what it was he was feeling. He had a sense that they all were racing madly down a long roller coaster whose brakes had failed, and yet he knew that someone was in control, that someone had planned the ride from the beginning. But to what end? Offensive missiles in Mexico? It was impossible for him to believe even now, although the Russians had gotten what they had wanted in Cuba. In exchange for removing their missiles they had extracted a promise from us that we would never intervene militarily with the Castro government. Perhaps the same things were happening in Mexico. But there was something else as well. Something more. He could feel it. He'd been glad to get out of the agency because of what it had done to him, and what he had seen it do to others. Yet when Trotter and Day had shown up in Switzerland he had almost gladly followed them. Hell, he had damned near jumped into their laps. His retirement had already begun to break down before they'd shown up. But now he wondered if coming back had been the right thing for him.

"You're forty-four and your life is passing you

by. You're no longer in the fray, is that it?" Marta
had asked, coming very close to the mark.

His life *had* passed him by in Switzerland, at
least five years of it had. He had become anxious
without admitting why. Or at least without admitting that he missed the business. "You are either a
part of the problem or a part of the solution," his
father used to say. He'd tried to step out of himself,
and in the end it had been impossible.

Day had ordered him to step aside. But that,
too, was impossible now.

The day had seemed six months long. Eight
o'clock in the evening seemed never to come. Yet
when it did and Leonard Day found himself driving
onto the grounds of Gallaudet College in Brentwood
Park, he wished he could somehow stop time. Powers had seemed preoccupied on the telephone, but
he'd agreed to meet Day at eight at his home. "Only
if it's very important, Leonard," Powers had said at
the last. "It's getting just a bit hairy around here at
the moment, if you catch my drift." How many
crises had he weathered in this town? he wondered.
How many late night meetings, private conferences,
for-your-eyes-only memos passed hand-to-hand had
he seen? Here in Washington at the top, among the
elite—the policy makers, the movers and shakers
—the big decisions were made, but so were the
colossal blunders. The U-2 flight of Francis Gary
Powers, the Bay of Pigs, the entire Vietnam debacle,
the abortive hostage-rescue attempt from Tehran,
Watergate, the Iran-Contra Affair. The list was endless. This small town on the Potomac was very
nearly an exclusively all-white Anglo-Saxon Protes-
tant male enclave. The chosen few belonged to
comfortable clubs where they could rest from the
vigors of leadership. Golf courses came with bar

service out on the fairways. Restaurants and hotels were so exclusive that eighty percent of the city (the blacks) could not gain entrance except through the service doors as busboys and waiters and bellhops. But God, it was exciting to be a part of it. First California, Day thought, now the center of the universe.

Driving past the college it was dark inside the car. The narrow road wound its way deep into the park, the trees and pathways mysterious in the warm night. Day lowered his window as he turned up the driveway to Powers's home. Lights shone through the trees as he reached the security gate. He'd been here many times in the night. But never quite like this. Never with this intent. Never with this edge of fear that rode with him like some dark entity.

From the gate house the security man came over. A handgun was holstered at his hip. "Good evening, Mr. Day," he said.

"I'm a little late."

"Yes, sir. So is the director, but you can go on up; I'll tell them you're coming."

Them? Day wondered as he proceeded up from the gate to the main house. Two cars were parked in the long circular driveway in front of the big three-story brick Colonial that Powers had taken over since becoming DCI. "A big rambling wreck of a mansion," was how he described it. But with a certain fondness, Day had always suspected. Of course Powers had been raised with the proverbial silver spoon in his mouth and expected always to live this way. It was his due. Getting out of the car, however, Day thought again that the house was ostentatious in its size, in its location, and certainly in its security precautions.

In the distance he suddenly could hear the dull chop of helicopter rotors beating the air. On the front step of the house he stopped and looked up as the DCI's machine came low over the trees from the southwest, its landing lights coming on as it swung left and settled in for a landing on the helipad at the rear of the house.

"Just this way, sir," someone from the open door said. Day turned. "They're in the study," the houseman said politely.

Day followed the man through the great hall beneath the U-shaped balcony and back along a narrow corridor to a pair of open doors that led into Powers's study, a large, book-lined room with French doors leading to a veranda, a long leather-covered desk, and a grouping of couches, chairs, and Queen Anne tables in front of the fireplace. A high tension room. Not a retreat. The man who occupied this place was under the gun twenty-four hours a day, and Day had a huge respect for him. A lot of them were carried out feet first, but not Powers.

"Would you care for a drink, sir?" the houseman asked.

"No," Day said at the doorway.

Lawrence Danielle stood at the French doors, holding the curtain back as he watched outside, and General Murphy, the deputy director of Central Intelligence, spoke on the telephone at the desk, his voice low and gruff. The room smelled of stale cigars and polished wood, and the only light was on the desk, casting the room in deep shadows. They were in crisis here, Day saw. All of them, each for a different reason, or perhaps the same one, had come to Powers for their salvation. Supplicants to the great man who sat on the seventh floor at Langley at the right hand of the president himself. In the days and nights to come he would always remember this exact moment as a watershed, as a bloody continental divide.

"He's just now touched down—" Danielle started to say, dropping the curtain and turning around. He stopped in midsentence.

"Hello, Lawrence," Day said.

"What are you doing here?"

"Donald agreed to see me."

"About what?" Danielle demanded, remaining by the window. Danielle was always the dapper dresser. This evening, however, his tie was loose, his collar open, and his face was red and looked as if he had just run up six flights of stairs. His eyes were bloodshot.

How far to go with this? There was a leak, according to McGarvey. One they hadn't found yet. One at high levels within the agency. Danielle was number three. General Murphy was number two. And number one had just now landed.

"When did you speak with him?" Danielle asked harshly. "We're busy here. Maybe yours can wait."

"This morning," Day said. "He asked me not to come if it wasn't terribly important."

Danielle didn't move, seeming as if he were listening for something, waiting for something to happen. He hadn't shaved; a bit of stubble darkened his chin.

"Mexico?" Danielle asked softly.

Day remembered a bit of T. S. Eliot from the old days.

It was from a poem called "The Hollow Men."

He remembered the exact moment that Trotter had come to him, what seemed like centuries ago, with his story. "Because I trust you," he'd explained. "Because you're close to Powers and Yarnell."

"Yes," he said, nodding slightly.

General Murphy was gazing across the room at him. "He's just arrived," he said into the telephone. "I'll call you later." He put down the telephone abruptly, his eyes narrow. He was a big man. An old friend of Powers who had pulled him from the army for duty as deputy director. Where Powers was sophisticated, Murphy was blunt. They made a wonderful team.

"What about Mexico?" he asked menacingly.

"I have some information," Day said hesitantly. "For the director," he added.

Murphy and Danielle exchanged glances. From out in the corridor they heard someone coming. Day stepped away from the doorway as Powers came around the corner, his bodyguard just behind him.

"Hello, Leonard," he said. His bodyguard closed the doors behind him. "It's confirmed, then?" he asked Murphy.

"I'm afraid it is, Donald," the DDCI replied.

"Has the president been notified?"

"No."

"Perhaps you should speak with Leonard first, and then we can get on with it, Mr. Director," Danielle suggested.

Powers took Day by the arm and led him the rest of the way into the room. "Leonard is a very old friend. My eyes and ears over at Justice, as a matter of fact. Didn't you know? He understands the essentials. I believe we can trust him on this one." He turned back to Day. "Isn't that right?"

Day felt as if he were standing next to a live high-tension wire. A wrong move and he would be killed. Instantly. "Yes, Mr. Director."

"We've discussed the missile crisis, from the legal standpoint," Powers said. "The latest now is that one of our SR-71 spy planes has unfortunately been shot down thirty miles south of the Mexican border. Not a pleasant bit of news to bring to the president."

"There are actually missiles then, sir?" Day asked. "It's certain?"

"It looks like it."

"God."

"Yes," Powers said.

"He's come with something about Mexico," Danielle interjected in his quiet voice.

"I thought as much," Powers said. "What have you got for us, Leonard? What have you found out?"

"And from where?" Danielle added.

Day had always been a cautiously ambitious man. His father had been a banker, but had gone too far too fast and had lost everything he'd worked a lifetime for, after which he had committed suicide. At this moment Day felt as if he were standing on the edge of the same chasm.

"What I have to say is for your ears only, Mr. Director," he said, girding himself.

Powers patted him on the arm. "It's all right, believe me."

"We can step outside for a moment," Danielle suggested, breaking the sudden awkward silence.

"No," Powers said without taking his eyes off Day. "We're terribly busy here, Leonard. I've yet to get over to the White House. We're in a shambles at the moment. It's going to get rough around the edges."

Still Day hesitated. Perhaps McGarvey's original assessment about Basulto's story was correct. Perhaps there was nothing to it at all. But then who had killed Plónski, who had killed Owens, and why? Something was happening inside of Day. Something he couldn't quite put his finger on. Yet he knew it had to do with fear of the second kind. The first was concern for oneself, while the second was fear for the world. For existence.

"It's about Darby Yarnell, Mr. Director," he said. "I have reason to believe the man is a Soviet spy."

PART THREE

26

McGarvey had a small room in the Four Seasons Hotel. The place was old but well kept and the bed was reasonably comfortable, though he hadn't come to sleep. The day had closed in on him, and in the afternoon he had found himself wandering almost aimlessly around the city; first to the White House, as if he thought to catch another glimpse of Yarnell the diplomat; then out to Chevy Chase where he passed his ex-wife's house, but her Mercedes was not in the driveway and the windows were all dark; and finally, dangerously, past Yarnell's fortress a block up from the safe house where Trotter's team was— or had been—doing its job. He'd returned to take a shower and change his clothes, then went down to the bar where he had a beer and a sandwich. They'd wanted him to back down for the moment, the Mexican crisis would first have to be contained, was their argument. But it made increasingly less sense to McGarvey, who was beginning to see that Baranov and whoever worked for him *were* the Mexican crisis. Yarnell was their only viable lead. At nine he headed on foot back into Georgetown along 29th Street. The traffic was heavy; the air was thick and smelled of exhaust fumes. The brownstone houses were expensive and implacable in their rows, like soldiers at attention. He turned left on R Street, passing Oak Hill Cemetery, the trees standing as natural counterparts to the grave markers, some of which were ornate and monumental, some of which were small and sad, lost in the darkness. At 31st Street he stopped and looked up toward Dumbarton Oaks Park. He thought about Marta back in Lausanne. Alone, he hoped. Sad. He'd begun to believe that she had told him the truth, that in the beginning she had watched him for the federal police, but that later she had fallen in love with him. But there wasn't a thing he could do about, or for, her now. Even if he wanted to do something, which he wasn't at all sure he did.

A pale yellow Mercedes coupe pulled up in front of the Boynton Towers Apartments across the street, and a woman got out from the passenger side. McGarvey decided there was something familiar about her. She turned and looked back inside the car, the street light illuminating her face and hair. She was Lorraine Hawkins, the girl with the *sommersprossen*. This evening she was dressed elegantly in a tight-fitting evening dress and her hair was done up in the back. She was background noise, McGarvey thought. Cover. Yarnell might notice the setup. Might become suspicious. If and when he did, they hoped he would notice her. A normal girl with friends who came and went. Nothing suspicious here. She made a gesture, then shut the passenger door, crossed the sidewalk, and entered the building. A moment later the Mercedes moved off. McGarvey caught a glimpse of the man behind the wheel, but he didn't recognize him.

Day had told him that there were more important considerations now. That Powers and the president would have to be brought in on this. But Janos had not been Day's friend. Day would not have to face Pat and the children. Nor had Day come face-to-face with Owens; he hadn't listened to the old man's story, hadn't looked into his eyes, hadn't in the end been witness to the cold wind whipping the flames hundreds of feet above the beach house.

The block was quiet for the moment. The watchers and the watched. As had been happening to him all along, he had the feeling that someone was lurking in the shadows, their eyes on him. But no one was about. There were no odd cars or trucks or vans with too many aerials. No lingering pedestrians. Nothing at all to suggest that his feeling was anything other than paranoia, plain and simple. There was more here though. Something else in the equation. Something he felt he should be aware of. Some flash of intuition that would make all the pieces fit.

He crossed the street, a taxi rushing past just behind him, and he went inside. The elevator was on its way back down. Lorraine had taken it up to the eighth floor but had thoughtfully sent it back. They were paying attention to the details, McGarvey thought, which was very good. Their lives could very well depend on their tradecraft. No use in advertising her floor number. Yet he was surprised that they were still here. He would have thought that by now Trotter would have called them away. Unless his were not the only second thoughts.

Riding up he took out his gun and checked the action, holstering it finally when the door opened onto an empty corridor. The building was quiet. He made absolutely no noise on the carpeted floor as he approached the apartment door. From inside he could faintly hear the murmur of someone talking, but then it fell quiet. He knocked and a moment later it opened. Lorraine Hawkins, her hair down now, stood in the doorway, the Mexican, Gonzales, right behind her, a long-barreled Smith & Wesson .357 in his right hand. The apartment was in dark-

ness. McGarvey could smell the night air from an
open window. A big infrared Starlight scope was set
on a tripod across the room. The telephone monitoring equipment had been set up on the buffet. Sheets,
the tan mack from Lausanne, was speaking softly
into the other telephone.

"Anything from his phone calls?" McGarvey
asked.

"Nothing that's worth anything," Lorraine said,
moving back away from the door. "He came in an
hour and a half ago. His daughter is with him."

McGarvey stepped inside. Lorraine closed and
locked the door behind him. Gonzales holstered his
gun and went back to the scope that was trained
across 32nd Street on Yarnell's house. Sheets turned
his back to them and continued with his telephone
conversation.

"Anyone else?"

"I just arrived myself."

She was hiding something, he could see it in her
eyes. "Who else is down there?"

Gonzales looked away from the scope. "Your
ex-wife showed up about twenty minutes ago."

"Alone?"

"With a man named Phillip Brent," Lorraine
said.

"They're over there now?"

"Yes."

This was not how he had imagined it would be
coming back to the States, he thought; Kathleen
involved in this business, wittingly or not. From the
beginning she'd distanced herself from his work,
then later from him. Now she was in the middle of it.
At the dangerous core.

He went to the window and looked across
toward Yarnell's house. Even without the glasses he
could make out the lit upper-story windows and the
vague black squares of the dark attic windows. The

watchers and the watched. The listeners and the
listened to. A bit of De la Mare came to him; *Tell
them that I came, and no one answered/ That I kept
my word.* But that didn't matter. There was no
honor here, he thought. No one else kept his word.

But why Kathleen? he wondered. Why her of all
people? She had nothing to do with this. She'd never
had anything to do with it. And for years she hadn't
even had anything to do with him.

"Mr. Trotter is on his way over," Sheets said,
putting down the telephone. "Apparently he's been
trying to reach you all afternoon."

"Well, he's found me," McGarvey growled,
dragging his eyes away from Yarnell's house.

"Would you like something to drink, Mr.
McGarvey?" Lorraine asked abruptly.

"We're shutting down," Sheets said before
McGarvey could say a thing.

"Not with my wife down there you're not!"

"I'm sorry, sir, but——"

"We'll just wait until John gets here. You can
give me at least that much."

"He said break it down," Sheets insisted.

"Bingo," Gonzales said softly from the Starlight
scope. He straightened up and stepped aside, his
eyes narrow, his lips pursed. He glanced at Sheets
and then at McGarvey and shrugged. "Maybe you
want to take a look, maybe you don't." He nodded
toward the scope. "But it's something."

He walked away and went down the hall to the
back bedroom. Lorraine and Sheets were watching
McGarvey, who felt as if he were on center stage in a
sideshow. He looked out the window. Nothing had
changed as far as he could tell with his naked eye.
Look, don't look. Stay, go. Think, don't think. Just
run away and keep running. Don't ever look back.
Christ, never look back.

Slowly he bent down to the scope's eyepiece. At

first the images were fuzzy, but when he adjusted the focus, the distant window frame leapt into sharp view, the open weave of the curtains like a patch-work gauze. He was looking into an upstairs bed-room of Yarnell's house. From this angle he could only see the forward half of the room. A man and a woman stood locked in an embrace next to a four-poster bed. It was a dangerous game they were playing. They had probably snuck off, leaving the others downstairs. The man's back was toward the window. When they parted, McGarvey was looking into the face of his ex-wife. Because of the effects of the infrared scope, Kathleen looked flushed, which in any event, he supposed she was. The man half turned, as if by request, giving McGarvey a clear view of him. Yarnell.

Oh, Kathleen, he thought. She'd always played dangerous games, but this time she could not know how precarious her position really was. For her as well as for Elizabeth. With nothing to lose, nothing seemed important. All of a sudden he felt a rush of protectiveness toward his ex-wife, and he didn't know why.

"What is it, Mr. McGarvey?" Lorraine asked.

Yarnell tenderly caressed Kathleen's cheek with his fingertips, and then kissed her forehead, her nose and again her lips, as if she were the most important person in the world to him, as if this were the most important moment, as if no one else in the world existed. Even from here McGarvey could feel the man's power. Kathleen would be helpless. Except, he suspected, she'd gone looking for it. But she didn't know, she could not know Yarnell's power.

Lorraine was beside him. "Is it your ex-wife?" she asked softly.

McGarvey looked up into her eyes. She seemed like a kind, sensitive girl, genuinely concerned for him. She was one of the good ones, he supposed, who cared. Unless she watched her step very carefully, she wouldn't last long in this business. The kind ones never did. There was no room for such sentiment.

"She's with Yarnell," he said, and he stepped away from the scope.

Lorraine watched him for a moment or two. "She couldn't know about him."

"I don't think so."

Lorraine looked through the scope for just a second, then straightened up. "Looks like they're putting on a show down there." She turned to Sheets. "We'll stick around at least until Mr. Trotter shows up. Did he say when?"

Sheets had already backed off for whatever reason. "He's in town. Said he'd be here in a minute or two."

McGarvey lit a cigarette. He stood beside the window looking out into the night, the city glowing in every direction, even up toward the Naval Observatory in the center of its own big park along with the vice president's mansion. The only darkness seemed to be in his own mind. Unwanted light was everywhere else. Strange and unfair, he thought. Thankfully Elizabeth was away at school. At least she would be spared the immediate hurt. Once again he was reminded of the women in his life: his sister, his ex-wife, his Swiss police watchdog, and Evita Perez, waiting for him in New York. They were all of a kind; judgmental women who in the end were very weak. Or, he wondered, was it merely his own chauvinism which made him think so?

Trotter was all out of breath when he barged into the apartment, as if he had just run up the eight flights of stairs. He stood puffing in the center of the room while he mopped the sweat off his brow with a handkerchief. He was flushed, and his glasses were steamed up. McGarvey noticed that he hadn't shaved since this morning and that he still wore the same clothes he had worn at their lakeside meeting with Leonard Day. He had to wonder what his old friend had been up to.

"I need time, John," McGarvey said.

"You were there this morning!" Trotter cried, his sudden emotion all out of proportion with what he was saying. "You heard him!"

"Forty-eight hours is all I need."

"To do what—?" Trotter started, but then realizing exactly what it was he was saying, and in front of whom, he cut it off.

"I'll get you and Leonard your proof, and you won't have to do a thing except keep watch on Yarnell from here. Just like you've been doing for the past three days. Just like you've done today."

"We can't, Kirk, don't you understand? It's over now."

Someone had gotten to Trotter. It was written all over the man's face. "What happened, John? Today? Who'd you see? Who else knows about this now?"

"We cannot go on."

"My wife is down there!"

Trotter seemed genuinely pained. "I'm sorry, Kirk. My hands are truly tied. In this you must believe me. Just get out while you still can."

"Disappear, you mean?"

"Yes."

McGarvey shook his head. "Who was it who got to you, John? Who'd you see today?"

"I have my orders . . ."

"From the bureau, John? From Day? Who?"

Trotter was cornered. He seemed to be all arms and legs. Gangly. "The president," he whispered. "The president told me to stop."

27

Time had truly and honestly run out. Winter, spring, day, night; it no longer made any difference to McGarvey. He was a man who had finally come face to face with his own demons, who had come foursquare against his own inner voice, which whispered like some troll in the scuppers that he was not master of his own fate let alone the future of others. Kathleen would say—and had—that he was a man driven by unseen forces. Insanity or simple willfulness, who could say. In the morning he took the shuttle flight up to New York after spending an intense evening with a new Trotter; a Trotter he'd never imagined existed, a man beside himself with fright, cowed into submission by the awfulness of the situation. "Here we have the potential for the ultimate disaster," he'd cried at one point, not knowing where to turn or in whom to seek comfort or solace. All the forces were aligned against them. What did it matter if they *believed* they had the blessing of being right right on their side? What did it matter the distance they had come? Or the lives that hung in the balance? Trotter had no answer. No guarantees, in the end—and who among us could expect such assurances, had any right to expect such assurances?—but Trotter would do what he could. Basulto would be held for another forty-eight hours and the team at the Washington safe house would unofficially continue their surveillance. (They'd volunteered for it, with no backup should the situation fall apart!) Lastly, Basulto would be released on McGarvey's recognizance with travel funds and documents when the time came. "If he ran, I would say good riddance," a defeated Trotter said. "Nor at this point do I wish to know what you have in mind, where you would be taking him, or for what purpose."

"We may not be much, John, but we are honorable men."

Trotter shook his head. "There is no such animal, didn't you know?"

"Did the president talk to you directly, John? Did he telephone you, send you a memo? Did a messenger come? What?"

But Trotter never answered, and as he entered the city through the Midtown Tunnel, he put his old friend out of mind. Just for now, just until he had all the pieces lined up. By then what he was setting in motion would have a life of its own. He would be able to step back and watch and wait for the end of the world or for his salvation, for all their salvations, though he didn't think there'd be any thanks handed round at the end.

He paid the cabbie on the corner around the block from Evita's club and went the rest of the way on foot. SoHo was not a morning neighborhood in the sense of *daylight*. There were people out and about, workmen, students on their way to school, mothers with their children, but the majority of the residents, the well-to-do artists, the connected businessmen, the chic women with their entourages, were still indoors, sleeping.

The front door to St. Christopher's was locked. There was no bell and it took nearly five minutes of pounding before the big black man who acted as Evita's bodyguard opened the door to McGarvey's summons. He wore a gray jogging suit and a sweatband around his massive forehead. He had a permanent scowl on his face.

"She's asleep," he said before McGarvey could say anything. "You'll have to come back tonight." He started to close the door, but McGarvey blocked it.

"I have to talk to her. This morning. Now."

"Motherfucker," the big man said, the word drawn out. "You don't hear so good." He yanked the door all the way open and poked a massive paw into McGarvey's chest, shoving him backward and nearly off the step. "Come back tonight."

"I don't want any trouble with you, Harry," McGarvey said, spreading his hands in front of him. "So if you'll just be a good boy and run upstairs and tell Ms. Perez that I'm here . . ."

The big man shoved McGarvey back another step. "I'm getting powerful tired of you, white boy. I want your lily white ass out of here now."

McGarvey didn't want this. It was stupid, and yet he had been feeling a confrontation building up inside of him ever since Trotter had shown up in Lausanne. Even before that.

"This is important, Harry," he said, trying one last time to be reasonable. He put his overnight bag down on the stoop.

"Shit," the big man swore, coming forward. He grabbed a handful of McGarvey's jacket and swung him around, bouncing him hard off the door frame. McGarvey didn't resist; he went with it. He sagged as if his legs were giving out. The bouncer was very strong, but he wasn't very sophisticated. A street brawler, McGarvey figured.

Harry hauled him to his feet, leaving himself wide open. McGarvey drove a knee into the big man's groin. All the air went out of him and he

staggered backward. McGarvey hit him in the solar
plexus, the force of the blow sending the big man
sprawling back into the vestibule. McGarvey came
after him, driving a right into the man's face, then a
left and two more solid right jabs, causing blood to
gush from the big man's nose and mouth where his
lip was all cut up. He sank to the floor, his eyes
fluttering, his breath coming in big blubbering gasps.

McGarvey hauled the bouncer the rest of the
way into the vestibule, looked around on the street to
make sure that no one had witnessed the confrontation, grabbed his bag, then closed and locked the
door.

Except for the bouncer's labored breathing, the
building was quiet. The man was unarmed. He
hadn't been expecting trouble, or at least he hadn't
been expecting someone too tough for him.

McGarvey's right shoulder ached from where he
had been slammed into the doorway. He hauled the
bouncer across the vestibule and into the darkened
club room, where he dumped him behind the bar.
He'd be out for a while yet, and McGarvey didn't
think he would be in much shape to continue the
fight when he did finally come around.

Leaving his bag by the entry to the vestibule, he
went upstairs to Evita's apartment. The living room
was a mess. There'd apparently been a party here last
night and no one had bothered picking up afterward.
The place smelled of stale booze and cigarettes, and
the sweeter, burned-leaves odor of marijuana.
Evita's cocaine paraphernalia was out on the coffee
table in front of the fireplace; the vial lay open and
empty. He listened but heard nothing, not even
noises from out on the street. St. Christopher's was
taking a holiday.

He went to the back of the apartment, past an
efficiency kitchen, the sinks and counters filled with

dirty dishes, and down a short corridor to the rear bedroom. The door was open. He stepped inside. The curtains were closed over the four tall windows, leaving the large room in semidarkness. A raised platform at the center was dominated by a large circular bed. Evita was sprawled out asleep on the bed, her arms and legs spread. She was naked. In sleep her body seemed dissipated, tinged a little in blue as if she had circulatory problems, sagging here and there, flattened out, her neck too thin, her knees and ankles too bony.

For a moment McGarvey nearly turned around and walked away. She'd suffered enough. But he couldn't think of any other way of doing what had to be done; of calling Yarnell out, of exposing the mole in the CIA and of stopping Baranov once and for all. Looking down at her on the bed he had trouble seeing her as the little girl in Mexico City, as Yarnell's and Baranov's plaything, yet he knew it was true.

He went into the bathroom, switched on the light, and turned on the cold water in the shower. He laid out a towel and a robe, then went back into the bedroom. Evita was just beginning to stir. He picked her up. She was surprisingly light.

"What?" she mumbled, her eyes fluttering.

McGarvey carried her into the bathroom, opened the shower door with his toe and put her down on her feet at the edge of the spray. She reared back all of a sudden, but he shoved her under the cold stream and shut the door. She screamed at the top of her lungs and then thumped against the door.

"You sonofabitch! Cristo!"

"We're leaving in twenty minutes," McGarvey called. "I'll put on the coffee."

Evita was still crying and sputtering when he went back out to the apartment. Harry, the bouncer, stood in the doorway weaving on his feet. His nose and mouth were bloody. He had a gun.

"I didn't kill her," McGarvey said. "I just put her in the shower."

"Get out of here," the big man growled.

"I'm trying to help her."

"She don't need your kind of help, you sonofabitch."

McGarvey didn't move. "I'm going to make some coffee. Then we'll be leaving."

"Not with her."

"Someone is trying to kill her, Harry. I'm trying to stop it."

"All sorts of people trying to do that lady harm . . ."

"Herself included," McGarvey said. "I'm here to put a stop to it. Give her some peace."

"Shit."

"I'm not leaving without her, Harry. One way or the other."

The bouncer raised his pistol. It looked like a toy in his massive paw. But the edge of his anger was gone. This was beyond his ken. He didn't know what to do or say.

"Ask her, Harry. As soon as she's out of the shower, listen to her."

"Who the hell are you? You a cop or something?"

McGarvey shook his head. "You don't want to know. Believe me. I'll bring her back in a couple of days and you'll never be bothered again."

"Fuck you!"

"Save your breath, Harry, you don't have a chance in hell," Evita said from the bedroom doorway. She had put on a robe and wrapped a towel around her hair.

"You all right?" Harry asked.

"None of us has a chance in hell," she said. "Go get your face fixed. And put away that gun, for Christ's sake." She turned and went back into the bedroom.

Harry seemed deflated. He lowered his pistol and looked from the bedroom door to McGarvey. He shook his head. "What have you people done to that woman? You fucked her up royal, that's what." He shook his head again.

"What people?" McGarvey asked softly.

"Shit."

"Who else has come up here?"

"There's always someone here. Someone after her. Pushing her. Telling her stories. Making her do . . . things."

"Who?"

"I don't know. Names don't matter. But I see things. I watch things. We all do."

"Her husband?"

"I would have killed the bastard if he ever showed up here," the big man said with sudden feeling.

"Baranov? Does that name ring a bell, Harry? Have you heard that one? Was he here?"

"I don't know shit," the bouncer said. "You want her? You can have her. I don't need this shit anymore."

"I'll bring her back . . ."

"She'll never leave Mexico. Not this time." The bouncer stuffed the gun in his pocket and went to the door.

"When was she in Mexico last, Harry? It's important." McGarvey hadn't expected this.

The big man looked at him. His shoulders had sagged. He was carrying an impossibly heavy burden. "A year ago," he said softly. "Maybe a little longer."

"Did she go alone?"

"She was looking for him."

"Who?"

"Baranov."

"Did she find him?"

"Don't ask me. But she's been fucked up ever since."

"Did he come here? Did he come to see her?"

"I don't know, I've already told you. And I'll tell you something else. If you're taking her to see him, you'll lose her. She's right, you know."

"About what?"

"She hasn't got a chance in hell."

McGarvey watched him leave. He heard him on the steps, his tread slow and even, as if he were a man either starting out on a very long journey or just returning from one.

"He's a good man," Evita said from the bedroom door.

McGarvey turned to her. She had gotten dressed, but she looked like hell, her eyes red, her face wan, drawn. "It's time for the truth now," he said. "All of it."

"Are we going after Darby and Valentin? Is that why you've come?"

"Yes."

She seemed to think about it for a long moment. "Then the truth is what you'll get," she said. "Only I don't think you're going to like it very much."

It was late afternoon. Their flight was due to touch down in Mexico City a few minutes before eight. The plane was barely half-filled so they had three seats to themselves in the smoking section near the rear. A thin haze hung over them. They had drinks, but had passed on the dinner. The stews had left them alone for the past half hour. Evita was strung out. "I don't know what will happen to me if I have to meet face-to-face with him again. You can't imagine what he's like."

They were all bastards, McGarvey thought.

"He's worse than Darby," she said, looking out the window. "More ruthless. More sure of himself." She turned back. "He gets what he wants. Always."

"Why didn't you tell me that you went to Mexico City to see him?"

"It wasn't important." She shrugged. "It had nothing to do with what you wanted."

"Did you see him?"

"No. But I found him. That part was easy. He's living in our old house. Same staff for all I know," she said bitterly. "I had to find out."

McGarvey hadn't been following her until that moment when it suddenly occurred to him what she was talking about. "It was your daughter, Juanita."

"Someone told me she was there."

"With Baranov?"

"I didn't know. She went down with some of her friends from school. He would know she was there."

"Was she with him?"

"What do you want from me?" Evita flared. "Cristo!"

"Was she there? Was your daughter with Baranov?"

"Yes," she said in a small voice. "She and her friends were there. But I didn't find out about it until later. I didn't know at the time." She shook her head. "She was proud of herself. For all I know Darby made the introductions."

"Why didn't you do something about it?"

"I wanted to," she flared again. "I wanted to take a gun and shoot him dead. I wanted to make him suffer like I had. But it wasn't possible. Nothing is possible against him."

"Why did he come to you in New York, then?"

"He offered to give her back," she said. Her eyes were filling. "Do you understand me? He offered to sell me my own daughter. Which was a laugh because when she finally did come back to the States she went straight to her father. So everything I've done in the past nine months has been for nothing."

It was coming now, McGarvey thought. The truth, so far as Evita knew it. And he thought he had a good guess what it might be. All a part of Baranov's plan. The Russian had made his calculations well.

"What was the price?" he asked. "That you spy for him?"

"I had been his whore in the early days. It was time to graduate. To grow up. It was important that we all expand, that each among us finds our place, our purpose in life."

"You supplied the club and the call girls?"

She nodded. "And Valentin arranged for the marks. Most of them were diplomats from the UN. But we got a steady Washington crowd, too, especially on the weekends."

"The tables are wired for sound?"

"That's right. The cameras are in the ceilings and in my apartment, of course."

"Who collects the film?"

"No film. It's all electronic this time. Goes out over a phone line to somewhere in the city."

"No one comes to maintain the equipment?"

"Not in the nine months since it was installed."

"Do you have a switch so that you can turn the system off?" McGarvey asked. "When you want privacy?"

She shook her head.

"Everything that's said or done in the club, in your apartment, is transmitted?"

She nodded.

"Including our conversations?"

"Yes," she said. She smiled wanly. "I tried to warn you."

"But I wouldn't listen," McGarvey mumbled to fill the gap.

"Men never do."

He might not have heard her. He was thinking of everything that had gone before. The unexplained, the unexplainable had come clear. Or at least a significant portion had. But he hadn't told her everything. She hadn't been told, for instance, about Janos. She was a leak, but she wasn't the only one. He wondered then, about his own stupidity. He had made a colossal blunder with Evita. What other blunders had he made? In how many other instances had Baranov forseen his moves; in how many other places had Baranov anticipated his actions and lain in the bushes waiting for him? Somewhere a long time ago he had heard the notion that some lives are inevitable and that of those lives some are terrible yet necessary. It wasn't fate; rather it was more akin to the ball rolling downhill—once it began its journey nothing short of catastrophe could stop it, which was ironic because at the bottom of the hill lay another sort of catastrophe. McGarvey felt at that moment as if he were rushing headlong down his own path of inevitability, and had been ever since Santiago.

Evita told him a story about a young boy who lived in the small town of Bellavista and dreamed someday of going to the big city and doing great things. The problem was, he had no idea what a big city was and even less of an idea what a great thing might be. Nevertheless, he prayed every night for his dreams to come true and eventually they did. Only they turned into nightmares because of his stupidity.

It was clear she was telling a story about herself. "What happened?" McGarvey asked.

"It's simple. He got in over his head. He attracted too much attention and the vultures came after him."

"And?"

"In all of his life, the young boy never had more than a single centavo to call his own. One coin in his pocket. So his wish was that as often as he put his hand in his pocket, there would be a centavo for him. Hundreds of centavos. Thousands of centavos. Millions. But still only one centavo at a time."

"So he went to the big city. Did he do great things?"

"You don't understand. Who cares about a single centavo at a time, no matter how many of them there are? The little boy was not only very stupid, but he turned out to be a freak and finally an outcast among his own people."

"The problem is, I can't figure out what it is that Baranov is really after," McGarvey said. "He's been working on it for months, perhaps even years, and something is about to happen. Do the names Ted Asher or Arthur Jules mean anything to you? Anything at all?"

"Never heard of them," she said. "What have they got to do with this? Are they friends of Darby's?"

"They were murdered last year on their way to Mexico City."

Her eyes widened. "Valentin?"

"Most likely."

"Why? Were they investigating him?"

"I don't know," McGarvey said. "But I'd guess they were."

"He'll kill us, too, you know."

"He might try."

"He'd be crazy not to," Evita said. "And why are we going to him like this? What exactly do you hope to accomplish? Are you going to try to kill him?"

McGarvey thought again about Janos and Owens, and about himself. Baranov had had plenty of opportunities to have him killed. But not so much as one attempt had been made on his life. Baranov knew about him and so did Yarnell, through the surveillance equipment in Evita's club if nothing else. So why hadn't someone come after him in the middle of the night? Why hadn't someone planted a bomb in one of the cars he had rented? Why hadn't his hotel been staked out? Why hadn't they come after him and Basulto in Miami? Especially Basulto. It was the Cuban who blew the whistle, who fingered Yarnell and therefore Baranov.

"He owns Mexico City," Evita said. "He's been there twenty years or more. What do you think you can do against him?"

McGarvey just looked at her.

"What are you doing? You an ex-CIA officer and me a whore."

"He knew I was coming. He knew that someone like me would be talking to you."

"He knows everything."

"How, Evita? How could he know? Nine months ago I didn't even know."

"He's a magician."

"He's a Soviet spy, nothing more."

"He has friends everywhere."

"Like you?"

"I'm no friend of his!" she flared.

"But you worked for him."

She passed a hand over her eyes. "You don't understand, you can't understand even after everything I told you." She looked up. "But you will if you ever meet him face-to-face. Then you'll see."

"Does the name Basulto mean anything to you, Evita?" he asked. She stiffened. "Yes?" he prompted.

"It's a cubano name," she said. "Fairly common." She wasn't convincing.

"Francisco Artimé Basulto. He was in Mexico City in the old days."

She closed her eyes. "Maybe," she said hesitantly. "Did he say he'd gone to the Ateneo Español? Was he ever there? Did he know the names and places?"

"Yes. Do you remember him?"

"He was young. A fancy dresser. Threw his money around."

"That's the one," McGarvey said. "Did you know him?"

"He was around."

"You saw him, at the Ateneo?"

"At some of the parties, too."

"Was he ever with Baranov?"

She nodded. "And Darby. He was one of the regular crowd for a while."

"Baranov knew him?"

"Yes."

"Did he ever talk about Basulto with you? Did he ever mention his name? Say what kind of a person he was? Who he worked for?"

She was trying to remember. She shrugged her shoulders. "I don't know. Maybe. But he wasn't much, or I would remember him better. There were so many of them."

"Did he ever do any work for Baranov, that you know of? Or maybe for your husband?"

"I don't know."

"What happened to him?"

"He just left, I guess. I wasn't paying much attention in those days, I've already told you. Most of them were leaving then anyway. It wasn't the same any longer."

"Would you recognize him if you saw him now?"

"I might," she said.

"Did Baranov ever mention his name to you? In New York, perhaps, nine months ago?"

She was finally catching his drift. She looked a little closer at him. "No he didn't. What does Basulto have to do with this?"

"He told me that he saw your husband and Baranov together in Mexico City, when the Ateneo was going strong. Before the Bay of Pigs."

"So?"

"But he didn't know who your husband was, only that he was an American."

"That's hard to believe. Everyone knew Darby in those days."

"Basulto was arrested in Miami a few weeks ago. He told the FBI that your husband was working for the Russians. He said your husband was on the beach at the Bay of Pigs, where he murdered a CIA case officer who might have had certain suspicions."

"He's lying to you."

"About what?"

"About not knowing Darby and probably about everything else. He was at our house. More than once."

"He's coming to Mexico City to help us."

She laughed. "Then you are a bigger fool than I thought you were. If that Cuban is in on this, you've been led into a trap. All of us have."

"That's what we're going to find out," McGarvey said.

The night was very hot and still. A dense smog hung over the great city. Riding in from the airport in a beat up old taxi, McGarvey could taste the air and feel it at the back of his throat and in his eyes. Evita sat next to him, looking straight ahead, her slight body held rigidly erect. She had not said a thing since they landed except when the customs official asked if she had anything to declare. She did not, and she was passed through. Traffic was very heavy. The city was ablaze with lights. Much of the damage from the recent earthquake was still evident, and poverty was apparent everywhere from the side of the road. They came to the Hotel del Prado, across from La Alameda Park downtown, and McGarvey paid off the cabbie. Evita did not want to go upstairs immediately, so McGarvey gave their bags to an oddly reticent doorman and they walked across the street.

"It doesn't feel like home and yet it does," she said. "It's all different now."

"How?"

"I'm not a little girl anymore, and there's no one left for me."

"Harry didn't think you'd leave if you came back here."

"He's probably right, because there is nothing for me in New York or Washington, either."

"Your daughter . . ."

"Was lost to me the day Darby took over. And if she's been with Valentin, she's doubly lost."

Some sort of demonstration was going on across the park along the Avenida Hidalgo. People were hurrying toward the noise from all over the park and the surrounding streets. McGarvey thought the crowd sounded angry, but Evita didn't seem to notice at first.

"You'll be safe once this is finished," McGarvey said, trying to sound convincing. A bonfire was burning in the street. They could see the flames through the trees. "You're her mother. Once her father and Baranov are exposed, she'll come back to you."

"I don't think so."

"Everything will be different . . ."

They suddenly came within sight of the large crowd choking the avenue. Evita pulled up short. Long banners had been hung in the trees and between the streetlights. A lot of people carried signs.

"I think we should go to the hotel," she said.

"What do the banners say?"

"'Glory to work,'" she read. "'The party and the people are united. Long live the Soviet people, builders of Communism.'"

McGarvey took her by the arm and they headed back toward the protective darkness of the park. A huge roar went up from the crowd. McGarvey turned around in time to see a straw-filled figure dressed in tails, red-striped trousers and a top hat, a white goatee on its chin, burst into flames over the bonfire.

"*Libertad!*" the crowd screamed. "*Libertad!*"

28

At ten that evening McGarvey called Hialeah. "Morgan here, who's calling?"

"This is Kirk McGarvey. Let me talk to Artimé."

"Oh, they said you'd be calling," the FBI field man said. "When do we get rid of this scumbail?"

"In the morning. I want him on the first plane to Mexico City. But stay with him until the plane actually takes off."

"We've babysat the bastard this long, another ten or twelve hours won't hurt much. How much money do you want us to give him?"

"Fifty bucks. I don't want him having enough to wander off on me."

"Listen pal, once we get him aboard that plane in the morning and watch it take off, he's no longer our responsibility. I just want to get that straight with you. Once he leaves, he's your headache."

"Has anyone else called or tried to come up there?"

"No one except Washington."

"Trotter?"

"Yes."

"Put Basulto on, would you?"

"Yeah," the cop said. "It's for you," McGarvey

heard the man say away from the phone.

"Yes?" Basulto answered the phone cautiously.

"It's me. You're coming to Mexico City. We've got some work to do."

"Are we going to nail that bastard, Mr. McGarvey? Are we finally going to get him? Is he down there now? I thought he would be in Washington."

"I'll tell you about it when you get there. They'll take you out to the airport in the morning. I want you in Mexico as soon as possible."

"Sure thing. Will you be meeting me?"

"I want you to take a cab downtown. To the Hotel Del Prado just across from La Alameda."

Basulto laughed. It was the same hotel at which he had met his case officer, Roger Harris, in the sixties. "Sure," he said. "I think I can find the place. What room?"

"I haven't checked in yet. I'll leave word for you at the desk."

"Are you in Washington?"

"That's right," McGarvey lied. "We'll be flying down in the morning."

"We?"

"An old friend. Anxious to meet you as a matter of fact."

"Who is this . . .?"

"Tomorrow, Artimé. We'll talk tomorrow." McGarvey hung up.

Their room was on the small side, but clean and reasonably well furnished. A crucifix hung over the bed, and on the opposite wall, over the bureau, was a large print of the Last Supper. A braided rug covered most of the tiled floor, and the large windows opened inward from a tiny balcony. Evita stood at the balcony's ornamental grillwork and looked across the park at the demonstration still going on.

"They don't like Americans," she said. "They've always blamed their poverty—and even their earthquakes—on the Americans."

"Is there anything more I should know about Basulto before he gets here?"

"Kirk McGarvey is a good name," she said seriously. "Better than Glynn, I think."

"Evita?"

"I told you everything I know." She turned around. "Nobody liked him. I don't think anybody trusted him. There was a rumor that he had worked for the Batista government. We were surprised that Castro's people didn't assassinate him."

She'd been a naïve little girl, intimidated by events around her, yet she remembered Basulto from twenty-five years ago even though she'd said she only saw him a few times. Who could he trust? Who could he believe? He didn't know any longer. Perhaps he'd never really known.

"Let's take a drive." McGarvey removed his pistol from the false bottom of his toiletries kit. "We've talked enough about Baranov; I want to see him."

Despite the lateness of the hour, McGarvey was able to arrange for a rental car through the hotel. The desk clerk asked him twice how long he would be staying in Mexico City and seemed pleased when McGarvey replied that unfortunately business would probably be taking him back to Washington in a day, two at the most.

The clerk looked at Evita as if he knew her, or wanted to. She said something to him in Spanish and he reared back as if he had been slapped. Leaving the hotel she refused to talk about it. McGarvey thought she looked ashamed.

Their car was a gray Volkswagen beetle with a

very loud muffler and a radio that did not work. McGarvey found a street map in the glove compartment.

"It's in the south," Evita said. Her face was pale in the light from the hotel entrance. The doorman was watching them.

"What?" McGarvey asked, looking up.

"Valentin's house. Our old house. San Juan Ixtayopan. In the mountains."

"We'll get out there. First I want to swing past the Soviet embassy."

"It's just around the corner," she said automatically.

McGarvey put down the map. "You have been there?"

"Yes. With Valentin," she said defensively. "He sometimes took me there at night. To the *referentura*. He was showing me off."

The *referentura* in all Soviet embassies was the equivalent of a safe room or screened room. Physically and electronically secure from the rest of the facility, it was the room in which KGB plans were formulated and carried out. It was the heart of KGB operations in any country. Even Baranov had to have taken chances bringing her there. But then the Russian was young in those days. And brash?

"Did you ever go over there with your husband?"

Evita shook her head.

"Did he ever go there alone to meet with Baranov?"

"I don't know. He never said and I never asked."

Traffic along the Avenida Juárez was heavy. Even over the blare of their muffler, they could hear the crowd noises from across the park. McGarvey waited for a break and then pulled out.

"What are we going to do at the embassy?" Evita asked.

"Maybe they'll offer us a nightcap if they recognize you," McGarvey said, not bothering to hide the sarcasm in his voice. Still she was lying to him. Even now she was holding back, telling him only what she thought he wanted to hear at the moment. It was habit from a lifetime of lying. A lifetime of deceit for fear that she would be found out for what she really was; a poor silly girl without a mind of her own. He wanted to despise her, yet he found he couldn't. If anything he felt sorry for her.

He turned left on López which ran along the east end of the park, then right onto the broad Calzada de Tacubaya after the traffic light changed. Behind them they could see the huge mass of the crowd completely filling the Avenida Hidalgo, several bonfires now lighting up the night sky, armed policemen behind barricades at all the corners leading toward the disturbance.

The Russians would be pleased with this latest round of unrest. In 1971 they nearly succeeded in maneuvering Mexico into a civil war. This time it seemed possible they might succeed. Certainly the mood of the Mexican government was different now than it had been in 1971; more hostile toward the U.S., under seige this time because of falling oil prices, massive unemployment, and several devastating earthquakes over the past few years, not to mention the continuing strife over the drug issue.

They passed behind the Palace of Fine Arts and across San Juan Letrán, the main post office. A statue of Charles IV stood in front of the College of Mines. Traffic was moving at a breakneck pace. McGarvey wanted to slow down, but the drivers behind him honked their horns impatiently.

"It's number 204, behind the tall iron fence on

the next block," Evita said. "Valentin's office will be on the second floor."

McGarvey pulled over out of traffic and parked across the street. The Soviet embassy was housed in an old Victorian villa complete with shuttered windows, ornate cupolas, tall brick chimneys, the roof bristling with antennae and aerials. Two light globes were perched above the entry gate, and inside the grounds were ablaze with light. Something big was happening at the embassy, something very big. McGarvey thought about the crises he had weathered at other embassies around the world. It was the same as this. Every window in the building was lit. The cipher machines would be running full tilt. Messages would be streaming back and forth between Moscow. The Mexican unrest, the missile crisis.

A dark Ford van came down the avenue and turned in at the embassy gate. The driver flashed his headlights and moments later the gates swung open and the van drove through, the gates closing behind it.

"He's probably inside now," Evita said in a small voice.

McGarvey glanced at her. Her eyes were wide, her lips pursed. She was shivering. "There's trouble. He'll be preoccupied. Time now for him to make a mistake."

She shook her head. "He never makes mistakes."

"We'll see," McGarvey said.

A man inside the compound came to the gate and looked across the street at them. He didn't move. A second man joined him, they said something to each other, and he turned and went away.

"They've seen us," Evita said.

"But they can't know who we are. Not yet."

"What are you waiting for? For Valentin to show up? Let's get out of here. We can't do anything."

McGarvey stared across at the other man for a long time. He wanted the Russians to see them. He wanted them to know they'd come. He wanted them to know that everything wasn't going to go their way this time. At least in this one thing, Baranov was going to lose.

"Please, Kirk," Evita said. "I am becoming frightened."

"Where is the American embassy?" McGarvey asked. "Is it far from here?"

"Not far," she said. "On the Paseo de la Reforma. Back the way we came."

McGarvey put the car in gear, waited for a gap in the traffic, and made a U-turn so that they passed directly in front of the Soviet embassy gate. Evita turned her head so that she would not be seen, but McGarvey looked directly at the Russian guard. Tell Baranov I've come for him. Tell him it won't be long now. And then they were past and turning again at the barricades blocking Hidalgo, the demonstration still building. Even more police had arrived, and they were anxiously directing traffic away from the park.

The crowd had spilled clear across the park onto the Avenida Juárez. They had to drive two blocks farther south before they could turn back to the west past the Hotel Metropol.

"What can you hope to accomplish here like this?" Evita asked. "Just driving around the city at night. Sooner or later someone will spot us. Valentin has his spies everywhere."

"I want him to know that we're here."

"This is insanity!"

"The insanity, Evita, has been going on for twenty-five years. I'm going to end it."

"It'll end when you're dead," she cried. "He'll kill us all, and in the end he'll get his way."

She was beginning to come apart. It was too soon. He needed her for a little while longer. "Listen to me, Evita. You're going to have to be strong, but just for a couple of days."

"I can't," she cried.

"You won't have to do a thing except make a phone call. One call tomorrow night. After that you can come back to New York. I promise you."

"Then what are we doing out here like this tonight?" she screeched. She held out her hand. "No, you don't have to tell me, you bastard! You're provoking him! You're parading around his city with me. You're showing him that you aren't afraid of him. Well I am!"

She was right. But he needed her. "I'll put you on a plane first thing in the morning, if that's what you want."

"You're goddamned right that's what I want!"

"He and your husband will have won."

"I don't care!"

"And Juanita will be theirs. Body and soul. She'll have about as much chance as you had." He was thinking about his ex-wife, Kathleen, and his daughter. They didn't have much of a chance either. Maybe it was too late for them after all. Maybe he was charging at windmills. Maybe he should have remained with Marta in Switzerland. Lausanne seemed so terribly far away just now. Unattainable. Unreal. As if that part of his life had never occurred.

"Oh, you bastard," she said.

"Forty-eight hours, maybe less," he told her, turning the corner onto the Paseo de la Reforma. She buried her face in her hands and began to sob.

A double row of tall trees lined the main boulevard, Mexico City's most magnificent. Stone and bronze statues of national heroes seemed to be everywhere. It reminded McGarvey of Rome's Via Vento or Paris's Champs Elysées. He expected to see legions marching in broad phalanxes to the roar of cheering crowds.

They came around a traffic circle at the center of which was a towering monument to Cristóbal Colón, which was the Spanish name for Christopher Columbus. If anything, traffic was much heavier now. There seemed to be an urgency throughout the city. A stridency to the note of the horns, to the snarl of the engines, to the movement of the pedestrians crossing against the lights and in the middle of the blocks.

Banners still proclaimed the opening of a new gallery in the Banco International next to the Hotel Continental and the statue of Cuauhtemoc, the last Aztec emperor, still rose above the intersection with Avenida Insurgentes—and all of it was cast in a violet glow from the streetlights. Mexico City was a pagan arena.

They could hear the roar of the crowd before they could see it. Traffic began immediately to slow. Evita looked up and sat forward.

"What is it now?" she asked.

"I think it's our embassy," McGarvey replied absently as he looked for a place to turn around. He did not want to get caught in a traffic jam here.

A blue and white police car, its lights flashing and its sirens blaring, raced past, followed by three ambulances. In the distance they could hear gunfire.

"What's happening?" Evita cried, holding her ears.

Two canvas-covered army trucks roared up from a side street and careened around the traffic circle, pulling to a halt on the grass. Immediately two dozen armed soldiers leaped from the trucks and on their officer's orders took up positions across the boulevard. Traffic came to a complete standstill and began to back up. A huge explosion lit the night sky with a tremendous flash and a heavy thump. A ball of fire rose from a building on the next block. Some of the soldiers looked over their shoulders, while others ran forward up the broad boulevard, motioning with their weapons for the cars and trucks to turn around. But it was impossible. Already traffic was backed up for several blocks.

People began piling out of their cars, talking excitedly with each other, shouting at the soldiers and pointing toward the flames and sparks shooting up into the sky. In the distance, from all directions, it seemed, they could hear sirens converging on the scene of the explosion. McGarvey had little doubt that it was the American embassy. Already he was considering the danger he was in because of his nationality. Evita might get by, but he didn't know more than a dozen words in Spanish. The mood of the crowd on this side of the army barrier was rapidly turning ugly. He'd found out what he wanted to find out in any event. The mood in Mexico City was rabidly anti-American, and the Soviet embassy had seemed to be on standby for an emergency.

They were near the head of the traffic jam. McGarvey eased the Volkswagen out from behind a taxi and bumped slowly up onto the median strip, ignoring the shouts for him to go back. One of the soldiers rushed down from the traffic circle, brandishing his rifle and shouting for them to stop.

"You're sick," McGarvey told Evita. "We have to get you to the hospital."

Evita's eyes were wide. She looked from the advancing soldier to McGarvey and back.

"Hospital! Hospital!" McGarvey shouted out the window.

Another grim-faced soldier raced over. Evita

suddenly held her gut and doubled over, screaming in what sounded like agony.

McGarvey took his pistol out of his pocket and laid it on the seat beside his right leg. He'd come too far, he decided, to be caught like this without a fight.

"Hospital," he shouted out the window again. And Evita moaned as if she were half-dead. It was a convincing performance.

A crowd was beginning to gather around them. The soldiers held a hurried conference and then stepped aside, waving McGarvey onto the traffic circle toward a side street that headed north.

"Hospital de la Raza," one soldier shouted. "De la Raza." He was gesturing toward the north. "Insurgentes Norte," he shouted as McGarvey passed.

The other soldiers watched them curiously as they drove past. Before they turned up Calles Rhin, McGarvey got a clear view down the broad boulevard at the huge crowd. The front of the U.S. embassy had been blown away and had collapsed into the street. Half the block was engulfed in flames. Soldiers seemed to be everywhere. The sounds of gunfire were clearly audible over the screaming and shouting of the crowd, the sirens, and the blaring bullhorns warning the people back.

They had to wait for three army trucks racing down from Avenida Lerma before they were able to cross and head back east, making a wide circle around the traffic backed up along the Paseo de la Reforma.

"Where are we going now?" Evita shouted.

"I want to see Baranov's house," McGarvey said, turning south along Avenida Bucareli. Traffic was heavy here, too, but in the opposite direction. The entire city, it seemed, was rushing toward the U.S. embassy.

"You're crazy. Let's go to the airport. Now. We've got to get out of here."

"First Baranov. And then we'll return to the hotel and stay there, out of sight."

"No."

"Yes, Evita. We've come too far to be stopped now. He's not going to win this time."

"He already has," she cried. "It wasn't the Russian embassy that was blown up. He's won, can't you see it? What use will it be if we're killed?"

McGarvey looked over at her. She had pinned up her long hair, but it was coming loose and hung in wisps around her face. She looked vulnerable. There was an hysterical edge to her voice now, and her eyes were a little wild.

"Do you think it'll make any difference if we return to New York? If he wants us, he'll get us no matter where we are."

"Then what are we doing here?"

"Maybe he'll make a mistake."

"And then you'll kill him? Is that it? Is that what you're doing here?"

"If need be."

"But it's not just him you're after," she said. "You want Darby, too, and maybe someone else. Is that it? Is there someone else? Another spy?"

"I don't know."

"Then what are we doing here like this? I'm supposed to telephone someone tomorrow? Who? What am I supposed to tell this person?"

They turned onto the broad Fray Servando Teresa de Mier; traffic was still heavy but moving much faster now, allowing McGarvey to speed up.

"If I'm to help you, I need to know what I'm supposed to do." She was trying to be reasonable.

"I want to see Baranov's house. I want to see where he lives."

She looked out the window. "What if I don't give you directions?"

"He's near Ixtayopan," McGarvey said tiredly. "I'll ask around."

"You're completely crazy."

"Probably. But I'm not going to stop."

"You'd never find him."

"It would take time, but I'd find him," McGarvey said. "Because he wants to be found. He knew that I was coming to see you, and he knew that you would help me."

She closed her eyes. "I don't understand."

"Neither do I," McGarvey said.

"What?" she asked, opening her eyes.

"Did Baranov tell you why I would be coming to see you?" he asked her. "Did he tell you that I would be coming after your husband and that you were to cooperate with me? Did he make you promise to tell me all about Mexico City in the early days? How your husband was a spy and how he worked for the Russians as well as the Americans?"

"It doesn't make any sense." She was avoiding his questions.

"It's all right if it scares you, Evita, it scares the hell out of me, too."

"But what is he after? What kind of a plot has he hatched?"

"It has something to do with the Soviet missiles here. And something else. Someone he may be trying to protect."

"Valentin wants Darby to be found out. He wants you to arrest him."

"I think so."

"But why?"

"I don't know, Evita. But that's why we're here. It's the one thing Baranov did not expect us to do."

* * *

To the southeast the road rose in tiers from the high plateau valley toward snow-capped mountains. Back the way they had come the city spread itself out across half the horizon, wonderfully lit avenues and streets stretching across the valley like long necklaces; tall buildings, radio towers, and even moving traffic along the broader avenues were clear despite the smog that blanketed the valley. They passed through Culhuacan, Tezonco, Zapotitlan, Tlalenco, Tlahuac, and Tulyehualco—cities that had been all but swallowed by the city's sprawl. Each was a little smaller than the previous one, and each had its own character, but they all seemed in a touristy way to want to return to the days of the Aztecs. Eighteen miles out from the center of the city traffic had finally thinned out so that now, driving southwest out of San Juan Ixtayopan toward the peak of Cerro Tuehtli, they were finally alone on the dark road. Their car was very loud as they crossed the mountains, but then McGarvey wasn't interested in hiding his presence; he wanted Baranov to know that someone was coming, that his Mexican fortress wasn't as impregnable as he might suspect it was. So what are you trying, you bastard? Everything points toward Darby Yarnell, your old pal and confidante, even your lover if Evita is to be believed (and he thought she was). Did he quit on you? Did he get too big for his britches, demand too much? Or did he want asylum just when you finally tired of him and wanted to get rid of him? Or had Darby Yarnell simply outlived his usefulness, and now it was time to dump him? What was he missing? McGarvey asked himself. Where was the one twist, the one fact, the one lie that in the light of day would make everything clear?

As they crossed a bridge spanning a deep ravine, they could see a large house alive with lights perched on the edge of the mountain above them. The road entered the trees and curved left before switching back. Suddenly they could see the house again, much closer now, and they could pick out dozens of automobiles parked in a front courtyard. Japanese lanterns hung in the trees, and they could see people dancing on a broad veranda that was cantilevered out over the side of the hill.

McGarvey pulled up a hundred yards below the house, doused his lights, and shut off the engine. In the sudden silence they could hear music and laughter and even bits of conversation, voices raised in celebration. Baranov was Nero: he was throwing a party while Mexico City burned.

He hadn't expected this. Baranov should have been at his embassy. The country was in crisis. And yet there seemed to be a logic to it. Baranov had envisioned some master plan, and now he was apparently celebrating his victory. The notion made the hair on the back of McGarvey's neck stand on end.

Evita sat back in her seat, shivering. She was remembering what it had been like for her in the old days.

"He's an arrogant sonofabitch," McGarvey said, reading her thoughts. "He *does* think he's won."

The band stopped playing and they could hear applause. McGarvey got out of the car and walked around to the passenger side. He took out two cigarettes, lit them both, and handed her one through the open window. At first she didn't move, but then she reached up and accepted the cigarette from him.

"The question is, what has he won?" McGarvey drew deeply on his cigarette. He stepped a few feet down the road so that he could better see the house above. "He must really impress the Kremlin. Do you know that the Russians have apparently constructed missile bases just south of our border? Mexico has come a long way since the sixties." Someone laughed from above and the music started again; this time the tune was a rumba. "He likes people. Have you any idea what he's up to?"

"He wants to take over the world," Evita said from just behind him.

McGarvey didn't bother to turn around. But he knew she had gotten out of the car. He heard the door close softly.

"He was afraid that the moderates would someday take control of the Soviet Union and give away everything they had gained since the war," she said.

"He wanted to speed things up."

"He wanted to be first secretary and premier."

"Maybe he will be." McGarvey flipped his cigarette off the side of the road and walked back to the car. Evita stood, one hand on the roof, her hip leaning against the door as if she needed support, which in a way she certainly did.

"I could go up there now and he would welcome me with open arms."

"Do you want to take the car, or walk?"

She looked up toward the house. "Who's to say he isn't right?"

"And I'm wrong?"

She looked at him. "Yes."

"Depends upon the geography. If we were standing below his dacha outside Moscow, I'd have to concede that he was right. But we're not."

She thought about this for a moment, then shook her head. "Can it be that simple?"

"Probably not. But I've run out of answers. Two good people have been murdered in the last few days because of him. One of them was my friend. He left a wife and children." He started for the other side of the car.

"No, don't," Evita said.

"Whatever you do or don't do, I can't leave it," McGarvey said. He thought again about Kathleen and about Marta. Both were strong women. And yet he couldn't get over the feeling that Evita was vulnerable, that she needed someone to hold her close, that that was all she had ever needed.

"Then go up and kill him!"

"I need the answers first."

"They won't do anyone any good."

"I think they will."

"No."

"Yes, Evita," he said softly. "I want your help. I need your help."

"I can't," she cried in anguish.

"Then go to him," McGarvey said harshly. "I'll do it myself."

He got in the car, started the engine, and switched on the headlights. Evita stood at the side of the road for another moment or two, then turned, opened the door, and got in. She hunched down in the seat, silent and pale, a little leaf of Autumn caught against her will in the ocean currents, totally without hope or control.

29

It was after two in the morning by the time they got back into the city. Traffic was still heavy. Fires could be seen here and there. Big crowds had gathered on many of the street corners, in some of the plazas and squares, and in front of American business establishments and offices. Banners seemed to be everywhere, proclaiming "Liberty from North American Aggressors," "Freedom From American Colonialism," and "True Independence At Last." Ordinary traffic was still barred from a wide area around the U.S. embassy so they couldn't get close enough to see what was happening. They returned to the hotel instead.

"What happened between you and that desk clerk earlier this evening?" McGarvey asked as they rode up in the elevator.

"Nothing," Evita said woodenly.

"Did he say something to you? I couldn't hear it."

She looked up. "Nothing. It was in his eyes." She looked away again. "He thought I was your whore."

"I'm sorry."

"Don't be," she said. "You know the funny thing about it is that I've been nearly everyone's whore except yours."

"What did you say to him?"

She actually smiled a little. "I told him that if he couldn't keep his dirty little thoughts to himself I would cut off his balls and stuff them down his throat."

McGarvey sat in a chair by the open window smoking a cigarette and watching the dawn break over the city as Evita slept on the bed. She was keyed up. She had wanted to talk, to be comforted by him, but he had made her take a bath and crawl in between the clean sheets. "You're going to need your strength when Basulto shows up," he told her. She wore one of his shirts as a nightgown. He had tucked her in and had kissed her on the forehead as he might a young child. She was asleep within a minute or two.

The demonstrations across the park had broken up sometime in the early morning hours, and from here the only traces of unrest he could detect were the lingering odors of smoke from the fires. Blue and white police cars continued to cruise past at regular intervals, each time a different car. Most of Mexico City's police force seemed to be on duty this morning. At four o'clock a convoy of army trucks rumbled past. At four-thirty a big automatic street washer lumbered by. At five the morning delivery vans and trucks began coming, bringing milk and bread and laundry and fresh meat and vegetables to the hotels and restaurants. At five-thirty the eastern sky began to lighten perceptibly.

His mood darkened with the morning. It was exhaustion, he knew, yet he could not help himself from sliding toward the edge of despair, where he began to doubt his abilities as well as his sanity. He was frightened that he no longer had anyone to trust and just a little intimidated by a sudden inability to envision Marta's face in his mind's eye. When he tried to think of her, he could only see Evita's face and eyes framed by her long dark hair. Thinking that way was nonsense because in truth she *had* been everyone's whore except his. And he felt more pity for her, he thought, than lust.

He turned around. Evita was sitting up in bed, the covers gathered in her lap. She was watching him, her eyes wide, her face almost serene, guileless in this light.

"I want you," he said, surprised by his own words.

"I don't want charity."

"It's not charity."

"The spoils of war, then." Her voice was flat, dull.

"Not that either. I don't think I give a damn about any of it now. If Baranov wants Mexico he can have it. It's not up to me to decide, or to change the world. I don't care if there is a traitor in the CIA. That's not up to me to fix, either. And I don't know if I really care about you. I don't know if I'm still capable of caring, if I was ever capable of it. I only know that I want you."

She pushed the covers back. Without taking her eyes off his, she took off his shirt and let it fall to the floor. Her chest was heaving, her nipples were erect, there was a faint flush to her forehead and cheeks, and her lips shimmered. She lay back on the pillow and reached out a hand for him.

"Come," she said. "I will be your whore as well."

He got up and took off his clothes. She watched him. When he came across the room she spread her legs and reached up to him, pulling him down. He entered her immediately, gathering her in his arms, kissing her deeply, her tongue darting against his.

Her hips rose to meet his, and she wrapped her long dancer's legs around his waist, drawing him even more deeply inside of her.

"It will never be all right between us," she said softly. A low moan escaped her lips as he thrust against her, trying to bury himself in her.

"Only now matters," he said.

"We may be dead tomorrow."

He wanted to say they were dead already, but he was losing himself with her, and nothing truly mattered except for this moment.

"I don't love you," she cried.

"No."

"I've never loved anyone."

They lay in each other's arms watching the sun rise, listening to the sounds of the city coming alive beneath their open window.

"As a young girl I studied to become a classical guitarist." She touched a scar on his chest with a long, delicate finger. "I used to wonder how my life would have turned out had I never met Darby or Valentin."

A car horn beeped outside and in the distance they could hear a siren. But it was much quieter than it had been last night. He reached over and kissed her breast. She lay back and held his head in her hands.

"I don't know what you want me to do," she said. "I don't know what you expect of me with this Cubano coming, but I'll do it. I think from the moment you showed up at the club I knew that I would do something for you."

McGarvey looked into her eyes. "I'm returning to Washington this afternoon."

"Leaving me here with Basulto?"

He nodded. Her eyes were very dark and very deep. He felt as if he might fall into them. If that happened he knew he would never get back out.

"You didn't mean what you said before, about not caring any longer."

He shrugged.

She smiled sadly. "I understand how it is with your kind. It's the Holy Grail you're all after. Only most of the time you never get it. You never even come close."

"I have to see it to the end."

"Naturally," she said. "Who will I call for you?"

"Your husband."

She closed her eyes and opened them. "And tell him what?"

"That you're down here with a Cuban who knew him from the Bay of Pigs. That it was I who brought you both down here, and that I know everything about him and about Baranov and about the other one in the CIA."

"He'll run."

"Tell him that I want to make a deal. It's no longer safe for him up there and he'd better get out while he can still save himself. Tell him Baranov is here waiting for him, too. That you'll all be together again like in the old days."

"When? What time?"

"Eleven in the evening; nine local time. This evening." Mexico City time was two hours behind U.S. eastern daylight time.

"And you'll be there. Watching him. Waiting to see who he runs to."

McGarvey touched her hip. She shivered.

"Maybe he won't run after all," she said, covering his hand with hers.

"He will."

"And then you'll know who else has been corrupted. And it'll be finished for you."

"Hopefully," McGarvey said. He wondered though if he truly cared, or if he had just been going through the motions. Except for poor Janos Plónski and the old man, Owens, he might not have come this far. Might not have pushed as hard as he had. Might have backed down when Day ordered him to.

"Valentin will know that I am here," she said softly.

"He doesn't want you any longer. You've served his purpose."

"He'll warn Darby. Maybe he's already warned him."

"No," McGarvey said. He reached over and lit a cigarette. "He wants Darby to fall."

"Why?"

"I don't know yet."

She sat up, her eyes suddenly bright. "He knew you'd find out. He wanted you to find out. Which means there's something else happening. He never does anything without a purpose."

"It looks like it."

"Is Basulto working for Valentin?"

McGarvey had thought about it, of course. Now he weighed the possibilities again. On the surface it seemed likely that the Cuban had been working for the Russians in the old days, and that he had set up his case officer, Roger Harris, to be killed at the Bay of Pigs. But it was just as possible that Basulto wanted out now. He had watched Harris fall, and he was at least in part the reason why Yarnell would fall. Maybe he saw his own future in the same terms. The game had gotten too rough for him, so he was trading Yarnell's life for his own. The coincidental timing was hard to accept, unless of course Baranov's sources had told him about Basulto's defection and he had worked up his own program to take advantage of Yarnell's fall.

"I don't know that either," he said quietly.

"I see."

Where did it fit? he asked himself, watching how the light made Evita's skin take on a golden glow. He had felt the Russian's presence almost from the beginning, and he supposed he had behaved badly in not protecting the people who had helped him.

"You want me to stay here with him, is that it?"

"Not in the same room."

She laughed.

"I'll leave you my gun."

"Maybe I'll save us all a lot of trouble."

"How?"

"By shooting him and then myself."

The clerk was clearly hostile when McGarvey went down to the desk to arrange and pay for Basulto's room. Evita had promised not to leave the hotel, but it was clear that she was barely hanging onto her nerves. He promised that it would be over by morning, but she didn't believe it, and he wondered if he did.

"I'll be leaving tomorrow," McGarvey told the clerk. He would be out and back before anyone knew that he was gone.

"Perhaps it would be wiser, señor, if you left Mexico today." He was young, with an olive complexion and a pencil-thin mustache. His manner was oily. "The hotel, of course, cannot guarantee your safety under the circumstances."

"What circumstances?" McGarvey asked stepping a little closer.

"There is unrest here, señor." The man's eyes strayed to a pile of newspapers at the end of the counter. One of them, the *Mexico City News*, was in English. Its headlines blared: AMERICAN SPY PLANE SHOT DOWN OVER MEXICO.

McGarvey quickly scanned the article. An SR-71 spy plane had been shot down sometime yesterday thirty miles inside Mexican territory. The information was scant; the story obviously censored by the government. But the plane was definitely American. The pilot's body had been recovered and identified.

McGarvey looked up. The clerk was staring at him.

"Have my bill prepared. I'll be leaving before noon."

"And Miss Perez?"

"Her brother-in-law is coming this morning. He will stay with her."

"He is cubano."

"Are you at war with Cuba as well?"

The clerk reared back. "Your bill will be waiting for you."

"When Señor Basulto arrives, tell him to meet me at Roger Harris's. He knows the place."

"Yes, señor."

The clerk went back into his office. McGarvey crossed the lobby and went outside, conscious of the pressure of the gun in his belt at the small of his back.

He found a public telephone three blocks away, across the street from the national lottery building. The international lines, especially to the States, were jammed, and it took more than ten minutes to get through to the number Trotter had given him.

It was answered, as before, on the first ring by the same man. "Yes?"

"Basulto is on his way to Mexico City. What time does he arrive?"

"Pan Am, 9:05 local."

"Tell Trotter to meet me at the safe house tonight at ten-thirty."

"He wants to talk to you . . ."

McGarvey hung up. It was already nine o'clock. If Basulto's plane was on time and there were no delays with customs, he would be at the hotel sometime between 9:30 and 10:00. His own flight left at 1:25, getting him in at Washington's National Airport at 9:40. The timing was tight, but it was coming to a head finally. By tonight it would be over, with only the repercussions to deal with. This time when he thought about Marta he could see her face. Switzerland was out, but perhaps she wouldn't mind living in France or Greece. Or was it simply wishful thinking; another product of his exhausted state?

By ten McGarvey, waiting across from the hotel in the park, was becoming impatient. Something might have gone wrong in Miami. Baranov certainly knew by now that Basulto was there. Perhaps he had ordered the man assassinated. It wasn't unthinkable considering everything else that had gone on. The Cuban had outlived his usefulness, hadn't he? Or was there a flaw in that thinking? Baranov had been celebrating last night, or at least he had put up a damned good show of it. Which meant, as far as Baranov was concerned, this business was as good as done. As it had last night on the mountain road below the Russian's villa, the thought raised the hair at the back of McGarvey's neck. Circles within circles. Lies within lies. Plots within plots. Baranov was the master.

Sitting on a bench watching the busy traffic he turned his thoughts to Evita; poor, frightened, abused little Evita waiting upstairs in the hotel room. He was astonished at his own behavior, and all the more guilty because he knew with certainty that Marta would understand. Or at least she would pretend to understand though he suspected she would secretly be hurt. But even more astonishing to him were his feelings toward Marta which had surfaced in the morning. He was allowing himself to think for the first time in a very long time that he was actually in love with someone.

In Lausanne the apartment would have been cleared out by now and Marta would be in her own place. He wondered what her real home was like and if she went back there when he was away at work, only returning to their apartment when he was coming back. It made him sad to think how he had treated her during their last years, especially the last weeks.

He had taught her how to ski after she had cheerfully admitted she was probably the only Swiss in history who didn't know how. It was in the early days of their relationship. He had learned to ski as a boy in Colorado and Montana. They spent a week in Zermatt working every morning on the lower slopes, making love in their room all afternoon, and dancing in the evening in the lodge. On the first day he had spent a frustrating two hours trying to teach her the basic snowplow turn. Out of the corner of his eye he had seen an older man in knickers, a bright red and blue sweater and a Tyrollean hat leaning against his ski poles watching them. Each time Marta would lean into the turn she would fall until at last she got it right, and he had hugged her, lifting her right out of her skis. The man watching them executed a perfect jump turn and schussed off down the hill yodeling in the best Swiss tradition. Marta had noticed him from the beginning. She laughed.

"I don't know who had more patience, him or you," she said.

The next week they found an apartment together and she learned just how impatient he really was.

A taxicab pulled up in front of the Hotel Del Prado, and Basulto, wearing a collarless gray sport coat, the sleeves pushed up nearly to his elbows, a small black overnight bag clutched in his left hand, got out and went inside. It was fifteen minutes after ten. McGarvey remained seated on the park bench in plain sight. The morning was already beginning to get warm, and traffic had picked up. Behind him a couple of banners from last night still hung in the trees. By tonight there would be another demonstration here, but by then he figured he would be long gone and this business finished. He had been in other cities like this before. Cities under stress, cities in crisis. Santiago came to mind. He didn't speak Spanish, but no one seemed to mind. Keep a low profile when the bullets start to fly and you'll be all right. Strange advice for an assassin, he'd always thought. But then it was war; and one country's holy mission was another's terrorist attack.

The two doormen in front of the hotel were talking with each other when Basulto came back out. They didn't bother looking up. He walked to the curb and looked across the street directly at McGarvey. He started to wave but then thought better of it, turning instead and hurrying to the corner. The light changed and he crossed the avenue.

McGarvey watched him coming, watched him trying to maintain an air of nonchalance. But it was obvious the Cuban was excited. McGarvey could see it in his walk, in the way he held himself like a boxer ready to dodge the next jab, and in the way he kept looking around, his eyes always moving, watching for a tail. But there was no one behind him. No one watching them, no one to care, yet.

"Is it so good meeting out in the open like this?" Basulto asked nervously, coming up.

"Sit down, Artimé," McGarvey said, not bothering to look at him.

Time, he thought, like truth, was such a precious

commodity and yet everyone seemed to abuse it, to squander it. Once it was lost, there was no going back. The same with truth. He was short on both just now.

"You called and I came. I'm here. Are we going to burn him now? What's the plan?"

"Tonight. He should be down here by morning at the latest. Him and his pal Baranov."

"Why here?"

"It'll be just like old days."

"Why not Washington? Just shoot the bastard. Or arrest him. Why here?"

"His wife is across the street just now. She's going to telephone him at nine. Tell him that she's here waiting for him. That you're here, too, and want to make a deal."

McGarvey glanced over at Basulto, whose eyes had grown wide. He looked as if he would jump off the bench at any moment and run, screaming, out into the street.

"What wife?" he squeaked.

"You might have to talk to him on the telephone. Convince him that you mean business. Convince him that you want to trade. But when he gets here, you're going to kill him instead."

"You're crazy. He's got no wife."

"Her name is Evita."

"Never heard of her."

"You knew her from the old days, Artimé. She didn't think much of you. Thought you'd been working for Batista before you signed on with Yarnell and Baranov."

"She's lying. I swear to God, Mr. McGarvey."

"I don't think so," McGarvey said quietly. He wanted to be almost anywhere but here.

"What can I say or do to convince you . . . ?"

"It doesn't matter. When Yarnell gets here tomorrow, you're going to have to kill him. I'll give you the gun."

"What about you?"

"I'm going to kill Baranov."

"I don't need this shit," Basulto said starting to get up.

"Where will you go?"

"I got friends."

"So do I," McGarvey said, looking up. "And so does Yarnell. He knows you fingered him. Just like you fingered your case officer, Roger Harris."

Basulto stood very still, as if he were afraid he would break something if he moved so much as a muscle. The morning sun glinted on his forehead and pomaded black hair. His eyes were filled with fear.

"You knew Darby Yarnell in those days. You knew who he was, and you knew that he worked for Baranov. But when Roger Harris came to you looking for a fellow agency officer who had turned traitor, it wasn't Yarnell he was after. It must have come as a big shock to you all. A big relief."

"I don't know what you're talking about."

"I think you do. I think that Baranov told you to lie. You were all biding your time, waiting for the right moment to get rid of Harris."

"I swear to God . . ."

"I know all about it, Artimé. So do Trotter and Day. But our deal with you still stands if you'll cooperate. Nothing has changed. We still want Yarnell. After all, it was he who actually pulled the trigger on Harris. Not you."

Tears began to fill Basulto's eyes. He sat down. "I loved Roger Harris. He was a good man to me."

"He just got mixed up with something that put him in over his head," McGarvey suggested.

"They knew about me."

"Who did?"

"The Russians. Baranov. They were going to blackmail me. There was nothing else to do, nowhere to run." He shook his head. "I should have went up into the mountains with Uncle Fidel when I had the chance, you know. Maybe it would have been different for me. There were a lot of heroes."

"Dead heroes," McGarvey said.

"They had respect."

"So you told them about Harris?"

"Yeah, I told them."

"Did you ever know the name of the man Roger Harris was really looking for?"

"No. I swear to—" Basulto stopped. He shook his head. "No."

"Did Baranov or Yarnell?"

"I think so. They were excited about it."

"Frightened."

Basulto managed a slight smile. "No. Not Valentin. Nothing frightened him."

"Then what happened? I mean after the Bay of Pigs?"

"I ran, just like I told you."

"Into the hills?"

"Yes."

"But Cuba and the Soviet Union were allies. You must have known that Baranov would come looking for you."

"They weren't allies at first. Besides, I hadn't done anything wrong in their eyes. And Valentin told me that I could get out any time I wanted. So I did."

"And he never came looking for you?"

"Never."

"Not even nine months ago? He didn't look you up, which at this point would have been very easy for him. He didn't look you up and tell you that he needed your help? 'Just one more little job, Comrade

Basulto.' He didn't tell you to get yourself caught?"

"No," Basulto said.

"But if he had, you would have gone to work for him, like in the old days?"

Basulto's anger flared, but then he held himself in check. He lowered his head. "Probably. But it didn't happen, and I was sick of it. All of it. Living that way. I wanted out. I want out now."

The Cuban had not told the truth before, and there was no reason to believe that he had told the entire truth this time. But McGarvey had a feeling that this version of the story was a lot closer to the truth than the others. Yet there was something missing. Something else. Something beyond his understanding, still, and he suspected beyond the understanding even of Basulto, who after all had been and continued to be nothing more than one of Baranov's pawns in a very large and complicated game.

"Not yet," McGarvey said, "Not quite yet."

With a strange intensity, Basulto threw up an arm. "I'll do it, Mr. McGarvey. Whatever it is you want of me. Because I'm tired and I want it to end. All the years. *Cristo.* You can't know. If you want me to kill him, I will. Just get me out. As one man to another, I'm asking you, just get me out."

McGarvey got to his feet, suddenly ashamed of himself without admitting why. "Come on," he growled. "I want you to meet someone."

The sun shone in her hair from the open window, making it seem almost as if a halo surrounded her head. She turned, and McGarvey could see the shock of recognition in her eyes as she saw Basulto. Last night and this morning she had seemed vulnerable. At this moment she seemed diminished.

"You," she said as if it were an indictment.

"It's all changed, I swear it," Basulto said from the doorway.

She laughed. "Don't you know? Nothing changes."

McGarvey thought she looked beautiful just then, and tragic. A lost soul barely hanging on to her sanity and her life.

"I'll be here for you," McGarvey lied, looking into her eyes.

"We'll manage," she said. "We're old friends."

"By tomorrow it will be over."

"One way or the other."

It was getting late. Time to go, and yet McGarvey was having a hard time leaving her. He was getting old, he decided. And soft in the head.

"Call at nine tonight," he said. "Put Artimé on if you think it's necessary."

She said nothing. They'd already gone over this.

"I'll be here," he said unnecessarily.

Basulto had been standing just within the doorway. He backed out. Evita said something to him in Spanish and he smiled, his eyes narrowing a bit.

He replied. "Si."

She nodded, and Basulto turned and disappeared down the corridor to his own room.

"He is genuinely frightened," she said.

"I think so."

"So am I."

McGarvey felt like a bastard leaving her like this. He didn't know where this story would end, but he knew that he would have to see it to whatever the conclusion would be. They would all have to see it to the end. He took out his pistol, laid it on the table, and then crossed the room and took her into his arms. "They're the bad lot, not us," he said.

She looked up into his eyes. "I'm not so sure," she said. "Are you?"

30

His bill was ready. McGarvey crossed the lobby with his overnight bag in hand, stopped at the desk, and took out his wallet. The bill was for a lot more than it should have been, and the clerk refused to look up at him. McGarvey paid it without comment. There was a lot of activity in the hotel this morning. A lot more than there had been yesterday, or even last night. There were, however, very few foreigners around. A lot of military officers had come in, but no one paid him the slightest attention. He was a nonperson. The pile of newspapers at the end of the counter was gone. Across the lobby a group of civilians were gathered around a television set. They seemed very nervous and tense. He picked up his bag.

Out on Avenida Juárez he got a taxi immediately, though the driver didn't seem very happy that his fare was a *norteamericano*. Traffic was light for this time of day. More banners had been strung up, and at some of the intersections they passed crews putting up even more. "Libertad!" "Heroísmo!" "Reforma!" The city was taking a holiday. Most of the shops were closed, big placards in their windows. McGarvey could only guess at some of the words and slogans, but the overall meaning was clear. A big break was coming between Mexico and the U.S., and the Soviet Union was expecting to pick up the pieces. It was frightening everyone silly.

A military roadblock was set up on the entrance ramp to the international terminal at the airport. Traffic was backed up several hundred yards in front of the barricades. Everyone was being stopped and their papers scrutinized. Only a few cars were being allowed through; others were being turned back and still others were being shunted off the road onto a large grassy field. A shuttle bus seemed to be going back and forth between the barricade and the terminal about a mile away. McGarvey paid the cabbie and walked up to the soldiers. He held out his U.S. passport.

"My plane leaves at 1:25," he said.

A young lieutenant with a pockmarked face took his passport and closely compared the photograph with McGarvey's face. "Your ticket," he demanded.

"I have only reservations."

"Impossible," the lieutenant snapped hostilely. He handed McGarvey's passport back. "The airplane is full. All the airplanes are full." He rested his hand on his holstered gun.

McGarvey put down his bag, pulled a hundred-dollar bill out of his pocket, and stuffed it in his passport. The lieutenant watched him through pig eyes. His lips were wet with spittle.

"It is important that I leave on that airplane," McGarvey said, handing his passport back to the officer. "You will see that my passport is in order."

The lieutenant glanced over at the captain, whose back was turned to them at that moment. He slipped the bill into his pocket. "I could have you shot, señor," he said, a slight smile baring his teeth.

McGarvey said nothing.

The officer handed his passport back. "You will

have to hurry to catch your airplane. The shuttle will take you."

"Thank you."

"Don't return to Mexico," the lieutenant said, and he swaggered off.

McGarvey picked up his bag and started around the barricade. The shuttle was returning from the terminal. Half a dozen other people were nervously waiting for it to arrive. Several soldiers, their automatic rifles slung over their shoulders, were watching them. A military helicopter swooped overhead from beyond one of the big maintenance hangars and headed toward the city.

It was late now, nearly one o'clock. There was a distinct possibility, he thought, that his reservations had been canceled. A lot of people, it seemed, wanted to get out of Mexico at this moment.

"*Alto!*" someone behind McGarvey shouted.

He kept walking. The soldiers looked around. One of them unslung his rifle, though he seemed uncertain.

"*Alto!*" the man shouted again.

This time McGarvey stopped and turned back as the burly captain, brandishing a pistol, raced up from the other side of the barrier. He looked angry; his face was red as he squinted into the harsh sun. His khaki uniform was wet with sweat. The lieutenant was nowhere in sight.

"Your papers! Your papers!" the captain shouted.

McGarvey smiled reassuringly. He calmly handed over his passport. The other people waiting for the shuttle bus studiously avoided looking over. "Your lieutenant already checked my passport."

"Well now I'm checking it, too." The captain flipped through the passport. "What is your destination?"

"Washington."

"Your tickets. Let me see your tickets."

"My tickets are in the terminal."

"You do not have tickets? You cannot go through. Impossible."

McGarvey stepped forward a little. The captain's hand tightened on his pistol. "This has already been taken care of. What are you doing to me?"

"What are you saying?"

"The five thousand dollars. I gave it to your lieutenant. Didn't you get your share? Christ, talk to him, but I've got to be on that plane."

The captain grinned. "Five thousand dollars. What do you take me for, that I would fall for a little trick like this? . . ."

"Bullshit," McGarvey swore, raising his voice. "You keep the goddamned passport. Just take me to your colonel. Right now. We'll see what he's got to say. Maybe he'll want a piece of the action!"

The captain was suddenly alarmed. McGarvey made a move to step around him and go back to the barricade, but the captain handed back his passport.

"I don't want any trouble here, señor. You have tickets at the terminal, then you shall go."

For just a second McGarvey refused his passport, and the captain practically pressed it on him.

"Leave now. Your bus is waiting. Just go, señor, and—"

"I know," McGarvey said, pocketing his passport. "Don't return to Mexico."

There were no problems with his tickets; McGarvey picked them up at the airline counter and boarded his plane immediately. They were delayed taking off for nearly an hour, but once they were airborne the pilot told them that most of the lost time would be made up in the air. No one really cared. Everyone was simply glad to be out of Mexico.

McGarvey ordered a drink, and when it came he sat back in his seat and closed his eyes. He tried to think about his sister, about Kathleen, and with guilt about poor Evita behind him in Mexico City. Each time his thoughts returned, unbidden, to Marta waiting in Lausanne. She had been the strong one, but he had not recognized it, and now he was sorry.

Tonight Evita would telephone her ex-husband at his home in Georgetown. Now that he had set his plan into motion, he wasn't so sure that it would work. She was to say that she had come to Mexico City at McGarvey's orders, but that she wanted it to be like it was in the old days. It was too dangerous now for them in the States. Especially now with Soviet missiles along the southern border. If need be Basulto would be there to support her story. He knew everything from the old days. He knew about Harris and about the other one Yarnell was working with in the CIA. That was the key finally. Yarnell might have been the superstar within the agency at one time, but he was on the outside now. He spoke with presidents and was friends with Donald Powers, but the real harm was being done by whoever was inside. Someone Baranov was grooming as early as the late fifties to take over for Yarnell someday. Surely Baranov had seen how brightly Yarnell's flame burned in those days. Certainly he knew that it could not last, that Yarnell was bound to burn out—more likely sooner than later. Someone had been waiting in the wings even then. Someone young. Someone who twenty or twenty-five years later would take up where Yarnell had left off. A steadier hand perhaps. Someone from the East Coast. Old family? Money? The right schools?

On the other hand, Yarnell could very well

ignore her. Perhaps he had heard this sort of thing before. He wasn't a stupid man. He or someone else had marked McGarvey's trail the entire way.

Or he could run to his contact within the CIA and warn him. It is time to get out. Time to cut and run. Baranov is calling.

The plane touched down at Washington's National Airport, across the Potomac River from Bolling Air Force Base, a few minutes before ten.

In the airport McGarvey was cleared through customs with no delays. Crossing the busy terminal toward the waiting cabs, he got the feeling he was being followed. When he turned, John Trotter was coming his way, a grim, determined look on his face, his eyes large and moist behind his thick glasses.

"It's gone too far," Trotter said. "The team is gone. We'll dismantle the equipment tomorrow. But as of this moment, you're done."

It was about what he thought might happen, so he wasn't surprised, merely a little disappointed in his old friend, who had gotten in over his head after all. Trotter was a cop, not a politician, but he'd known that all along.

"Then you and I will finish it," he said.

"No, Kirk, it's truly over. And that is by a direct order from the president."

"Yarnell has gotten to him," McGarvey said.

Trotter looked away, as if by not facing his old friend he would not have to face up to his own troubles. "Apparently."

"Then he's won."

"It's not for me to decide."

"You'd already decided when you came to me in Lausanne."

"That was a hundred years ago."

McGarvey looked at his watch. "And now we're down to the last forty-five minutes."

"What do you mean by that?" Trotter said, alarmed. "Exactly what is it you're talking about?"

"Come on," McGarvey said. "We can talk on the way into town."

Trotter's car was parked across from the departing-passenger ramp. A lot of people had come up from Mexico City on the same flight, and the area was crowded. McGarvey watched for surveillance, a face, an attitude, or a posture out of the ordinary. Mexico was Baranov's for the moment; it wasn't impossible that he would know McGarvey had gotten out. But there was no one as far as he could tell. He tossed his bag in the back seat and they headed north up the George Washington Parkway, past the Marriott Twin Bridges Hotel, the Pentagon in the distance across the Boundary Channel and Lagoon.

"I can get you some money, Kirk," Trotter said. "Not much, but something. For what you've done already."

"Later."

"What's that supposed to mean?"

"We've still got work to do."

"No, goddamnit. It's over. I've already told you. Day has told you. Am I going to have to arrest you?"

"It's too late, John."

"I don't give a damn about Basulto, if that's what you're talking about. The little bastard can rot in hell for all anyone cares."

"Yarnell's ex-wife is down there, too. They're going to telephone Yarnell tonight at eleven our time. Less than an hour from now."

Trotter glanced over. "You'll just have to stop her. Tell her the deal is off."

"I'm not going to quit."

"It's because of Janos, isn't it," Trotter said gently. "We can't even prove that Yarnell or his people did it. Someone else could have been responsible. Use your head, Kirk."

"He's working with someone in the CIA, John. Someone we don't know about. Someone who Baranov turned in the late fifties. Now he's active."

"I don't believe it."

"You'd better. It's not going to stop just because we stop. Mexico is just the tip of the iceberg. Baranov has been planning this entire business for a lot of years, and he'll keep going until someone stops him. Everything he's worked for is finally coming to a head. If he wins he'll make even more points at home. The Kremlin is already in love with him. Think what his position will be if he hands them Mexico on a silver platter. Is that the sort of man you want running the Soviet Union? And he'll get it if he wins here."

They were approaching the Arlington Bridge, which would take them across the river. Trotter started to pull toward the off ramp. "What hotel are you staying at?"

"The safe house, John."

"No."

"I want to listen to that telephone conversation."

Trotter shook his head, but he didn't take the ramp.

"It's all I'm asking."

"And then what?" Trotter asked.

"See what he does. See how he reacts."

"What do you think he'll do? What do you want him to do, Kirk? Go to the president? Is he your inside man?"

"I'm hoping he'll call his contact. Warn him."

"And what if it was the president?" Trotter suggested wildly.

"It's not," McGarvey said. "He's from California, not the East Coast."

"Christ, what's that supposed to mean?"

He kept going back to Lausanne in his thoughts, and yet at the end there he hadn't been happy or satisfied. He'd been looking for change, for just this or something like this. The old magic. Now that he was here he wanted out. Be careful what you wish for, he'd heard, you just might get it.

"His contact within the agency has an East Coast accent," he said, watching Trotter for any sign of recognition.

"How do you know this?"

"Basulto told me. I finally got more of the truth from him. He was lying to you about almost everything."

"About the East Coast accent, I mean. How did he know?" There was something there, something in Trotter's myopic eyes. Some hint of a dawning recognition.

"Roger Harris told him. It wasn't Yarnell, though. It was someone else. Someone who showed up at the party Yarnell and Baranov threw outside of Mexico City. Evita Perez heard his voice that night."

"Did she say who it was? Did she know?"

"No. She only heard his voice, she was never allowed to see his face."

Trotter thought about it. "We can come up with the embassy staff directories for those years. Shouldn't be too hard to put together who was around then and now, and who has an East Coast accent."

"He might not have been stationed in Mexico City. He might have been visiting. Or he might have been down there on special assignment."

"He could have erased the records by now in

any event," Trotter said. He was getting caught up in it. "All these years," he mused.

"How has Leonard Day been taking it?"

"I don't know," Trotter said. "I haven't seen him all day. He won't return my calls." He glanced again at McGarvey. "It's the missile thing, isn't it? That was Baranov's plan from the start."

"That's part of it, but there's more."

"They won't get away with it," Trotter continued. "They didn't get away with it in Cuba, and they certainly won't succeed this time either. The situation must be very bad in Mexico City. Did you run into any trouble?"

"Jules and Asher, the CIA field officers killed in Havana last fall. Why were they going to Mexico City?"

Trotter blinked. "Replacements. Reinforcements. I don't know."

"One of our spy planes was shot down yesterday."

"Yes . . ."

"What else have we done to confirm those missile installations? Have we sent anyone down there?"

"How in God's name would I know, Kirk? I don't have any contacts over at the agency except for Larry Danielle, and he certainly wouldn't say anything. What is it?"

McGarvey looked at his watch. They had barely twenty minutes before Evita was due to place her call. But there was something else, always something else. He could feel it. He could practically taste it. Baranov never did anything by halves. At least McGarvey had got that impression listening to Evita. It was the timing that had bothered him all along. The murders of Jules and Asher, Basulto's coming out, and Baranov's visit to Evita in New

York (the trip itself very risky for the Russian); all had occurred in too narrow a time span for McGarvey's liking. Too coincidental not to be carefully orchestrated.

They merged with the traffic crossing the Key Bridge. Washington was a city bright and alive and vibrant. But beneath the surface it was a metropolis, like Mexico City, under siege, holding its collective breath, waiting for the outcome.

"I just want you to listen to the telephone call, John. After that it'll be up to you."

They crossed the canal and turned right on M Street past the City Tavern, and then the Rive Gauche Restaurant. People lined up around the block to get in.

"How sure are you about this, Kirk?" Trotter asked. He was looking for guarantees. He was a drowning man and he needed a lifeline. But there wasn't one within reach.

"I'm just guessing."

The Boynton Towers apartment was in darkness when Trotter let them in. McGarvey wouldn't allow him to switch on the lights. All the equipment had been turned off, but it was still in place, ready for the cleanup crew to come along in the morning and remove it. Trotter stood in the middle of the living room, while McGarvey went to the window and looked down across 31st Street toward Yarnell's fortress. Only a few of the windows were lit. No party tonight.

"If he calls his contact," Trotter asked softly, "then what, Kirk? I mean, how are we going to handle it? The same as before?"

McGarvey was thinking about his ex-wife over there in Yarnell's arms. It was going to come as a very large shock for her. He didn't know how well she would handle it, but he sincerely wished her well.

"Are you going to kill him? Nothing has changed, you know. He is still friends with the president and with Powers. The scandal would wreck our government. Christ, we can't let that happen, especially not now. We need our strength. Solidarity. This could ruin everything."

Trotter was truly frightened. "There's no proof of any of this. You were correct. Good Lord, it never was anything more than circumstantial. There could be a dozen different explanations, some of which might possibly be quite innocent."

No, McGarvey thought. Evita had been correct. No one was truly innocent.

"Once we step over that line, there'll be no going back, Kirk. Not for any of us. Not ever."

McGarvey turned away from the window. "It's time, John. Turn on the tape machine, would you?"

31

In the mews behind Scott Place, the streetlights cast a violet glow on the brick walls and buildings, and from where McGarvey stood in the safe house he imagined he could see eyes watching him from the attic windows of Yarnell's citadel. It was well after eleven, the recorder on the telephone tap was on and ready. Trotter stood poised, though the equipment was automatic. He hadn't said a thing in the last fifteen minutes. McGarvey could feel his fear and his impatience. Evita hadn't called. She couldn't go through with it; she was in trouble; Basulto had stopped her; she was lying dead in a pool of blood. All of it ran through McGarvey's mind as he brooded like an anxious father waiting for his daughter to come in out of the night after her first date. He'd erred in thinking she could actually betray Baranov and her ex-husband. He'd erred in trusting Basulto, he'd erred in listening to Trotter and Day in the first place. He'd erred all of his life because he had never found a place in which he felt that he belonged. Not Kansas, not Washington, not South America nor Europe; not the service, nor the agency, nor the bookstore. He supposed he might be considered a loner, and yet he could not stand being alone.

He could not see the actual driveway into Yarnell's place, but he could see where the mews opened south on Q Street and fifty yards north on Reservoir Road. Anything or anyone coming or going then, would be visible at either end of the lane. Of course there could be a back way for a man on foot, or even a front way across the mews into a fronting building, then through its rear door onto 32nd Street. Somehow McGarvey didn't think it would be necessary this evening to go down onto the street. At least not until Evita called. When she called. If she called. The night had deepened. Black clouds had rolled in from across the river, and a mist hung over Georgetown.

It was possible, of course, that Yarnell wasn't at home this evening. In fact, considering the Mexican crisis, he might already have cut and run. But for some reason McGarvey didn't believe it. Yarnell was there. He could feel the man's presence out ahead of him in the darkness, just as iron filings can feel the effect of a hidden magnet. The power was there.

Yarnell's telephone rang. The reels of the tape machine began to turn. McGarvey looked away from the window. Trotter's eyes were wide. The telephone rang again, the sound from the speaker soft, muted. "Have you got a gun with you?" McGarvey asked. Trotter nodded. The telephone rang a third time. "Maybe he's not home—" Trotter started to say.

"Hello," Darby Yarnell's calm, cultured, self-assured voice came from the machine. They could hear the hollow hiss of the long-distance connection.

"Darby?" Evita said. She sounded very far away. Frightened and very much alone. "Is that you? Can you hear me?"

"You just missed Juanita. She's off with her friends."

"I didn't call to speak to her."

"Oh?" Yarnell said without missing a beat. McGarvey could understand already, at least in a small measure, what they'd said about him. "Are you in New York, darling? The connection is awful."

Evita didn't answer. Come on, McGarvey said to himself.

"Evita?"

"I'm in Mexico City. We have trouble. You and I, you know."

"What in heaven's name are you doing down there, especially now? Are you at your sister's?"

"The Del Prado. Downtown. You remember it?"

"I think you should go to Maria. If you want I'll telephone her for you. Or at the very least get yourself over to our embassy and stay there."

"Darby, you're not listening to me," she said, and McGarvey could hear that she was trying to be strong, trying to hold on, but he could hear the fragility in her voice. She was on the verge of breaking.

"What is it?"

"You're going to have to come down here."

"I don't think that's such a good idea. Do you, darling?" McGarvey could almost hear him smiling. "Whatever it is you're doing down there in Mexico City, I'm sure that I can't help you by joining you. Why don't you take the first plane out in the morning. You can spend the weekend up here with us. Your daughter would love to see you."

"Goddamnit, you're still not listening," Evita shrieked. "You never listened. Just like Valentin. The two of you were quite the pair."

"I'm going to hang up now," Yarnell said patiently. "I'll telephone our embassy and tell them that you need assistance. Take care of yourself—"

"Don't you dare hang up, you bastard," Evita

interrupted. "Because I'm not down here to see my sister. McGarvey brought me here."

"What are you talking about? McGarvey who? Is he someone from your club? What?"

"Ex-Company. He was hired to assassinate you."

"Good God almighty," Trotter said. "What did you tell her?"

McGarvey motioned for him to be quiet.

"Are you drinking?" Yarnell asked, and McGarvey could hear genuine concern in his voice. "Or are you taking something else?"

"He knows everything, Darby. I swear to God. I'm not here alone. He brought someone else with him. Someone from the old days."

"I think you should go to bed and get some rest."

"Don't you want to know his name? He was the one who blew the whistle on you."

"For God's sake, Evita."

"That is, before I told McGarvey everything I knew." She laughed, the sound was brittle. "All about you and Valentin in the old days. And now you're in big trouble. You won't be able to talk your way out of this one so easily."

"You need help. Let me call someone."

"His name is Artimé Basulto. Remember him? The little scumbag. Says you killed a man named Roger Harris. Shot him dead. And now he wants to get back at you. He told someone in the Justice Department, who told someone in the FBI, who hired McGarvey to kill you. Just like the old days, Darby, lots of helpers."

Trotter had stepped away from the tape machine as if it were about ready to explode. "On an open line," he said in amazement.

Again McGarvey motioned him to keep quiet.

"Honestly I don't know what you're talking about," Yarnell said, not so much as a waver in his voice. McGarvey had to admire the man's presence of mind and control.

Except for the hiss and pop of the imperfect connection, the line was silent for a pregnant second or two.

"Evita?" Yarnell prompted again.

"Valentin came to New York nine months ago. Said McGarvey or someone like him would be coming asking questions, snooping around."

"Valentin who?"

"Come off it, Darby. I know everything now. I mean *everything*."

"Good-bye."

"I saw you and him that night," she said. Her voice was shaking badly now. "You didn't know it, but I walked in on the middle of your . . . lovemaking with Valentin. Oh, God."

For the first time Yarnell was at a loss for words. McGarvey turned and looked toward the man's house. He could imagine him holding the telephone to his ear, his mind racing to all the possibilities that he was suddenly faced with.

"They know it all, Darby," she cried. "I'm sorry. They know about Valentin and they even know about the one from the party that night in Ixtayopan. They know he's still with the Company and that you're working together. I swear to God, they know it all. You've got to get out of there. You can come down here. McGarvey will make a deal. Valentin will help us. It'll be just like the old days. Oh, God, please, Darby. You have to listen."

"I don't know what you're talking about, Evita. You always did have a wild imagination, but now I think it's finally gotten the better of you. I honestly think that you need professional help now. If you come back here, I'll arrange something for you. I promise . . ."

"You promise?" she cried, half laughing. "You're a traitor. A goddamned spy. And you promise? You don't know the meaning of the word."

"Goodbye, Evita. I'm truly sorry for you now."

"You'll burn in hell, Darby. They'll get you! I'll see to it . . ."

The connection was broken. For a moment they could hear the continued hiss of the long-distance line, but then the tape machine stopped and the speaker fell silent.

It came to McGarvey that for all the evidence, for all the testimony against him, Yarnell might be innocent after all. Or, if he *had* worked with Baranov in the old days, maybe he had long since quit. Maybe he had retired from Baranov's service on the same day he had retired from the CIA. Perhaps Baranov's visit to Evita had been nothing more than a manipulative effort to get Yarnell back into the game. Force him to run when McGarvey closed in on him. Force him back into the Russian's service by allowing him no other options. "Speculation will be the bane of your existence if you let it get ahold of you," one of the old hands had told him. "There's no end to it, boyo. Leads you down so many dark alleys that you might just as well give up ever seeing the light of day again." Good advice, if overcautious. So now what? What he had set in motion had a life of its own. It would continue on its path with or without his continued participation.

"Now what?" Trotter echoed his own thoughts softly.

"He's either a damned good actor, or he's innocent," McGarvey said.

"It would appear so."

"Whatever he is, he's got his choices now."

"If he ignores her call, there wouldn't be a thing we could do to him. No way of proving his innocence or guilt." Trotter glanced at the tape machine.

"He'll either call or he won't call."

"If he doesn't, we'll be right back where we started."

"Worse," McGarvey said glumly. "Now he knows my name, and knows what we know. If he holds tight, he's won."

At the window McGarvey once again looked down toward Yarnell's house. He wondered what the man was doing at this moment, what he was thinking. He wondered if someone was there with him. Perhaps Kathleen had stayed over. He realized now, too late, that he should have called her at home so that he could make sure that at least for tonight she would be out of the fray, insulated in some small way from whatever might happen. Too late, too late, he thought. Often we made the right decisions, but we delayed our choices until they no longer mattered. By omission we were often as guilty as the hotheads. He wondered if Yarnell was sitting next to his telephone, his hand perhaps hesitating over the instrument as he tried to make his own decision, a decision that stretched back, in all reality, more than twenty-five years to an initial indiscretion in Mexico City. At the very least he suspected Yarnell was looking back at his life, wondering where his own mistakes had been made. Wondering how he had come to be here and now.

A vision began to develop in McGarvey's breast of an older Yarnell looking back at himself as a young, arrogant, conceited man, filled with a desire to change the world singlehandedly. A lot of that had gone on in the late fifties and especially in the early sixties. Camelot, they'd called President Kennedy's administration. And everyone had believed it and believed *in* it. Nothing was impossible for the honorable men. A bit of verse from the French poet Boileau-Despéraux came to him: "Honor is like an island, rugged and without a beach; once we have left it, we can never return." It was a hearkening back to his own past, to a simpler time in college, when his own choices were unlimited. "They were men without honor," someone else had written. Finally he understood the *they.*

Yarnell's metallic gray Mercedes sedan appeared out of the mews onto Q Street and turned the corner onto 32nd, its taillights winking in the distance.

"Christ! He's on the move," McGarvey cried. He crossed the room in four steps, tore open the door, and was halfway down the corridor to the stairwell before Trotter emerged at a dead run from the apartment.

Yarnell had not made a telephone call. He had run instead. To whom? To where? McGarvey hadn't counted on this.

The stairwell was well lit and smelled of concrete. McGarvey raced headlong down the staircase, his feet barely touching the steps. He could hear Trotter above him. If Yarnell had stayed put, he would have won. The man had finally made a mistake. At the bottom he slammed open the door, waited until Trotter caught up, and then rushed across the lobby and out onto the street to the car.

Trotter climbed in behind the wheel, his hand fumbling with the keys until he got the engine started and they accelerated down 31st Street, slowing at the intersection of Q Street. A taxi was just turning the corner from Dumbarton Oaks, but there was no other traffic. Ignoring the stop sign Trotter gunned the engine, slamming on his brakes as they came to P

Street. The big Mercedes was just passing beneath a streetlight two blocks east.

"There he is. We've got him," McGarvey said. "Don't lose him."

"Where the hell is he going?" Trotter asked, turning the corner. "What is he doing?"

McGarvey was thinking about Evita, so he didn't bother to answer. He pulled out the card on which he had written the number for the Del Prado Hotel and picked up the cellular telephone receiver from its cradle. Trotter kept glancing over at him as he dialed.

They crossed Rock Creek and a few blocks later turned southeast onto Massachusetts Avenue. Traffic was heavier now. Trotter knew what he was doing. He kept two cars behind Yarnell, switching lanes from time to time so that he would present much less of a constant image in the Mercedes's rearview mirror.

The international circuits were busy. McGarvey had to dial the number four times before he finally got through. They'd passed Mt. Vernon Square, turning northeast onto New York Avenue, the Mercedes still half a block ahead of them. Yarnell wasn't going out to either National or Dulles airports. McGarvey realized that he was probably going to his CIA contact.

"Del Prado," the hotel operator answered.

McGarvey gave Evita's room number. After a slight hesitation, he supposed because he was an American, the connection was made and the phone was ringing.

"Where in God's name is he going?" Trotter mumbled again.

Evita answered on the first ring. She sounded all out of breath. "Yes?"

"It's me," McGarvey said. "Are you all right?"

"Cristo! Basulto is gone. The floor maid said he checked out about six o'clock. What's going on?"

"Listen to me carefully, Evita. I want you to get out of there right now." McGarvey was cold. "If there's no late-night flight out, check into another hotel and take the first flight out in the morning."

"I called him, just like you asked. But he didn't believe me."

"I know," McGarvey said. "I heard. Just get out of there now, Evita. Leave the gun and go."

They weren't too far from Union Station. McGarvey wondered if Yarnell was going to double back and take a train out of Washington. It didn't make sense.

"I'm scared. What's going on up there?"

"Get out right now. Hang up and leave. Don't even bother checking out. Just get away from the hotel."

"Where am I supposed to go?" she cried.

"New York," McGarvey said. The Mercedes had turned onto Florida Avenue, and he suddenly realized with a terrible clarity where Yarnell was headed and why he was headed there, who his contact was within the CIA and what it all meant. A deep, final pain pulled at his gut. God help us all, he thought in horror.

"Will you be there?" Evita was demanding.

"I'll be there," McGarvey said. "Go. Run!" He slowly hung up the telephone and looked at Trotter, whose complexion had turned ghostly pale in the darkness.

The Mercedes turned onto the grounds of Gallaudet College. Trotter followed at a respectful distance. "It's Powers," he said unnecessarily.

McGarvey wanted to say that he had known it all along. That he had suspected the director's complicity from the beginning. But he had not. This now came as a complete surprise. Powers was the very best. The brightest. The most trustworthy. He was the man with the right stuff. Handpicked by the president, with the trust not only of the government and of the general public, but of the case-hardened professionals who worked for him. It was as if the news had suddenly broke that Kennedy himself had been a Russian spy. The realization that Powers was a traitor was no less stunning.

Just for a moment McGarvey wanted to turn around, get his things, and go back to Europe. To the south of France, or Greece or even the Costa del Sol. Anywhere so that he could forget. I shouldn't have been involved with this in the first place, he thought. He had believed that he was inured to dishonor. Now he understood that he'd never known the first thing about it. Philby had been nothing by comparison.

Powers had betrayed not only his country, he had betrayed the very notion of the loyal American. The last bastion of truth and justice, it seemed, remaining in an age of betrayal. Powers had been, since the early sixties—perhaps even earlier—a traitor. And yet he had done fine things in defense of his country. The Russians had indeed suffered reverses at his hands. All a sham, McGarvey wondered, or had he traded one victory against several larger victories for Baranov? Like Kim Philby, Powers had been raised amongst the elite of his homeland; the finest upbringing, the most prestigious schools, the brightest future. And like Philby, his perfidy had come as the least suspected, most shocking of all surprises.

The college grounds were dark and mysterious at this time of the night; a fine mist lay in the trees and swirled across the road. They said nothing to each other as they followed Yarnell past the school buildings and then up the private road, where they doused their headlights and hung back as the Mercedes stopped at the gate house. The guard came out, said something to Yarnell (whose figure they could clearly see in the lights now), and then the gate opened and the Mercedes disappeared up toward the house, the lights of which were just visible through the trees.

For a long time they sat in their car not knowing what to say or really what to do now that they had come to this point. No way back, McGarvey thought. No way to erase what had gone on before. No way to expunge Yarnell's sins, or Powers's sins, or his own, for that matter. He glanced at Trotter.

"You'd better telephone Day," he said. "Tell him that we're going to need some help over here."

"Sure," Trotter said. "Sure." But he made no immediate move to reach for the telephone.

Evita Perez lost her virginity to Darby Yarnell when she was barely twenty years old. She lost another sort of virginity when she had been drawn into Baranov's circle. And once again she had sinned by betraying her past. She didn't know which had been worse; they had all hurt her deeply. Nor, she decided, had anything she'd done provided her with the satisfaction she'd gone looking for. "Just let go," Baranov's words from years earlier came back to her. "I will always be there for you. No matter where. No matter why."

She sat now staring at the telephone as she had for the past half hour, trying to let go, but knowing that she couldn't. Trying to believe that Valentin would be there for her, but knowing that, of course, he would not be. He had never been. Trying to force herself into an overt action that she'd known all along was the only path to her survival, yet realizing she hadn't the strength or resolve for it so she was trying to psychologically pump herself up for at least an attempt.

"Get out," McGarvey had told her. "Run!" She forced a smile. He didn't understand. Even now he had no real comprehension of what they were up against. We can't run, she'd wanted to tell him. None of us are innocents. None of us are free of sin. We're all of us by a certain age locked into a future whose parameters are fairly sharply defined. Plumbers might climb mountains but they seldom become artists. Artists make lousy accountants. And foolish little girls who sell their souls for imagined royalty end up bitter, indecisive old hags on some trash heap somewhere.

It was just midnight by the time she finally roused herself enough to change her clothes and put on a little makeup. McGarvey had left her his pistol. He'd shown her how to use it, but she still wasn't quite certain about the safety catch. She took the gun out of the night table drawer and hefted it. The metal was slightly cool, with an oily odor. It felt foreign to her and ridiculously heavy in her hands. Melodramatic. Yet deadly. She raised the gun and sighted along the receiver as he had shown her. "Pull the trigger and keep pulling the trigger," he said. "If nothing else, the noise will scare him to death." He'd meant Basulto, of course. She didn't think Valentin would frighten so easily. With him she would have to fire at point-blank range. To the head. Over and over again.

She lowered the pistol with shaking hands and then stuffed it in her purse. Before she left the room, she looked out the window. There were more demonstrations tonight in the park. She'd have to be careful crossing the city, but then this had been her

town, her country once upon a time, and she knew it
well. This time, she thought, she wasn't some naïve
little kid incapable of caring for herself.

At the door she stopped for a moment and
looked back at the few things she was leaving behind.
She wanted a drink and she wanted, even more than
that, a couple of lines of coke. She knew where to get
those things here, but she'd fought the urge. Now her
nerves were raw, her mouth was dry, and her stomach was fluttering. An hour ago her heart had begun
to palpitate, but she had steeled herself against the
outward symptoms. The pleasure principle, it was
called. She'd forgo the immediate pleasure of relief
for a much greater pleasure later.

She took the elevator down to the second floor
and crossed the empty ballroom to the rear stairs.
Once in the service corridor on the ground floor, she
hurried to the loading docks behind the kitchens and
outside into the still, muggy night. The sounds of the
demonstration in the park were loud, ominous.
Moving fast she walked around to the parking ramp
where McGarvey had left the rental Volkswagen. He
hadn't turned in the keys in case she needed a quick
way out. She found the car on the second level.
Again, as she had in the room, she hesitated.
McGarvey had told her to run. Meaning to "run
away from trouble, not toward it." But she was
repaying a long-standing debt wasn't she? It was up
to her now to make sure Valentin did not ultimately
win. Someone was going to have to stop him, and it
wasn't going to be McGarvey because he simply did
not understand what he was up against; what they
had all been up against from the beginning.

Traffic was light around Independencia, a block
south of the hotel, and along the broad Lázaro
Cárdenas, but a car was on fire at the Fray Servando
Teresa de Mier, so Evita had to make a broad detour

east before she could turn south again, picking up
San Antonio Abad, the main highway south out of
the city. She was able to speed up, a cloud of blue
smoke trailing the car, as she rattled into the quiet
night. Behind her when she bothered to look into the
rearview mirror, she could see Mexico City ablaze
with lights and fires and even fireworks rising on
long, ragged plumes into the sky. She had to admire,
despite herself, Baranov's handiwork. He had
wanted Mexico from the very beginning. It was one
of the reasons, she supposed, that he had targeted
Darby, who had practically owned Mexico City from
day one. And now at long last it seemed as if he was
going to get his wish.

It got dark south of Tezonco. It was a Thursday
night, everyone had gone up to the city for some
action. New York would be the same tonight, she
thought. The Thursday parties getting ready for the
weekend. No one gave a damn if they stumbled
around in a daze on Friday, because the week was
over and they had Saturday and Sunday to sleep in.
But it depressed the hell out of her, the meaningless
rat race. Monday came along and she hardly wanted
to open the club. Sometimes just for the hell of it she
didn't because on most Mondays there weren't
enough customers to pay for the staff let alone the
building mortgage or any kind of a profit. They all
lived for the weekends, Evita most of all. Or maybe
an occasional couple of days down in Atlantic City.
Once, she'd even thought about going down to
Florida in mid-February. But something had come
up. Something always comes up, doesn't it, she
thought. And it was a sweltering July before she realized that she had missed her chance. She was
babbling to herself now, but she couldn't help it. She
always got this way when she was frightened. The
mountains shimmered in the distance. Along some

stretches of highway they seemed so close she felt she could reach out of the car window and touch them. As she drove she was alternately freezing cold and boiling hot. Partly from fear, partly preliminary withdrawal symptoms from her cocaine habit. Just a little longer she told herself between bouts. She could hold on because she knew that she must.

Ixtayopan was all but deserted when she drove down the main street and then turned southwest up into the mountains, the air decidedly chillier here than it had been down in the valleys. The car's exhaust rumbled and crackled off the mountainsides as the narrow macadam road switched back and forth, rising higher and higher toward the peak of Cerro Tuehtli. She crossed the bridge and suddenly she could see the house above. There were not so many lights as before when she was here with McGarvey and a party had been in progress, but someone was in residence up there. She had been up this road hundreds of times. Yet she didn't feel as if she were coming home, or even returning to a place that once had been her home. This time she felt like a complete stranger. An intruder, in fact, come with intent to do harm. The law was on his side.

She had trouble downshifting and ground the gears badly coming through the trees. She headed up the steep driveway to the plateau on which the house and grounds had been constructed. All of a sudden, coming over the crest of the driveway into the front courtyard, it struck her what she had done and why she had come here tonight. The car bucked and stalled out, rolling to a stop in the middle of the parking area twenty yards from the house, the head-lights shining on the front veranda. Very little had changed in twenty-five years. The rambling one-story ranch-style house still seemed new and modern and prosperous. The living room windows were dark, but the east wing where Darby's study had been located and where the master suite looked back toward Mexico City, was lit up. There were no cars parked in the driveway. The garages were around back. He was probably in the city at the embassy. Tonight had been a fool's errand. Her hands shook very badly as she opened her purse and pulled out the automatic. She toyed with the safety catch, switching it down and then up and then down again. She couldn't remember about it and she could feel panic rising in her chest. He would have a staff out here. Perhaps even bodyguards. He was an important man. They would probably shoot first and ask questions later. Maybe she didn't care. She opened the door and got out of the car, standing for a moment on wobbly legs before she started up to the house, the pistol in her right hand hanging at her side.

"Trust in me," he had told her. "I have enough strength for you as well as for Darby." His words seemed to hang in the crisp mountain air. "Someone is coming," he'd told her in New York. "I need your help. It's time now to repay old debts." She'd laughed then and she laughed now, because if there had been any debt owed it was his debt to her for everything he and Darby had done to her. Yet she had done exactly what he had asked of her. She'd told McGarvey everything. She'd even slept with him. And now she felt truly dirty for the first time in her life. It was even worse for her now than it had been in the old days.

The sliding glass doors to the living room were open. Baranov stepped out of the darkness onto the veranda. Evita stopped short. He had changed and yet he hadn't. He was short and stocky, his thick neck was like a bull's, his features were dark and broad and very Russian. But even from a distance of

twenty feet, she could feel heat radiating from him as
if he were a furnace. She could feel his power, his
self-assurance, and even a bit of his humor from
where she stood. He wore khaki trousers and an
open-necked shirt. A bit of gold chain around his
neck was illuminated in the already fading glow of
the Volkswagen's headlights. She felt a silly urge to
run back to the car and switch off the lights before
the battery was fully dead. It would be hard starting
the engine when it was time to return to town.

"You are a wonderful girl," Baranov said softly.
"I thank you for your help. You did good."

Just let go, she thought, and there was a certain
comfort in the notion. Give in. Don't fight him,
because winning is impossible. She closed her eyes,
and she could see a kaleidoscopic image of her entire
life; Valentin, Darby and Juanita. All ruined. All
gone. All harshly used.

"McGarvey knows about Darby," she said,
opening her eyes again. "And about you. Everything."

"I know," he said.

"That doesn't matter to you?"

"On the contrary, it matters very much to me,
Evita. In this you must believe me. Before this night
is over, we will have triumphed, you and I." He
smiled. She could clearly see his perfectly white
teeth. He beckoned to her. "Come. We'll wait together."

"They're going to arrest Darby," she said.

"I know."

"They know that he's working with someone
inside the CIA."

"Worked," Baranov corrected her.

Evita felt light headed. "What?"

"Darby hasn't been active for years and years,
my dear. Didn't you know? Hadn't you guessed?"

"Then why . . .?"

"It wasn't him I was after. It was someone else."

"There were people killed."

"Not Darby's doing, believe me."

She shook her head.

He smiled sympathetically. "I'd sincerely hoped you would show up here tonight, you know. You can wait here. In the morning I'll drive you down to the airport. I don't think Mexico would be such a good place for you just now."

"You bastard," she said. She raised the gun and switched the safety catch down and fired, the pistol jumping in her hand. Baranov didn't move a muscle. She fired again, breaking something inside the living room. She started forward, firing a third time and a fourth, still Baranov didn't move, his eyes locked into hers, a slight smile creasing his features. She fired a fifth and sixth time, her elbow aching from the recoil, her ears ringing from the noise. He was invincible, invulnerable; nothing could hurt him. He was God, he was untouchable. She had known that from the very first day she had laid eyes on him, and here, now, the wild thought ran through her mind, was the living proof. He was not an ordinary mortal man. He could not be killed with bullets. He would live forever.

She held the pistol in both hands and sighted on the middle of his chest. She stood flat-footed about fifteen feet down from the veranda. He held up a hand, like a benediction.

"It's enough, Evita," he said sadly.

She squeezed slowly on the trigger, like McGarvey had told her to do, tears slipping down her cheeks, a great big hollow feeling inside of her. Her life had come down to this one act: either she would kill him and continue to live, or she could not and she would have to die.

He moved to the left at the same moment the gun went off, and he staggered backward against the edge of the doorway, a big splotch of blood suddenly appearing on his left arm, just above the elbow.

She took another step closer and fired a second shot, this one catching Baranov high in the left shoulder just below the collarbone. He cried out in pain and slumped to the floor, half in and half out of the house.

She came up on the veranda as Baranov was trying to crawl into the house. He stopped and looked up as she reached him.

"You sonofabitch," she cried. She raised the pistol to his head, the barrel inches away from his temple.

His eyes softened. "You will not kill me. Not after what we have been through together, you and I."

Her hands were shaking so badly that she could barely keep the gun pointed at him. There was no fear in his eyes, however, and it infuriated her. But it frightened her, too.

"I will require some medical assistance, so it will be best that you not stay here this evening after all."

"Fuck you," she said and she pulled the trigger. The hammer slapped on an empty chamber.

Baranov managed a slight, depreciating smile. "Mr. McGarvey has always had the habit of loading only eight bullets into his Walther. Fortunate for me, his predictability."

Evita pulled the trigger again, but nothing happened. She could not believe that she had come this far, had come this close, and still had lost. "No," she cried.

"Go," he said. "Killing me wouldn't have done much in any event, except land you in jail. The die is cast, my dear. You must see that now."

She looked down at him in sudden horror, thinking that she had ever believed in him, that she had slept with him and done his bidding. Perhaps it was the blood on his arm and shoulder, and the pain which she could clearly read in his eyes, that made him somehow more human for her than before. He wasn't a god, at all. Nor was he an infallible giant. He was only an ordinary man. An extraordinarily evil man. But simply a man for all of it. She stepped back and let the gun fall to the floor.

"No one will be coming after you," he said. "You are safe. Trust me."

She turned, crossed the veranda, and started for her car. He said something to her from the house, but she couldn't quite make out the words. She looked back but she couldn't see anything in the darkness, and now the house was a stranger's house to her. She had never been here, not to this place. Nor would she ever have a desire to return. That much she knew for certain. Everything else was a mystery to her.

Francisco Artimé Basulto stepped from the airplane at Havana's José Marti International Airport and breathed deeply of the warm, moist night air. He was home at last and he felt ten feet tall. At the very least he would get a medal along with his promotion. And he damned well deserved it and more, by his reckoning. The past few months had been bad for him, much worse than he had suspected, especially with McGarvey. He'd get that man's ass sooner or later. Baranov had promised him. "You will get everything coming to you, Artimé," the Russian had said at their first meeting nearly a year ago. "Believe me when I tell you that everyone will be satisfied." What's not to believe, he'd wondered. With Baranov anything was possible. The sky was the limit.

Twenty or thirty people had come on the late-night flight from Mexico City, and Basulto went with them across the parking ramp and into the customs hall of the big terminal. They'd been held on the plane for nearly a half hour while their luggage had been off-loaded and brought in. He would stay downtown for the weekend and have a little fun. He deserved it. Monday would be soon enough for him to check in. Baranov would be coming over and they would go through the debriefing together. Even the colonel would be impressed.

He stood in line at the check-in counter and when his turn came he surrendered his passport and baggage claim ticket. He was tired and wanted to get this over with as quickly as possible. He was out of cigarettes, he was hungry, and he needed a drink. A big drink.

The clerk, an older, horse-faced woman in a militia uniform was staring at him. There was something about the expression in her eyes that was bothersome.

"Is there something wrong?" he asked.

"I don't know, Comrade. Is there?" she asked.

A bulky man in civilian clothes came across the hall. He was smiling. "Ah, Comrade Basulto, welcome home, welcome home," he said effusively, and the knot that had suddenly tightened in Basulto's gut immediately began to loosen.

"Thank you," he said. "It's good to be back among friends."

"Colonel Alvarez would like a word with you before you go into town," the civilian said. He took Basulto's passport and baggage claim ticket from the woman and motioned for Basulto to come with him.

"I hope this won't take long. I'm tired and I—"

"Yes, we understand," the civilian said pleasantly. "It will take just a moment, believe me."

They went past the customs inspection counters to the back of the hall where a door to an office stood open. Several soldiers were gathered around a table on which Basulto's suitcase lay open. Ten feet away he could see that there was something packed in his suitcase that he hadn't put there. For just an instant he was confused. But then he recognized what he was seeing and he stopped short. Inside his suitcase there had to be at least twenty kilos of cocaine wrapped in one-kilo plastic packages. He'd handled the stuff enough to recognize it when he saw it. He had been set up.

"Comrade?" the civilian asked, turning around.

"No," Basulto said, taking a step backward. "That's not mine."

"Just come in and we'll straighten it out," the civilian said reasonably.

They didn't give a shit about him. He had served his purpose, and now they were throwing him on the trash heap. *Cristo!* He wasn't going to spend his life in Uncle Fidel's jail.

The civilian was reaching in his suit coat as Basulto turned and bolted for the main doors. Not like this, goddamnit! It wasn't going to end like this! Someone shouted to him, but he didn't understand. Not like this!

Something very hot and hard slammed into his back and he could feel himself being propelled forward, off his feet, the sound of a gunshot booming in his ears. Before he hit the floor a million stars burst in his head and he was dead.

32

McGarvey and Trotter sat in the darkened car watching the gate house and the driveway up to Powers's residence. Occasionally they would say something to each other, but for the most part they had kept their silence, each absorbed in his own glum thoughts. Powers the traitor. Still McGarvey found it difficult to fathom. Trotter had called a disbelieving Leonard Day, who nonetheless agreed to come over as soon as he possibly could, though it might take him an hour or more because he had guests who wouldn't be all that simple to shoo away. That had been nearly an hour ago. It had come to McGarvey, in the meantime, that at the very least Trotter and Day were treating this as nothing more than some sort of an unfortunate mistake. Powers simply could not be their traitor. Not Powers. There would be another explanation. There had to be. It also came to him that he had become a worrier. At times like this he thought about the people he knew and how they were making mistakes with their lives. He could see the way clear for each of them, the way out of their troubles. He thought about his sister for whom land, duty, and responsibility were more important than people, and he thought about

Kathleen, who was cut of much the same cloth and would never be completely happy until she learned to love herself a little less and a man—any man—a little more completely. Marta and Evita, on the other hand, were the direct opposites of his sister and ex-wife. They were women who loved too completely, at the nearly absolute exclusion of everything else, including their own previous loyalties and common sense. He thought also about Powers and Yarnell, men so far out of what might be considered a "normal" category that they lived their lives unaware of the realities of the majority of the people they had set themselves up to serve. It was not arrogance, he thought, so much as insularity. They were islands unto themselves, for the most part ignorant of the natives on the beaches but forever watching the distant horizons for threats from afar. These sorts, when they fell, were always surprised.

"At least he didn't bring his mob with him this time," Trotter said into the darkness.

McGarvey glanced over at him. "They'll have to be dealt with."

"That depends upon what happens tonight."

"I'm not going to assassinate him for you, John, if that's what you mean," McGarvey said. "It's gone beyond that now. No need any longer to protect Powers."

"I meant with Leonard. He'll have to talk to them."

"They'll deny it."

"Probably."

"Maybe they'll shoot him dead."

"Good Lord, it's not Donald Powers," Trotter blurted. "It simply cannot be. And let me remind you that you don't have a shred of proof linking him to any crime, to any wrongdoing."

Looking out the window again, McGarvey had

to admit that it was true. There was no proof. Not even proof against Yarnell now that Basulto had skipped out. Evita's testimony would be thrown out of any court; she was an ex-wife with a grudge, she was a prostitute, and a drug addict. Hardly a reliable witness. He was an assassin who had been fired by the Carter administration for political unreliability. Owens, with his testimony about the old days, was dead, as was poor Janos and his story about altered records. There was no one left. And all the while, lurking in the background, was Baranov. This was his doing. Why? What had he hoped to accomplish? What were they still missing?

"It's all such a mess," Trotter murmured. "An incredible, stinking mess."

They both heard the shot from up at the house, like a tiny firecracker popping.

"Good Lord," Trotter said, looking up.

"Give me your gun," McGarvey demanded, and he jumped out of the car.

Trotter fumbled in his jacket pocket, his eyes wide behind his glasses.

"Come on, John!" McGarvey snapped. He looked over his shoulder toward the house.

Trotter handed him the gun, a big, bulky nine-millimeter automatic. "What the hell is going on, Kirk?"

The guard had come out of the gate house. He was looking up toward the house, his pistol drawn.

"Block the driveway and then get the hell away from the car," McGarvey shouted over his shoulder as he raced across the street. He levered a round into the firing chamber and switched the safety off.

Behind him Trotter started the car and pulled up the street, screeching to a halt just in front of the gate house. The guard had spun around as Trotter, his badge held high over his head, jumped out of the car. "FBI," he shouted. "FBI!"

Automobile headlights appeared at the head of the driveway, flashing in the trees and illuminating the thickening fog. A powerful car engine was racing at top speed. Lights were coming on all over the house above, and a siren began to sound, its metallic wail piercing the night.

The gate guard was looking from Trotter, who had backed away from his car, to the driveway and back again, not quite sure what was happening but understanding that a situation of some sort was rapidly developing in front of his nose. He had not spotted McGarvey, who had taken up position in the shadows off to the side.

There had been only one shot, but any lingering doubt that tonight's meeting between Yarnell and Powers had been innocent in purpose was gone. Baranov had set up the mechanism, McGarvey had managed to push all the right buttons, and now the principle players had leapt into action.

The car's headlights suddenly backlit the iron bars of the gate, throwing long shadows across the road and over Trotter's car. McGarvey dropped into a shooter's crouch, both hands on the pistol, his arms extended. All at once Yarnell's Mercedes burst into view on the driveway, moving at a high rate of speed. The guard just barely managed to leap aside as the car hit the gate with a tremendous crash, sending one half of the heavy metal structure flying off to one side. At the last possible instant, the Mercedes swung very hard to the left in a futile effort to avoid crashing into Trotter's car, its right fender caving in Trotter's door, both cars skidding across the street and up onto the curb.

The gate guard rushed down the driveway as

Yarnell half rolled, half fell out of his car.

"Stop! Stop!" the guard shouted.

Yarnell was hidden behind the open car door. McGarvey started across the street as two shots were fired in rapid succession. The guard was thrown backward off his feet, a big geyser of blood erupting from the center of his chest.

"Yarnell!" McGarvey shouted.

Yarnell's figure filled the window opening and he fired, the shot ricochetting off the pavement. McGarvey fired three times, the first catching Yarnell in the chest, the second smacking into the door panel and catching him in the groin, and the third hitting him in the neck just above the sternum, destroying his throat and filling his lungs with blood.

Trotter was racing up the road.

"See about the guard," McGarvey shouted, approaching the Mercedes with caution.

Another car raced down the driveway from the house and skidded to a halt in the street.

"FBI! FBI!" Trotter shouted.

McGarvey didn't bother looking back. Yarnell half lay, half sat in a bloody heap beside the Mercedes, his head lolling back on the leather-upholstered seat. A beretta automatic lay beside him. He was dead, there was absolutely no doubt of it. His eyes were open and his tongue filled his mouth as if he were gagging on something. Even in death, however, McGarvey could feel the power of the man. For two and a half decades no one had been able to touch him. Twenty-five years or more he had been allowed to operate unchecked. McGarvey thought how the man should have seemed diminished in death. But he didn't.

Stuffing Trotter's pistol in his pocket, McGarvey bent down over Yarnell's body and went through his pockets. No proof. Still there was no proof of anything other than the fact that Yarnell may have tried to assassinate the director of Central Intelligence tonight.

In Yarnell's breast pocket he found a miniature tape recorder. It was still running. McGarvey switched it off, and glanced over his shoulder. Four guards had come down from the house. One of them had broken away and was coming this way. McGarvey quickly stuffed the tape recorder in his pocket and got to his feet. In the distance he could hear the sounds of the first sirens.

"An ambulance is coming," the guard said, out of breath.

"Yarnell won't need it," McGarvey said stepping aside.

The guard caught sight of Yarnell's body and he stopped short. "Christ," he said. "You two put it to him, didn't you?"

"He was trying to escape. Shot your gate guard."

"What the hell were you two doing here in the first place?" the bodyguard asked, his eyes narrow. "We weren't informed of any bureau operation."

"We were following Yarnell," McGarvey said. "What happened at the house? We heard the shot."

"Following Mr. Yarnell for what reason, exactly?" There would be an investigation, and the man was thinking about his own future.

"He was suspected of working for the Russians. How is Powers?"

"Damn," the guard said glancing down at Yarnell. He shook his head. "Not good, I'd say. This bastard shot him in the head from close range. We didn't know what the hell was going on. Christ, they're old friends. Have been for years. How the hell were we supposed to know?"

"How about your gate guard?" McGarvey asked.

"Charlie is dead. There'll be hell to pay for this all. A lot of hell for a long time."

"Shit runs downhill," McGarvey said.

"Yeah, ain't that just the truth now," the man said, walking off.

Trotter came across the street as the ambulance arrived and was directed up to the house. One of the guards went with it while the others kept a watchful eye. Other sirens could be heard in the distance.

"In a very few minutes this place is going to be crawling with some angry people who are going to have a lot of questions," McGarvey told him.

"And I don't know what the hell to tell them," Trotter said. He was staring down at Yarnell's body. He sighed. "What an incredible mess."

"We can try the truth, John, or at least some of it. But they're going to want to know who the hell I am."

Trotter looked up. "Powers probably won't make it from the way his bodyguards were talking. No need to prove anything now."

McGarvey thought about the tape recorder in his pocket. He took out the gun and handed it to Trotter. "For the record you shot him."

"There is enough circumstantial evidence, I suppose," Trotter said.

"Keep my ex-wife out of it,"

"I'll try, Kirk, that's all I can promise."

The first of the police cars showed up just ahead of Leonard Day in a stretch limousine. Powers was taken away in the ambulance, its lights flashing, its siren screaming. Two other ambulances showed up moments later. Trotter walked over to where Day was talking with a District of Columbia police lieutenant, a secret service agent, and a couple of Powers's bodyguards. For the moment they were ignoring McGarvey. Even more sirens were converging from around the city. The first of the television vans arrived, but the police had already blocked off the narrow street and wouldn't allow the reporters to cross the barriers.

McGarvey got his bag out of Trotter's car as the coroner came over and checked Yarnell's body. Police photographers took a series of pictures, the flash units blinding in the darkness. And then one of the ambulance crews respectfully lifted Yarnell's body onto a stretcher, strapped it in, and took it away.

A crowd had finally gathered. There were uniformed police officers and plainclothesmen everywhere, but everyone made a point of avoiding McGarvey. Confusion will come to the very end of every operation. Confusion and disdain. It was nearly axiomatic. The dustbin crew they were called. The investigating officers, the forensics specialists, the accountants of the business at hand, there to pick up the pieces and put them back together in neat, platable ledger books.

His part in it was done, or very nearly done. Yet he was less certain now of what had really happened than he had been at the very beginning. As he waited he tried to examine his feelings as an accident victim in shock might try to determine the extent of his injuries. But nothing came to mind, and he understood that he was numb, and whatever he was thinking now would all be changed by morning, or by next week, or next month.

It was nearly two in the morning. McGarvey sat in the back of the stretch limousine with a shaken Trotter and a pensive Leonard Day. They'd crossed Constitution Avenue on Third Street below the Capitol and headed toward the river. He was out. Day had taken care of everything so that he had become the invisible man as far as concerned the investigating officers. An extraneous object hardly worthy of a second glance. The man had the power, which was just as well because for all practical purposes the business was finished. And still he had no real idea what Baranov had hoped to accomplish. Yarnell might not have been able to provide the Russian with much in the way of hard intelligence these days, but my God, the director of Central Intelligence had to be the ultimate of gold seams.

"I want you to leave the country," Day said. "Back to Europe where we dug you up from under a rock."

A week ago he would have resented such a remark. It didn't matter any longer. "What's our story?"

Day looked at him, his lips compressed. "You, mister, have no story. Plain and simple, you keep your mouth shut. You were never here, you know nothing about it."

"Keep my ex-wife out of it," McGarvey said tiredly. "Other than that you're welcome to it."

"We'll just see now, won't we," Day said, puffed up with self-importance. "From what I can see she was very deeply—"

McGarvey reached over in the darkness and clamped his fingers around Day's throat, cutting off the man's wind. "If need be, I'll come back and kill you. It's easier than you think."

Day's eyes were bulging nearly out of their sockets, and his face was beginning to turn red. He tried to struggle, but McGarvey's grip was iron tight. Trotter had reared back, he didn't know what to do.

"Make certain my ex-wife isn't involved in any way, and I'll keep my end of the bargain. Do you understand me, Mr. Deputy Attorney General?"

Day nodded frantically and McGarvey let go.

He lit a cigarette and for the remainder of the trip over to the Marriott he sat back in his seat and stared out the window, ignoring the other two. In the morning he would leave. He found that he was actually anxious to see Marta again, hold her in his arms, if she would come away with him. Not Switzerland, of course, but they would find solace somewhere together. He resolved to be a better person. He'd stepped back into the fray and found that the rules of the game, if not the class of participants, had drastically changed. It wasn't for him. He might be dissatisfied in the future, there never could be a guarantee against that. But he didn't think he'd ever again pine away for the agency.

He reached in his pocket and felt for the miniature tape recorder he'd taken from Yarnell's body. He thought about turning it over to them, but had decided against it. At least for the moment. They had their story in any event. Yarnell had been a traitor. Donald Powers had somehow discovered his friend's duplicity and when he had confronted him with it, Yarnell shot him. Yarnell was killed during his attempt to escape. Spectacular headlines, but it was a story they all could live with. There'd be no one to dispute it, whether or not Powers died of his wound. He thought again that he didn't know a thing about honor.

"Good-bye, Kirk," Trotter said outside the hotel. They shook hands. Day remained in the car.

"Take care of yourself," McGarvey said, and he meant it.

"You too."

33

For the rest of the morning, McGarvey lived in a state that could only be called disbelief and horror. He had not gone to bed after Trotter and Day had dropped him off; instead, he had listened to the recording that Yarnell had made of his conversation with Powers. And then he had listened to it again. He had telephoned Evita's club twice, but there was no answer. He called the Del Prado in Mexico City, but the clerk knew nothing about Ms. Perez. She had not checked out, but she hadn't returned to her room either. No one had seen her leave the hotel. He ordered from room service with the gray, overcast dawn, but when his breakfast came he found he didn't have the stomach for it and drank barely a half a cup of coffee. He telephoned Trotter a few minutes before eight.

"I don't think there's anything left to be said, Kirk," Trotter growled.

"Is he still alive?"

"Powers? As of six when he came out of the operating theater he was in critical condition."

"Can he speak? Will he regain consciousness?"

"What the hell are you talking about?" Trotter demanded. "Just go, Kirk. Leave it be."

"I have to know."

"Maybe we treated you shabbily. I have no defense. It's just the way it went. But there's nothing to be gained—"

"Is he conscious?" McGarvey persisted.

Trotter sighed. "I don't think so. From what I understand he may never come out of it, and if he does he'll probably be a vegetable. It's all over. Go."

"But he was innocent."

"We know that."

"So was Yarnell."

"What are you talking about? What the hell are you saying? Good Lord, haven't we gone through enough?"

McGarvey looked at the tape recorder lying on the desk. "It was a Baranov plot," he said. "And he will have won if you publish the story that Yarnell was a traitor."

"We have the evidence."

"Circumstantial, all of it," McGarvey said. He was thinking about Basulto's story, about Owens's hatred of Yarnell, who was probably guilty of seducing his mentor's wife and of arrogance and of a certain hardness of character and purpose. He thought about Evita and everything she'd told him. She'd been manipulated all right, but by Baranov not by her husband, who had in his own way tried in the end to insulate her. And he thought about poor Janos, who had died on a fool's errand. Yarnell had not murdered them. Baranov had.

"John?"

"I'm here."

"I'll meet you at Leonard Day's house. Right now. This morning. Call him and tell him we're on the way out."

"I won't."

"I think you will." He hung up. It was all clear to

him now. All the pieces fit, from the hijacking of the flight out of Miami in which the two CIA officers were murdered to the incident last night. Yarnell had been doing his duty as he saw it up there. Nothing more.

McGarvey cleaned up, ordered a rental car through the hotel desk, and drove out of the city up to Day's palatial home on Lake Artemesia near College Park. The morning was cool and windy. The lake was dotted with whitecaps. No one was fishing. A plain gray Chevrolet sedan with government plates was parked under the overhang when McGarvey drove up. It was at places like this, he thought, that the real work of government service was often conducted. It didn't offer him much comfort.

Inside Trotter and Day were waiting for him in the study. They were drinking coffee. Trotter looked terrible; his eyes were bloodshot, his tie undone, his jacket disheveled. He hadn't changed from last night. Day, on the other hand, seemed fresh in his three-piece pinstriped suit. He also looked angry, even imperious, sitting behind his big leather-topped desk.

"I haven't got time for your asinine bullshit this morning, McGarvey. I want that straight from the beginning here," Day said. "You want money we'll give it to you, although John tells me that you refused his very generous offer."

There had been no offer, but it didn't matter. "Yarnell and Powers were both innocent," McGarvey said, facing him across the desk like a schoolboy before his masters.

"So John has told me. And what of your painstakingly gathered evidence?"

"I was wrong."

"He was wrong," Day hooted looking over at Trotter. "What do you suppose he was wrong about?

Darby Yarnell's guilt or his innocence?"

"It was a Soviet plot," McGarvey went on doggedly. He wanted to get this over with and leave before he did something truly stupid like going across the desk and smashing Day's pretty face.

The study was a pleasant room. It smelled of books, leather, Day's cologne, and coffee. A lot of the books were privately bound in matched covers. McGarvey wondered if anyone had ever read them.

"It began with the hijacking of the Aeromexico flight out of Miami," he said. "Planned and financed by the Soviet-run CESTA network."

Trotter sat forward a little. "The weapons were Soviet made. Supplied by CESTA."

"Because of the missile thing?" Day asked. "Is that why those two were shot down? Were the Russians afraid of an early discovery?"

"No," McGarvey said patiently. "I think the missile thing will turn out to be simply another Cuba."

"Simply," Day said in amazement.

"The Cuban missile crisis got the Russians exactly what they wanted all along. A promise from us to never again intervene in Cuban affairs. It worked then, and I suspect it will work in Mexico."

"If that wasn't the Soviet's goal, and I'm certainly not saying that I agree with you, then what?"

"How effective was Powers as a DCI?" McGarvey countered. He was thinking about the tape recording.

"Very," Day said. "The best we've ever had, bar none."

"Where is he now?"

"In the hospital, of course—"

"Baranov has won," McGarvey said quietly. "Powers was a thorn in his side. Has been for years and years, so he wanted to get rid of him. Cast doubt on his loyalty. Throw our entire secret service into shambles just at the moment we most need its services."

"But what did Jules and Asher have to do with it, Kirk," Trotter asked.

"I expect that operation was designed to do nothing more than get Powers's attention. He and Baranov have known each other for more than twenty-five years."

"It was him in Mexico City?" Trotter asked.

McGarvey nodded.

"What are you talking about?" Day demanded. "Who? What about Mexico City?"

"When Yarnell was in Mexico City he worked Baranov, who at the time was his counterpart at the Soviet embassy. One evening Powers apparently showed up at a party that Yarnell threw and at which Baranov had supplied the women."

Day's eyes narrowed. His sarcastic manner was gone. "And there was an indiscretion?"

McGarvey nodded. "Most likely. Just that one night. Yarnell might not have thought much about it at the time, but Baranov had, and so had Powers."

"It was the link between them all these years," Trotter said, understanding the situation at a much deeper level than Day because of his training.

"Why in God's name did he run to Powers last night? Why did he shoot him? It doesn't make sense, McGarvey."

"It didn't to me at first," McGarvey said. "Not until this morning. But first you have to understand that this entire affair, everything that has happened, was orchestrated by Baranov."

"He's that good?" Day asked.

McGarvey nodded.

"And it started, you say, with the deaths of Jules and Asher?"

"By killing them and making sure that Powers knew the weapons were Russian made and CESTA supplied, Baranov was putting Powers on notice that trouble was coming."

"He warned Powers."

"In effect. He wanted Powers to become defensive. Just one more link in a very long chain of evidence."

Day shook his head, and Trotter had to explain it for him. "Innocent men aren't generally defensive. Just another piece of circumstantial evidence."

"The Cuban was working for Baranov, of course," Day said.

"From the beginning," McGarvey said. "And you have to admire him. He did a fine job."

"Where is he now?"

"Havana, I suppose. Picking up a medal. Or a bullet."

"And Darby's ex-wife?" Trotter asked.

"Hopefully on her way to New York. Baranov actually came to New York about nine months ago to see her. He told her that someone like me would be coming around asking questions about her ex-husband. She had a grudge, and she had seen things in Mexico City that she couldn't possibly have understood. At the time Yarnell was very close to Baranov. They did everything together. Two young spies, both brilliant, both headstrong and arrogant, were working each other. Seducing each other, playing the game on a grand scale. What was a poor little Mexican princess supposed to believe when she saw them together?"

"How could Baranov possibly know that someone like you would be coming?" Day asked.

"He set Basulto on you and Trotter. He knew that you wouldn't take it to the CIA because of Powers's friendship with Yarnell. He figured that you might be calling in an outsider. Someone who knew the game. A radical."

"How do you know that Yarnell wasn't actually a traitor?"

"Because of the quality of the intelligence he sent back on every assignment he was ever given. His boss, Darrel Owens, had nothing but praise for his protégé's work in Mexico City and in Moscow, although he hated him."

"Why?" Day asked. They were leaving him behind again, but it didn't matter now. McGarvey figured that Trotter would explain it to him later.

"Yarnell was probably sleeping with his wife."

"Why in heaven's name?" Day chirped.

"He was hedging his bets," Trotter said. "He was an ambitious kid and wanted to get to the top as quickly as he possibly could. The cuckolded husband is almost always the first one to cooperate lest he make a public fool of himself."

Admiration and hate often went hand-in-hand in this business, McGarvey thought, recalling his afternoon with Owens. No one, he suspected, had ever been neutral about Darby Yarnell, who in the end had made the most tragic mistake of his life. He had simply out-thought himself. In the end neither he nor Powers had been a match for Baranov's skills.

"What about Janos Plónski?" Trotter asked, breaking into McGarvey's thoughts. "He'd found something in the records that got him killed."

"My fault," McGarvey said tiredly. He supposed Pat and the kids had returned to England where her mother still lived. Eventually, he knew, he would have to face them, but only after he found the right words.

"What did he discover?" Trotter prompted.

"He looked up Basulto's track. Several of his

operations had been pulled from their jackets. But it was done years ago."

"By whom, if Yarnell and Powers were innocent?"

"There wasn't time to get the dates straight, but I suspect Roger Harris did it. He was Basulto's case officer and he suspected there was a mole in the agency and he wanted to hide what Basulto was doing for him—namely finding the traitor."

"Who killed Harris in Cuba then . . ." Trotter started to ask, but a sudden understanding dawned on him. "Basulto," he said into the breach.

"Yeah," McGarvey replied.

"Well, what about Yarnell's bodyguards," Day wanted to know. "That's not what you would consider normal behavior for an innocent man."

"Yarnell was never what you would think of as normal," McGarvey countered. "He'd always surrounded himself with a crowd. Admirers, some of them, others actual bodyguards. Maybe he'd gotten paranoid in his old age. Maybe he thought Baranov would be coming after him someday. I don't know."

Day sat back in his chair, his hands in front of him on the desk. "Still doesn't answer the question of why Yarnell went to see Powers last night. Why he shot him. Not the actions of an innocent man."

Darby Yarnell had been an arrogant sonofabitch. But a romantic for all of it. An overzealous patriot who had thrown himself body and soul into being a spy in defense of his country. The ends, for him, justified the means. Any means. And it was those very qualities that Baranov had recognized early on, that he had used to manipulate Yarnell. All the signs were there, but McGarvey had seen them too late. As they all had. Only Baranov had known the outcome from the very beginning. Only Baranov truly knew about honor and dishonor, and how to use this understanding to the best advantage. McGarvey took the miniature tape recorder out of his jacket pocket and laid it gingerly on Day's desk.

"Yarnell remembered that night in Mexico City when Powers came to his house and was seduced," McGarvey began. "He remembered the party, the music, the girls, and mostly he remembered Baranov. We were led to believe that there was a mole in the CIA. A man at high levels who was selling us out to the Russians. Baranov's handmaiden. In Yarnell's mind, everything pointed to his old friend Powers, whom he thought was being blackmailed. He thought he understood Baranov. He thought Baranov had used that night to turn Powers. Or was about to do it. So he went to the house and shot him. It was his patriotic duty, as he saw it."

Day and Trotter were staring at the tape recorder as if it were a wild beast about to devour them.

"I took this from Yarnell's body last night. It was running. No one else knows about it. No one but us."

"You've heard it?" Trotter asked, looking up.

McGarvey nodded. "Yarnell had loved his country and had given his life in her defense. He thought he was thwarting Baranov when in actuality he had played the score the Russian had laid out for him, the first notes of which had been written twenty-five years ago."

"You can't expect us to believe such a story," Day said halfheartedly.

"Yes, I do," McGarvey replied. He switched on the tape recording, then turned and walked out as Darby Yarnell's voice came from the tiny speaker.

"*Hello Donald. We have a problem, you and I.*"

"*Yes, I suspect we do,*" Powers said.

* * *

McGarvey had gone from day into night with the same thoughts, the same voices in his head following him like a shadow, like an alter ego, at once frightening and somehow strangely comforting in that he finally understood. Riding in the taxi from LaGuardia Airport into Manhattan, he wondered how Day and Trotter were taking it. Powers had died shortly before noon. A counsel for the CIA had admitted the DCI had been assassinated by Darby Yarnell, a longtime friend, but a spokesman for the Bethesda Naval Hospital, where both men had been taken, hinted about a possible brain tumor in Yarnell's frontal lobe. It would be days, possibly weeks, before anything conclusive would be known, but Yarnell quite possibly had not been in control of his faculties at the time of the crime. Meanwhile, the president had given the Russians an ultimatum: The missiles in Mexico would have to be dismantled within the next forty-eight hours or a complete air and sea blockade of Mexico would commence. The United Nations was meeting in emergency session. Gorbachev had so far made no response. Nor had the Mexican government. The world, as it had in the sixties, was holding its breath.

"We have a problem, you and I," Yarnell had said on the tape.

"Yes, I suspect we do," Powers had replied.

"It's Valentin."

McGarvey would never forget the longish pause on the tape. On first hearing it, he had been concerned that something had gone wrong. That the machine had somehow malfunctioned. But then Powers made the first of his damning statements.

"I've been expecting this for a lot of years, Darby. You know, now that it's come I'm actually glad."

"It's been a burden," Yarnell said.

"Yes. It has."

Yarnell had gone there to accuse his old friend of being a traitor, and Powers had been expecting Yarnell to come forward finally and admit that he was the traitor. It should have been a comedy, but too many lives had already been lost—and more were in the balance—for it to be humorous.

The lights of Manhattan suddenly came into sight across the East River. McGarvey had always liked this view of the city; it was power, to him, and success and excitement. "The American dream," his father once told him, "is to light up the universe." We'd gotten a pretty good start in New York City. It made him sad to think how much he would miss it.

"... *knew he'd be coming for you,"* Yarnell's words stood out in McGarvey's head. *"I simply never imagined the lengths to which the man is willing to go. It staggers the imagination."*

"Even yours?" Powers had replied, and McGarvey had plainly heard the slight note of derision in the DCI's voice.

There was another longish pause on the tape until Yarnell said that Baranov had sent for them.

Powers laughed.

"Evita telephoned from Mexico City, Donald. She says she knows everything. Basulto is with her. And someone else, McGarvey something or other."

"Of course she could not know everything," Powers said.

"Not without Valentin's help and advice. Which brings us to an interesting juncture, you and I."

"Yes. I thought you'd be coming someday."

"Me, or someone like me."

"You," Powers had said. He sounded final, and so very sure of himself.

They passed through the Midtown tunnel and into Manhattan, and merged with traffic heading south on Second Avenue toward SoHo. It was a

Friday night. The daytime city of offices and businesses had fallen silent, while the nighttime city of restaurants and bars and clubs had come alive. A dangerous, wonderful place, he thought. Alive.

"Why me?" Yarnell had asked.

"You've been his lapdog all these years."

"What?"

"I never had the proof until tonight, until just now. Valentin called and you jumped. It's gotten too difficult for him in Mexico I suspect, so he sent you here."

"He's blackmailing you . . ."

"And you've come with the ransom demand."

"Don't be a fool," Yarnell had said, the words echoing again and again in McGarvey's head. *"Don't be a fool . . . A mole in the agency . . . at the highest levels. You, Donald. It has been you all these years . . ."*

"We were friends . . . Baranov has wanted me for a long time . . . you were the traitor, not me. . . ."

A single gunshot, the sound distorted in the tiny machine, cut Powers off in midsentence. For a moment there was silence on the tape, and then rushing sounds, like water over a cliff, the definite sound of a car door closing and the engine coming to life.

An East Coast accent, Evita had said, as had Basulto. Powers's accent was East Coast, but he'd been Baranov's mark from the first day. The Russian had bided his time, had saved the single indiscretion like money in the bank until it earned enough interest to make the withdrawal significant. He had wanted to destroy Powers, and he had.

The cabbie dropped McGarvey off in front of St. Christopher's on Broome Street. The club was dark, not a single window was lit. A couple of passersby glanced up at him as he mounted the single step and rang the bell. He could hear it inside. He glanced down the street as the taxi turned the corner and was gone. He had thought about calling ahead in Washington and again at LaGuardia, but had decided against it, wanting to come here in person to face her, though he had no real idea what he wanted to say to her.

He rang the bell again and then tried the door. It was open. Just inside the vestibule he closed and locked the door and, leaving his bag, passed through to the club where the only illumination came from the exit signs. He took the stairs up to Evita's apartment and let himself in. She was curled up on the couch, her hands clutched at her bosom. Her feet were bare and her silk nightgown was hiked up nearly to her hips. She was sleeping, McGarvey thought at first as he came across the living room. Her cocaine paraphernalia was laid out on the big coffee table in front of her. But there was an unnatural stillness about her. He stopped a few feet away and watched for her chest to rise and fall; for a movement, any movement, a little twitch, a flexed muscle in sleep. But she was absolutely motionless, and he knew that she was dead.

With Baranov out of reach and Darby Yarnell dead, there had been no reason for her to continue living. She had had her fantasies, as we all do, about somehow regaining her youth or whatever it was she perceived she had lost by growing older, until Baranov had set out on his mad plot to bring Powers down. She'd heard the news this morning, of course, and she had killed herself.

He gently touched her cheek. Her flesh was already stiff and cool. She had been dead for half a day at least. Probably since noon.

Baranov had let her leave Mexico City knowing

how she would end up. She had been the last link to the old days. The very last one who could do him any harm. But he'd known her better than anyone else.

It had been her hands that had tapped out the coke on the tiny mirror, her hands that had cut it into lines and her hands that had held the tiny straw to her nostrils. But Baranov had killed her as surely as if he had held a gun to her head and pulled the trigger himself.

Darby Yarnell had killed her, too, with his arrogance, with his mad energy, as if she had been a delicate moth attracted to a raging inferno.

The system had killed her. The bureaucracy of government, by its insensitivity to the people it was supposed to serve, had destroyed her. The aristocracy of lies and dishonor had proven to be a fatal attraction.

He thought about Baranov, who was surely celebrating by now. The magician, Evita had called him. He cannot lose. He cannot be beaten. Perhaps she had been right.

McGarvey turned and left the apartment. Downstairs he collected his bag, let himself out, and headed up toward Houston, where there would be more of a chance to catch a cab at this hour of the night. It was over, he thought. Time now to try to find the peace he had been searching for all of his life.